THE WURTENBERG AFFAIR

DAVID MEATON

The Book Guild Ltd

First published in Great Britain in 2023 by
The Book Guild Ltd
Unit E2 Airfield Business Park,
Harrison Road, Market Harborough,
Leicestershire. LE16 7UL
Tel: 0116 2792299
www.bookguild.co.uk
Email: info@bookguild.co.uk
Twitter: @bookguild

Copyright © 2023 David Meaton

The right of David Meaton to be identified as the author of this
work has been asserted by them in accordance with the
Copyright, Design and Patents Act 1988.

All rights reserved. No part of this publication may be
reproduced, transmitted, or stored in a retrieval system, in any form or by any means,
without permission in writing from the publisher, nor be otherwise circulated in
any form of binding or cover other than that in which it is published and without
a similar condition being imposed on the subsequent purchaser.

Typeset in 11pt Minion Pro

Printed and bound in the UK by TJ Books LTD, Padstow, Cornwall

ISBN 978 1915853 424

British Library Cataloguing in Publication Data.
A catalogue record for this book is available from the British Library.

For my Grandfather
George Meaton
1896 - 1961

ONE

The Morgan family had given much to the Great War, and the loss of the two eldest sons fighting with the 2nd Battalion, the South Wales Borderers on the Somme in 1916, and the tragic death of another son killed when the roof collapsed on him in the pit had a great effect on the Morgan family. However, it was the continual threat of the death or serious wounding of their youngest son, Derfal, serving in France at the Ypres Salient, that weighed most heavily on the Morgan parents. They were both hard-working chapel people and desperately prayed for all their sons but especially for their youngest, who was a corporal in the South Monmouth Siege Company based at Passchendaele. Some comfort was felt within the Morgan household, though, because they still had two other sons who remained relatively safe at home. Wesley, who was serving as a police constable in Cardiff, and Gwyn, who was still working underground in the pit, and neither of them could be called up because of their reserved occupations, which should keep them safe at home.

The war had been dragging into a third long year with scarcely any good news at all coming from the front, and the mood of people in the country was close to rock bottom. The South Wales pit valleys had not suffered such high levels of casualties, dead or wounded, because so many men were conscripted to keep the coalfields working at full capacity. Even so, by the third year of fighting, every village was mourning families who had lost sons, brothers and husbands and who had received back men broken in body or spirit who were then thrust into a world quite unprepared to receive them or cater for their needs effectively.

Although Wesley had not had the benefit of the scholarship to attend the County School in Newport like his younger brother Derfal, who was able to complement his elementary education from the village school, he was a boy who enjoyed reading widely and was not afraid to use his brain to solve problems. He was supremely disappointed when he had to go to the colliery as a pit boy at the age of thirteen and endure the drudgery of the back-breaking work underground. Luckily for him, this experience spurred him to pursue his studies even more when he was not working, and he became a regular reader at the library and signed up for courses at the Mechanics Institute to further his personal knowledge. He knew implicitly that he would not be able to escape from the colliery unless he had something more to offer in terms of skill or learning that would convince a potential employer that he was worth taking a chance on. He trained his mind to be sharp and to think quickly and practised puzzles and solved mathematical problems to keep his brain supple. He had developed an ambition to join the South Wales Constabulary, which he considered a useful occupation that would benefit the community and guaranteed a fair income, quality accommodation for single officers and a good house for married ones and a comfortable pension when he retired. Constables, whilst not rich, seemed to live rather better than the colliers in the valleys and enjoyed a kind of status in the community. He knew that not all of his neighbours in the village would be well disposed towards the police, but he was not the kind of person who courted popularity, and he believed that the work of the local constable provided such positive outcomes for the community in keeping people safe and protected that it far outweighed any negative feelings from a minority of people. Wesley knew he could not apply to become a constable until he was twenty-one years of age, which meant he must build an exemplary work record in the pit for seven years or so before he could apply.

His younger brother Gwyn was far less diligent and followed him into the pit two years after, when he left the village school. Gwyn was as sharp and intelligent as most but had little inclination to study and preferred to spend his time on the rugby field and chasing the girls. He just accepted that it was inevitable that he would spend his working life grafting underground and he would spend his non-working hours enjoying himself at the rugby club or at the bar of the Miners' Welfare Club. When the war came, he tried to volunteer but his reserved occupation kept him out of the army, much to his disappointment. Gwyn, however, coped well with the work underground and was a happy and popular member of his shift. He was quite pleased that the departure of a fair number of local lads to the army or navy had meant there were more lovely young girls to go around, and Gwyn Morgan saw it as his mission to get to know as many of them as he could. He was handsome and charming and had always found it easy to talk to young women and to charm their mothers also.

Derfal was the youngest and was lucky to have enjoyed a more privileged upbringing than his elder brothers, largely because of the advice and support from the headmaster of the village school, Yanto Richards, who had managed to persuade his parents that they had a boy with a potential to excel academically. Mr Richards prepared Derfal for the scholarship examination for entrance to the County School in Newport very effectively, and it was no surprise when he won a place in this celebrated school at the first attempt. The opportunity to get a secondary education was only rarely available to working-class boys in this part of Wales, and his parents went without much to ensure that their youngest was able to participate fully and gain the maximum advantage from this once-in-a-lifetime chance. They were convinced that their sacrifice would enable Derfal to have a better start in life and to avoid a lifetime of drudgery down the pit, which was the prospect for so many of his friends and neighbours. They had little idea what advantage it would give him but when he passed the School Certificate Examination, he was able to gain a position as an office boy in the gas company with prospects to advance to junior clerk in time. They knew that this would prove a solid start for Derfal's working life and although the initial salary was not princely, the prospects were good. Mr Morgan was intensely proud that his youngest son went to work clean and tidy in a suit, collar and tie and came home as smart as he had left in the morning. He felt a strong pride that at least two of his sons had managed to break free from the colliery and find employment which could lead somewhere and give them a future.

Derfal, however, was intensely bored with the deadly routine of office work in the gas company and desperately tried to join up, and like many village boys, the lure of the infantry was foremost in his mind. On the morning of his eighteenth birthday, he ran away from the office and volunteered at the local drill hall but was saved from the infantry when one of his old schoolmasters, now serving as the local recruiting officer, intervened to redirect Derfal to the Royal Engineers, feeling that it would be a waste of his talent in the infantry. Derfal's enlistment led to him winning a place at the Army Technical College and studying for the Mechanician's Diploma, equivalent to the Higher School Certificate, in Aero and Motor Vehicle Engineering, resulting in a promotion to corporal and posting to join the Monmouth Siege Company as the NCO i/c , the transport section at Passchendaele in the Ypres Salient.

1917 saw a spectacular initial success on the first day of the 1st Battle of Passchendaele turn into failure when the high command failed to capitalise on their initial success but instead chose to sit on their laurels, consolidating the new-won positions just a few hundred yards forward from the previously held ones. Lord Kitchener's subway strategy had worked fantastically well, and the German machine guns had been outflanked and could not be brought to bear on the first wave of British attackers who broke through the enemy lines without heavy casualties. There was massive frustration and reticence amongst the allied soldiers, particularly the British, who had endured a terrible and long autumn and winter in the mud and sludge without any meaningful advance. The cautiousness of the British generals led to stalemate, which lasted through the autumn and winter, and a second attack was not launched until the spring of 1918, and both opposing armies became bogged down in the mud of an extremely wet winter that made living conditions extremely uncomfortable for the troops and movement almost impossible. Many troops lost confidence in their generals' ability to bring this war to a conclusion.

The autumn of 1917 saw the October Revolution in Russia and the overthrow of the worst dictator in modern history by the Bolsheviks. There was considerable embarrassment amongst many allied leaders who had felt extremely uncomfortable with the worst excesses of the Tsar in the oppression of his own people. There was some relief that the Tsar had been overthrown, and the Bolsheviks were quietly welcomed by the allied leaders. Lloyd George even welcomed the victory of the Bolsheviks as a great triumph for the principle for which the war was being fought. He stated that it signalled the end of the corruption, excess and inefficiency of the Tsar's reign, and similarly the impact of the rise of the Bolsheviks was not lost on the ordinary soldiers either. For many in the trenches there was an upsurge of hope and support amongst those on the front line who dared to hope that a similar overthrow of the established order might occur at home too. The whole notion of a country governed by ordinary men and women was such a radical overturning of the way that things were done that few of them were convinced it would happen in Britain too. The British establishment were glad to be released from the great embarrassment endured by the allied powers, whose claim to be fighting for the preservation of freedom and democracy looked somewhat suspect whilst one of the worst despots in the modern world was numbered amongst their ranks. However, it was soon evident that the positive feelings felt by the western governments towards the new Bolshevik government in Russia were dissipating as they came to realise the potential danger that the spread of their idealism would cause within their own countries, proving a major threat, probably greater than that posed by the war, to the continuance of their beloved status quo. Britain's liberal values had made it a welcoming place for political émigrés and refugees over the previous forty years or so and as a result there was an abundance of radical and socialist societies and journals operating in and around London that took up the Bolshevik cause and spread the word amongst the working people through the support of the trade unions.

Against this background of potential unrest within unionised British industry and the working class more generally, PC Wesley Morgan found himself propelled forward within the constabulary. Wesley had undergone his training and probation at Cardiff Central Police Station, but when the war came, he was transferred to the station located in Tiger Bay to patrol the docklands and surrounding streets. Wesley was glad to move away from the city centre station and to focus his attentions on the prevention of smuggling, pilfering and, more seriously, to keep a watch for enemy espionage activity tracking the movements of British and neutral merchant shipping bringing much-needed war supplies to Britain from the Empire, and shipping men, ammunition and stores to the armies in Europe. There was a strong sense that enemy agents were already operating in and around the major seaports of Britain and were channelling valuable intelligence back to the German military about British supply lines and identifying suitable targets for sabotage. This seemed much more like valuable war work to Wesley and much preferable to chasing petty criminals or putting drunken soldiers on leave into the cells to sober up for the night. He was looking forward to this assignment and was extremely happy to be given the chance to take on this work. He packed his kit and cleared out of his room in the section house accommodation in the police compound near Cardiff Castle and cycled through the city streets towards the docklands to report for his new duty. He was joining Red Watch and was to report to the watch commander, Inspector George Bennett, at nine this morning. He had left early for he knew with all his kit on his back and strapped on his bike, he would be slower than usual on his ride. However, he was outside the inspector's door in good time and knocked and waited as the clock struck nine. A strong voice called him in and, smoothing down his uniform, he entered the office to face a large red-faced man with bushy grey side-whiskers but nevertheless neat and tidy in his inspector's uniform. First impressions were of an imposing presence, but Wesley could see that the inspector's eyes were warm and his smile friendly when he stood and shook hands and welcomed him into the watch. He said that Wesley's fitness report from the superintendent at Central Police Station was exemplary and suggested that he may have the potential to be promoted into the criminal investigation department as a detective with a little more experience. Inspector Bennett explained that he had been posted here to join a team of young constables who were being put together to undertake a secondary undercover role in addition to their normal patrolling duties.

*

"You have been selected to be one of these special officers because of your quickness of mind and attention to detail and potential to become a detective. This role is not compulsory and if you decide that you do not wish to commit yourself to the extra work then that will be fine, and you will continue to undertake the uniformed constable role in the dock area as normal. However, if you choose to join this team, you will have a real chance to advance your career into the CID as a plain clothes officer much faster than would otherwise happen."

I asked if he could tell me a little more about the undercover work and he replied that unfortunately he could not divulge any details until I had volunteered to join the team. I was cautious by nature, but I was also ambitious and knew that this might prove to be the opportunity I was looking for to make a career in the constabulary. After a few moments of thought, I nodded my head and said that I wanted to be part of this team. The inspector beamed and congratulated me on the right choice and said that when I was dismissed, I was to report to Detective Sergeant Powell, who would arrange the transport to a secluded country house which was used as a police training facility near the village of Llanthony in the Black Mountains above Abergavenny.

"You will be there for four weeks undergoing thorough briefings, firearms training, a vehicle driving course and intensive German language to prepare you for the work you will undertake in and around the docks and the Welsh coastline." He shook my hand again and said he looked forward to meeting me again at Llanthony House in the next couple of days. He reminded me not to divulge to my friends, relations or other constables where I was going and what I was going to be doing.

Detective Sergeant Powell was only in his mid-twenties and was tall and slim with a bright and handsome smile and an air of confidence which made my nerves disappear. He greeted me in a friendly manner and said that from now on during the training we would dismiss the use of ranks and surnames and I would be addressed as Wesley, and he was Bryn. He said there was going to be six of us in the undercover team who would be placed inside both the red and blue watches at Tiger Bay Police Station to combat the threat posed by enemy spies and agents and fifth columnists to British merchant shipping and military supply intelligence. He directed me to the canteen where he said I should enjoy a cooked breakfast as it would be early evening before we arrived at Llanthony House and our next meal. "You are only the second candidate to accept so far, and you will find the first volunteer in the canteen already, and the inspector has more to interview before we can set off." He pointed me in the direction of the canteen and said he would see me later. I could smell the delicious aroma of frying bacon as I turned the corner at the top of the stairs and made my way towards the seat of that glorious smell. The canteen was small but cosy and the kitchen was busy preparing the hot lunch for the watch currently on duty. I could see that the daily menu was quite limited but was different every day and comprised favourite wholesome dishes designed to provide the necessary fuel for the constables out in all weathers. There was only one other person in the dining room and he, like me, was encumbered with a suitcase and rucksack containing his kit, so I guessed he was joining the same team as me. He was short and stocky with the kind of build that suggested he played wing forward judging by his square and strong appearance. He was also in uniform and was a constable, and I could see from his number that he was from the Swansea Division and not Cardiff. I asked if I could join him and he nodded his assent, so I deposited my kit and introduced myself as Wesley Morgan and he shook hands and said his name was Carwyn Jones and he was from Llanelli. I went up to the counter and ordered a full cooked breakfast from the middle-aged serving lady and two cups of tea. She smiled and said that as I was a new lad today, I was to sit down at the table and she would bring the drinks and food over when it was ready, but in future when it was busy, I would have to collect it myself. I nodded my agreement and wandered back to the table with Carwyn, who appeared quite taciturn and not quite an easy conversationalist, but I am not particularly voluble myself during first meetings, so we got on quite well during those first few moments together. He seemed to be as steady and cautious as me, and these were the qualities I respected the most, seeming to me to be ideal traits for a police constable.

We were soon joined by the third and fourth members of the team, Colin Evans and Tudor Williams, and then after a longer wait, Ivor Bethal, and then the biggest surprise of all when the final candidate to join us was a WPC Alicia Bell. We were all a bit shocked to see this young and pretty girl ranked amongst our number, but she was soon to show us how good she really was when we got into our training, and any thoughts we might have had about her ability to cope were very quickly smoothed away. The team was now assembled and, soon after, Bryn Powell collected us about 3.30pm and we made our way to the transport waiting to take us to the training school. This journey would probably take nearly three hours and it would be dark before we arrived at our destination, and I took the opportunity to catch up on my sleep, urged on by the steady hum of the engine and the heat inside the cabin of the truck. I was shaken awake when the tone of the engine changed and the vibrations through the chassis increased as the truck changed down to tackle the steep climb up the mountain road from Abergavenny to Llanthony. It was getting dark now, but it was possible to make out the steep sides of the valley on each side of the road and the dense thickness of the forest on the mountainside. I knew that there was a famous abbey in the village of Llanthony but little more than this about the area. Finally, the truck pulled through some imposing gates leading down to a Georgian country house surrounded by rugged parkland and pasture inhabited by thousands of sheep. The façade of this house and the steps leading up to the double front doors was nothing like anything I had ever experienced before, for even the largest houses around my village were small compared to this. It was even more impressive when we entered the splendid mosaic-tiled entrance hall, where we were greeted by a Colonel Russell Stewart who introduced himself as from the Security Service and whose staff would be leading the briefings over the next few days. The housekeeper, Mrs Engleton, and her staff then showed us to our rooms, and we had a free hour to unpack and get ready for dinner at eight in the dining room. My room was on the third floor and although quite small had a good view of the park and the mountain and there was a comfortable bed and a desk for studying, and it was certainly much better than sharing a bed with two other brothers during my childhood at home or the cell-like accommodation provided in the section house for unmarried officers.

Dinner was served at eight sharp and was three courses, consisting of soup, roast beef and vegetables followed by an apple tart and cream. Wine was served but Col. Stewart made it clear that there would be no more alcohol after tonight until the final dinner when the course was concluded. Most of us were not great wine drinkers, preferring a pint in the pub, but sipped at a single glass more out of politeness than pleasure. After the meal was over, we were introduced to the directing staff for the course and there was an opportunity to begin to get to know the people we would be spending the next month with. Col. Stewart introduced Major Harcourt-Evans, who was from the Intelligence Corps; Sergeant Major Albert Martin, who would teach us to use firearms safely and some unarmed combat; Sergeant Gareth Hughes from the South Wales Constabulary, who would teach us to drive motor vehicles safely and at speed; Fraulein Irma Von Spitzer, who would attempt to teach us the rudiments of the German language and Doctor Rhodri Williams, who would teach us rudimentary coding and how to break it. Corporal Freddy Miller, who would be our PT and fitness instructor, was the last to be introduced, and he sent us off to bed with the news that we needed to meet him outside the front door in running kit for a cross-country run of four miles' duration before breakfast. This was to become our routine every morning and was certainly a good way to clear one's head and lungs for the active days that followed. Training was to begin the following morning and we were to dress ourselves in the coveralls provided in our rooms for the work of the day, and we all went off to bed excited about what lay before us.

Dawn was still some thirty minutes away, although the traces of lightness were beginning to show through the surrounding woodland when we assembled just before six the following morning. We shivered and our breath could be seen in streams when we exhaled as we stomped around trying to keep warm, waiting for Corporal Miller to arrive. It seemed an age that we waited, but he appeared right on time and led us down the driveway and into the woods to start our morning run. We were soon to discover that he had mapped out several different routes; through the woods, along by the river, up one side of the valley and across the top of the dam at the head of the Llanthony reservoir, and the most difficult of all involving a steep climb to the moor above the village. He set a steady pace and his object was to test out how fit we were whilst ensuring that we all kept up and finished together. His routes were intended to take about thirty minutes to complete, and he intended to gently increase the pace as the weeks went on to stretch us all and build our stamina. He frowned on racing and stressed teamwork so that we all worked together to ensure we all made the grade, just as we would out in the field. Corporal Miller was a cheery young man and chivvied us along good-naturedly, and I think we all got to like him from day one. He had been detached from the Army School of Infantry, where he was a physical training instructor for the duration of our training, and then he was rejoining his regiment for service on the Western Front. The path through the woods was quite damp after the recent rain, which meant we had to be extra careful not to slip over as we ran, although the wet conditions meant that my ankles and lower legs became spattered with mud. I was looking forward to the plentiful hot water back at the house and the chance to clean up and change my clothes before our first classroom session after breakfast. I no longer felt cold and had warmed up sufficiently to run smoothly and this morning the pace suited me fine, for although I considered myself to be physically fit, I had the build of a front-row prop forward and was more used to short bursts of running and had developed my upper body strength and leg muscles for pushing and scrimmaging rather than for long-distance running. I noticed that Carwyn was pushing ahead and had to be held back a little by Corporal Miller. Alicia Bell seemed a comfortable runner and stayed within the middle of the pack, but Ivor Bethal was blowing hard and having trouble keeping up, but again I noticed that Corporal Miller just slowed the pace a little to make it easier for Ivor to keep up. It took us just twenty-eight minutes to complete the circuit and we all rushed up to our rooms to get washed and dressed ready for breakfast at seven. Ivor was in the room opposite mine and as I was dressing, I could hear him coughing violently, and when I entered the corridor on my way to breakfast, I could smell cigarette smoke coming from under his door. We had not been banned from smoking, although it was only permitted on the terrace overlooking the rose gardens and was expressly forbidden anywhere inside the house. I enjoyed filling my old briar pipe and smoking some tobacco as I read the newspaper during an off-duty moment but never smoked cigarettes. I had left my pipe and pouch in my kitbag and had decided that I would, like alcohol, forgo the pleasure of a smoke until the course was completed successfully.

The breakfast table was laid out with hot porridge, fresh bread, eggs, bacon and sausages and plentiful cups of tea. At first, I thought that I would never eat all that was on offer but when I sat down, I realised that the morning run had prompted my appetite and that I was feeling quite hungry. As we tucked into the hot food, we started to relax, and the conversation began to flow in an easier fashion. None of us knew what lay before us but we were anxious to know what we were being trained for and to understand why we had been selected. Corporal Miller came and joined us and chatted about the run and how he was impressed with our first outing and would try to test us a little harder tomorrow morning. I noticed that he sat next to Ivor, and they became engaged in a quiet but purposeful conversation as they ate their breakfast. Later in the day, Ivor confided in me that the corporal had noticed his lack of fitness and shortness of breath during the run and had indicated that he had to improve his respiratory fitness or fail the course. Miller was certain that the cause of Ivor's lack of puff was that he smoked too much and had recommended that he cut down drastically or give up altogether. Ivor was in a quandary because he knew that the corporal had worked out exactly why he was struggling on the cross-country run, but it wasn't quite as easy to cut down or stop as he made it sound. Ivor said he had been smoking heavily for over ten years and would often smoke forty cigarettes in one day and was frightened that if he tried to cut down, as the corporal suggested, the cravings would be so bad that he would not function that well. I tried to counsel him to heed the advice he had been given and perhaps try to find something else to occupy his mind instead of smoking.

The first session of the day was taken up with briefings and we were all assembled in the library, which had been converted into a kind of schoolroom with enough tables and chairs for each of us to sit and make notes, a podium for the speaker and large maps of the docks at Newport, Cardiff and Swansea and charts of the Severn Estuary, the Bristol Channel and the Welsh coastline as far as St David's Head. There were smaller maps of the less important ports also and photographs of half a dozen or so ordinary-looking men and women which caught our interest. The first session was led by Colonel Stewart at eight o'clock sharp, and he led straight into the reasons why this small unit was being set up and why we had been specifically selected to be part of it. He stressed that although we were all members of the South Wales Constabulary, if we were to successfully complete the initial training course, we would be required to enlist in the newly formed secret security service, although we would continue to serve within the constabulary. He was at pains to suggest that the counter-espionage work that the security service would undertake would grow exponentially on home territory as our enemies sought to gain advantage over us at home rather than just on foreign battlefields. He predicted that security service work would expand even after the war was concluded and would have a vital role to play in ensuring that we would be able to maintain the peace successfully in the years after the war was over.

He described how, in 1914 and 1915, naval intelligence had identified that there had been considerable enemy activity centred around our seaports and supply lines. At first, it was thought that this was sporadic and largely a coincidence that the enemy was able to intercept shipping coming to and from Welsh seaports, although valiant attempts had been made by the Royal Navy to patrol our coastal waters to deter U-boats from operating close inshore. However, as the war progressed, the daily value of the tonnage lost steadily increased and it was becoming apparent that the attacks were not a result of chance but carefully coordinated and targeted on specific high-value cargoes chosen to have most impact on our war effort. Our ability to continue to fight this war was dependent on continuing support from all parts of the Empire providing us with raw materials, food, resources and men and the ships of the Merchant Marine to bring these goods here.

"We simply cannot afford the continued loss of vital supplies, ships and men at this rate if we wish to win this war. In addition, there is the imperative to maintain a constant supply line to our armies fighting in Europe, Palestine and Africa, which is also sent by ships. The major Welsh ports are particularly busy in handling war traffic with the fast turnaround of merchant vessels through the three largest ports daily, and we have noticed that ships arriving at and leaving these ports are particularly vulnerable in the sea approaches to the Welsh coast from the Atlantic Ocean or through the Irish Sea. It has long been known that German U-boats boats operate in this area in significant numbers, taking advantage of the rugged and largely sparsely populated coastline to operate close inshore and hide in the many small bays and coves or seek refuge in southern Irish waters, where the high level of anti-British feeling means they can operate with impunity.

"The major question is how can the enemy U-boats have such accurate information about shipping movements in and out of British ports that they can effectively lay in wait for our unsuspecting vessels to sail over the horizon into their sights? They have certainly infiltrated their own spies into Britain to observe our shipping movements more closely, but this strategy has never allowed for their operatives to gather the amount of accurate and detailed knowledge necessary to provide the U-boats with such an effective advantage. Our own experience in attempting to infiltrate British agents into Germany has shown us clearly how difficult it is for a foreign individual, however fluent in the culture and language, to suddenly appear in a new place and build the antecedents and contacts to blend into a new community without attracting the attention of people around him or the suspicion of the local police. The only proven method that we have found is to follow the adage that to avoid detection, hide in plain sight, and that suggests that the enemy agents gathering the intelligence for the Germans are above suspicion because they are natives, born here or have lived here for a long time. They will be respectable people with jobs that give them access to ship manifests and movements, who have been recruited by the enemy to pass this information on to the spy network operated by German agents in this country. The most likely suspects are people who may have connections with Germany or have sympathies with the German cause, but they may also be vulnerable to coercion, hold a grudge against the British or simply be working for monetary reward. The German spies will have set up a network operating throughout South Wales to gather this intelligence and to pass it on so that it can be transmitted to the U-boats by wireless or signal lamp. Each member of the network will have only a limited knowledge of other members and will simply pass the messages on to their immediate contact. We believe that only the actual German operatives themselves will code the information for transmission to the U-boats. A series of rendezvous locations will have been set up so that a designated U-boat can lie off a deserted stretch of the coast and receive the messages by signal lamp or wireless direct from the spy. The exchange of more detailed information in writing or the ingress or exfiltration of German personnel could also be affected by small boats directly to the beach.

"Our priority must be to identify each member of the network rather than apprehend the German spies themselves, although I am not, in the least, suggesting that their capture is not important, but it is far more important to cut off the supply of information to the network in the first instance. This will take painstaking work by this team to identify each member of the network or networks as evidence is gathered of their involvement, bearing in mind that each link in the chain is only aware of one or possibly two other members of the network. At this stage, we do not know whether there is just one network operating across South Wales or whether there are several networks clustered around each of the major ports. The main objective of this team is to roll up the networks and halt the ability of German agents to coordinate attacks on British shipping. The operational command will be in the hands of Inspector George Bennett and his second-in-command is Detective Sergeant Bryn Powell, and these two officers will report to me. To begin to focus our thinking, George has already drawn up a list of suspects for our attention and their photographs are on the blackboard here, and you will receive a file of background information regarding each suspect. I will not go through them in detail now but will only make comment that they are just the kind of ordinary, hard-working, respectable people who would appear beyond reproach. They all have one thing in common, that through their normal daily activities they have access to the knowledge of the daily shipping arrivals and departures and the cargoes carried. Do not assume that they are guilty just because there is a file on them, because as policemen and women, you know full well that although you can arrest on reasonable suspicion, you cannot secure a conviction without proof. Your job is to build on the suspicion and find the evidence that will confine them to prison to face the executioner for their treason in time of war."

The first suspect was Ernest Sullivan, who was originally from Cork but who had lived in Newport for fifteen years and had worked in the dock management office as a manifest clerk for over ten years. He had never come to the attention of the police and had an exemplary work record with the Dock Company. He was a regular member of St Jude's Roman Catholic Church in the city and was known to have relatives back in Ireland who he visited several times a year. One of his brothers, Declan, was known to be a fugitive republican activist who was wanted by the British authorities in Dublin for leading violent attacks on British troops in the suburbs of the capital.

The second suspect was David Taylor, who was one of the berthing masters at Newport Docks and had intimate knowledge of the arrival, departure and loading of all ships entering and leaving Newport Docks. He was born in Caldicott, a small village ten miles or so from Newport, and after ten years serving in the Merchant Navy as second mate on a tramp steamer, he married and settled down with his wife, Rachel, in Newport and went to work on the docks. He was a man of good character also, but although he called himself Taylor, his actual family name was Rabinowitz, and he was only the first generation to have used an anglicised name. His grandfather, Benjamin, had emigrated from Stuttgart in 1868 and set up a small tailor's shop in Newport, and his father, Solomon, carried the business on to this day. David had no interest in tailoring and entered the Mercantile Marine as an apprentice deck officer in 1900 and served as a mate on a number of small steamers trading between Cardiff and Hamburg until his marriage in 1910 to Rachel Wiseman, whose family also originated from Stuttgart.

Third on the list was Jonathan Pugh, who was a clerk for the Lloyd's of London Register whose job it was to report a full record of the ships and tonnage of cargo that passed through the docks at Swansea and surrounding areas. Pugh had worked for Lloyd's for over twenty years, both at Cardiff and now Swansea Docks. There was some talk of problems arising over gambling debts that he had accrued from betting on greyhound racing and that this was the reason for his hasty transfer to Swansea from Cardiff. Pugh continued to be trusted by his employers because he appeared to be as diligent and conscientious at work as ever, but the rumours about his gambling habits and rising debts continued to circulate.

The fourth was Hilda Williams, the wife of Mordred Williams, who worked as a haberdasher at Bennett's Department Store in Swansea, but her maiden name was Mueller and she originated from the small village of Brüggen on the Dutch border with Germany. Mrs Williams was fluent in Dutch and German and since the war started, she liked to tell people she was Dutch. She had studied as an interpreter in her native country and had come to Britain to find work in 1896. She had worked as secretary to the chairman of the Cardiff Dock Company since 1906. Before the war, she and her husband made frequent trips to Germany to visit her family, at least three times in the preceding years before the war. Her youngest brother and three cousins were serving in the German Army and were believed to be serving on the Western Front at this time.

Number five was Manfred Gruber, born in Caerphilly in 1898 into a German family who settled in Wales in 1860. Apart from his German name, everything about Manfred was Welsh; a passion for rugby and he sang in a male-voice choir. He worked as a junior clerk in the shipping office at Cardiff Docks and had been in this job since leaving school. He did not have much responsibility, but his main role was to collate the shipping movements in the Cardiff dock area each day and, therefore, he had detailed knowledge of merchant shipping movements that the U-boat commanders were seeking.

The final character pinned to the blackboard was a middle-aged man with strong character in his expression and of stern appearance, and he was introduced to us as Sir Wilhelm Branden, who was the current chairman of the South Wales Docks and Wharfage Company, which operated all the major ports along the South Wales coast. Sir Wilhelm's family was one of the leading Anglo-German families who diversified into Britain at the time of Prince Albert's marriage to the young Queen Victoria in the early part of the previous century. After twenty or so years, the family managed to establish themselves as successful mine and factory owners, and landowners, and over the next fifty years or so consolidated the family as one of the richest and most powerful in Wales. They had always kept close association with the German side of their family, and several of his cousins were serving as field officers in the Kaiser's army. However, they quickly followed the lead given by the royal family when they changed their name from Battenberg de Saxe-Coburg to Windsor. Sir Wilhelm shortened their name from von Brandenburg to the much more British-sounding Branden at the start of the war to detach themselves publicly from their German roots. Again, it was stressed that there was no direct evidence to suggest that anyone in Sir Wilhelm's family was disloyal to their adopted country other than the fact they continued to maintain family connections to family members in Germany, and Sir Wilhelm himself certainly had access to the information that was being passed to the enemy.

After the break, Major Harcourt-Evans began the first lessons in what he called tradecraft, and over the next few weeks he taught us how to conduct covert surveillance, follow suspects, monitor dead-letter sites, coding and decoding and how to look beyond what appeared to be normal or usual, ever remembering that the best spies use their ability to blend in and avoid attracting attention as their best cover. We were encouraged to be good listeners and to become quietly active in the neighbourhoods where our suspects lived and worked, and by keeping our ears to the ground, we might be able to cultivate a network of watchers and informers who would keep us informed of the movements of our targets more effectively than we could. He also stressed that we all needed to be able to drive cars, vans and motorcycles to ensure that we had the mobility to cover the whole area at speed, and also to be fully familiar with the use of small arms. Sgt. Maj. Martin and Sergeant Hughes were to lead us through the acquisition of these new skills, and our group were split into two sections and alternated time behind the wheel and on the range daily. I was put into a section with Ivor Bethal and Alicia Bell, and Ivor proved that he could drive any motor vehicle fearlessly at breakneck speed, whilst Alicia was the absolute marksman with whatever weapon she fired. Our training moved at such a pace that we soon lost track of what day it was as we fell into bed at the end of each day tired out. I felt that I was able to cope with almost all aspects of the course, although I must admit that the cross-country run each morning was a struggle some mornings, although I did manage to keep up with the pack. Ivor improved enough to satisfy Corporal Miller, but it took a physical toll on him each day, and the bouts of coughing could be heard all over the top floor. I liked the sessions on coding and decoding the best and enjoyed learning the rudiments of German enough to recognise basic messages written in German that were similar to the kind of messages that might be sent by the spy network.

We were surprised when Col. Stewart announced that Friday was to be our last day of training and there was to be a celebration dinner that evening to recognise the good standard of readiness we had achieved. "Transport will be laid on to take you back to Cardiff on Saturday morning, and you will begin your undercover work from next Monday morning. Carwyn and Ivor will be based in Swansea, Colin and Tudor will cover Newport, and Alicia and Wesley will focus on Cardiff in the first instance, but there will be occasions when you will concentrate your efforts in response to promising leads."

I was pleased to be working with Alicia, whom I had come to respect very much as a professional colleague over the past weeks, although I did not know very much about her socially. I had become quite fond of Ivor and would miss his company but not his severe coughing bouts, which had kept me awake on many nights during the course. I was also sorry to say farewell to my comfortable bedroom in Llanthony House and exchange it for the austere bedroom provided in the Tiger Bay Single Man's Section House. I thought that to soften the transition, I might catch the valley train to my home village and enjoy a pint with my dad and brother Gwyn in the Miners' Welfare Club and enjoy Mum's Sunday dinner before returning for duty on Monday.

TWO

The three suspects that Alicia and I were to focus on had several things in common: they all worked at Cardiff Docks, all had access to the shipping movements information that was being leaked to the enemy and all were of German extraction. These things in themselves were not proof of any wrongdoing but provided just cause for them to be scrutinised more carefully and included in our investigation, if only to rule them out of suspicion. On our first day at Tiger Bay station, Alicia and I spent several hours discussing our strategies with Inspector Bennett, and it was agreed that we would first try to establish whether there was any connection between the three of them through their German connection outside of a purely professional relationship at work. George Bennett felt that Manfred Gruber was probably the least likely of all the suspects given his age and lowly position, and the close working relationship between the chairman of the Dock Company and his secretary would provide the most fruitful avenue for our early investigation. Alicia and I were not so sure, and we believed that they would be the most difficult to observe closely because of their privileged positions as chairman and his secretary at the Dock Company, and although we were sure that employees of the company would probably speak to us about their boss, we would need to use our discretion as to what was believable or just gossip. We also believed it would be difficult to keep track of Sir Wilhelm's movements outside his office since he operated within a very different social circle from us and had access to many places we could not follow. He lived in Craddock Park, a large 700-acre estate consisting of a twenty-five-bedroom mansion house and six farms. The estate was largely open parkland but Craddock House itself was within an 18-acre enclave surrounded by high walls, and the map showed clearly there were at least four different entrances and exits which we were unable to monitor twenty-four hours a day. However, Hilda Williams was much easier to observe closely as she lived in Penylyn in a modern, three-storey terraced house built about ten years previously. This area of the city was distinctly middle class and renowned as a quiet and comfortable area in which to bring up children. It was conveniently situated to the north of the city centre, and Hilda was able to travel to her office on the docks by bicycle. This neighbourhood seemed to be a little too expensive for the combined salaries of Mordred and Hilda to purchase or rent, and we decided that this would be where we would start, with an in-depth look at their finances. Alicia also volunteered to try to establish some greater understanding of where Hilda went and who she had met with on her last three visits to Germany in 1913 and 1914.

I also had a niggling feeling in the back of my head that the inspector was wrong to dismiss Manfred too quickly. I also thought it unlikely that he was working alone, and in his lowly clerical position he may not have the opportunity to access and copy the shipping movements and manifests secretly whilst keeping up with his normal work schedule. However, I had a hunch that if the information was recorded for him by someone else who did have the opportunity and time to do so without detection, he was the most likely suspect to act as the conduit for passing the vital intelligence down the line into the hands of the German agent. The other avenue of investigation I wanted to check out was why Manfred was not serving in the army or the navy by this time. Manfred certainly appeared to be young and fit and was within the call-up age bracket. His job in the dock office could be considered as important war work in working to keep the supply lines open, but it was a role that could be undertaken easily by older men or those less fit than him, thus releasing Manfred for conscription. The more we talked around the three suspects, the more detailed our strategy was becoming, and I could see that with just two of us working on this together, this case was going to be a long one unless vital evidence fell into our laps quite easily. We decided that Alicia initially would investigate the finances of the Williamses and I would establish Manfred's status with regard to conscription, and we would come together again at the end of the shift to pool what we had found out.

After a quick lunch in the canteen, I set off to the personnel record office at the Cardiff Dock Company to enquire about the employment status of Manfred Gruber. Even with the power of my warrant card, I was unable to get much further than the personnel clerk on the front desk, who made it emphatically clear that I would have to make a written request to view any personnel records to the personnel manager, stating the reason why I wanted access to them. I tried to hint that there was an issue of security involved, but he was not willing to waver from his stated position. However, just as I was about to give up, he asked me for the name of the person I was interested in, and I told him it was Manfred Gruber. He immediately replied, "Oh, that conchie, I…" but when I tried to press him for more detail, he became tight-lipped and wouldn't say any more. It was obvious to me that he knew exactly who I was enquiring about and that there was some gossip or notoriety around his status in relation to the war. I realised that I would have to go through the conscientious objector files at the main police station to see whether Manfred had applied for this official status to avoid conscription in the army, or whether this was just office gossip by busybodies wondering out loud why a young fit rugby player was not serving at the front. The whole question of conscientious objectors was a vexed one, and many of the people who publicly declared themselves to be against killing and war in general were pilloried by the public and denigrated as craven cowards. I had never met anyone who had declared themselves publicly to be a conscientious objector, but I was aware that there were people who for reasons of religion or belief were implacably against killing in all forms and refused to take part in it. However, many of these people volunteered and served unarmed, in the front line as ambulance drivers and stretcher bearers throughout the war. I knew that it was probably fair to say that in addition there were some people who pretended to be unfit medically to fight. The law allowed for citizens to register as conscientious objectors and to volunteer to undertake valuable war work, and for those who didn't volunteer, their status was left for the courts to decide. Those who lost their cases could be imprisoned and made to work in detention camps, and it was not surprising that people in general had a low regard for conscientious objectors.

 I was turning ideas over in my head as I cycled into the city to the main police station at Cardiff Castle, and so many questions were revolving in my head that I was wondering whether the whole "conchie" idea was a false trail leading nowhere. The records of applications, court cases and verdicts did not throw up Manfred's name and I was beginning to get despondent that I was wasting my time when the elderly constable in charge of the records suggested I look at the list of conscriptions exemptions medical for Cardiff. I found Gruber's recorded in January 1915 as exempted from military service because of a family history of epilepsy stretching back through the male line for three generations and that in all there were four Grubers included in the exemption certificate: Helmut Gruber and his three sons, Joachim, Manfred and Freidrich. The medical board considered their case in late 1914 based on the medical records received from the Mannheim Children's Hospital in Germany that both Helmut and his father suffered regular seizures that were thought to be epileptic in nature. There were sworn statements submitted by a Cardiff physician, Dr. Julius Matthias, who said that all three of the Gruber boys had suffered intermittent seizures and fits during their childhood years. He had written that although the frequency of these fits was slowing, there was no reason to expect that they would cease altogether and therefore they must be considered unfit for military service. The medical board accepted the medical evidence placed before it and discounted the suggestion that all three boys were fit and healthy with excellent attendance records at their places of employment and had not experienced any kind of epileptic episodes since starting work. The board considered in their judgement that there was a significant risk of further epileptic fits which would prove a danger to others within the military setting. I now had my answer as to why Manfred Gruber was not in the army and why some of his workmates thought he was a "conchie" shirking his duty. I thought that I would make the written request to see his personnel record, and I was willing to wager that it would contain a certificate of medical exemption but that this information had been kept confidential. I decided that I would follow up on Dr. Julius Matthias and how he came to have this significant knowledge of the Gruber boys' health and was willing to swear an oath to the medical board on their behalf.

Around six, I met again with George Bennett and Alicia, and we lay on the table what we had discovered during the afternoon. Alicia hadn't got all that far with her investigations of Mordred and Hilda Williams' finances but had established that Mordred earned three pounds a week plus 5% commission on sales and Hilda earned 38/6d, providing a combined annual income of around £230 a year. She had not yet been able to discover the titles to the house they lived in, which would indicate whether they were buying or renting the property, but in both cases their income would be stretched greatly in either circumstance. Alicia had a contact in the head office of the South Wales Bank, where the Williamses kept their accounts, who would have a look at their account and forward balances of total transactions, current and savings accounts at close of business that day for our information. She told me that any more detailed access would have to be by written request in future. Alicia said she was meeting her friend that evening to take possession of these figures and we could get a better picture in the morning.

I explained how far I had got with investigating Manfred Gruber and that if we wished to view his personnel record, we would need to apply in writing. However, gossip at the Dock Company suggested that some colleagues thought that Manfred was a "conchie" and used a bogus medical condition to avoid conscription. Four male members of his family were given exemption from military service at the same time, in January 1915, on the grounds of hereditary risk of epileptic seizures. From the evidence that I could see in the file at central registry, the only detailed evidence of epilepsy was contained in the hospital medical records of treatment for epilepsy of Manfred's father, Helmut, and his father. There was a suggestion from a specialist in Mannheim that epilepsy might be hereditary and that if Helmut had sons in the future, he was to be sure to test them for epilepsy. There was no evidence presented that Joachim, Manfred or Friedrich had ever suffered seizures or fits except for a sworn statement from a Dr. Julius Matthias of Cardiff asserting that the risk of epilepsy was too great to allow them to serve in the army. I wanted to investigate Dr Matthias a little further to establish the bona fides of his evidence. It was agreed that we had established quite quickly that there were legitimate lines of enquiry for us to follow for these two suspects, although we were still looking for any link with Sir Wilhelm Branden. Inspector Bennett said that he did not need to be briefed every day unless we uncovered some startling new information he needed to see but that we should meet every other day.

This arrangement suited me fine as I was anxious to pursue my enquiries speedily and to follow my instincts where possible without having to share every little piece of information gleaned with the boss. I felt that Alicia felt somewhat similarly, but when we met in the dock canteen at seven the next morning, we were able to review what we had discovered and agreed we should try to share what we had found at least once a day. Alicia had kept up a friendship with a former colleague at the branch of the South Wales Bank where they had both worked together in Penarth. Her friend, Ruth Maddock, had been promoted into a junior management role at the headquarters of the bank. Ruth had passed to Alicia the previous evening the account details and balances at the close of business the previous day. She was sorry that this only provided a snapshot of the financial affairs of the couple they were interested in, but she was unable to release any further information without a written request or a magistrates' warrant. Ruth reassured Alicia that the bank would fully cooperate in any police investigation on this basis. Alicia showed me the note, which showed that the Williamses had three accounts with the bank – a banking account for day-to-day expenses which had a balance of £378.00, a savings account in the name of Mordred Williams with a balance of £765.00 and a second savings account in the name of Hilda with a balance of £540.00. This information, although interesting, raised far more questions than it gave answers, but we were both sure that it was highly unusual for a couple with a combined income of less than five pounds a week to have accrued a total cash balance of £1683.00, more than seven times their annual combined income. We were careful not to read too much into this as there could well be perfectly legitimate reasons for their apparent wealth. They could have had an inheritance or some other windfall that had improved their financial situation, but without more detailed knowledge from their bank regarding their financial affairs, we could not make any strong suppositions about these sums. It was certainly an interesting question to find an answer to, and we agreed that we should put it before the inspector at our next meeting later in the week and press him to seek a warrant to investigate the account more thoroughly. Alicia was going to search the Cardiff property register to try to establish who was the actual owner of 36 Taffview Avenue and if it was not owned by the Williamses, whether it was let to them by the owner on a rental contract.

Over a second cup of tea, I explained that I intended to try to track down the Dr. Julius Matthias who had testified to the medical board that Manfred Gruber and his brothers were epileptics and unfit for military service. The absence of any other medical evidence that any of the brothers had suffered a seizure or fit worried me greatly. I found that a sworn statement from a single doctor was not that convincing by itself, but if his statement had been accompanied by the medical records of the three brothers, documenting when the epileptic episodes had occurred and what treatment was given, etc., I would have been satisfied. There was plenty of evidence in the Mannheim Hospital records of frequent epileptic seizures experienced by Helmut Gruber and his father which was recorded in detail, but it was only a suggestion from a German doctor that this condition might be passed on to any male children Helmut might have in the future. I wanted to ask Dr. Matthias what additional knowledge he possessed that would demonstrate categorically the risk that epilepsy had been passed from father to son in this case. "Firstly, I am going to meet with Professor Byron Meredith at the university hospital where he is a specialist in epilepsy to discuss hereditary epilepsy as I have a nagging feeling that whilst epilepsy can be passed through the generations, it is not usual for it to pass to all sons or daughters in the same family. Professor Meredith has agreed to speak with me in the break between his lectures at eleven this morning, and I hope that he will give me a better understanding of the risk of passing the condition from one generation to another."

I left Alicia at ten so that I would have time to cycle to the university hospital in time for my meeting with the professor, and Alicia made her way to City Hall to follow her leads, and we agreed to meet back at the station by five in the afternoon. I found my way to the hospital quickly, but the buildings were a rabbit warren, and it took me nearly twenty minutes to find the correct lecture theatre, but I arrived just as the students were filing out at the end of his session. I made my way into the lecture hall and descended the stairs to the front where the professor was answering some last questions from some eager medical students. When he was finished with the students, I stepped forward, introduced myself and showed him my warrant card. I could see he was interested in what the police wanted to know about epileptic conditions, and he asked me what I wished to know. I explained my confusion around the issue of hereditary illnesses and asked if a father had epilepsy, what the risk would be that this would be passed on to his children. He smiled and said that was an interesting question and he had to admit that research evidence so far could not give a quantitative answer to the extent of the risk of transmission between parents and their children. "However, the answer would have to be that there is a risk of such transmission, but we do not think that this is overwhelming and in most cases the transmission does not occur at all." I asked a further question, whether there was any difference in risk between male or female children, and he smiled and said that this was much easier to answer because there was a marked difference, with boys being almost twice as likely to develop epilepsy from their fathers than girls. The professor wanted to move on to his next lecture and was anxious to go, but I held him back with one final question. If a father was epileptic, what would be the risk of him passing the condition on to all three of his sons? He thought for a minute and then replied that in his opinion this was highly unlikely and there were hardly any recorded cases of multiple transmission within a single family, and he was certain that there had never been an incidence of three sons all being diagnosed with epilepsy from their father. If such a case was reported, it would be investigated with alacrity and reported widely. I thanked him for his expert opinion and said that he had clarified something for me in an important case I was working on. We shook hands and he rushed off to find his next lecture room where a group of medical students were waiting. I weighed up what he had told me and how it influenced my thoughts about Gruber's medical board evidence. I now knew that the risk of hereditary transmission was not high, although it was possible, and that there had never been a recorded case of multiple transmission involving three sons of an epileptic father, which directly contradicted the sworn statement given by Dr. Matthias to the medical board. It was now imperative that I contact the good doctor to interview him about why he gave the statement that he did.

I headed for the university library where I looked for the medical register for South Wales in the reference section. I pored over the pages which gave names, qualifications, specialisms and locations of all qualified medical practitioners practising anywhere in Wales. I looked through all of the entries under M three times, but there was only one Matthias listed and it wasn't Julius. The entry was for Dr. Sabine Matthias, who had qualified in medicine at the University of Wurtenberg in 1882 and had studied for post-graduate qualification in Orthopaedics in Lucerne and finally, Children's Medicine at Cardiff University in 1895. I was disappointed that this was not the Doctor Matthias I was looking for, but my attention was struck by the inference that this Doctor Matthias had German connections too. There was an address for her consulting rooms where she was in general practice in a very fashionable part of the city. I copied the information down and was about to put the book back when I noticed that there was a list of retired doctors, and a quick look bore fruit. I found the name I was looking for, listed as retired from general practice at the end of last year. He had also studied at the universities of Wurtenberg and Lucerne at the same time as Sabine and had practised, as a neurological surgeon, at Waverley Hospital and ran his private practice from the same address as Sabine Matthias. I guessed that Sabine and Julius were either married or siblings and that I would be able to find him at the address listed in the record. Dr Julius had also studied in Germany and maybe he and Sabine were of German extraction even though they had lived and worked in Cardiff for over twenty years.

I thought that I would look for a small café to get some lunch and plan the format of the questions I wished to ask Dr Julius Matthias if I could get a chance to meet him that day. It took me some time to cycle to the area where his consulting rooms were situated, in a rather upmarket area of the city, and I could see that he and Sabine must have very lucrative practices judging by the opulence of their consulting rooms. I entered a lavishly decorated receiving area and was greeted by a young woman who was acting as the receptionist. I introduced myself and showed my warrant card and said that I needed to ask Dr. Julius Matthias some questions about an old case he had consulted on in 1914. The receptionist smiled and said that Dr Julius had retired and no longer practised medicine and it would not be possible to consult him. I smiled back but made it known to her firmly that I wasn't asking for an appointment as a patient and that it was a matter of extreme urgency in an ongoing enquiry that I interview Julius Matthias that day. "I am sure you have a means of contacting him by telephone and I insist that you contact him now and tell him I wish to speak with him now." She looked as if she was about to resist, and I was sure that one of her main responsibilities was to provide a polite barrier between the patients and the doctors during the normal course of the day. I don't think she had ever dealt with a persistent policeman before and was in a quandary as to what to do. Her discomfort was eased by the interruption of a tall middle-aged lady who spoke with a slight accent and asked if she could help. She introduced herself as Dr Matthias and went on to say that her husband had retired at the end of last year and was no longer available for consultation. I replied that I did not wish to consult him about a medical matter but to clarify some evidence that he had given to the Conscription Medical Exemptions Board in January 1915 which had arisen during an ongoing investigation. "I would be extremely grateful if Dr. Julius could clear up some questions about the evidence he gave to the medical board at that time and to discover whether he has in his possession any further information that might help us with our enquiries about our suspect."

She considered for a minute and then asked me to wait whilst she telephoned her husband. When she returned, she said that her husband could spare me fifteen minutes now but had an appointment in half an hour. She turned to the receptionist and said, "Heidi will show you through to our private apartments where my husband is waiting in his study."

Dr. Julius Matthias was in his sixties and was a small, wiry man who certainly looked much fitter than many men of his age. He received me into his study warmly, although I could sense that this was out of politeness rather than a genuine desire to be of assistance to the police. I did not want to reveal my hand too much, and I was at pains not to alert his attention to the fact that I was investigating Manfred Gruber in case the doctor was also involved in the spy network. I spun him a story that as part of the process of medical exemptions from military service, a regular review of cases was undertaken each year. The cases were chosen at random and approximately ten per cent of exemptions were reviewed each year to ensure that the medical conditions still applied. I said this year one case for review was that of the Grubers and that he had provided a sworn statement that Joachim, Manfred and Friedrich Gruber were unfit for military service because of the high risk of epileptic seizures and fits because their father was a chronic epileptic and had suffered epileptic episodes frequently since his childhood. He replied that he remembered the case because it had been three brothers and it was unusual for all the sons in one family to be affected by the same condition that rendered them unfit for service in the military. I recounted that the file I had reviewed contained detailed evidence documenting the course of epilepsy in Helmut Gruber and his father from Mannheim Hospital, but there was a lack of any documentation recording epileptic episodes in any of his sons. "You were unequivocal in your statement that all three sons had a high risk of contracting epilepsy, and which would develop into frequent fits similar to that of their father, so I am sure that you had access to detailed records of epileptic issues that occurred in childhood and in the young adult lives of these three young men. The adjudicator on the medical board has asked if you could share this evidence with the board so that the board decision can be upheld. Otherwise, there is a possibility that exemption will be revoked immediately, and the Grubers will become eligible for call-up."

The doctor was affronted and said that he had never had his medical judgement questioned by a policeman who knew nothing about the medical consequences of epilepsy. He went on to say that, of course, he had seen the medical records of the Gruber boys, which documented the epileptic episodes they had all experienced during their early years, suggesting that they were at high risk of contracting a severe version of the condition as they moved into adulthood. I asked if he still had copies of these records in his possession, but he shook his head and said he had returned them to the family doctor as they were subject to patient confidentiality. I suggested that he would, doubtless, have a record of the family doctor concerned so I could get sight of the files at his office. He apologised and said that he did not have such a record as the medical files were provided by Helmut Gruber when he attended his office, and he returned them through him. "Did you examine Joachim, Manfred and

Friedrich at any time before you issued the sworn statement on their behalf?" He said that there was absolutely no need to examine them in person because the evidence presented in their medical records was clear that all three of them were at high risk of developing full-blown epilepsy as they grew older. I thanked him for his cooperation and was disappointed that he had not been able to settle this matter on that day, but I would pursue my enquiries with Mr Helmut Gruber and hopefully the medical records would be made available for review. I thanked him for his help again and for giving up his time. I could see that he had relaxed somewhat and was now smiling as he said farewell, suggesting I might call again if I had any further questions for him.

I realised when I looked at my watch that I had spent nearly forty-five minutes with Doctor Julius, and although he was supposed to have limited time available because of a prior appointment, he had not seemed in any hurry to be elsewhere. I did not think that he had been entirely truthful in his answers to my questions other than to confirm that he had written the statement in support of the Grubers' exemption from military service. I suspect that Helmut Gruber came to Dr. Julius for a certificate stating that he was a chronic epileptic, for which there was clear documentary evidence, and whether by Gruber's request or Matthias' suggestion, the statement came to include the three sons as well. I did not find the suggestion that the medical records were provided by Helmut Gruber from his family doctor particularly credible, and the fact that they were not attached to the application to the medical board, as the records of the elder Gruber were, backed up my suspicion that something was wrong here. I also found it strange that Matthias was unable to remember the name of the family doctor concerned as the medical network within the city would suggest that he would likely recognise the name of the practice concerned even if he did not know the doctor personally. Finally, I could not believe that any doctor would swear a statement as evidence before a medical board without examining the patients concerned before putting pen to paper.

I was back at the police station by 3.30pm and found a spare desk to write up my reports of the interviews with Professor Meredith and Doctor Julius Matthias before meeting with Alicia again at 5.30pm. I felt pleased with myself because I had appeared to cover a lot of ground today and felt confident that the evidence used to gain exemption from conscription for Manfred Gruber and his brothers was false, but the nagging question was why? Helmut Gruber may have simply wanted to ensure that he had security of care from his sons given his chronic condition and advancing age. The German factor may also have been an influence, and I could understand that migrants from Germany, whilst loyal to their adopted home, would not want to fight against their relations from the land of their birth. Finally, logically, if Manfred had been recruited by German intelligence to gather vital information about British shipping movements, then they would want to ensure that he remained in his position at the docks and wasn't conscripted into the army. I was still somewhat frustrated because whilst I had found a great deal more circumstantial evidence, I had not yet found too many hard facts to prove my version of events was true. I laid my reports out before Alicia and we discussed them in detail, and she was less despondent than I was about what we now knew that we did not know that, morning and she listed the points for me. "We know from Professor Meredith that the transmission of epilepsy between generations does happen, although multiple transmissions in the same family are very rare. He also stated categorically that there are no documented cases where three siblings have contracted epilepsy from their father, and if such a case existed, it would have been investigated immediately by the medical community. If the medical records of Joachim, Manfred and Freidrich Gruber showed that they had all contracted epilepsy from their father, this would be recognised immediately as unusual and become the subject of immediate research interest amongst doctors specialising in this disease. Secondly, Doctor Julius Matthias was willing to swear that the three Gruber brothers were unfit for military service because of the high risk of developing chronic epilepsy from their father without even examining them. Thirdly, their medical records could not be produced for your examination, nor could Matthias remember the name of the family doctor who provided these records, and Matthias told you he met with Helmut Gruber, who provided him with his sons' medical records. Finally, you have now established that the German connection now extends beyond Hilda Williams and Manfred Gruber to the Matthias household."

Alicia's comments had made me feel considerably better and I was anxious to hear what she had managed to find out in her enquiries at the Cardiff property register. She seemed to have had a harder time than me breaking through the bureaucracy of local government but was eventually able to look at the title deeds for the house in Taffview Avenue, where the Williamses lived. The house was registered as owned by a Mrs S Matthews c/o the Empire and Colonial Bank, Cardiff Central branch since January

1908, but the records contained no more information about who she was and where she currently resided. The titles had not been transferred since that date, so she was still the legal owner of the property. The property register was in City Hall and so Alicia was able to consult the ratings office, which was on the same floor, to establish who the current ratepayer was for the property, and this also returned the same answer: Mrs S Matthews. Alicia then decided to consult the 1911 census record for Taffview Avenue, which clearly showed that the house was occupied by Mordred Williams and Hilda and their two children. This suggested that they had rented the house from Mrs Matthews sometime before the last census in 1911 and so after briefly calling into the Empire and Colonial Bank in Castle Street to enquire after Mrs Matthews, she spent the rest of the afternoon examining house rental agreements at the City Estate Office. The bank manager was reluctant to say much but indicated that Mrs Matthews had opened the account in 1907 when she was living in Wurtenberg in Germany but had since moved on, but as far as he could remember she was still living abroad. I asked how they kept in contact with her, and the bank indicated that there was a contact address in Cardiff for correspondence but would not divulge the details without a warrant. The Estate Office was far more helpful and were happy to open their records for my perusal, and I searched for nearly three hours and was unable to find any record of a rental contract existing between Mrs S Matthews and Mordred or Hilda Williams. The knowledge of who Mrs S Matthews was and where she was living remained a mystery, but there was one snippet of information that was quite interesting because the bank manager was sure that when Matthews opened the account, she was living in Germany, although he did not think she was there now. We could be sure that Mrs Matthews could be placed in Germany in 1907 but we couldn't be sure where she was now. There were some pieces of the jigsaw that did not fit well together about the domestic arrangements of the Williamses, which needed further investigation. We needed to establish how they came to live in a house they could not afford to rent or own on their combined income and what their relationship was with Mrs S Matthews, who was the legal owner of the property. There could be perfectly innocent explanations for this, but without the opportunity to examine, in detail, the Williamses' bank accounts, we could get no further. It would be necessary to obtain a magistrates' warrant to get the South Wales Bank to give us the access we desired. We also agreed the need to understand more about the mysterious Mrs Matthews so we could make contact with her in order to verify the status of Mordred and Hilda as the occupiers of her house. This would need a second magistrates' warrant to get the Empire and Colonial Bank to release Mrs Matthews' contact address to us. Finally, we both agreed that Helmut Gruber should be interviewed and asked to reveal the source of the medical records that he allegedly shared with Dr. Julius Matthias and to reveal the name of the family doctor who had treated his three sons and could verify the diagnosis of high risk of onset of epilepsy. We decided that we would put this before Inspector Bennett in the morning and hopefully he would agree with our course of action.

I had the germ of an idea in my head that might enable us to confirm or rule out Hilda or Manfred from our enquiries. I had the notion that if we could insert some false information into the shipping movements documentation that only went through Hilda and to Manfred and was not shared with anyone else in the dock office, we might have a chance to identify if the information passed on contained the false information or not. I imagined that if the false information suggested the arrival of two fast, independent sailing ammunition ships coming in from the United States on a particular date and ETA, this might prove to be a very tempting set of cargoes for the U-boats to attack. Of course, there would be no ships to attack, but if the navy were to discover a U-boat or two in the designated area at the projected time then it would suggest that the information had got through. I did not know whether naval intelligence would think this a worthwhile ploy, but I thought it might be worth a try. I outlined my thoughts to Alicia, and she recognised my enthusiasm but didn't think that it would work as I intended. She was sure that there were flaws in the plan that would need to be rectified and she explained what she meant. Her first thoughts were that it was a little premature to be planning this kind of operation without firmer suspicions pointing at Hilda and Manfred, for we did not know at this stage whether they are working alone, together, or were indeed innocent. Secondly, we needed to know much more about U-boat operations and Royal Navy patrolling and what the likelihood was of our patrol craft intercepting U-boats in the exact area at the precise time. Thirdly, she thought that a single operation would not be enough to establish the guilt of our suspects categorically, and too many falsehoods would alert the U-boats' commanders to the prospect of false information from our side. She was sure that the German intelligence people would be expecting a certain percentage of the information they received through their agents to be false, inserted deliberately by us to put them off track. She thought we should concentrate on steady police work and build a case against our suspects if it proved there was one to be made. I was a little deflated by Alicia's reaction but over the next few hours I began to see that she was correct in her cautious approach and that my idea could always be brought forward later when it was more appropriate.

    Inspector Bennett listened carefully to our reports the next morning, and he was satisfied that we had made enough progress with our lines of enquiry to request the warrants from the magistrate and he would arrange for them to be acquired that day and we could execute them immediately. He said he approved of my deception with Julius Matthias in suggesting that we were investigating the exemption of Joachim Gruber as a part of the random annual review of exemption decisions made by the Conscription Medical Exemption Board but offered a word of caution regarding interviewing Helmut Gruber. "Keep strictly to the same story and keep the focus on the Joachim decision." Alicia and I were grateful for the wise words and the approval for our course of action from the inspector and after the meeting we sat together to plan our next steps. As soon as the magistrates' warrants were obtained, we would serve them and would gain access to the information we wanted to scrutinise further. In the meantime, I decided to visit Helmut Gruber and, keeping to the same story as I used with Dr. Julius Matthias, try to gain access to the medical records that he allegedly used to convince Dr. Matthias of the risk of epilepsy being passed to Joachim, making him unfit for military service. I would embellish the story about the routine nature of the random review of decisions made by the medical board where approximately ten per cent of decisions were reviewed annually. My objective was to convince Helmut Gruber that this enquiry was purely a routine matter, and a thorough check of the documents would settle the issue once and for all. I tried to assure him that this was just an administrative procedure that was held as a check on the decisions of the medical board and was not an attempt to overthrow the original decision in the case.

    Mr Gruber's tailor's shop was in an area close to the docks, and from the display in the front window I could see that he specialised in Merchant Marine uniforms and worsted suits suitable for work purposes rather than leisurewear. A bell over the front door jangled as I pushed it open and entered the tiny shop area, which was deserted, although I could hear the sound of sewing machines and pressing machines from the workshop at the rear of the premises. After thirty seconds or so, a small middle-aged man in a dark suit but wearing a work apron over the top and with a tape measure around his neck came from the back of the shop. He looked pale and quite haggard, and his complexion showed that he didn't get out into the sunshine very often. He was wearing thick-lensed spectacles halfway down his nose, but when he spoke his voice was low and heavy with a German accent. I introduced myself and showed my warrant card and said that I wished to speak with Helmut Gruber, and he indicated that he was Helmut. I explained to him simply the reason for my visit, and I could see from his eyes that he was frightened and suspected that something far worse lay behind the reason for the attention of the police. I was at pains to reassure him that this was a routine enquiry designed to ensure that the Medical Exemptions Board had completed its work fairly and was not intended to review the cases brought before the board for a second time. "However, in the case of Joachim Gruber, it has been noted that although there was a sworn statement from Dr. Julius Matthias that Joachim is unfit for medical service because of the high risk of epilepsy being passed through the male line of your family, the doctor never actually examined Joachim and based his opinion, solely, on the medical records you provided for him from your family doctor. The medical adjudicator has ruled that Joachim's medical records should have been shown to the Medical Exemptions Board accompanying Dr Matthias' statement at the time of the board hearing. He has also ruled that if the record could be retrieved and shown to the adjudicator's office then the case would be resolved without any further action being necessary." Helmut Gruber seemed to relax a little bit and then stuttered that he didn't have the records anymore. I replied pleasantly that this was not a particular problem if he could provide me with the name and address of his family doctor and I could gain access there and need not trouble him any further. He seemed to get a little flustered and said that he couldn't remember the name and address of the surgery offhand but would be able to get it for me when he returned to his home after work that evening. I was rather suspicious that a man with such a chronic medical condition and with three sons allegedly with the same condition did not have the contact details of his doctor close at hand, but I did not wish to arouse his suspicions any further and replied that this would be fine, and I gave him my card and suggested that he drop in the name and address of the doctor or copies of Joachim's medical records at the front desk at Tiger Bay Police Station, addressed for my attention, in the next couple of days. I could see from his face that he was visibly relieved, and he quickly agreed that he would do this as soon as possible. I thanked him for his cooperation and bid him good morning and left the shop. Feeling thirsty and wishing to reflect on my meeting with Mr Gruber, I crossed the road to a tea stall and got a mug of tea and began to weigh up what had just transpired.

Initially, I thought that I was little further forward after this encounter, but on reflection I began to see that the short meeting with Gruber had been quite informative. Even though the medical exemption was obviously of major importance to him and his family, whether genuine or not, he was unable to provide me with either the medical records for Joachim or the name and address of his doctor. I felt that this was strange that a family so afflicted by such a chronic medical condition as epilepsy did not have the name of their doctor easily to hand. I decided that I would give him forty-eight hours to comply before applying a little more pressure. Before I had completed half of my mug of tea, I was surprised to see the figure of Helmut Gruber, wearing a heavy overcoat and a Homburg hat, locking up the front of his shop and scuttling off down the street at some speed. I retrieved my bicycle and set off slowly after him as I was anxious to see where he was going in such a hurry. It was difficult to ride slowly enough not to overhaul my prey so, after a few hundred yards, I dismounted and walked alongside my bike, keeping Gruber in sight about seventy-five yards ahead. I toyed with the idea of ditching my bike but had a feeling that Gruber may hail a cab or catch an omnibus, and I would not be able to follow on foot. Sure enough, as he turned the corner into Courtney Road, I saw him hail a cab and I mounted my bike again and cycled after the taxi, keeping it in clear sight. After a few minutes, I began to have a strong idea of his destination as he seemed to be making his way to the area where Dr. Julius Matthias lived, and this may well prove to be an interesting development if I was right. I kept a safe distance back from the cab, but I was sure that Helmut Gruber would not be aware of my presence because of the heavy traffic of horse-drawn and motorised vehicles and bicycles in the city centre. My suspicions were confirmed when the cab turned into the avenue where the Matthias residence was located and came to stop at the front of their building. I dismounted and remained about fifty yards away on the other side of the road, where I had a good view of the entrance to the Matthias surgery. Helmut Gruber hurried up to the door and was admitted swiftly by Julius Matthias himself, and I settled to wait for Gruber to emerge. I would have loved to be able to hear what they were saying, but my impatience had to be curbed for the present and I settled to wait for him to emerge.

I wondered why Gruber had rushed here instead of to his family doctor and couldn't help thinking that it was possibly because neither the medical records nor the family doctor ever actually existed and were totally fictitious, but at this moment I was unable to prove this to be so. It was over forty-five minutes before I observed Gruber coming out of the side gate of the Matthias property and walking swiftly away in the direction of the city centre, where he clambered onto the rear stage of a passing omnibus at the next corner, but in the melee of buses and taxi cabs, I was unable to see which one he was on as he had disappeared inside the lower deck cabin, hidden away from my view from my bicycle seat. I resolved that I was unable to continue following him with any certainty and decided to return to the station.

THREE

I had given Gruber a couple of days to send me the name and address of his doctor or provide copies of Joachim's medical records at the police station, and I decided that I should be patient and allow him a little time to do this before visiting him again. I knew that this period of grace would put pressure on Gruber as he knew that if he didn't comply with my request I would be back, and on the second visit I would probably not be as accommodating as in the first instance. I surmised that the hurried visit to Dr. Julius Matthias was to discuss exactly what course of action they should take, assuming that they were both lying about the existence of these medical documents. All I really had for sure was the German connection in that both the Grubers and Matthias were fellow countrymen, but this, alone, would not be proof of espionage and might easily be explained as community support intended to keep German boys out of the army, where the good doctor was willing to swear a false statement to secure the medical exemption certificate. This, if true, was a serious breach of medical ethics and conduct and would probably result, if proven, in proceedings against Matthias for medical misconduct, but this was not the case I was investigating. It seemed a good idea to spend a few days scrutinising the information that we would have access to after the serving of the magistrates' warrants approved by Inspector Bennett.

I collected the warrant for the South Wales Dock Company and served it myself at the personnel office of the Dock Company that afternoon, and Alicia had taken the various warrants for the opening of the Williamses' bank accounts and to find the current address for Mrs S Matthews. I saw the same clerk at the personnel office, and he was reluctant to do anything further than before, but when I warned him that he was in danger of being arrested for obstructing an officer in the discharge of his duty backed by a court warrant, he looked askance at me and turned on his heel and almost ran into the back office, returning immediately with an older man with more authority. He took the warrant from me, read its contents thoroughly and turned to the junior clerk, instructing him to fetch the file for Manfred Gruber immediately. The personnel manager, who had introduced himself as Mr Allan Powell, asked whether I wished to take the file away or just view its contents in the office, and I replied that I couldn't be sure until I had read the file and decided whether there was the evidence I was looking for. My thoughts were that viewing the file would probably serve for now, but if any of its contents were needed for evidence in court, they would be requested in time for the hearing. He smiled coldly and said that would be in order. The clerk returned with the file and showed me to a table and chair where I could sit and read it through and make my notes. The file was not particularly extensive, but I was able to establish that Manfred was an excellent employee with good timekeeping and a diligent attitude to his work and that there was, indeed, a medical exemption certificate for military service lodged in his file. I copied down the personal details provided by Manfred to his employers and noted the details of his exemption certificate.

I asked the manager what kind of work Manfred did for the Dock Company, and he replied that he worked in the shipping office compiling the register of all shipping movements inward and outbound. This information established, without any doubt, that Manfred Gruber had access to the very information vital to our enemies but did not yet provide any proof that he was the source passing this information on to the German agents. I sought some detail as to what his duties comprised and was told that Manfred maintained the register of shipping movements for the whole Cardiff dock complex, making extra copies of the entries each day for circulation to the various department heads within the Dock Company. This established that he had plenty of opportunity to make additional copies for his own use if he wanted to, but this was still not reliable enough proof in itself, although the circumstantial evidence was beginning to build up and pointed strongly to some involvement of Manfred in the German spy network. I asked the personnel manager whether there was a record of how many copies of the register entries were made by Manfred each day and he said that there was such a record, and they were sent out according to a set circulation list and signed for in each department that received them. I asked what happened to them at the end of each reporting period and he replied that on receipt of the next day's entries, the previous sheet was destroyed and certified by the head of that department as having been destroyed. The only complete record of shipping movements at Cardiff Docks was held in the central register of shipping compiled by Manfred Gruber. I asked for a copy of the circulation list, and he sent the junior clerk to get me a copy. I could now see that Manfred clearly had the opportunity to make an additional copy of the daily entries for himself if he wished to pass them on to the German spy network, but perusal of the circulation list showed me that both Hilda Williams and her boss, Sir Wilhelm Branden, were signatories on the list. This confused the issue somewhat and widened the number of suspects just when I was hoping that the list would show that Manfred was the only suspect with access to the information. I realised that I was being too presumptuous and was allowing my feelings to cloud my judgement instead of following the facts. Manfred was still a suspect but so were Hilda and Sir Wilhelm, and I would have to drill deeper if I was to find out who the real culprit or culprits were. I thanked Mr Powell for his cooperation and returned the file to his keeping but kept the circulation list and my notes on the contents of the file with me as I made my leave. As I cycled back to the station, I found that I was looking forward to seeing Alicia and finding out what she had managed to discover from the Williamses' finances and about the address for Mrs S Matthews. I also started to realise that I was thinking about Alicia not just as a colleague but also as a female companion, although I was not confident that she had any such interest in me other than as a fellow investigator.

    I met Alicia in the canteen, and we found a table in the corner where we could talk privately and share what we had managed to uncover during the investigations that day. Alicia begged me to go first, and I explained what I had discovered at the Dock Company's personnel office from Manfred Gruber's file. She agreed with me that the information was only circumstantial but was positive that it provided another step forward and showed that we were right to focus our attention on these three suspects at Cardiff Docks. I was anxious to hear what she had discovered, and she laid out the bank statements of Mordred and Hilda Williams for the past year and said that although she had not yet had much chance to study them carefully, they clearly showed that far more money passed through their accounts than they earned from their employment, but she had not yet been able to trace where the additional payments paid into their accounts regularly were coming from and that this would take a more detailed investigation. She had, however, noticed that Hilda and Mordred paid no rent or rates or any other utility bills for the house they lived in, and this was something else that needed to be looked at carefully. She would start to look at the accounts in greater detail in the morning and try to make some sense of their financial affairs, and she would be grateful for some help with this. I willingly agreed to anything which allowed me to spend more time with Alicia and looked forward to a very pleasant day tomorrow in her company. She produced a bank letter, headed with an address written in a clear hand:

> Mrs Sabine Matthews
> c/o Wurtenberg Holdings
> PO Box 23576, Castle Park
> Cardiff

This was a little disappointing as it only gave us a PO Box number to work with and not an actual address, but I felt that some enquiries at the general post office might enable us to establish who rented this PO Box, and the companies register may be able to give us further information about the directors of the holding company. There were a couple of things that struck me as rather odd or coincidental about this address – one was that this was the second time I had come across the name Sabine in the past twenty-four hours, and it was hardly a common female name in Wales. Secondly, the woman named Sabine I had met so recently lived in the Castle Park district of the city. Thirdly, her married name was Matthias, which was very similar to Matthews, and finally she and her husband had both studied at Wurtenberg University when they were younger. The Matthiases already featured in our investigation, and we had established that they were already linked to the Grubers and could now also be a possible link with the Williamses. We were both excited that we seemed to have made significant advances in our investigation and began planning out what we had to accomplish in the morning, and it soon became clear that far from spending my day working closely with Alicia, I would be out and about on my bicycle trying to track down the actual address of Wurtenberg Holdings and to firmly establish the link we suspected between Matthias, Gruber and the Williamses.

My first call was to the general post office in central Cardiff where after several abortive enquiries I was finally directed to the office of the official who controlled the renting of all the post office boxes within the city. The GPO being a government department and an offshoot of the Home Office, there was no difficulty about releasing information to the police as part of their enquiries. The PO Box supervisor was a garrulous and friendly chap who had worked for the post office since boyhood and seemed to have an almost photographic memory about who rented his boxes. It did not take him more than a few minutes to track down the file for PO Box 23576 in Castle Park, and he confirmed that this was rented in the name of a company, Wurtenberg Holdings, which was located at 176 Gwdonkin Road, Castle Park by an applicant named S Matthews. As I wrote this down in my notebook, I had a notion that I had come across this address or something similar very recently and enquired of the post office official whether it was usual for companies to rent post boxes in such proximity to their actual business address. He said that it was not usual, especially where there was a post restante delivery service provided in this part of the city, but he guessed that it was probably because this address was shared with a doctor's surgery. All sorts of lights were switching on in my head and I could feel the excitement rising inside when I asked him if he could remember the name of the doctor. He smiled and said that it was the German doctors called Matthias, who ran their surgery from the front of the house where they lived at the rear. I thanked him profusely for his cooperation and made my way out into the street, jubilant that the connection between the Williamses, Gruber and Matthias was becoming clearer.

 I needed to go to the companies register to discover the company status of Wurtenberg Holdings and see who its directors were. I suspected I would find that the Matthiases were members of the board of directors, which would be the first piece of conclusive evidence of the link between our current suspects. The registers at Companies House were open for public perusal and despite identifying myself as a policeman, I was directed to join the queue of waiting people wishing to consult the register. I waited over an hour before I was called forward to the reading desk, where a copy of the latest register was available for me to consult. I quickly turned to the W section and scrolled down until I found Wurtenberg Holdings and quickly read through the complete entry and then jotted down what I had discovered. Wurtenberg Holdings was listed as a General Importer and Exporter comprising four companies controlled by a central board of directors. The holding company was based in Gwdonkin Road in Cardiff with three subsidiary companies based in Cardiff, Swansea and Newport Docks respectively. The holding company was financially secure, with assets over £250,000, and the chairman of the board was listed as Sir Wilhelm Branden, with six directors – Julius Matthias, Sabine Matthias, Hilda Williams, Helmut Gruber, David Taylor and Jonathan Pugh. The company secretary was Heidi Weisse and their legal representatives were Kruger and Randolph, Solicitors of Cardiff. I was struck immediately by the fact that there was no mention of a Mrs S Matthews, and I was now confident that this name was fictitious, invented purely to detract attention away from Sabine Matthias, and I knew that I needed an official from her bank to confirm that she and Sabine Matthias were one and the same person to establish this categorically to be true. Secondly, I now realised that Sir Wilhelm could now be linked directly to the Grubers and Matthias, and Jonathan Pugh and David Taylor were names that I recollected from the security briefings at Llanthony.

I was now anxious to get back to Alicia to share what I had discovered but before I rushed back to the police station, however, I decided to try to find out a little more about Kruger and Randolph Solicitors and try to establish who Heidi Weisse might be also. It proved relatively easy to find out the details of the firm of solicitors from the companies register, and I quickly found the relevant entry and copied the details into my notebook. The firm was an old established practice and had been based in St David's Square in the business quarter of the city for fifty years or so. The firm had been started by Herbert Randolph and his son Rhys and had practised successfully for many years. Herbert Randolph had died in 1892 and his son Rhys had become the senior partner and had taken over the running of the firm, but Rhys Randolph did not seem to enjoy the strong reputation of his father and the fortunes of the firm had declined under his leadership. However, it seemed that the fortunes of the firm were revived somewhat when the firm took on a new partner, Anton Kruger, in 1908, a young lawyer who had qualified in Stuttgart but had moved to Wales with his family in 1907. It appeared to me that Kruger had taken over the managing of the firm and that Rhys Randolph had taken a step back in the running of the firm. The reputation of the firm and the volume of business increased steadily over the next five years, and they had secured a place as one of the leading law firms in the city. Here was another character in this circle who appeared to be of German origin. Each member of the circle had come to Wales around the same time, and I was certainly wondering whether this was simply coincidence or part of a complex plan to place people sympathetic to Germany in British life. I knew that if I wanted to find out more about Kruger and Heidi Weisse, I would need to do some more legwork at the public records office and look at the 1911 Census results to see what further information I could dig up on the background of these two people. I had a nagging feeling, however, that as the circle of people of German origin were uncovered as interacting together there were too many coincidences to accept that this was completely innocent.

The Census documents showed that Anton Kruger lived in an imposing terrace near the city centre in an area much favoured by wealthy business and professional people as a popular place to live. Anton was shown as the head of the household and was married to Agnes Randolph in 1910 and they had three children under the age of five. It now seemed clear that Anton, in becoming Rhys Randolph's son-in-law, had secured his place as the senior partner of the law firm also. I noticed that Anton's nationality was listed as Polish and not German, and I was unsure as to how I could discover whether this was true or just a ruse to confuse the issue. He was only in his mid-thirties and was well within the age for call-up, and I needed to recheck the military exemption records to see if he was exempt from military service on grounds of nationality or medical grounds. There was only one Weisse family listed in the 1911 Census, and Rabbi Aaron Weisse was listed as the head of household, and he appeared to be a widower and was living in a house attached to the synagogue in East Terrace. Also listed were his daughter Heidi, who was married to Joachim Schultz, who was not resident at this address, and Mathilde and Rachel, her two daughters. This seemed to fit the person I was searching for, but I was a little perturbed because she used her mother's maiden name rather than the family name of her father in her directorship of Wurtenberg Holdings. I decided that I would mention Joachim Schultz' name to the sergeant who kept archive records at Cardiff Criminal Records to see if it prompted any reasons why Schultz was no longer in Wales. I knew that this might be a long shot, but it might turn up some useful information that I could use.

On my way back to the station, I cycled close to Helmut Gruber's shop and decided it might be useful to exert some additional pressure on the old man to come up with the missing medical records. The shop was dark and empty as it was on my first visit, and as I pushed the door open, I heard the bell ringing at the rear of the shop. Helmut Gruber came out from the workshop as before with an expectant look on his face, which soon disappeared when he realised that I was not a customer. He turned pale and appeared to be shaking when he saw who was standing in his shop, but I tried to reassure him by telling him that I had only dropped in tonight to save him a journey to the police station with the information I required. Helmut could hardly breathe but managed to speak in a breathy whisper that he would collect the files in the morning and drop them into the police station for me as arranged. I responded that as he had obviously now remembered who the doctor was, if he gave me the surgery address, I could call there to collect the medical records that evening and I need not trouble him anymore. I thought he was going to faint and fall on the floor, but he stammered that this was not possible as he had arranged it with the doctor and could not contact him so late in the afternoon to alter the arrangements. I was sure that he was lying but thought I would go along with the pretence, and if he did not produce these records as promised in the morning, I would discuss his arrest with Inspector Bennett tomorrow afternoon. I thought it best to be cautious and not to reveal our hand too early.

I left the shop and crossed over to where I had left my bicycle and decided to stand back in the shadows to see if my visit prompted another hasty visit to Dr Julius Matthias as on the previous occasion. I waited for over fifteen minutes but there was no movement from the shop, and I decided to head back to the police station to write up my notes. As I pushed away from the kerb and started to put pressure on the pedals and gain some speed, I heard the clattering of horses' hooves resounding on the cobbles in the street behind me. I twisted my head round to look over my right shoulder and could see a cart pulled by two large horses hurtling towards me at a gallop. The driver had a large black cloak wrapped around him and I could not see his face clearly, but there was something familiar about his appearance. He seemed to be struggling to control the horses as if they were running away out of control, and in this narrow cobbled street it would be difficult to avoid crashing into shop frontages or into anyone who got in their way at this breakneck speed. I realised I was in the greatest danger as I could not find anywhere to go to avoid this juggernaut. I frantically searched for some small niche that might give me refuge if I could manage to dismount in time, but I could already smell and feel the horses' breath so close behind me as the nearest horse was overtaking me and squeezing me against the walls of the buildings on my left side. I suddenly became aware of a shop doorway coming up fast and reconciled myself to leaping from the bicycle and into the relative safety of the door recess if possible. As I drew my weight upwards, ready to push with my legs to leap sideways, the driver's whip caught me across the back of my neck and a violent pain seared up into my head and across my shoulder and I fell towards the ground. The use of the whip had convinced me that this was no accident and that a deliberate attempt was being made to kill me, or at the very least remove me from the investigation, and as this thought flashed through my mind, I saw the front wheel of the cart mangle the rear of my bicycle and felt a massive thump in my back, which propelled me with some velocity into the doorway recess of a haberdasher's shop. I hit the wall and door with some force and was knocked unconscious for at least two or three minutes, and when I regained consciousness, I ached all over my body and the wreckage of my bicycle was laying on top of me. The street appeared to be deserted, which gave me the chance to check for any broken bones and pull myself slowly onto my feet. I searched in my pocket to make sure I still had my precious notebook and then drew out my whistle and managed to blow three loud blasts, which was the policeman's call for assistance. I knew that any constable in the vicinity, hearing my call, would respond immediately. Almost at once, I heard a response which told me that help was on its way and then a second blast a little further away, which reassured me that I was not alone. The responding whistles would also warn my assailants that more police were on their way and make them reluctant to remain close by. I sank back down as the exertion of getting up and blowing the whistle had taken all my strength away, but it only seemed an instant before the sound of hobnails ringing out on the cobbles, running quickly towards me, could be heard. The first on the scene was a young local constable who was quite out of breath after running so hard to my aid, but through great gulps of air he managed to calm me down and told me not to try to speak too much, but I insisted he look at my warrant card in my pocket. Thirty seconds later, a second constable arrived, and he was older and took charge and together they did their best to make me as comfortable as possible with a little first aid and an assessment of my injuries. My mind was fuddled, and I thought I heard horses' hooves again and desperately tried to warn my two colleagues that the horse and cart that had run me down was on its way back to finish the job, but they didn't seem to be bothered that much, for I was wrong, as they could see it was the police ambulance with the police surgeon on board approaching from the corner of the street. The doctor gave me a quick examination and administered an injection of painkillers and generally patched me up to be able to make the journey to Cardiff General Hospital. I felt them lift me onto the stretcher and place me gently in the back of the wagon, but before the cart had moved twenty yards, I had succumbed to the sedative the doctor had given me a few minutes earlier and I was asleep. I learnt much later that I was lucky that the ambulance was close by and on its way back to base after another call when they heard a police whistle calling for assistance.

When I recovered consciousness, I was already in a hospital bed at one end of a ward with the screens pulled tightly around the bed, which cut me off from the rest of the ward, and I could see that I already had a drip attached to my arm. I felt somewhat detached from what was going on around, almost as if I was watching what was going on from under the sea or through a frosted glass window. I could see the young doctor and two nurses working urgently and administering to my injuries and heard their voices as they spoke to each other but could not decipher more than a small percentage of what they were saying. The seriousness of their expressions suggested, however, that my wounds were serious enough but were probably not terminal. As my consciousness returned more fully, I could feel that I was heavily strapped up around my chest, my left wrist and right foot, and there was a bandage around my forehead which suggested a head wound of some sort, but I could not feel any pain. My memory was beginning to return and a picture of what had happened to me in the dark street outside Gruber's shop was beginning to form in my mind. Just as the doctor seemed to have completed his initial treatment, I became aware of a movement in the curtain as Inspector Bennett stepped into the space by my bed, accompanied by Bryn Powell. It now felt extremely crowded in this small space with their arrival, but the doctor dismissed the nurses to their duties. Bennett and the doctor began to speak quietly, and I realised that the doctor was giving the inspector an assessment of my injuries, so I strained my hearing to try to catch the gist of what they were saying. It was difficult to get the full picture, but from what I managed to hear, it seemed that I had suffered a heavy blow to the head as I crashed into the haberdasher's shop entrance wall and had four broken ribs, a dislocated wrist and a sprained ankle which, considering the impact from a collision with a large cart and two horses moving at high speed, was thankfully less serious than could have been expected. I had suffered cuts and bruises to my face and hands, but these were largely superficial and would heal quickly. Most of my more serious injuries would need rest to aid my recovery but the strapping-up of my ribs, wrist and ankle would ease the pain. "Constable Morgan will need to come to the hospital to have the bandages changed regularly. These injuries will heal within a month or so and he should be able to return to full fitness. He is receiving painkiller sedatives to manage the pain, but these should only be necessary for a few days as the level of pain will decrease as the healing process begins." The doctor put on a serious expression and said that the one thing that concerned him was the blow to the head, and it was still too early to tell whether there may be any longer-term effects caused by the concussion but that he would try to assess the potential for this as I returned to full consciousness. The inspector was keen to interview me about what had transpired that night, but the doctor insisted he wait until the morning to see if I returned to full consciousness and was strong enough to talk about what had happened in the dark street earlier. The inspector was not happy but reluctantly agreed to wait until the morning but said that he would post a constable here at my bedside in case I said anything during the night, and he would return to interview me first thing in the morning. The doctor said that the constable could sit at the door of the ward rather than at my bedside if this was acceptable, and I saw the inspector nod his head in agreement.

I now felt relieved to be left alone and I lay back and tried to feel what my injuries amounted to; I could feel the tight bandages around my head and ribs and felt that my left wrist and right ankle had immobilised, but I knew I could still hear and my eyesight was rapidly returning to normal, and I seemed to recollect that the doctor had suggested to Bennett that I would be fit again in a couple of months so, perhaps, I had been fortunate tonight. I was certain that I had been run down deliberately by the driver of the horse and cart, who seemed to direct the charging horses directly at me without shouting any warning. He had been disguised by a huge cloak wrapped around him to hide his clothes and face and had intentionally flicked his whip to catch me across my shoulders and neck, causing me to stumble and fall from my bicycle into the path of his horses or under his cartwheels. Luckily for me, I had a kind of second sense and had lifted myself up on the pedals ready to leap clear when a suitable refuge presented itself. Although I seemed to be able to see what happened as a series of images, as if they were presented in a book, I realised now that it had all happened at such breakneck speed that there was no time for rational thinking at any stage. I was glad that my reactions were fast and thank goodness for the fitness training I had received at Llanthony, which undoubtedly contributed to my ability to act so quickly. Although it was pitch black and the driver was covered by the cloak, there was something vaguely familiar about him, but I was unable to think where I had seen him before. My mind was whirling with all the events of the night but eventually my eyes drooped, and I succumbed to a deep and restful sleep.

As far as I could tell, I slept peacefully throughout the night, but a recurring thought kept nagging at the back of my head; that someone had come into my room during the night and spoken to me. The notion was vague but would not go away when, at first, I tried to dismiss it as only the young doctor checking on his patient in the night. This explanation did not sit right as I felt a distinct sense that my night visitor was not there for the good of my health, and I had the distinct impression that the visitor was a female. This would be very unusual as I was in a men's ward, and female doctors would not attend to male patients unless there was a very pressing reason for doing so, and would certainly not attend male patients alone without a chaperone. This question was taxing my brain considerably and I determined to approach the young doctor and share my thoughts with the inspector when he arrived in the morning. Doctor Grieves came to see me just after I had received a small portion of breakfast and a mug of tea, and I was sitting up a little in the bed and feeling a little better for my rest, although I ached all over, and the exertion of lifting myself up on the pillows was almost too much for me. The doctor checked me over and expressed satisfaction at my improvement overnight and said that many people underestimate the recuperative powers of sleep. He thought that I must have slept right through the night until the morning. I said that I was woken up in the night when the lady doctor came to see me. He looked a little confused and replied that there were no lady doctors practising medicine in the men's wing of the hospital, although there were plenty working in the women's and children's wings. He thought that I was mistaken and that I had probably confused this mystery visitor with one of the nurses whom he had asked to check on my responses every couple of hours during the night, which is standard practice for patients with head injuries. He picked up the chart at the end of my bed and confirmed that I was checked at midnight, 2 and 4am and woken at six-thirty. I asked him if the nurses would need to speak to me to check my response and he confirmed that if you were sleeping peacefully, they would only check pulse, breathing and eye movement. "Your reactions were completely normal, and they have recorded their findings and signed against their entry. The normal finding is a good sign and suggests that the concussion is not as serious as we first thought."

I heard what the young doctor had said but I was not too convinced because I had a clear picture in my mind of a middle-aged female doctor, possibly with grey hair and wearing a long white coat over her normal clothes, standing at the end of my bed and reading my chart in detail. The mysterious figure was certainly not one of the nurses on duty in the ward because she was not wearing the distinctive nurses' uniform and even in the dim light, I could discern this clearly. When she realised that I was watching her, she drew back a pace and spoke quietly with a low threatening growl, saying, "You have been fortunate to survive the terrible incident tonight, Constable Morgan, but be careful because other accidents could be arranged for you if you fail to keep your nose out of our business." The light was behind her, and I could only see a silhouette, which meant I was unable to see the features of her face, but I was certain that her accent suggested a slight Germanic sound, although I didn't have enough information to positively identify my mystery guest. I was confused again by the visit because initially I thought that her visit was an attempt to find out how serious my injuries were because they had failed to kill me, but her message suggested that it was more of a warning to persuade me to drop the case. I knew that I had much to tell Inspector Bennett but was less than certain that he would believe my version of events and take the action against the Gruber and Matthias families, who I thought were the guilty parties in this matter.

The hospital routines began early in the day, and I found that I had been fed, washed and cared for and was propped up in bed ready to face the day by seven-thirty, chomping at the bit impatiently, waiting for the routine of the rest of the world to catch up. I thought it would be several hours before Inspector Bennett or Detective Sergeant Powell made an appearance to take my statement, and my mind was working overtime trying to make sense of all that happened to me yesterday and to make sense of the information I had uncovered at the Public Records Office and on the companies register. I needed to ensure that Alicia would follow up on Joachim Schultz with the Criminal Records Department and establish whether Kruger was a Polish national as the census records seemed to suggest and whether he was exempted from military service or not. There was, however, one question still bothering me about the incident the night before, as to whether it was premeditated or just spur of the moment. The idea that Gruber and Matthias had conspired together to give me a warning or kill me was difficult to believe unless they had my movements under surveillance, and I was certain that I would have been aware of being followed over the past days. I had only decided to visit Gruber's shop again on the spur of the moment and I was beginning to think that old man Gruber had become so unnerved by my persistence that he was moved to take decisive action to remove me from the enquiry. I was certain that Helmut was not the driver of the horses and cart, but he had three sons who were certainly young and strong enough to have been the driver. Although I did not see the face of the driver clearly enough for the purpose of identification, there was a certain familiarity about him, and the only Gruber brother with whom I was vaguely familiar was Manfred, who seemed to be the most likely suspect in my mind. I knew that suspicion was not enough to arrest Manfred Gruber and I was sure that Inspector Bennett would wish to act with caution to ensure that we did not reveal what we knew too early and risk rolling up the whole spy network rather than just one member of it. This was the risk that if the spy network became aware of a major ongoing police investigation into their activities, they would be likely to disappear completely from view, but as far as we knew at this point, they thought that I was acting alone on behalf of the Medical Exemptions Board as part of their routine audit of cases. It seemed obvious to me now that the medical records for the Gruber boys did not exist and that Dr Julius Matthias had faked the statement he had given to the board.

FOUR

Later that morning, I was interviewed by the inspector and Bryn Powell at length from the relative comfort of my hospital bed. The screens had been pulled tight around my bed space and a constable stationed outside to ensure that we weren't interrupted or overheard. I was feeling much better than when I was first brought into the ward, and a good night's sleep had worked wonders in my recovery, allowing me to tell my story of the events in the street outside Helmut Gruber's shop with clarity. The inspector was very patient and skilled at letting me talk freely but also extremely attentive to the small details that came out through the story as he made me go over the events as I remembered them several times. He was very quick to downgrade the notion that this was an accident caused by a pair of runaway horses or a desperate carter trying frantically to control them. The failure to find both the horses and cart or the driver in the immediate vicinity, or anyone coming forward to report the accident, suggested that this was so. The attempt to disguise his face and the use of the whip to strike me on the back of the neck and head to force me to fall under the charging horses and cartwheels also added to his suspicion that this was no accident. Any innocent cart driver would have reported the incident to the police immediately after hitting a cyclist. No such report had been received at any police station in the city and the cart and horses had not been found, although some broken pieces of the cart had been recovered from the street in the immediate vicinity of the impact, which might lead us to identify the perpetrator. He confided in me that he felt a strong policeman's intuition that there were too many coincidental events linked to the Grubers and the investigation we were engaged in for this to be so. He had formed an opinion that I was the victim of a deliberate attack that had been clumsily or hastily carried out, designed to remove me from the scene, and he was already convinced that my line of investigation provided the motive for the attack. He hoped that this was a precipitous attack prompted by Helmut Gruber's fear that he was about to be exposed as conspiring with Julius Matthias to give false evidence to the Medical Exemptions Board. It seems highly likely that the alleged medical records for the three Gruber sons were fictitious or did not contain the incidence of epilepsy alleged by the sworn statement made by Dr Julius Matthias to the Medical Exemptions Board. "The impromptu visit to Gruber's shop last evening must have been the last straw for Gruber, who saw that time was running out fast as he was convinced that your persistence meant that you were not going to let this matter drop. He needed to act fast if he was going to stop you, and I believe that he had three young and able sons who could have driven these horses and cart, but at this moment we do not have evidence to prove it was them."

I shared with them my thoughts about the identity of the driver, although I could not swear to a definite recognition, but there was a familiar look about him suggesting a Gruber family resemblance, and the only Gruber son whom I had seen before was Manfred. I also recounted my recollection of the mysterious night visitor by my bed in the middle of the night but again under the influence of sedatives, half asleep and still feeling the effects of trauma, I knew that my account would not stand up to examination in court. However, I was as certain as I could be that it had taken place and I emphasised that the mysterious visitor was a middle-aged woman who spoke with a hint of a German accent and warned me quite emphatically to step back from investigating their affairs or something worse might happen to me. I had spoken with Doctor Grieves and he had confirmed that the night nurses had checked my vital signs every two hours during the night whilst I was asleep and recorded their observations on my chart. The young doctor was also emphatic that female doctors did not work in the male wing of the hospital but were largely confined to working in the female or children's wards. When I asked him if female doctors ever attended male patients, he told me that they did when they were accompanied by male colleagues or nurses but never alone or in the middle of the night. According to the doctor, the night nurses had been busy carrying out observations on patients throughout the night and were not aware of any visitors to the ward, but he pointed out that the constable stationed at the ward door would have been aware of anyone who entered or left the ward during the dark hours. The inspector said that they would interview the night nurses, Dr Grieve and the night duty constable as soon as they could and try to follow up on what I had alleged. I understood that they would not just take my word for what had happened and would look for corroborative evidence to back up my story, but I couldn't help doubting myself and my version of events. I was sure that I had been visited by Dr Sabine Matthias, who had come with the express intention of warning me off and to threaten me with dire consequences if I failed to do so. Helmut Gruber would probably only face a fine or internment if it was proved that he had deceived the Medical Exemptions Board, but her husband stood to lose his professional reputation and standing in the community as well as a fine and possible internment should it be established that he had lied on oath to the tribunal. I could see how they would want to avoid these consequences as far as possible and that this is what prompted them to act so rashly. I could not see any evidence that they were aware of the additional enquiries we had been making into their financial affairs and connections with Hilda Williams, Sir Wilhelm Branden, Anton Kruger and Wurtenberg Holdings.

Inspector Bennett eyed me sternly and said that I should forget about the enquiry for the moment and that I should concentrate on my recovery as my priority. He reassured me that the investigation would continue under the lead of Alicia Bell and that he would draft in Ivor Bethal to support her in this work but as soon as I was fit to return to duty I would be back on this case. "We have invested a great deal in training you for this role and you are already showing such great potential as an undercover investigator that we would be reluctant to lose you." I was comforted a little by his words but still hoped that I would get a chance to talk to Alicia about the case sometime soon. Before he left, Inspector Bennett said that he had sent a telegram to my father informing him that I was in hospital and recovering from a road accident and he expected that they would visit me sometime today. He reminded me about the need for secrecy about the work we were involved in, but I could say that I had sustained my injuries in a road accident involving a collision with a horse and cart. I would be pleased to see my parents but didn't like the idea of hiding the truth from them but understood the reason why. I doubted that Dad would miss a shift at the colliery to visit me in Cardiff, but I was sure that my mum would make the journey today or tomorrow on the train. After the inspector left, I was feeling tired and ready for some further sleep, and looking up at the ward clock, I realised that we had been in close conversation for nearly three hours but as I settled into my pillow, I was interrupted by the attention of the nurses taking their observations and doctors' rounds and then lunch before I could relax and drift off to sleep.

Mum and Dad had received the telegram around eleven last night and had immediately determined that they would travel to Cardiff on the train to visit me in the hospital. Dad was not a good sick visitor at the best of times but was also reluctant to miss his shift without giving prior notice to the colliery management. He said that he would arrange to go on Saturday, which was his day off, as they could not afford to miss a day's wages because of the extra expenses accrued by Derfal's scholarship at Newport County School. Mum decided that nothing was going to stop her going and that she would take Derfal with her for company on the journey. Once Mum had made up her mind, it became final, and nothing could stop her doing what she said she would do. It was about three-thirty that afternoon when I was shaken awake by my nurse to tell me I had visitors and she plumped up my pillow and straightened my sheets so that I was presentable to receive them. I was genuinely pleased to see Mum and the smiling face of Derfal, my youngest brother, who was still a schoolboy, and although Mum's expression was serious, I could see the love and care in her eyes as she looked at my battered and bandaged bulk laying in the bed. As I started to talk, however, she relaxed a little and I think she began to see that although my injuries looked quite severe, I would soon recover with few long-term issues. It simply looked worse than it was, and they were both eager to know how it happened, so I described how it happened with as much accuracy as I was allowed to divulge but was pleased that they readily believed that the driver of the cart had lost control when his horses were startled and bolted, and I was the unfortunate cyclist who got in their way. Mum said that she thought riding a bike in a big town or city was much more dangerous than in a small village because of the motor- and horse-traffic all mixed up together. I pointed out that riding a bicycle was an essential part of my duties as a constable, although I did walk the beat sometimes and had learnt to drive a car. She said that I needed to be more careful and be aware of the dangers around me when riding a bike. I reassured her that I would not be getting onto a bicycle for some time in the future, not until my wrist and ankle had healed fully, and that I would be probably restricted to administrative duties in the police station until the police surgeon passed me fully fit for resuming full police duties. Mum spent about an hour giving me all the gossip about the village that she had picked up through the chapel, which bored me, and news about my older brothers in the army in France. Gwyn, my younger brother who worked in the pit, had been playing well as the first XV scrumhalf for the rugby club this season. I was glad to hear this news from home but grateful that I had left the village and didn't have to endure this small talk on a too-regular basis, although I was happy to see Derfal, who was coming up to his sixteenth birthday and would be taking his school certificate examinations in a couple of months. Around five, Mum and Derfal said their farewells and headed out of the hospital to catch a bus to the railway station. I was pleased that they had made the effort to visit me today, but I was also glad that they had gone as I needed to relax and gather my thoughts before Alicia came to visit me so I could talk things through carefully and compare notes with her.

Alicia did not visit me until the following morning when she came out of patient visiting hours and used her warrant card to gain entry to the ward. I found that I was very pleased to see her and although I couldn't bring myself to say so out loud, my pleasure was more than just professional. However, I was glad to find that she was as anxious as I to hear what I had discovered at Companies House and at the Public Records Office, and she listened carefully when I explained what I had found out about Wurtenberg Holdings and the board of directors. The company was registered at the same address as the Matthias surgery and residence, and both doctors were directors, plus their receptionist, Heidi Weisse. The chairman of the board was Sir Wilhelm Branden and Hilda Williams was the company secretary, and I was surprised to find Jonathan Pugh and David Taylor, in our list of original suspects during our training, also members of the board. The legal representatives were a firm of solicitors called Randolph and Kruger, whose senior partner, Anton Kruger, was registered as Polish but had studied and qualified as a lawyer in Stuttgart before moving to Cardiff in 1907. Almost every board member had a strong German connection by birth or association, although they had all been living in Wales for some time. The holding company was well financed and held considerable assets in the bank and was listed as a general importer and exporter and had premises in all three major docking facilities along the South Wales coast. The companies register contained little further information and I was unable to ascertain any details about their employees or annual turnover, but I was sure that we could get access to their company accounts via their bankers with a further magistrates' warrant. I explained to Alicia that I didn't believe that Anton Kruger was Polish and strongly suspected that he was German, or if he was a Pole, he was from a Polish/German family as his family name was more Germanic than Polish and he came to Britain direct from Germany, like many of the other directors of Wurtenberg Holdings. Alicia was sure that she could make discreet enquiries amongst the Polish community in Cardiff about Mr Kruger and see what she could turn up. I told her about Heidi Weisse, who worked for the Matthiases as their receptionist at the surgery but didn't use her married name, which was Schultz. "She is the granddaughter of one of the rabbis at the East Street Synagogue, Aaron Weisse, and is married to Joachim Schultz. The 1911 Census did not list Joachim as a resident at the East Terrace address, although Heidi and her children were listed." I found it a little suspicious that Heidi chose to use her mother's maiden name rather than her actual surname, which should be Heidi Schultz, and would have liked to know when and why Joachim Schultz was no longer with his family. Alicia suggested that Schultz was not a particularly Jewish-sounding name and that most Jews who had moved to Britain tended to anglicise their names to sound less Germanic. If Joachim Schultz was not Jewish, this might be the reason for the break-up of the family and the reluctance to use his name within the local Jewish community after he had departed. She noted this down in her notebook for future attention.

She said that she had learnt a great deal from the scrutiny of the Williamses' bank accounts, which had opened new avenues of investigation about the regular cash flow in and out of their bank accounts, which was far in excess of their earnings. The house they lived in was paid for entirely by Mrs S Matthews, whose forwarding address was the same as that of the Matthias household and we now knew was also the address of Wurtenberg Holdings, where Mrs Williams held the position of company secretary. "Most of the transactions through their accounts, deposits and withdrawals, are made in cash, with cheques used only occasionally. I am trying to track down as far as possible who the beneficiaries of payments were and who was paying money into their accounts on a regular basis, but this will take time."

Alicia told me that Ivor Bethal would be joining her tomorrow and together they would analyse the financial affairs of the members of the board of Wurtenberg Holdings to establish how closely their affairs were linked. She explained that Inspector Bennett had instructed them to take a step back from the Grubers to convey a false impression that their warning had been heeded and to let the heat cool a little. The last thing we wished to do was to frighten them off so that they ran to ground before we were in a position to arrest the whole network and secure multiple convictions for espionage. "Bennett believes that if we use your recovery and recuperation as a time just to keep a watching brief from a distance on the activities of the Grubers, they may be lulled into a false sense of security, and we will be in a much stronger position to tackle them head-on when you return to duty." I could see the sense in this strategy. Although my own sense of impatience would have directed more immediate action, I was content to recover from my injuries and bide my time until I was able to be part of the investigation again. The Grubers had not seen Alicia or Ivor before so I thought they should be able to keep a surreptitious surveillance without being discovered whilst I was off duty. With our business concluded, Alicia was anxious to slip away and get back to her investigations, although I would have welcomed her staying a little longer.

Even just less than forty-eight hours since I was brought into the hospital, Doctor Grieve was encouraged by my improvement in such a short time and was optimistic that I had not really suffered any significant long-term injuries that would prevent me from returning to duty within about four weeks. His fears about a serious head injury were now receding, but he was concerned that my ankle and wrist were knitting together properly before he let me out of hospital. He reassured me that I should be able to go home within a couple of days if things went well and I was able to walk with crutches without putting too much weight on my ankle. He was sure that within a couple of weeks I would be walking again without the aid of crutches and could start exercising my ankle gently to rebuild its strength. He felt that the wrist would take a little longer but as I was right-handed, this should not cause me too much inconvenience. He said that the orthopaedic consultant would see me on Friday morning to decide whether I should be discharged that afternoon or kept until next week. He said he hoped that I would be discharged on Friday afternoon but that depended on whether I had somewhere to go where I could be looked after properly. I lived in accommodation for single men provided by the police, which I knew was certainly not suitable for my recuperation or recovery, but I was certain that I could spend a few weeks at my parents' house in Bedwas if that was at all possible. The young doctor said that this sounded a possibility, but Bedwas was rather too far to travel for the physiotherapy sessions that I would need to get full movement back into my ankle and wrist. He said he would try to arrange for the therapy to be carried out at the General Hospital in Caerphilly, if possible. He then left me to sleep, and I drifted off with so many ideas about the case, going home to my parents for a while and, of course, Alicia whirling around in my head.

The next two days passed in a flash and on Friday morning I was spruced up and sitting up in bed for the rounds by the consultant at ten in the morning. The consultant seemed quite elderly with grey hair and big side-whiskers, which were popular at the end of the last century. He was portly and dressed immaculately in morning dress with a formal wing collar. His progress around the ward was like a royal procession with his large entourage of junior doctors and nurses paying due deference to their leader as he moved on from bed to bed. When he finally approached my bed in the far corner, he spent two or three minutes studying my charts and checking my observations and then asked the sister to lift the covers over my ankle, and he gently manipulated my ankle and gave a sigh of satisfaction, which I supposed was because I didn't jump up with too much pain rather than because of an improvement in its condition. He then looked at my wrist and moved it around and this did hurt considerably, and he tutted under his breath every time I flinched and then he passed on to the next patient without a word to me, which left me rather confused as to the outcome of his examination. I watched his progress down the other side of the ward for the next twenty minutes and then he left the ward as he had arrived. Eventually, Doctor Grieve came up to the side of my bed to give me a briefing on the consultant's diagnosis. I was eager to hear the verdict and the young doctor explained that my ankle was healing well and Professor Watkins was extremely pleased, but he was concerned that the swelling in my wrist had not yet dissipated enough to allow free movement of the joint. I was not sure whether I had made enough progress to leave hospital that day, or would it be next week, but I waited anxiously for the verdict. However, given his concerns about my wrist, he had decided that he would discharge me on Monday and would prescribe some anti-inflammatory treatments to reduce the swelling enough for me to cope outside the hospital. The consultant had made it clear that my injuries were less severe than many of the wounded soldiers being admitted to the hospital after repatriation from the front, and I could not take up a valuable bed after Monday. I was delighted to hear this as I would have enough time to arrange police transport to take me to Bedwas on Monday afternoon and prewarn my mother and father that I was returning home for a while.

Saturday visiting hours came and Mum, accompanied by Dad, came in as soon as the doors were open, and they seemed delighted to hear my news. Mum busied herself with working out how she was going to fit me into the already cramped bedroom shared by Gwyn and Derfal. She decided that I should have Gwyn's bed as he was always the last to go to bed at night and up early for his shift in the morning, so this would cause the least inconvenience to the rest of the household; she would make up a temporary bed for him in the back kitchen, which would be warm enough for him to sleep well for a few weeks. I had some misgivings about this because Gwyn was working long shifts in the pit and needed his rest but when I objected, Mum would not listen and had made up her mind. I knew better than to push it any further because when Mum made up her mind, there was no chance of changing it. I tried to appeal to Dad, but he just shrugged his shoulders because he knew that Mum knew best and went on to tell me all about what was doing well in the allotment this year and how when I was able to get about a little more easily, I could accompany him and help him with planting and weeding as a bit of therapy for my injuries. I did not yet know what time the police transport would come for me, but I suspected that I would be at home by mid-afternoon on Monday, but Mum said everything would be ready for me. Dad suddenly remembered to pass on apologies from Gwyn for not coming to see me but he was playing scrum half for the village team that afternoon at Maesteg, but he looked forward to seeing me next week. I thought he might not be so happy to see me when he realised that he had been kicked out of his bed and had to sleep on the put-you-up in the back kitchen for the next three weeks or so. After an hour, Dad started getting restless and Mum said that they ought to be on their way as it would take nearly two hours to get back home by the time they'd caught a bus to the station and the valley train to Bedwas. I was so pleased that they had made such an effort to come to see me that day, but I was also glad that they were leaving as I was feeling tired and would welcome a chance to close my eyes and snooze for an hour before the evening meal.

Detective Sergeant Bryn Powell dropped in just before the close of visiting time to see how I was getting on, and I was able to arrange for a police car to drive me home on Monday and he said he would book the car for two in the afternoon. We then spent ten minutes reviewing the progress of the case and he told me that they had discovered the cart that had probably run me down by matching the broken pieces of the tailboard to missing pieces on the suspect vehicle. The cart belonged to a Geraint Jones, the butcher who owned a shop and slaughterhouse just two doors away from Gruber's shop and, coincidentally, they shared a communal back entry and yard. "Jones closes his shop at four in the afternoon and the horses are stabled in the yard behind his shop when he goes home at night. He was mystified when he opened up in the morning to find damage on the tailboard of his cart and he had a feeling that the horses were in the reverse stalls to the ones he had put them in the night before. He felt that he was not going mad and, when he got a chance during the day, he called into the police station to say he thought someone may have used his cart and horses without his permission. He was treated with some suspicion at first until his alibi checked out that he could not possibly be the cart driver at the time you were run down. However, Ivor Bethal was poking around in the yard when he happened to notice Manfred Gruber coming out of a gate opposite the stable and he recognised him from the briefings at Llanthony House. Gruber had never seen Ivor before and didn't recognise him as a policeman and just passed on his way, unaware that he had been recognised as a person of real interest as having easy access to Mr Jones' horses and cart."

This was good news and backed up my suspicions that Manfred was the driver of the cart that ran me down that night. "The police surgeon has inspected the damage on the side and rear of the cart and has found some blood samples on the nearside of the cart that struck you and which he will analyse in his laboratory, but he wasn't overly optimistic as the wood of the butcher's cart was covered in blood spatters from the butchered animals it regularly transports, so this might not prove conclusive."

Sunday in hospital passed very slowly and every time I looked up at the ward clock, the hands seemed only to have moved an inch or two. I tried to concentrate on reading from a book I found in the bedside drawer, but its chapel religious tone was not much to my liking, so I tried to sum up in my head all the evidence we had discovered against this potential German spy ring, but in my state of boredom I found it too difficult to really concentrate properly, so in the end I just dozed and waited. There were no visitors allowed on the Sabbath and successions of lay preachers from various local chapels came around trying to make the bedridden sinners repent, with the pain of dire consequences for those who ignored the call. I thought that most of the poor souls in the beds around this ward had probably experienced a fate worse than death through disease or wounds in warfare to be all that interested in the message they were spinning, but the preachers were not put off and delivered their fire-and-brimstone and wages-of-sin sermons anyhow. I was reminded of those long Sunday sermons delivered by the Reverend Lewis at the Miners' Chapel in Bedwas which I endured with such bottom-numbing regularity every Sunday when I was growing up. It struck me life would be a little better if there was more pleasure and fun instead of this deadly stern and serious approach to life. Finally, it was time to serve our evening meal and the holy rollers were sent on their way, and I almost enjoyed the meal served that evening and felt glad that I would be out of hospital by two in the afternoon tomorrow, when I knew that with my Mum's home cooking and loving care I would soon return to my old self, although I knew that too much home cosseting would soon send me back to Cardiff and bring some normality back into my life. I knew that having me at home would put extra strain on the family finances, whilst I suffered no loss of pay being injured on duty, and I would give Mum some extra housekeeping money to ease the financial burden for them.

In the end, I stayed just over three weeks at home and enjoyed being at the heart of the family again a great deal. It was reassuring that the routine of the family had not changed too much since I had moved to Cardiff, but neither had the love and warmth that bound us all together as Morgans diminished in any way. It was gratifying to see my mother confidently controlling everything that went on in our house whilst cleverly letting Dad think he was in charge. She worked from morning until night to make sure that our house was clean and as comfortable and warm as she could make it and that there was a hot meal ready for Dad and Gwyn when they came off shift six days a week. The water was hot and the tin bath ready for them to bathe when they came in from the pit so they could scrub off the coal dust and dress in clean clothes before entering the parlour to enjoy their food and relax by the fire. Dad liked to pore over the newspaper, reading every story in minute detail, following the news from the front and particularly the politics of the working-class tension around poor working conditions, workers' rights and low wages. Gwyn would chat for a while but was always anxious to get out of the house as quickly as possible to meet up with some girl or other, go drinking at the Miners' Welfare Club or rugby training every Wednesday. Dad's lifetime in the pit had made him militant for better working conditions and greater safety, and he believed that the sacrifices made by ordinary folk, whether they were fighting or keeping the wheels of the war turning at home, demanded that the ruling classes must change, and society must become fairer for all. He believed that wealth should be more evenly spread amongst all so that the scourge of poverty would be eradicated and that privilege by birth would end, and he often talked about the formation of a political party to challenge the elite ruling class for a fairer share in the running of our country, so often talked about by miners in the colliery and at the club. He had worked forty-five years in the pit since he was a boy, and conditions for miners had changed little and wages were still as poor as ever. He knew that his working life was coming to an end as his fitness and strength were already beginning to decline, and he knew the day would come when he would be cast aside by the bosses and would lose his livelihood, unless some small job could be found on the surface to keep him going for a few more years as a cleaner or lamp trimmer. He was a proud man, and he would be reluctant to accept such a demeaning loss of status by taking one of these easy jobs even though it would mean a drastic reduction in income for the family if he was made redundant. He felt he was secure whilst the war lasted but when it ended and lots of able-bodied young men returned home, he knew he would be surplus to requirements at the pit. Thankfully, they were savers and they had over the years always managed to live within their means and save enough for emergencies and although there was no pension for his service in the pit, they would be able to continue to live in their colliery house rent-free and would still receive his allocation of free coal each week. Thankfully, the miners themselves contributed from their wages to the welfare fund, which supported retired miners and those injured or sick through work and this would help a little.

One of the things I enjoyed the most was getting to know my youngest brother, Derfal, a little better. There was a gap of six years between us, and he was still at school and would be sixteen within a month. He was a very bright boy with an immense interest in literature and spent much of his spare time with his head in a book. He also had an enquiring mind and the curiosity to know how things worked. I had a great affinity with him as I too had enjoyed reading and enjoyed using my brain rather than my physical strength to solve problems. He was interested in my job as a police detective and whilst I couldn't tell him a great deal about my current investigation, I did explain how we searched for evidence that we would build into a case that would stand up in a court of law. I taught Derfal how to play chess and he became quite addicted to the game and within a few days had understood the basic tactics of the game sufficiently to make me think seriously about how to overcome his strategies to win the game. Of course, during the daytime when they were all going about their daily tasks, I spent much time alone and began to rethink the evidence in the case so far, but this only led to frustration as I had no contact with Alicia or Ivor to keep me abreast of any new evidence that they had uncovered since I had been away. To keep me occupied, I tried to exercise my ankle as much as possible and after a week I was able to walk reasonably well using only a walking stick, and I discarded the crutches. I received a letter from Caerphilly Hospital calling me for physiotherapy on my wrist the following Thursday, and so I redoubled my walking exercise because I knew that I would have to walk to the station to catch the train and then walk to the hospital from Caerphilly station. Every day, I practised walking down High Street to the station and back up the hill home until I felt confident that I had the stamina to make the journey. On Thursday morning, I dressed in my suit and set off in good time to catch the 09:00 train to Caerphilly. The journey was only three miles and took barely ten minutes, but I was glad of the opportunity to sit for that short time to get my breath back. I was pleasantly surprised when I came out of the main door into the station yard at Caerphilly to see a horse-drawn bus with the hospital name on its destination board, so I was glad to climb aboard. It was my good fortune as the journey to the hospital was about a mile or so, but it was all uphill and would have certainly tired me considerably before my appointment. The hospital was busy with local people coming for their appointments but also crowded with large numbers of wounded soldiers who were recovering from their wounds, waiting at every clinic. I found the room where I was to report and handed my letter to the nurse who manned the reception desk. She directed me to a seat and said that they were busy today but I should be seen within an hour. I had bought a newspaper from the stand at the railway station, so I settled to read the news whilst I waited.

The therapist was a man of about forty years of age who told me that he had lost the lower part of his left leg when he stepped on a mine whilst running across no man's land at the first battle of Ypres in 1915 but had recovered and returned to the job he had done before the war because he was no longer fit for military service. He asked me rather pointedly why I was not in the military, and I told him that I was a policeman and this injury had been sustained when a criminal I was chasing had tried to run me down with a horse and cart. He became more friendly and sympathetic then and worked efficiently and expertly to manipulate my wrist more freely. He was satisfied that the inflammation had dramatically reduced and was confident that I would get full use of the wrist and hand again in a month or so. I was booked for two more sessions the next week on Tuesday and Thursday at the same time as today. These sessions proved equally useful, and he was almost ready to sign me off as fit after the third session but said that he would make an appointment for me to see the police surgeon, who would confirm my fitness to return to duty. The letter calling me to the police surgeon's office in Cardiff came a week later, and I was confident that he would sign me off ready for duty on that day because I was now walking without the aid of a stick and could use my hand and wrist as normal again. The bruising and scratches had all but disappeared and I felt fit again. I knew Mum would be sad to see my return to Cardiff as she had become used to having me around every day, but I was anxious to get back on the case.

The police surgeon's department was on the floor above the central morgue in Cardiff and four or five doctors worked there, supported by a score of administrative staff. I wore my uniform for the first time in ages and was able to travel free on the train and buses as a result and travelled down to the city on the train. I was due to meet with Doctor Clarke at 11:00 and was waiting outside his office ten minutes before the appointed time, but I didn't wait long because at the exact time he opened the door and invited me into his office. He asked me to remove my tunic and shirt and proceeded to test the strength and movement of my wrist by asking me to perform certain manipulative tasks and then to lift some small weights. He made some approving noises and then sat and completed his notes on my records. He then repeated similar tests on my ankle and filled in the notes again and finally he looked up and smiled and said I could return to duty on the following Monday morning, and he would inform Inspector Bennett of his decision. I was delighted as I made my way back to the station and couldn't wait to get back to work the next week.

FIVE

The atmosphere around the boardroom table at the emergency meeting of Wurtenberg Holdings, hastily called the day after the attack on Wesley Morgan, was tense, and everyone seated around the table knew that tempers were frayed and feelings running very high. Sir Wilhelm called the meeting to order as chairman of the holding company, but it was soon clear who the commanding force was amongst this group of people when Anton Kruger switched to speaking in German and directed proceedings from then on. The first item on the agenda was the attack on the British policeman, and Kruger was furious that this attempt on his life had been made precipitously without the knowledge or approval of members of the board. His voice was raised in volume as he directed his remarks to all sitting around the table, but they were especially directed at Helmut Gruber and his son Manfred. He accused them of utter stupidity for acting so rashly and for forgetting all they had been taught in their training, reminding them that they were at war, and as German soldiers, operating behind enemy lines, it was their duty not to draw attention to themselves and to act cautiously in all dealings that might raise the suspicions of the police. They looked back at him sheepishly as he condemned them for being so overcome with fear that they acted without thinking and put them all at risk. Helmut stammered and spluttered and almost burst into tears as he tried to excuse himself from blame… but the policeman was so persistent, and time was almost running out to provide him with the medical records he was asking for. He said that he was at his wits' end and desperate and did not know what to do, and when Manfred said he would take care of it he was relieved, but he didn't realise that he was going to attempt to kill the annoying policeman. Kruger's anger spilled out of him as he shouted his admonishments across the table, directed principally at Helmut but meant equally for the ears of everyone around the table.

Kruger continued without stopping and pointed out that the policeman was only following up a routine check-up as part of the annual audit of decisions made by the Medical Exemptions Board. "Had you and Dr Julius Matthias given him straight answers, he would have been satisfied and we would have heard no more. Julius, you have proved yourself equally as stupid and cowardly as Gruber and you could have easily produced a falsified copy of the medical records required and passed it to Constable Morgan and that would have been an end to it. Your prevarication when added to the lack of straight answers from Gruber made Morgan even more determined to get to the bottom of this case and not to let it go. What kind of doctor makes a diagnosis without examining the patient first or at least receiving written records or case notes to guide his thoughts? What parent of boys who were alleged to suffer from epileptic fits from childhood and who was a chronic epileptic himself could not remember the name of his family doctor or produce their medical records for examination when it was requested by the legal authorities?"

He now turned his attention to Manfred Gruber and said that up until now he had an exemplary record, and one of the reasons that he was selected for his role was that he was calm and cautious and had not been prone to any rash action or behaviour previously and had not attracted any adverse attention towards himself by his behaviour so far. "However, what possessed you to act so out of character, stealing the butcher's cart from your neighbour's stable and attempting to run the constable down in the street only a few short yards from the front door of your father's shop? The Cardiff police are not stupid and will quickly look for local connections, and this may well have attracted suspicion on you and your father that might put us all in some jeopardy. Even then, your actions were carried out so poorly that you failed to deliver a decisive blow and kill the unfortunate policeman. He lies in hospital with multiple injuries, but the prognosis does not look too bad for this young man, who is likely to recover and return to duty sometime in the future, so we are reliably informed by the other good doctor Matthias, Sabine, who further exposed us by covertly visiting Morgan in his hospital bed in the middle of the night. This was highly risky, and we can only hope that young Morgan was heavily sedated and unable to recognise her as the mysterious night visitor. It seems that collective stupidity reigned in your heads again that night.

"Finally, if we are lucky, we may not be too troubled by these events if we act cautiously from now onwards. If Morgan had recognised Manfred or

Sabine, the police would have raided your premises by now and all remains quiet, and we are fortunate that there were no witnesses to the attack. Manfred returned the cart and the horses to their stable under the cover of darkness and even if the police find the cart, it should not tell them very much." He then dropped his voice into a more sinister and threatening tone and said that they all knew the power invested in him as a colonel in the Kaiser's secret service and that if any one of them threatened the safety of their mission by such stupidity again, he would have them relieved of their post and shot.

They all knew that he meant what he said and all nodded and mumbles of, "*Jawohl*, Herr Oberst," were heard around the table. "If we keep our heads and behave as we were taught to do, as undercover operatives, we can weather this enough to be able to carry out the important missions entrusted to us. The police will make enquiries in the street during the next few days, and you must have your stories prepared and consistent with each other. Julius will produce a false medical record for Helmut should the police persist in asking for it, but I will guess that after a couple of days the interest in this matter will decrease as the police concern themselves with more serious cases."

They then moved on to the second main item on the agenda which was Operation Worm's Head and involved preparations for receiving two German officers who were being landed by boat from a U-boat in Rhossili Bay on the remote Gower Peninsula within the following week. Details were still uncertain because weather and visibility were the overriding factors as to the date and time of the landing and whether they could go ahead or not. Jonathan Pugh and Manfred Gruber were to receive the two *Hauptleute* on the beach and transport them by van to the safe house at Llangellis Farm near King Arthur's Stone. Dependent on the time of landing, it was hoped that Jonathan and Manfred would have time to make it back to Cardiff during the hours of darkness, but if this wasn't possible, they were to leave the van and travel back by train in the morning. "The two officers who are joining our group are sabotage and demolition specialists and their task is to survey likely military and civilian targets to be attacked in the South Wales region and prepare proposals for attacks to be launched with the support of this group." The atmosphere in the room lightened considerably at this news and some lively and excited chatter broke out around the table as they began to think that they were finally going to strike at the heart of the enemy on his home ground. For many of them it had been a long time waiting to answer the call of their mother country over the many years living quietly amongst their enemies, and now they had a chance to make a difference and strike back.

"The third item concerns the return of one of our group members who has been undergoing specialist signals and coding training in Germany. He is well known to most of us as he is Heidi Weiss' husband, Joachim Schultz, who has been serving in the Imperial Army since 1910 and undergone specialist signalling and coding and code breaking training. For the past year, he has been part of another group working around the Port of London but has been seconded to us for communication with the U-boats. Feldwebel Schulz is taking up a post as Sir Wilhelm's chauffeur and will be arriving by train from London tomorrow afternoon and will join the meetings here by virtue of his office. He knows the Cardiff area very well, having lived here before 1910, and speaks excellent English and carries a Swiss passport. His role will be to code the messages of shipping movements and take them to the rendezvous with the U-boats if they are able to land a small boat, or communicate them by light if they are unable to land. He is an expert marksman and will support the two officers in their sabotage work also. His job as a chauffeur will give him access to the motor vehicles kept by Sir Wilhelm and the opportunity to drive about the region on Sir Wilhelm's business, which should act as excellent cover when he is out and about driving on our business as well."

Before the meeting broke up, there was a general discussion about the need for greater caution and security. "The recent incidents with Constable Morgan and our reaction to his enquiries could have resulted in the arrest of members of our network through carelessness. We must be extra careful about how we react in our dealings with the enemy and especially when dealing with enquiries from the police. No actions should be taken without the authority of the board unless it becomes an absolute necessity. Sir Wilhelm, Hilda and Manfred are most at risk because they are at the heart of the operation and are the ones who have the access and take the greatest risks to get the vital shipping information out of the docks. The rest of the team are to support and protect them in this vital work and do nothing that will jeopardise their positions. Keep contact between each other to a minimum and try to restrict communications to within the shell company activities, for you are all listed as directors or employees of Wurtenberg Holdings, which gives us all legitimate reasons for communicating about company business."

Whilst this meeting was extremely tense, it was clear that Herr Oberst Kruger had underestimated the interest of the Cardiff police in members of his group. It was obvious that he believed that their deep cover, established over eight or nine years, was still effective and that the interest of the police was purely routine and had Gruber and Matthias acted sensibly would have attracted no further attention. He believed that Wesley was just a local constable given this task to check up on a decision made by the Medical Exemptions Board as part of their annual audit and no more than that, and as all the members of their clandestine group lived exemplary law-abiding lives within the local community, there was nothing to fear. It was obvious that they were as yet unaware of the existence of an undercover police unit set up specifically to investigate the passing of vital shipping intelligence to the U-boats operating in the Bristol Channel and the Irish Sea. The British Secret Service had long suspected that German agents had infiltrated the major ports around the British coast and were gaining access to expected arrivals and departures of merchant ships and their cargoes and passing this information on to the German Navy. The regular incidence of attacks on British ships carrying vital war cargoes on their way into port or leaving ports had long been considered more than just coincidence but rather that the U-boat commanders were directed to specific targets by the information secretly passed to them by German spies. Although Kruger had vented his anger fully at the meeting, and he meant what he threatened would happen to the Grubers and Matthias if it happened again, he had lulled himself into a false sense of security and believed that this incident would blow over quite quickly, dismissing it as an unfortunate accident.

Inspector Bennett, on the other hand, was playing the cautious game and not revealing what they knew about what had happened to Wesley on that fateful night. He was happy to play this down and give the impression that they believed this to be an unfortunate accident and thankfully the officer would recover from his injuries in due course. He believed that this would take the pressure off Wesley and discourage the Grubers, aided by the Matthiases, from making a second attempt on the life of his young officer. He had already prepared the misleading statement that he would release to the newspapers that Constable Morgan had been the victim of a hit and run accident and had been run down by a careering horse and cart which had not yet been found. Enquiries were still ongoing in the search for the driver, but without witnesses, the chances of apprehending him were small. The inspector was certain that Manfred Gruber was the driver and that he had used his neighbour's butcher's cart, but he had no compelling evidence he could take into court and get a conviction. He had no intention of revealing at this early stage of the investigation the many leads and lines of enquiry that Wesley and Alicia had discovered and were actively working on and how just a focus on Williams and Gruber had led them to the Matthiases and then to Wurtenberg Holdings and to at least six other persons of interest, with German connections, linked to these two. He was sure that by biding their time and continuing to work covertly they would build the case he was looking for, and he was also certain that the group may be emboldened by getting away with the attack on Wesley, which might give them a false sense that they were untouchable and might lead to further mistakes. He knew that thorough legwork was the basis of good police work, and he was certain that they would have them all in custody in due time. There was a mass of information to sift through in the financial and commercial records that had already been obtained, and the recuperation period for Wesley would give Alicia and Bethal ample opportunity to come up with some answers.

Constable Jenkins, who had been on duty at the door of the ward providing protection for Wesley that night, was interviewed by Detective Sergeant Powell and he was definite that no one, other than the sister and her nurses, had entered the ward during the night. Finally, Inspector Bennett managed to get the truth out of him when he admitted that he had fallen asleep at his post for a few minutes and was fully awake a few seconds later when the ward door creaked open as someone was leaving. This was of no concern as it was only a female doctor with grey hair leaving the ward and hurrying away down the corridor. He did not see her face, nor did he speak to her, but he thought there was no harm done as he assumed she was a member of the medical staff. Bennett was apoplectic with anger and suspended Jenkins, to be called before a disciplinary hearing. Jenkins had failed in his duty for he had not seen her enter the ward, had not checked her identity and failed to challenge her on leaving. His final words to Jenkins as he left the interview room were that he should think himself lucky that this mysterious woman had not murdered Constable Morgan in his sleep. It was now certain that Wesley's less than perfect recollection of the mysterious night visitor was probably true. Although there was a strong likelihood that this was Dr Sabine Matthias, it fell below the threshold of what could be called definite evidence. Unless they could find a witness or some written evidence putting Sabine Matthias in the ward at that time, this information added little to their case. Public interest in the case declined quite quickly when the press statement was released suggesting that this was a hit and run accident rather than a deliberate attack on the police. As the days passed and the story disappeared from the newspapers and the police had not approached the Grubers or the Matthiases again, Anton Kruger was further reassured that their cover was still intact and they were free to carry out their operations as planned.

As the weeks of Wesley's rest and recuperation were dragging by in Bedwas, Colonel Kruger was satisfied that his assessment of the situation had been correct, and although he still cursed the incompetence and cowardice shown by some of his team, he focused more closely on Operation Worm's Head. Plans were fully in place, and everything was ready for the arrival of the two officers from Germany. The weather and visibility were the overriding factors in setting the date for their arrival, and Jonathan Pugh and Manfred Gruber had to be ready at short notice to travel to the rendezvous with the U-boat landing crew as soon as they received the signal to go. The safe house had been set up and provisioned by Heidi Weisse in an isolated location in one of the more remote parts of the Gower Peninsula, and the two officers would work the farm as part of their cover for being there. Stories had been put about the local villages as supplies were ordered and accounts set up of two wounded soldiers taking over the farm. Before the war, this part of Wales was popular with walkers, hikers and birdwatchers, but the number of visitors had declined dramatically since the war began, so this became an excellent place to operate without being troubled too much by nosy neighbours. The arrival of Joachim Schultz should be invaluable, and Anton would use him to drive the van on the evening of the pickup if possible. The van would be loaded with farm equipment and supplies for delivery to the farm, which should not attract any adverse attention if they were stopped by the police or army checkpoint en route to the Gower. Routine checks were frequently carried out on the main roads out of Cardiff and Swansea during nighttime, primarily to curb the activities of the black market and to deter poachers and burglars from targeting empty properties in the country. The latest signal from Berlin suggested that the most likely period for the landing would be on Tuesday or Wednesday of the following week, and the two operatives, codenamed Otto and Heinrich, would be bringing with them a cache of weapons and explosives to be hidden on the farm for their use during operations. Manfred, accompanied by Joachim, was sent to the farm that weekend to *reconnaitre* the landing beach and to find a suitable hiding place for the weapons and explosives that would not be obvious to anyone unless they were pre-warned what to look for. The stretch of beach was isolated, with no houses or farm buildings within at least a mile, and they were both sure that it was ideal for their purposes. Access to the beach was by way of some winding steps that had been dug out of the cliff face and provided a private and secluded way to and from the beach, and there was a space just off the farm track on the clifftop to park the van where it would not be obvious to any passer-by, although it seemed unlikely that this would be a possibility. The only slight problem was with how much equipment, weapons and explosives Otto and Heinrich would be bringing with them. Joachim was sure that it would not be a large amount in weight because they were coming from a submarine where space was extremely limited and being rowed ashore in a small boat. There would be five of them on the beach so they reckoned they would be able to manage to lift it all in one go, up the steps and into the back of the van.

However, the search for a suitable hiding place proved much more difficult and although there were many potential hiding places in the outbuildings of the farm, there were very few that were large enough to contain all the weapons and explosives together and still provide ease of access when required. After several hours of frustration searching every inch of the farm, it was Manfred who spotted a likely solution when he was examining a disused slurry pit at the rear of the main barn and went to have a closer look. The slurry pit, although abandoned, was still quite a noxious place to visit, and although the pit was empty, the smell was sickening and guaranteed to keep people at a fair distance. He reckoned that a searcher would need to have some real persistence to give the pit more than a cursory inspection, but would it provide ease of access for Otto and Heinrich? Three sides of the pit were overgrown with thick briars which made it difficult to approach the pit too closely, but Joachim noticed that, vaguely distinguishable through the briars, there seemed to be a door. They found some shears in the shed and cut away at the root of the briars nearest this wall and pulled the briars far enough away from the wall that they could reach the door, which seemed to provide an entrance to a space underneath the pit for cleaning and maintenance purposes. The door was unlocked and although it was hard to push open, the room inside was clean and dry and the smell was much less nauseous than outside. They both knew that this would be a good hiding place and if they carefully replaced the briars back against the wall, the entrance would be hidden again. They were careful to remove all the clippings and burn them so as not to leave any trace that they had been cutting there, and returned the shears to the shed. They were both tired after a busy day and were anxious to return to Cardiff as soon as possible and certainly before darkness fell.

Although they had not seen anyone all day, their visit to the farm had not gone unnoticed as they had been observed walking around the farm by the local bobby from Port Eynon Police Station, who passed by in the lane on his bicycle earlier that afternoon. Constable Evans had heard the rumours about the wounded soldiers coming to be the new tenants for the farm and made a mental note to drop in and introduce himself on his return journey later in the day. Unfortunately for him, an incident involving farm labourers fighting at the Gower Arms pub kept him busy for the rest of the afternoon and he had to postpone his social call at the farm until another day. Evans was a diligent policeman and entered the sighting of the two newcomers at Llangellis Farm into his notebook, which would get included in his weekly report to police headquarters in Swansea, and he also made a note to call in at the farm next time he cycled that way early next week.

A message was received on Sunday evening that the weather was just right for the landing at Rhossili Bay on Tuesday next when the U-boat would attempt to rendezvous at 23:00 when there was no moon because of maximum cloud cover. The U-boat would signal by light the code word "Valkyrie" and Joachim would reply "Wagner" from the beach and the boat would come onto the shore. If this was unsuccessful on Tuesday, the U-boat would rendezvous again at the same location on Thursday when the weather was much the same, and a new set of code words would be sent on Wednesday evening just in case. Jonathan, Manfred and Joachim were all prepared to travel up to Llangellis Farm early on Tuesday evening to get everything ready for the arrival of the two German officers later that evening. Joachim had arranged for the issue of Lugers to Jonathan and Manfred in case of any trouble and he carried a Mauser himself. The farm equipment and supplies were packed into the back of the van, and they set off from Cardiff around five in the afternoon to make the two-and-a-half-hour journey to the Gower, which would give them plenty of time to stow the farm supplies and light the fires and cook a supper for their new arrivals. Jonathan Pugh proved to be a good cook and the three of them enjoyed a Welsh lamb stew whilst they were waiting, and at 22:30, they were ready to make their way to the beach. The night was still and very dark as no moon showed through the complete overcast cloud cover and they were thankful that there was no wind to blow away the clouds. It was not too cold, although they were all wearing heavy woollen coats, caps and gloves and were still warm inside from the wonderful stew. Joachim parked in an appropriate secluded spot and then made a quick circuit of the immediate area to ensure they were completely alone. Joachim was satisfied that they were not being watched and they all checked that their weapons were loaded and slowly made their way down to the beach to wait for the U-boat's signal. The time dragged by so slowly and by the time the watch hands crawled round to 23:00, it seemed as if they had been waiting for hours already but still no signal had come and they were all getting a little unsettled until at 23:10 a bright stab of light flashed from low on the horizon and Joachim repeated the code word Valkyrie out loud and then sent Wagner as the correct reply. The U-boat was probably very low in the water with only the conning tower above the surface to make themselves as small a target as possible to coast watchers or passing ships. There followed a quick flurry of flashes which Joachim acknowledged and then repeated for their benefit, indicating that the ship's boat was over the side and would hit the beach in about eight to ten minutes. Joachim would shine his light seawards every two minutes to allow the boat to vector directly to them on the beach. They were all excited but also on edge because this was the most dangerous part of the operation so far and they were most vulnerable when receiving men and contraband from the boat as all their attention was on getting the men, equipment and weapons ashore safely. It was nearly fourteen minutes later before the boat could be seen about fifty yards from the beach attempting to cut through the first line of the breakers without broaching, but the seaman on the tiller knew his stuff and neatly brought the boat ashore safely, only five or six yards from where they were standing. The boat's crew were all in uniform but there were two tall figures dressed in dark civilian clothes who clambered over the prow and waded forward whilst the boat's crew passed forward the boxes containing the weapons and explosives. After very quick greetings, Joachim led them back up the steps whilst Manfred followed at the rear with his Luger in his hand, ready to fire if they were challenged and the boat's crew were already rowing hard back to the relative safety of their U-boat. It was a further ten minutes before the van was loaded and they set off for the farm, where the boxes were unloaded and hidden away underneath the slurry pit whilst Jonathan got supper on the table to welcome Otto and Heinrich. Introductions were made but were restricted to first names only for security reasons. The two new arrivals were captains in the German Army and were combat engineers and sabotage specialists and could speak fluent

English with little trace of an accent. Otto told them that they had brought six Mauser rifles and ammunition, three Medson light machine guns, ten Lugers and a plentiful supply of 1915-type grenades and various explosive substances and detonators. After a little chatter, everyone turned in as Otto was to take the three of them to Swansea railway station to catch the early train to Cardiff at 05:45 so that they wouldn't be missed at work in the morning and so they could keep the van at the farm for their personal use, if necessary. Sir Wilhelm had taken the precaution of registering this vehicle to Llangellis Farm so that it would cause no suspicion if stopped by the police.

At 04:45 in the morning, Otto drove Jonathan, Manfred and Joachim into Swansea station so they could catch the first train back to Cardiff and make their way to their respective workplaces as usual. The colonel had stressed how important it was not to draw attention to themselves in any way, and a break from normal routine could draw unwanted attention and lead to increased scrutiny of them as unreliable persons. Otto was nervous driving on British roads for the first time and had to remember to drive on the left, although there was so little other traffic on the country roads leading from the Gower towards Swansea that he soon gained confidence. He was aware that there might be increased security around transport hubs so chose roads that kept him away from the docks and dropped his three compatriots 200 yards short of the station, driving away quickly before they attracted any attention. He returned to Llangellis Farm by following the same route that he had taken on the way out and apart from one wrong turning in a country lane about a mile short of the farm was safely back at the farm within forty-five minutes.

The other three just split up and made their way individually to the station and purchased their tickets singly as they felt that three men travelling together might attract attention, whereas three individuals travelling to work in Cardiff was likely to go unnoticed. They ensured that they sat in different carriages of the train and made no indication that they knew each other during the journey. The train was an express and only stopped once on the way to the capital city before continuing to London, so the journey time was less than an hour and although the train was not deserted, there were only a handful of passengers in each carriage. Jonathan did not alight at Cardiff but continued to Newport, where he was working at the docks that day, whilst Manfred and Joachim got off at Cardiff Central and went their separate ways. Manfred had managed to sleep for most of the journey time, being woken only by the ticket collector who clipped his ticket, so felt a little more refreshed than when he got on. Joachim, with his military training, resolved to be more vigilant and did not sleep at all but kept a constant lookout for anyone paying him any particular attention. Nothing unusual caught his attention but he did not drop his guard and kept up this cautious behaviour until he was safely back in his room at Sir Wilhelm's estate. He was excused work that day because the work rota showed he had been working late the night before on a delivery job of farm supplies for Sir Wilhelm that involved him travelling back by train. No one expected him at work that day, so he was able to catch up with a few hours of sleep in the privacy of his room above the garage and stables at the rear of the main house. As he drifted off to sleep, he thought amorously of the reunion he would have with his wife, Heidi, whom he had not seen for nearly five years. He wondered if she was still as attractive as she was when he left in 1910 and whether she would be as receptive to his advances as she had been before he returned to Germany, and he relished the opportunity to find out, reckoning that this was a bonus of this posting. Joachim had always enjoyed a full sexual life with Heidi and always said he was in love with her, although they had only been brought together, as a couple, by the German secret service to set up home as a married couple in Cardiff in 1907. Heidi was the daughter of a well-known Jewish rabbi who had moved to Wales to minister to the Jewish ex-pat community in Cardiff in 1905. Heidi did not accompany her family at that time as she was still studying at the university where she was recruited into the German secret service and paired with Joachim, and they came to join Heidi's family in 1907 as a married couple. Joachim had many lovers during the five years they had been apart but still felt a lustful longing to lay with Heidi again.

Manfred headed straight to his father's shop where the family lived in the apartment over the shop and was able to find the time to wash and shave and dress in business clothes and make it to the office by eight for his day's work. Although Sir Wilhelm and Hilda Williams knew where he had been last night, no one who he worked alongside had any knowledge of their connections and they were careful to keep it that way. Manfred's desk was at the back of the shipping office and all the signal flimsies and telegrams regarding shipping movements, cargoes and tonnages came to his desk first where he painstakingly made up the register for the ensuing twenty-four hours for circulation to the various department heads in the docks. This work required great precision and accuracy and some subterfuge too as he had to make an extra copy to pass through his secret network without anyone being aware that this was happening. Fortunately, although his colleagues knew that Manfred enjoyed the office banter and chatter, they did not disturb him whilst he was engaged in this aspect of his work. The first couple of hours each day required the register to be updated accurately and the copies circulated, and that morning Manfred cursed because he could see from the pile of signal flimsies and telegraphs that there would be a lot of arrivals and departures to enter into the register and that he would have to work more quickly than usual to meet his deadline. Most of the signals were routine arrivals and departures and Manfred recognised many of the ships as they were frequent visitors to Cardiff Docks, but he also noticed when ships stopped coming and although he did not know why, he guessed that some had been torpedoed by U-boats operating off the Welsh coast and this gave him some satisfaction to know that maybe he had played some small part in it. Today was no different than usual, but he did notice that a special convoy of ammunition ships was due to enter the port early the next morning. The convoy consisted of five large American-registered cargo ships carrying tanks, motor vehicles and artillery shells from factories in the USA to boost the British war effort, and Manfred was sure that they might be an urgent target for their U-boats. The convoy, code "Homerun", was escorted by Royal Navy destroyers across the Atlantic until they reached the approaches to the Irish Sea, when they were left to enter port alone as the destroyers headed back into the Atlantic to escort the next convoy. This seemed to provide a golden opportunity for the U-boats to strike at some more significant targets and sink them before they reached the safety of Cardiff Docks. Manfred was excited but still worked meticulously to get his work done and could hardly control his impatience to deliver the completed copies to the respective department heads. He left his office at 10:40 and walked around the docks delivering the daily register update and at five to eleven entered Hilda Williams' office and delivered her copy and that of Sir Wilhelm and collected their signatures of receipt. Manfred was eager to draw her attention to convoy Homerun, and she confirmed that she would confer with Sir Wilhelm and expected that he would send a messenger to Colonel Kruger with this intelligence immediately and that he should go back to his office and continue to work as normal so as not to draw any attention to himself.

Sir Wilhelm received the news of the convoy with immediate interest and as soon as Hilda had returned to her office, telephoned Anton Kruger at his law office. The colonel was delighted to receive this news and said that he would send a message to the Kriegsmarine U-boat HQ immediately and needed Sergeant Schultz to come to his office within the hour to encode the signal for transmission. Joachim was rudely awaked by loud banging on his door, which made him grumpy and bad-tempered, but he climbed out of bed and put on his dressing gown and opened the door to find Enid, one of the parlourmaids, standing at his door. She conveyed the message that he was urgently required to telephone Sir Wilhelm at the office within the next five minutes and he could use the telephone in the hallway of the big house. Joachim washed and dressed as quickly as he could and then called Sir Wilhelm at his office to be told to get to Col. Kruger's office immediately and take his code books with him. Twenty-five minutes later, he was ushered into the colonel's office by his secretary and when the door was firmly closed, the colonel switched to German and explained that it was urgent to send a signal to Berlin that afternoon on the expected arrival of the ammunition ships off the Welsh coast in the early hours of tomorrow. The colonel had already drafted the signal in German and Joachim set to work putting it into a German naval code for transmission by wireless to U-boat command that day. Kruger stressed to Joachim that speed was of the essence, so he must take this signal to Llangellis Farm immediately so that Heinrich could send it on to Germany using their secret wireless transmitter. Twenty minutes after he had arrived at the law office, Joachim was back in the driving seat and heading along the main coast road to Swansea, feeling anxious because the congestion of buses, lorries and horse traffic was slowing down the speed of the traffic. However, once he was clear of the Cardiff city limits, the volume of vehicles on the road reduced greatly and he was able to speed up. Even so, the journey was going to take at least two hours, and that was dependent on no hold-ups around Swansea before he got out onto the Gower Peninsula. He knew he had chosen wisely when he'd selected the Pierce-Arrow small touring car from the garage because it was fast when on the open road. He had been tempted to take one of the Bentleys but rejected them because he thought they would attract too much attention, especially on the Gower Peninsula where such vehicles were rarely seen.

The journey passed without incident and he pulled onto the track leading up to the farmyard at about 15:30 to find Otto already in the yard but fully engaged in conversation with a uniformed constable. Joachim was a little unsure of what to do because he had no prepared cover story for why he had come to the farm today, and his first reaction was to turn around and head off in the opposite direction. He was sure that this would certainly catch the attention of the policeman, which would be disastrous for them all, so he decided that he would brazen it out in the open and drove into the middle of the farmyard and approached Otto. They both turned to look at the new arrival and Joachim introduced himself as Joe Schultz, representative of the Branden Farm Machinery Company of Cardiff and said he was looking for Mr Henry Crawford, who had asked for him to call to discuss the purchase of a tractor. Otto smiled and shook hands and said he was pleased to meet him and said that Mr Crawford was inside the farmhouse and that if he went to the front door and knocked, he would come out. Just as Joachim was about to walk towards the door, the constable said that he didn't sound as if he came from these parts, and Joachim knew he should be as near to the truth as possible in his reply to avoid being caught out in the lie and said that he was a Swiss national who had settled in Cardiff with his family in 1905. Constable Evans remarked, "That explains why a young man like you is not in the army," and Joachim jokingly replied that Switzerland were neutrals as he approached the front door and knocked. His voice could be heard introducing himself as Joe Schultz from the Branden Farm Machinery Company, and Henry invited him in and closed the door. Evans drew his attention back to Otto and continued finding out as much about him and his co-tenant as he could. Otto had told him that he was Lieutenant Oliver King, recently of the Welsh Fusiliers, who had lost the lower part of his left leg in France when he stepped on a mine in no man's land, and he had met Captain Henry Crawford of the Oxfordshire Regiment in hospital, who was now completely deaf as a consequence of being blown up in his dugout. The noise of the explosion in such an enclosed space had burst both his eardrums and although he could still speak clearly enough, he had the greatest difficulty communicating unless he could read the lips of the person speaking to him. "Both being from farming backgrounds, we decided we would try to aid the war effort by taking on a farm." Otto had been given a special boot contraption that he wore over his left foot and ankle, simulating a false foot and ankle and guaranteeing that he always walked with a limp when he was in public, but it was so uncomfortable to wear that he tended not to put it on when working around the farm. It needed all his concentration not to hop around on his left leg whilst he stood talking to the policeman, and he needed to remember to limp when he did move about. After a little more social chit-chat, Evans seemed satisfied and made his farewells, saluting Otto as he mounted his bicycle and rode away down the track away from a relieved Otto and a worried pair of co-conspirators inside the house.

Otto's relief was to prove false because Constable Evans was certainly not satisfied by all he had discovered during his short visit, and he had got off his bike once he was out of view of the farm to make some notes of the points he wished to follow up when he got back to the station, and then he had made his way surreptitiously back up the lane until he could read the registration number of the vehicle Mr Schultz was driving when he arrived at the farm. Their stories seemed plausible enough, but something didn't ring true, but he wasn't sure what it could be other than Mr King seemed remarkably fit and healthy for someone who had undergone major amputation surgery comparatively recently, and Mr Schultz seemed an unlikely character to be the representative of a farm machinery company as he didn't have the look or demeanour of a country person at all. Perhaps he was making too much of nothing, but it wouldn't hurt just to check up on these three characters to satisfy his curiosity.

Henry and Joachim were reticent and wary because any attention from the police was unwelcome in their kind of work, but Otto was so confident that the constable had accepted without question what he had been told and said they should stop worrying. They reluctantly agreed because Joachim had an important mission to conclude and was anxious to explain the reason for his unannounced visit this afternoon. Henry was the wireless operator and took the coded message and disappeared upstairs to make the transmission immediately, and they knew that he would be a little time as the message was longer than what was usually transmitted by wireless. He was away for over twenty minutes but when he returned, he told them that he had been told to stand by to wait for a reply. This was a break from their strict wireless protocols and did increase the risk of discovery of secret wireless transmitters by the enemy, but HQ wished to pass instructions to them if the U-boats were to be vectored onto the convoy. They had confirmed that every effort was to be made to attack this convoy and orders were being sent out to U-boat commanders immediately, but this did not guarantee that all the U-boats would be available to mount an attack on this convoy at such short notice. Wireless transmissions could only be received when the U-boat was on the surface, and all U-boats were required to acknowledge when they received a signal so it would be some time before they would know whether they had received the message and how many were able to mount an attack.

Otto now took command and ordered Joachim to put the car out of sight in the barn and told him that he would have to stay in case further signals needed to be encrypted. It was nearly an hour before the first confirmation came in when U-17 acknowledged that it was at least eight hours away from the track of the convoy on electric motors underwater but would try to surface for greater speed after nightfall. U-765 declined due to lack of ammunition, but three U-boats were perfectly placed in the path of the convoy and would position themselves for a three-pronged attack as the convoy sailed towards them. All three of them were excited that this might turn into more than just an opportunist attack, with three or possibly four U-boats converging onto this convoy. The night was going to prove to be a long one as they waited for news of the progress of the attack, although Joachim could not help worrying about the presence of the police constable at the farm earlier in the day. He was much less prone to write this off as a coincidence, and if it was just a social call to welcome new residents into the area, there was still a serious security presence behind the call. He was certain that the constable would check out their stories carefully over the next few days before making his decision, but he would almost certainly pass on any suspicions he might have in his reports to higher authority. He did not like it one bit because he was aware that Manfred Gruber and the Matthias doctors had been at the centre of some recent attention from Cardiff police, and he did not like it when what might appear to be unrelated incidents suddenly become related as the police begin to join the dots. He confided with Otto and Heinrich about his misgivings, and they were less concerned than he was but agreed that they needed to be exceedingly cautious about their behaviour and movements around the area and try not to draw unwanted attention their way. Joachim said that he would report his concerns to the colonel on his return to Cardiff and to Sir Wilhelm.

Around three in the morning, Joachim was woken by the sound of distant rumbling like thunder a fair distance away and he got up to see what it was. He climbed the small hill behind the house which gave a distant view towards the sea, and he could see the sky lit up by flickering lights, like the reflection of flames in the clouds, and could distinctly hear naval guns firing. He could not discern what was happening at sea and estimated that the action was at least ten miles offshore. By now, Otto and Heinrich had struggled into their clothes and joined Joachim on the hill and had brought a strong pair of binoculars to try to get a better view of the action at sea. Another huge explosion, followed by many smaller ones, flashed across the sky in front of their eyes whilst they had to wait a few seconds before the rumbling sound of the explosions reached their ears. There was certainly a naval battle going on but whether it involved their U-boats attacking the convoy or not, they were unable to see. Even through these powerful glasses, they could not make out very much, although Otto was sure he could see the outline of a burning ship, but neither Henry nor Joachim could see anything when they looked. The noise of battle died away, but the flashing flames reflected in the sky remained for a long time after. They returned to the house and Henry listened to the radio transmissions from Germany to find out what had been going on. Berlin Radio were broadcasting a major naval victory with their heroic U-boat forces destroying a major ammunition convoy en route from the United States to British ports in the early hours of that morning. They claimed that a concerted attack by three U-boats had sunk three ammunition ships, *SS Brooklyn Star, SS Hudson Bay* and *SS Bunker Hill*, and crippled two other merchant ships so badly that they would not reach port. These ships were US registered and were carrying war materials, which was against international law for a neutral. The broadcast concluded that this was a major strike against the British war effort and that all their U-boats had survived the battle safely. The news was so welcome that a bottle of schnapps was produced to toast their brave submariners, but their celebrations were to be short-lived because as the day rolled on, a clearer picture emerged of what had happened the night before off the Pembroke coast.

Sir Wilhelm could see the evidence with his own eyes at 07:30 that morning when four ships of the convoy docked in Cardiff shepherded by a tenacious frigate, *HMS Penarth*, with a newly bent front end, which had come out from the Welsh inshore squadron based at Pembroke Dock to escort the convoy the last few miles into port. The lieutenant in command of the *Penarth* had been expecting a routine escort job and had the surprise of his life when the convoy was attacked by at least four U-boats who seemed to be waiting for them to sail onto their torpedoes. It soon became clear from the reports made by the masters of the merchant ships that they had been attacked by three U-boats on the surface twelve miles west of Worm's Head, and *SS Bunker Hill* had been torpedoed and set on fire. She lay stopped on the surface for over thirty minutes, which enabled most of the ship's company to escape into the lifeboats before she was torpedoed twice more and broke her back and sank. The captain of *HMS Penarth* immediately ordered the convoy to turn away and zigzag at a speed of eleven knots, which could outrun even the fastest U-boat, whilst he turned and engaged the attacking U-boats in true Nelsonian tradition. The U-boats outnumbered the *Penarth* but were at the slight disadvantage that they were unable to dive, having chosen to attack from the landward side to achieve maximum surprise but remaining in shallow water because of the shoals nearer the coast. The *Penarth* was positioned between the convoy and the coastline so they would have to take on the frigate in a gun action, hoping to sink her if at least one of the U-boats was able to fire a spread of torpedoes at the small ship. The frigate was a lively ship and a good sea boat and at full speed could reach nearly seventeen knots, and her two gun crews were eager and competent and soon bracketed the first U-boat before making two direct hits on the conning tower of the first submarine. Whilst they were still running at full speed at the target, a vigilant lookout spotted a torpedo track coming from the starboard and the *Penarth* flung herself into a fantastic tight turn to parallel the torpedo track, and watchers on the wing of the bridge were relieved to see it miss the ship by ten feet or so. The *Penarth* was now racing straight at the U-boat that had fired the torpedo down the reverse torpedo track with every intention of depth, charging his adversary, but to their amazement the submarine did not dive but attempted to turn across the bows of the *Penarth* and engage her with their forward gun. The German captain had made his move too late, and the bows of the *Penarth* caught the U-boat just aft of the conning tower and heeled her over as the racing frigate's bow raked over the submarine's deck, punching several large holes in the plating and saddle tanks. Water was pouring into the submarine and although the *Penarth* had bent her bows, she had suffered little serious damage, nothing that a naval dockyard couldn't put right in a few days. U-138, which was hit by gunfire, was left stopped and on fire off Worm's Head, and U-345 sank with only a few survivors six miles south of this position.

SIX

Cardiff Docks were alive with stories of how the valiant little ship tied alongside, waiting to get into the dry dock for a proper inspection of the damage to her bent bows, had saved the convoy from almost certain destruction by quick thinking and exemplary seamanship. Accounts of the action varied greatly and the further away the storytellers were from the action, the more outrageous and exaggerated the stories became. However, the reports on the desk of flag officer South Wales Command were clear and objective, and it was evident that the actions taken by Lieutenant E J Palfrey RN, a retired naval officer recalled into the navy for the duration of the war, had outwitted the U-boats' commanders completely. His boldness had been supported equally by the skills and determination displayed by the crew of the *Penarth* in sinking one U-boat with gunfire and ramming a second, which had been saved from sinking and successfully brought into harbour and the German crew were now prisoners of war. Admiral Hastings was delighted that one of the little ships under his command had performed so well in action and he resolved to ensure that Palfrey would be rewarded with a medal and maybe a promotion onto a larger vessel should the opportunity arise. The *Penarth* was likely to be in the hands of the dockyard for several months to come whilst a new bow was fitted, so she would most likely be paid off and her officers and men reassigned to other ships within a week or two. However, something was niggling at the back of his mind that was far more serious and more urgent to understand. He was aware that German submarines operated in the approaches to the west of England and Wales in the Atlantic and Irish seas, but this was the first occasion that a concerted attack had been made on a convoy so close inshore by three or more U-boats working together. Was this a sign that the Germans were getting lucky and just happened to be in the right place at the right time? He knew that luck played an enormous part in warfare but when it involved a pack of submarines mounting an attack together, this suggested that they were working on intelligence that had been received beforehand which vectored them onto the right position at the right time to intercept this vital convoy. This is what troubled the admiral and his staff that morning as they assembled in the operations room to bring their minds to bear on this question, and after the initial excitement and satisfaction that only one merchant ship had been sunk by the U-boats to the loss of two enemy submarines, they started to wrestle with the notion that there was a security breach somewhere between South Wales Command and civilian agencies acceptedwith knowledge of shipping movements. There had been isolated attacks on merchantmen and convoys by submarines at frequent intervals since the war began, but they were largely put down to chance rather than a direct strategy driven by intelligence, as they tended to have taken place in much deeper water involving U-boats attacking with torpedoes whilst submerged. There was little evidence to suggest that the attacks were getting more frequent or that there was any pattern emerging suggesting a naval strategy based on intelligence was in place. Some of those present were convinced that this was just luck, and the U-boats were patrolling the approaches to the Welsh coast in the knowledge that there were three large deep-water ports that could receive and turn round merchant ships at high speed, so ships carrying war supplies would be directed here. They believed that the longer the U-boats patrolled these approaches, the higher the chances became of intercepting their ships. The answer was to increase their patrolling activity with specialist anti-submarine vessels deployed in greater numbers to deter the U-boats from entering this area. The admiral was not so sure that this view was correct because no one in South Wales Command or in the civilian agencies was aware of the arrival of convoy Homerun until eighteen hours before their estimated time of arrival at Cardiff Docks that morning. This tended to suggest that if there was a breach of security, it was more likely to have been in the United States where the information concerning this convoy's passage and ETA could have been made six days ago, giving the Germans ample opportunity to assemble their attack boats off the Welsh coast ready to intercept the convoy. Admiral Hastings had invited Colonel Stewart from the Secret Security Service to address them, and he would be with them within half an hour as his train was due into Central Station about ten minutes ago. He might have some interesting details to share with them about breaches in security and what they could do to prevent them. The meeting broke up and was scheduled to reassemble when Colonel Stewart arrived.

The room was by now quite smoky when the admiral called the meeting to order and introduced Colonel Stewart to address them. The colonel was dressed in tweeds and looked more like a country squire than a staff officer, and he was accompanied by another man whom he introduced as Detective Inspector George Bennett of Cardiff Constabulary. The colonel began with an apology of sorts by saying that the secret service had been aware of the activities of the German submarines in their waters for some time and from the outset rejected any notion that there was any luck or chance involved in the U-boat operations around the coast of Britain. The strike rate success of attacks on British and allied shipping was having a significant effect on the supply of essential war supplies vital to the effective operations of their ships at sea and soldiers on land. Ships were being sunk close to their shores on an almost daily basis and as the submarine-building programme increased in German shipyards, the situation would only get worse. He explained that to combat this threat they had set up small teams of specially trained police officers and military personnel working undercover in several areas where merchant ship traffic was at its busiest and where U-boat activity had been on the increase, just like recently in South Wales. "There are teams operating in London, Hull, Newcastle, Edinburgh, Glasgow, Liverpool, South Wales, Plymouth and Southampton because in every one of these shipping areas the tonnage sunk by enemy submarines within less than three hours steaming from port has been on the increase. Fortunately for us, a breakthrough was made in the Port of London which alerted us to the secret operations of German espionage agents or German sympathisers. These networks were working together in gathering information about the movement of ships in and out of our ports with details of cargo manifests and destinations. At first, we thought it likely that the information was obtained largely by surveillance and that German operatives were watching our ports and logging movements of shipping at our major ports, but this did not provide us with an adequate enough answer as to why the U-boats could lay in wait for ships on the dates and times they were due to arrive or leave our ports on such a high number of occasions."

Then came the fortunate breakthrough that he had mentioned earlier when a man was stopped in a routine search leaving the East India Docks in London by the dockyard police one night during last November but when questioned he prevaricated with his answers and then assaulted the constable and made a run for it. The man had been selected for a random search and the officer concerned had no particular reason to have stopped him that night, but his behaviour certainly attracted their attention afterwards. Three officers gave chase, and their prompt action meant he was apprehended before he had made 300 yards. Under questioning at the dock police station, the man had put up a wall of silence, but a check through the items in his pocket revealed his identity and where he worked. The contents of his pockets suggested he was born locally in the East London docklands area and had come to work in the harbour master's office straight from school as the office boy and had worked there for ten years with an exemplary record. He was one of the clerks who supported the work of the harbour master and had full sight of the arrivals and departures of ships entering and leaving the Pool of London as well as cargo manifests, tonnage and destinations. This information would be of vital interest to their enemies and coupled with the mystery of why he chose to run rather than face down the enquiries of the dockyard constable, their attention was alerted. His ID and employment papers appeared to be in order so why did he run? The lack of cooperation from the suspect increased their suspicion that something was not right and led to the setting-up of an in-depth investigation into this man, his family and friends. Was it likely that he was a German spy infiltrated into Britain some time before the war to go underground and live quietly and respectably and to get into jobs which gave access to vital information that could be leaked to the enemy, or was he simply a German sympathiser who was happy to work against the interests of his country?

The investigation was led by some talented detectives from Scotland Yard who discovered that the suspect, Thomas Smith, was a member of a well-known family of stevedores and tug-boat men who lived in the terraced streets within a stone's throw of the dock gates. However, digging into the background of this family history turned up some interesting information that although to all external appearances they purported to be typical cockney London folk, this branch of the family had only been started by the marriage of Winifred Watters, daughter of Joseph Watters, a costermonger from Brick Lane, to Ludwig Smitt, an able seaman on the Hamburg-London ferry service in 1881. They settled down in London and Ludwig changed his name to Smith and to all external eyes they appeared to be a cockney family. However, a more eagle-eyed member of the investigation team happened to notice a clipping in the local paper at Southend-on-Sea dated 1904, which reported that a young man on an excursion from East London was swept away by the tide in the flood tide in the estuary, but no body was found. The boy was thought to be Thomas Smith, fourteen, son of Ludwig and Winifred Smith. This was a significant development because no record could be found of the registration of the death of Thomas Smith or any burial or funeral service in his name, and the 1911 Census recorded him as still living as a member of the Smith family, now aged twenty-two. When Ludwig and Winifred were interviewed by the police teams, they were both vehement in their denials that anything had happened to their Tommy and that the local newspaper had got it all wrong. How could they have been right, because Tommy had been nowhere and had been there all the time, they said. Comparison of family photographs showed that there was little family resemblance between Thomas and his brothers and his parents and that there appeared to be a gap in records of Thomas' activities between the summer of 1904 when he was supposed to have drowned in the Thames Estuary and starting work as an office boy over a year later in early 1906. He was not at school, nor was he in any other kind of employment, although the family swore that he was with them all the time. There was no definite proof that Thomas Smith was not who he said he was, but something didn't quite add up properly in their story.

A thorough search of the Smith family house came up with the conclusive evidence that they had been looking for with the discovery of a wireless transmitter and code books in German under the floorboards of the bedroom slept in by Thomas and his brother Henry. "It was inconceivable that Thomas could have operated this radio without his brother Henry or other members of the family being aware of it. It was most likely that they were all involved in the espionage, and they were all arrested and are being held in custody as we try to break the whole network before they go to ground. You are aware that most German nationals are interned for the duration of the war, but we now believe that there could be many more living secretly undercover, who we did not previously suspect of having German ancestry or connections because they appeared to be as British as you or I. The secret service commissioned a review of all people who had access to vital shipping information in the docks around our country and have compiled an extensive list of suspects to be kept under close surveillance. We have positively identified six people of interest in the South Wales area who fall into this category, and we strongly suspect that a German spy network is operating in South Wales.

We have detected radio transmissions from inland positions on the U-boat frequencies, but their radio discipline is good and, so far, they have not stayed on air long enough to be pinpointed by our operatives. We are certain that the intelligence concerning convoy Homerun was intercepted and transmitted to Berlin almost immediately after it was received in Cardiff. I will hand over to Inspector Bennett to give you the details of the local operation and how we can work together in future."

Inspector Bennett looked an imposing figure in his dress uniform as he rose to address the assembly of naval officers in the operations room. He began by describing how a small group of talented young police officers had been trained by the secret service in a secret location with the express mission of searching for the German spy network operating in South Wales. "This group has been at work for just two months and has already discovered another eight persons of interest connected to the original six suspects identified by the secret service and has established without doubt that the spy network has infiltrated the docks at Cardiff, Newport and Swansea and placed their own people in positions of trust and with access to vital shipping movement information. We have enough evidence to arrest the main protagonists at Cardiff Docks who we believe were responsible for the passing on of the Homerun convoy intelligence yesterday, but we wish to roll up the whole of the spy network, not just pick off one or two operatives who could easily be replaced. A leading member of my team was seriously injured in a hit and run attack when he was run down by a two-horse-drawn wagon in a Cardiff Street, and we are certain that this was retaliation by some members of the network who had become rattled when Cardiff police started asking questions about some false documents concerning one of the main suspects.

"Fortunately, my officer, although injured severely in the attack, has recovered well and will return to duty soon and renew the pressure on these particular suspects. He was largely instrumental in opening up the enquiry by discovering that the medical exemption certificate granted to one of the leading suspects was almost certainly obtained falsely, and it was his dogged pursuit of the truth in this matter that led to the discovery of further members of the network and that there was at least a dozen or more German nationals living openly in Cardiff using false identities. He was further able to identify that these people operated in full sight by acting as the members of the board of a holding company that operates at all three major docks in South Wales. Whilst my officer has been on sick leave, other members of his team have continued to dig further into the background of these new suspects, and we have kept up as much surveillance of their activities as possible. It is difficult to watch some of them that closely as they are socially and professionally well placed and have access to places that my officers do not, but we are keeping a close watch on those we can watch more thoroughly.

"Additionally, my officers are also supported by our own network of local police and coast watchers in more remote stretches of our coastline, keeping watch for sightings of U-boats and unusual activity on or near isolated beaches. The particularly keen attention to duty of the local bobby at Port Eynon on the Gower Peninsula has enabled us to identify probable landing sites where U-boats are able to approach close enough to the shore to row a small boat to the beach to bring new personnel and equipment from Germany and receive messages from spy groups operating onshore. Local fishermen have often heard diesel motors close inshore and think they have heard German voices carrying through the silence of the night. These occurrences always seemed to be when cloud cover was at its maximum and visibility was poor. Some of the boatmen had tried to get closer to these strange noises but had not managed to catch sight of a U-boat on the surface but could smell the exhaust fumes from their engines lingering over the sea in the still night air after they had dived. The local fishermen will make any sighting reports to the local police station, who will forward them on to us in due course. The local bobby has also highlighted some unusual happenings at a remote farm about a mile or so from the coast that will warrant our further attention over the next few days." He concluded his remarks by saying that it was imperative that the existence of the special police task force remain a secret and that the German spy network did not become aware of their activities and how close they were to uncovering their activities. We now had the capacity to track the wireless frequencies used by the German U-boats for sending Morse messages, and they had employed some specialist trackers who were listening in for the passing on of messages from inland locations. This equipment would enable them to know when messages were passed directly to U-boats at sea or direct to Kriegsmarine HQ in Germany and be forewarned that possible U-boat action may be taking place, and as they could see from the events of the past thirty-six hours, this network was able to pass messages directly to Germany and call up U-boat action almost immediately. He finished by reassuring all present that they would share all information with the admiral's office and then they expected to roll up the whole German operation in South Wales within a few weeks, before too much further damage could be inflicted on more allied ships. "The loss of the two U-boats yesterday will reduce their potential to operate along our coast for a few days and give us a respite to move ahead together. We would ask that the navy keeps up the level of inshore patrolling because we are sure that the U-boats will be back within a few days and from our end we will endeavour to put an end to their spying at the earliest opportunity." After George Bennett had completed his remarks there were a few questions and then the meeting broke up with a great deal of optimism that finally they were on the cusp of striking a blow back at the enemy.

At the same time as the meeting was underway at naval headquarters, there was a hasty meeting in Anton Kruger's office with Sir Wilhelm Branden where they were at a loss to understand how the attack on an unguarded convoy should have such disastrous results. They were mystified as to how a small inshore frigate could strike such a blow and sink two of their submarines so easily, most of the merchant ships escaping unharmed. Eventually, they began to realise that the operation had been put together far too hastily without any real planning, and the tactics adopted by the U-boat commanders of attacking from the landward side in the shallower water had the advantage of providing surprise but the major disadvantage that the convoy was in deeper water, where it could easily manoeuvre and use their superior speed to outrun the attacking U-boats. The U-boats would have stood a far better chance if they could have attacked from underwater rather than on the surface, but being so close to the shore, they did not have the depth of water to dive safely. This passed the advantage to the frigate captain, who knew that the U-boats on the surface could not escape from him. The presence of the frigate between the U-boats and the convoy was also a complete surprise to them as the intelligence suggested that the convoy would be unescorted for the last few miles into port. Being caught on the surface with little room to manoeuvre had contributed greatly to their defeat in this action, and they resolved to be more cautious and to plan more carefully in the future. Their agents in the Dock Company only had sight of the shipping movements in real time within a daily window, and this made it difficult for U-boat command to plan ahead and to respond reactively. The sinking of two of their submarines meant that there would be a delay whilst two additional submarines were dispatched to replace the stricken vessels, which would mean several days before regular patrolling near the Welsh coast would resume. Longer-term convoy planning and shipping schedules were controlled by the Admiralty, and although they were always looking for opportunities to infiltrate agents into the naval organisation, they had been largely unsuccessful. Colonel Kruger did resolve, however, to make his criticisms known about the poor performance of the two U-boat commanders who had been sunk at the hands of HMS *Penarth* and let the convoy escape largely unscathed. It would seem obvious that the British would always have the merchant ships stand out at sea whilst the anti-submarine frigate of the inshore squadron would place themselves between the convoys and the coast to provide protection from stealth attacks on the surface, which seemed to be the chosen mode of attack used in these waters. Kruger requested a long-overdue change of tactics to outsmart the British if they were to increase the losses inflicted on convoys heading for or leaving Welsh ports. As they were bringing their meeting to a close, Kruger's secretary interrupted to say that Joachim Schultz was in the outer office and wished to speak with them. Schultz had rushed back from Llangellis Farm and was anxious to impart what he had witnessed the previous evening. His account of the action at sea backed up the version of events circulating in Cardiff that morning, but Kruger was most concerned when he heard that the farm had been visited by the local policeman from the sub-station at Port Eynon. Schultz had had no choice but to use the cover story of the Branden Farm Machinery Company, using the persona of Joe Schultz, a Swiss national and representative of the company. "The policeman seemed satisfied with my story, but I felt that he was more interested in the identity of Otto and Heinrich and why they had suddenly appeared at the farm so recently."

Kruger was concerned too and suggested that Otto and Heinrich could start earning their living by arranging a small accident to befall the inquisitive policeman that would make the scent go cold. Schultz added that he felt that Otto was finding it hard to carry off the impersonation of a wounded amputee, and the boot arrangement that he was supposed to wear to immobilise his foot to make it appear as if it was false was uncomfortable to wear for long periods and Otto preferred to leave it off. This would be satisfactory if he remembered to limp properly, but he often forgot and the freedom of movement of his supposed false foot did not appear to be all that effective. He was not sure whether the policeman had noticed, but it was plainly obvious that Otto was not an amputee the minute that Joachim saw him walk. Kruger was angry when he heard this and thought that it would be best to have chosen a genuinely wounded German soldier rather than one who was obviously unable to play the part effectively. "I will send him a message that if he does not wear the false foot mechanism, I will personally amputate his foot to make him appear more believable as the safety of our whole network depends on every one of us remaining undercover and not attracting any attention from the local authorities."

Wesley Morgan was returning to duty on the following Monday morning and all these events were unknown to him as he made his way back to his room at the section house attached to Tiger Bay Police Station. Even though the room was sparse and cramped, he was glad to be back and eager to get into the case and be reunited with the team the next morning. He was tired after his journey from Bedwas and decided to eat in the police canteen and get an early night. His first job in the morning was to rejoin the team by reporting to Inspector Bennett at 08:00. George was glad to see him back and was sure that the team had missed Wesley's sharp mind and determination whilst he was off. Although they had still made good progress, they had lacked some of the drive that Wesley brought to the team. He explained the strategy he had undertaken to convince the Grubers that the hit and run attack on Wesley was being treated as a traffic accident and that no suspicion had fallen on them as statements were issued to the press that this was purely an accident where the unfortunate officer was struck by a runaway cart. Enquiries to find the driver and his cart had continued but had reached a dead end and the case had been dropped after a few days. He explained that this was a ruse to give the false impression that the police were mystified and had concluded that Constable Morgan was unlucky enough to be in the wrong place at the wrong time. He continued that he was satisfied that the attack was deliberate and may have been a botched attempt to kill him or simply to warn him off but either way it was a massive overreaction to the enquiries being made about the missing medical records. He also stated that he was sure that Manfred Gruber was the driver of the cart and had acted rashly, using the cart belonging to Mr Jones the butcher. He was also sure that the Matthias doctors knew about the attack after it had been carried out and that Dr Sabine Matthias was the secret midnight visitor who came to see how serious his injuries were and warned him off when she discovered that he would make a full recovery. He concluded by saying that he had been at pains to give them the impression that they were clueless to reassure the German group that they had no suspicions about them and that their cover was still secure. He finished by saying that he had recommended to the chief constable's office that he be appointed as detective constable with immediate effect because of the exceptional work he had put into the case so far, and the letter of appointment had been received last Friday. He said that there was no need for him to wear his uniform from today as from now on he was a plain clothes officer, and he would also receive an increase in pay and allowances due to his higher rank.

*

Alicia and Ivor were waiting for me when I came out of the inspector's office and their smiles of welcome and their congratulations meant that I was the last to know about my promotion, for they already seemed to know. We spent the rest of the day going through all the evidence that they had accumulated about the affairs of our suspects and introducing the other characters that had appeared since I had been away. I was impressed by the meticulous way in which Alicia had sifted through all the financial records and documentary evidence and catalogued it all so we could cross-reference what we had discovered and make new connections easily if they arose. It was now glaringly obvious that this seemingly diverse group of people were inextricably linked financially, professionally and by origin, and we had the conclusive evidence to prove it, but we didn't have the definitive evidence to prove that they were spying against us and that was to be our next task.

The first task was to find out more about Joachim Schultz, the estranged husband of Heidi Weisse, who had been missing for five years and had suddenly reappeared in Cardiff without warning. Where had he been for the past five years? Had he kept in contact with his wife and her family? How did he come to be employed by Sir Wilhelm Branden, the chairman of the holding company of which Heidi was a director?

The second task was to follow up on the reports made by Constable Evans from Port Eynon on the Gower Peninsula about two ex-soldiers who had suddenly taken over the running of an isolated farm in a remote part of the Gower just about a mile from the beaches at Rhossili Bay, which was where mysterious sounds of U-boat engines had been heard by local fishermen close to the shore several times over recent weeks.

The third task was to put pressure back on Helmut Gruber for the medical records of his three sons or for the name of his family doctor. I felt that Helmut was the weakest link and felt that the renewed police interest in this matter would jolt him back to reality with a shock. I suspected that these records did not exist, nor was there a family doctor who could corroborate Dr Julius Matthias' diagnosis, and Helmut would either be forced into another reckless action, or he would have produced false documents to satisfy our interest during the time I was away.

Alicia volunteered to investigate Schultz, and Ivor Bethal would visit Helmut Gruber at his shop, and I would take a trip to Port Eynon to speak with Constable Evans, and we set about planning how we would approach each of the tasks in detail. I needed to requisition some transport to get to Port Eynon and went in search of the station sergeant to see what was available for our use. Sergeant Lewis said that there wasn't much call for motor vehicles in our manor and we mainly used horse-drawn vehicles, but he did have an Arrol-Johnston 11.9 horsepower four-seater car that we could have the use of as it was only rarely used. I was delighted because this was a fine car with a leather soft top, headlights and was very powerful. I signed it out for the use of my team and decided that I would set off for Port Eynon early the next morning to glean all I could from Constable Evans about his suspicions and the reasons for his concern. I did not want to give away too much information about our investigation but felt that I would have to confide a little in Evans because I would need him to keep up some surveillance on the farm over the next few weeks.

It was a fine morning, and I was warm enough with the hood down because I was wearing an overcoat and scarf over my suit. The car bore no police markings so I was not worried that I might be spotted on the country roads on the Gower Peninsula, and I had left early so the roads were quiet and I made good progress along the coastal road towards Swansea and was heading out onto the Gower by nine-thirty or so. I was tempted to pass by the farm before I went to Port Eynon but decided against it because there were not too many non- agricultural vehicles in this part of Wales, and I did not want to attract attention to myself by accidently exposing myself to the suspects at the farm. Port Eynon was a charming and quiet fishing village on the shore facing across Swansea Bay towards industrial Port Talbot and it wasn't difficult to find the small police office at the top of the hill leading down to the harbour. Constable Rhys Evans was in the police office, which was attached to the side of the police house where he lived with his wife and three children. He was a pleasant- looking man in his mid-thirties with an open face but possessed sharp eyes, which suggested that he didn't miss much. He was a little surprised when I entered the office as there were not too many city dwellers driving around the Gower these days, but a quick look out of the window at the car and another at the way I was dressed, and he guessed that I was a policeman too. I introduced myself and began the conversation by saying that my interest had been caught by several snippets of information that he had reported to headquarters that had filtered through to my investigation office. "I am particularly interested in the sightings of U-boats operating close inshore that have come from the fishermen hereabouts and to know more about your suspicions concerning the new tenants at Llangellis farm and the third man that you met there, Joe Schultz." I couldn't divulge too much about my investigation, but I hinted that it was a vital matter of national security, and we were on the track of enemy agents or fifth columnists working against us by collaborating with the enemy in this part of Wales. He understood my need for discretion and was happy to discuss what he had observed at the farm and share the reports from the local boatmen, and we spent a couple of hours deep in conversation during which he elaborated what the fishermen suspected from the strange sounds and smell of diesel they had experienced on several occasions and at several locations, and he showed me a chart of Rhossili Bay where these sightings had been plotted, which I found fascinating. I could see, if the boatmen's sightings were accurate, that the unidentified vessels had approached to within several hundred yards of the beaches around the bay at least sixteen times in the past twelve weeks, which suggested a regular deployment in the area. The sightings were only logged on nights with poor visibility and no moonlight and when the fishermen had headed towards the location of the sounds that they had heard, but the only evidence that a vessel had ever been there was the smell of the fumes from their diesel engines. This evidence pointed reasonably towards these vessels being enemy submarines operating secretly in our waters. I agreed with their conclusions, and the events of a few nights ago just off this coast had borne this out to be true.

I asked him to explain what made him so suspicious of the new tenants at Llangellis Farm and to try to be specific as to why he wanted to look at them more closely. Was he motivated because they were newcomers to the area and he was inquisitive, or was there something that he felt was definitely wrong about these two young men that didn't appear to be right with him? He said that he only called in at the farm, initially, to say hello and to introduce himself as the local bobby and to see if they needed any assistance or introductions to people in the area. "I was surprised that two wounded soldiers with no previous farming background would take on this farm, which had been empty since the war started and was overgrown and run-down. There was a fair bit of work that needed doing before the land could be worked or animals raised again, and I wasn't even sure that the farmhouse was habitable. I cycled over to the farm to see if they were settling in and met Mr Crawford in the farmyard, and although he referred several times to his co-tenant, Oliver King, I never met him. Crawford didn't invite me into the house and Mr King didn't venture out of doors, although I could see him moving around inside through the parlour window. Crawford was friendly enough, but I detected a little reluctance to say too much about himself other than that he was wounded and invalided out of the army and had met Mr King, who was also wounded, at the convalescent hospital. I tried to press him gently to divulge more but my attempt was thwarted by the arrival of a third man, who announced himself as Joe Schultz, a sales representative for a farm machinery company in Cardiff. This man was friendly and said he had an appointment with Mr King to discuss requirements for the farm. He referred to his notebook and looked up the relevant page and said that he worked for the Branden Farm Machinery Company and gave me the address for my notebook. It was obvious to me that Mr Crawford was not expecting the visit from Joe Schultz, and he was anxious to pass him on to Mr King and shepherded him towards the front door, which was opened swiftly, and Schultz went inside."

He thought it was a little strange, but even stranger was that Schultz was obviously of call-up age, had the bearing of a soldier yet was working as an agricultural salesman and, stranger still, he spoke English with a strong German accent. He said he was confused by all this and determined to pass on a report to headquarters of his suspicions. He also remembered that Crawford had lost the lower part of his left leg and foot to an exploding German shell during their artillery barrage and now walked with a false foot made of metal which enabled him to be quite mobile, although he walked with a pronounced limp. He was surprised, however, to discover that Crawford appeared to be able to move with the agility of an able-bodied person and he had no recollection of a limp at all.

I found Constable Evans' observations interesting and was determined to follow up the leads he had given me in the next couple of days from my desk in Cardiff. Before I left, I asked if Evans would accompany me in the car to show me the beach locations where it was believed U-boat crews had made landings and then pass by the farm on the way back, just to get my bearings clear. He was happy to agree and for the next hour we took a tour along the edge of the bay and stopped at several locations where there was clear access to the beaches below, and I was beginning to get an understanding as to why the Gower Peninsula was an excellent location for clandestine operations. I left Port Eynon after lunch and drove back to Cardiff, excited to impart what I had discovered to Alicia and Ivor before the end of the day. I knew that Ivor intended to call on Helmut Gruber that afternoon and I was anxious to hear from him how the old tailor had reacted to his request for the medical records. I was sure that as the weeks went by with no requests from the police for the medical records, he had probably thought he was safe and had got away with it, but he was in for a surprise today. Alicia would have been following up on Joachim Schultz, but I don't think that she had much chance of getting very far with these enquiries quickly, but the information about the Branden Farm Machinery Company may provide an avenue to follow.

Ivor was already in the office when I reached the station and he gave me a full account of his visit to Helmut Gruber that afternoon. "The old man was quite helpful and cooperative at first until he realised that I was following up on the enquiries you were making concerning the medical records of Friedrich Gruber to be submitted to the Medical Exemptions Board. The mention of your name seemed to frighten him somewhat, so I laid it on thick and told him that if the medical records for Friedrich Gruber were not received at the medical board within the next forty-eight hours his medical exemption would be revoked, and he would be called up in the next wave of conscripts. I stressed that in that event the exemption certificates for Manfred and Joachim Gruber would be revoked too as they were based on the same medical evidence, and they would be called up too. I also suggested that the medical board would probably wish to take proceedings against the doctor who provided the sworn statements as to the boys' epilepsy without examining any of them or seeing their medical records. Old man Gruber was a quivering mess as I left the shop and as a last word, I said that I hoped he would submit them at Tiger Bay Police Station tomorrow morning." Ivor laughed and said that he didn't hang around in the street outside in case they were tempted to try the hit and run again.

SEVEN

Alicia had a much more difficult day and had not been able to follow her planned schedule of investigation around Joachim Schultz as she was detailed to assist in another investigation where a female officer was required. A young woman had been found unconscious in Cathays Park in a poor and dishevelled state in the early hours of the morning. The victim had been found by a patrolling beat constable who arranged immediate medical assistance and she was taken to the General Hospital. After receiving medical attention, her injuries were found to be less severe than first thought, but it was apparent that she had been sexually assaulted, and the woman alleged that she had been raped and beaten by her ex-husband. Alicia was annoyed to be taken off her case to follow up on the sexual assault case, which she hoped would be an open and shut case as the perpetrator was known to the victim and was her ex-husband. She made her way to the General Hospital, which was where Derfal had been taken after his attack, but this time she went to the women's section and met the male detective in charge of the case, Detective Sergeant Bevan, who briefed her on what was already known about the incident. The victim's name was Heidi Schultz but since she and her husband had been estranged for the past five years or so, she had reverted to using her maiden name, which was Weisse. Her husband was Joachim Schultz, sometimes known as Joe, who had left her nearly six years ago but had recently returned to work in the local area and had made contact again just a few days before the incident took place. Alicia knew immediately that this case might prove to be significant for the main enquiry as both Heidi and Joachim were persons of interest to them, but was also quite sure that the leaders of the German spy ring would not wish the police to become too involved in the affairs of two of their members if they could avoid it. However, this was early days and Alicia knew that she needed to interview Heidi before there was any opportunity for her to be contacted by members of the spy network to stop her pursuing the case against Joachim Schultz. The doctor in charge had given assent to Heidi being interviewed and Alicia was given the use of a small office to meet with Heidi. It was obvious from first sight that Heidi had undergone a considerable ordeal as she looked haggard and drawn, with bruising around her left eye, and she had read from the initial medical report that she had bruising to her breasts and wrists and blood on her inner thighs and vagina, which suggested a violent sexual attack. The doctor was sure that penetrative sex had taken place and that it was not consensual, judging by the signs of struggle evident on her body. He was sure that when the attacker was apprehended there would be signs of the victim's fight to defend herself, probably in terms of scratches to his face and hands.

Alicia decided to play the sympathetic woman and gently drew from Heidi her account of what had happened the previous evening and how she had ended up unconscious in Cathays Park. Heidi was reluctant to say too much initially but as Alicia gained her confidence and trust, the story gradually began to come out. Joachim and Heidi had been married about ten years previously when she was only eighteen, when she was swept off her feet by this handsome and experienced man some ten years older than herself. Joachim was always fun to be with and was forever up to different schemes to try to get rich quick, none of which ever amounted to much but nevertheless she was deeply in love with him. They moved into her father's house in East Street near to the Cardiff Synagogue, where her father was the rabbi, and although Joachim was not Jewish, they got on well and he was accepted as a member of the family. She had always suspected that he had affairs with other women as he seemed to have to travel a lot with his job, and she also suspected that he was also involved in some criminal activities, like house-breaking and burglary. He was known to have a strong temper and had been banned from some of the most notorious pubs in Cardiff for brawling in their bars. Joachim had never treated Heidi brutally, although he could be quite rough in their lovemaking, especially if he had been drinking. After about four years together, Joachim suddenly disappeared one night on the pretext of a business trip to Swansea, and she had not seen or heard anything from him or about him until he turned up again a few days ago. She said she was visited by detectives from the City Police who were looking for him two days or so after he had left and felt that this was hardly a coincidence and was probably the reason that he had left so hurriedly. Alicia made a note to check police records from that time to see why Schultz was of interest to police at that time and to see if he had a criminal record.

Alicia gently coaxed Heidi to go on by asking her how she felt when she heard he had returned to Cardiff just recently. Was she angry that he just walked back into her life without even a word of explanation for his conduct? She said she had almost rid him from her mind, and it was an unpleasant shock when she heard he was back, but she was prepared to meet him to hear his explanation about where he had been for the past five years. She agreed to meet him in the private bar of the Cross Keys Hotel in Newport Road at eight o'clock last night, and although she had no desire to take him back as her husband, she was eager to hear what he had to say for himself. They met at eight and he was unusually pleasant and courteous and not at all like the Joachim she remembered from their early days together.

"He didn't give any explanation for his prolonged absence other than to say it was because of his work commitments but kept saying that I was never out of his thoughts, and he just dreamed of getting back together during his enforced absence, which made me wonder whether he had been in prison because I remembered the police were looking for him when he ran away. He assured me that it was nothing like that but it was difficult to contact me during that time but that he was back now and wouldn't go away again." She said she didn't believe him, but he was not being unpleasant, so they enjoyed a few more drinks before she had to leave to catch the last tram going back towards East Street. Joachim offered to walk with her to the tram stop and they left the bar together about ten-thirty or so to take the ten-minute walk to the stop when he suggested they take a short cut through the park, which would get them to the tram stop in under five minutes. She said that if she was on her own, she wouldn't dare walk alone through the park at night but accompanied by Joachim she felt that no harm could come to her. They walked around the perimeter pathway for a couple of minutes until they came to a bench by the side of the path, secluded amongst some tall shrubs and trees, and Joachim pulled her down to sit on the seat and kissed her hard on the lips. "I did not ask for this kiss but when I felt the passion in his lips and the tightness of his grip, I succumbed and opened my mouth and let his tongue meet with mine and we kissed deeply for some few minutes. Although I was enjoying the kissing, I began to worry about missing the tram and tried to break away from his embrace, but he just gripped me tighter and kissed me harder, biting my lips and forcing his tongue further into my throat. By now, I was beginning to get worried because I knew I was powerless to break free as he was physically stronger than me. He was now fumbling at the buttons of my blouse under my coat, and I could feel him roughly rip away the material of my blouse and undergarments to pull my breasts free and into his hands. He squeezed my nipples so hard I cried out loud, and he punched me several times in the face to silence my objections and by now I realised what his intentions were as he lifted me bodily and pushed me back against the trunk of a large tree where he lifted up my skirts and petticoat until his way lay open and he lifted me onto his erect penis and penetrated me deeply. I tried to scream but he stuffed his handkerchief in my mouth as he wound my legs around his waist so that he could pound deeper into me until, after what seemed an age, he ejaculated with a massive sigh and then forced me onto my knees and made me submit to the final indignity of licking the semen from his penis with my tongue, which seemed to revive him, and this time he entered me from behind and raped me a second time. When he had finally finished, he wiped himself on my blouse and rearranged his clothing and as a parting gift hit me so hard on the back of the head that I lost consciousness and collapsed to the ground."

Alicia found this account truly harrowing and had a growing sense of sympathy for Heidi, who had been the victim of a truly horrific attack. She felt that this would be a difficult case to bring to court because Joachim and Heidi were still married and in some courts in Wales, it would be difficult to argue against the conjugal rights defence. Nowhere in her account did Heidi specifically say no and by her own admission enjoyed the heavy kissing, and maybe Joachim took this to be a green light for what happened next. However, now that they were in possession of Heidi's statement of the alleged rape, they had a perfect opportunity to interview Joachim Schultz about a serious matter that was in no way related to his potential involvement in espionage. She shared the statement with Sergeant Bevan and filed it in the case notes, and he was more than willing for her to take the lead on this because he found rape cases uncomfortable to work on and more suited to women officers. This suited her fine and she returned to Tiger Bay to discuss these developments with Wesley and Ivor, but she couldn't help thinking that Heidi Weisse, spy and enemy of the state or not, had undergone a terrible attack at the hands of Joachim Schultz and he should be brought to justice for this crime, whatever happened. She was not sure whether they would be as certain of this as her as they may prefer to prosecute the espionage case as a priority.

Wesley and Ivor had less enthusiasm for pursuing the rape case but did agree that it provided a golden opportunity to legitimately investigate Joachim and Heidi without giving away any information regarding their suspicions about the spy ring. Wesley was certain that they should strike immediately and get an arrest warrant from a magistrate that night and immediately drive over to Sir Wilhelm's estate and bring Joachim in for questioning before he had any opportunity to escape. Wesley went immediately to arrange the warrant and asked them to inform George Bennett of what actions they were taking and why. Within a couple of hours, Wesley had found a magistrate willing to sign the arrest warrant and they planned to arrest Joachim at Sir Wilhelm Branden's country estate at about 11pm.

Inspector Bennett had authorised some extra resources for making the arrest and search of his room and three uniformed constables from the night shift were allocated to their operation. It wasn't thought likely that Joachim Schultz would be armed but they couldn't be sure, so Wesley and Ivor drew revolvers from the armoury, just in case. They drove out to a holding point about half a mile from Sir Wilhelm's estate, Craddock Park, and were in position by ten-thirty or so and this gave Wesley a few minutes to brief the team on the purpose of this operation. It was of paramount importance to apprehend Joachim Schultz, who was one of Sir Wilhelm Branden's chauffeurs who lived on the estate in a room located above the garage and stable block to the rear of the house. It was explained that their intention was to approach the front of the house and to inform Sir Wilhelm Branden that they were about to serve the arrest warrant on Joachim Schultz for the rape and assault on Heidi Weisse. The two vehicles were to remain on the main driveway at the front of the house around a hundred yards from the front door. This was only a matter of protocol, for Sir Wilhelm was an influential man and Joachim's employer but as soon as he was aware, he would come out of the front door and flash his torch three times in quick succession as their signal to go. They would enter the garage block and climb the stairs and proceed to Schultz's room. There was only one entrance and exit but it was possible that Schultz could jump out of the rear window and make good his escape, so two of the constables were to position themselves at the rear of the building to apprehend Schultz should he attempt to escape custody this way.

Sir Branden was not very pleased to have his evening disturbed by the police at this late hour and was full of bluster and threats, but when he realised the seriousness of the crime that Schultz was charged with, he became a little more compliant. He did not give away that he knew Heidi Weisse and Joachim were in fact married, or that he knew Heidi at all, although, of course, the police knew that he and Heidi were both members of the board of Wurtenberg Holdings, but they were sure that he did not realise that they knew about the existence of the holding company at all. Many thoughts must have been going through Sir Wilhelm's mind in rapid time as he realised that he could not deter them from their task of arresting and questioning Schultz for the rape and assault of Heidi, and if he were to show anything other than outrage and shock that Schultz could have committed such a heinous crime, this might appear suspicious to the police. He took comfort from the fact that this crime was totally detached from the espionage activities that his group were engaged in and there was no reason to think that the police would pursue any enquiries other than the sexual crime and violence that he had allegedly committed. Sir Wilhelm reasoned that there was a good chance that he and Anton Kruger could persuade Heidi not to press charges against her estranged husband or for Joachim to argue that he was only exercising his conjugal rights. The biggest worry was whether Joachim could be trusted to follow orders to the letter as he was not imbued with the highest levels of intelligence and may not have the resolve to just remain silent and make the police work doubly hard to prove a case against him. He thought it imperative that Anton Kruger act as his lawyer and use the pretext of legal advice to tell Joachim exactly what he needed to do. He felt sympathy for Heidi for her ordeal at Joachim's hand, but he was sure that it was in their best interests to get Joachim released as quickly as possible before it became a danger to the whole mission. Heidi would be ordered to withdraw the charges against Schultz and to say that she had consented and they had got a little overexcited, not having seen each other for six years. Schultz was now expendable and when the police interest had passed, some small accident could be arranged and he could easily join the corpses of the two wounded British veterans buried in the woods near Talybont. Sir Wilhelm said he would accompany them to show them the way, but they thanked him and said for his own safety he should remain in the house because Schultz had shown himself to be a desperate and violent man.

With that, Wesley gave his leave and headed out of the front door and signalled the waiting vehicles, which he could hear immediately start their motors and move swiftly towards the rear of the main house. Wesley ran as fast as he could to meet up with the arresting party at the foot of the stairs leading to the first floor above the garage area.

*

Schultz was living in room 5 and we approached stealthily and positioned ourselves either side of the door. Ivor and I drew our revolvers, and Alicia and the third constable drew their truncheons. As I hammered on the door, I shouted that we were the police, and he was to open his door immediately. There was shouting from inside but no movement to open the door, so Ivor and I kicked the door in and smashed our way into the room just in time to catch Schultz with one leg up on the window ledge ready to climb out. However, we were far too quick for him and darted across the room and pulled him bodily back through the window and into the room. He was squirming and throwing out punches in all directions and certainly had no intention of coming quietly. Had he connected with any of his punches, he might have laid out one or other of us and make his escape, but Alicia's cool head put a stop to his resistance by giving him two resounding whacks across the kneecaps with her truncheon with all the strength she could muster. The pain must have been excruciating, for Schultz immediately stopped fighting, drew his legs into his body and wrapped his arms around his knees, presumably to protect them from further attacks from Alicia's truncheon. It was now relatively straightforward to pull his arms behind his back and handcuff his hands securely and to lift him up on his feet. I now read out to him the contents of the arrest warrant and told him that he had the right to remain silent but if he chose to speak, anything he said could be used against him in court. He was led away by the constable to be locked in the back of the Black Maria for the journey back to Cardiff, and I congratulated the team for an efficient operation, and we made our way happily back to Tiger Bay to begin interviewing Schultz as soon as possible.

I booked Schultz into custody with the station sergeant, and he was locked up in a cell whilst Alicia, Ivor and I held a short conversation to plan out our interrogation strategy overnight and in the morning. I was certain that Sir Wilhelm would have already contacted Anton Kruger, the lawyer, within a short time of the arrest, and I was certain that Kruger would appear at the police station at the earliest possible moment to prevent us speaking to the suspect before he had the opportunity to direct him what to say. It was now after two-thirty in the morning and I would not expect Kruger to turn up at the station until eight in the morning at the earliest. We agreed that the best option was for us all to try to grab a few hours of sleep so that we would be refreshed and ready to conduct the interviews the following morning with clear heads. We could guess what Kruger would advise Schultz to do, which meant he wouldn't talk to us anyway, and I was sure that they would try to get Heidi Weisse to withdraw the charges to stop the enquiry dead in its tracks. Alicia was convinced that Heidi was so traumatised by the attack that she didn't think she would withdraw the charges whatever pressure they put on her, but when dealing with these rape cases involving husband and wife, you can never be sure. Anton Kruger may have been a German spy, but we knew for sure that he was an excellent lawyer with a successful practice in Cardiff and we could expect him to use all his considerable skills to get his client off the hook. Schultz was surly and aggressive and treated our enquiries with a certain flippancy as he did not think that a man having sex with his wife was against the law, and he was confident that Heidi would never bring charges against him. I for one was happy to shut the steel door of his cell on his smirking and arrogant face until the morning.

*

Sir Wilhelm waited until the police had arrested Schultz and removed him from Craddock Park before he made the call to Anton Kruger. It was a long time before the telephone was answered and Kruger was less than happy to have been woken in the middle of the night and made his bad temper known immediately, but he soon quietened down when he heard what Sir Wilhelm had to say about the arrest of Schultz on rape charges. Kruger was furious that Schultz had been so stupid and exposed them all to great risk. "I thought I made it so clear to them all after the last incident with the hit and run on the policeman that we needed to keep a low profile and avoid attracting the attention of the police by all the means in our power." He began to think now as a lawyer and said that he would take Schultz's case and attend the police station first thing to brief him on what he must not do or say. The police would be unlikely to interview Schultz in the middle of the night but would begin first thing in the morning and he would make sure that he was there. Meanwhile, he instructed Sir Wilhelm to drive over to Dr Julius Matthias and inform him what was happening and get him to use his influence with Heidi to get her to drop the charges against Schultz immediately and to threaten her with dire consequences should she be reluctant to do so. He also suggested that Schultz was now a liability, and if they managed to get the case closed, they could no longer use him because he was too well known to the police, so perhaps Sullivan, Otto or Heinrich could be relied on to deal with him on their behalf. When he put the receiver back on the cradle, he began to realise the seriousness of the situation and he poured himself a schnapps and sat in the drawing room whilst he thought through his next steps. The situation was precarious for the whole network because the police would be thorough and put pressure on Schultz in ways designed to provoke ill-judged outbursts from him. Kruger knew that Schultz was a drunkard, a brawler and a womaniser as this was clear from his file but, most dangerous of all, he was hot-headed and motivated by a strong sense of self-preservation. He was volatile and he could easily imagine situations where he could make unguarded remarks or be drawn into giving away incriminating information on members of the group to gain more favourable treatment from the police or to secure his release. He knew that his superiors in Berlin would be less than satisfied with the turn of events and would want Schultz dealt with quickly and efficiently before he could reveal any vital information about the operations in South Wales. Kruger also knew that Schultz possessed skills crucial to the successful completion of their mission and he would need to be replaced immediately. Kruger had already used the services of Ernest Sullivan, an accomplished assassin, to deal with the two wounded British veterans who were murdered by him to establish false identities for Otto and Heinrich, and he realised that he would have to call upon his special services again to deal with Schultz, and Heidi Weisse too if she proved to be difficult.

Several months before, the story of the two wounded lieutenants, Crawford and King, who wished to become farmers despite their wounds, became known to Kruger via a distant relative who worked as a nurse at the Moreton Park Convalescent Hospital for Wounded Officers in Llantwit Major. Crawford had lost the lower part of his left leg and King was now profoundly deaf as a result of their injuries incurred on the battlefield. They had met and become friends at the hospital and as they were both deemed to be medically unfit for continued military service, they began to think about what they could do in civilian life once they were discharged from the army. They both agreed that it was possible for them despite their disabilities to make a go of it in civilian life if they could decide on some employment that they were capable of doing reasonably well. Crawford had been a schoolmaster and King an accounting trainee, but after their time on the Western Front neither felt like returning to their previous occupations. They dreamed of become tenant farmers and talked enthusiastically all the time about learning to become farmers and still helping the war effort. Their enthusiasm was infectious and soon their ambition was talked about all through the hospital. When the story filtered through to Kruger, he immediately saw a golden opportunity to substitute two German operatives in their identities, and it was a coincidence that he had already earmarked Llangellis Farm as a suitable venue for a future safe house because of its isolation and proximity to a beach where the U-boats could land a boat. A watch was maintained on the two British officers and when they were discharged from the hospital, they were kidnapped by Sullivan and some of his men from their hotel and driven away to Llangellis Farm in secret. Sullivan killed them both with one shot to the back of the head and disposed of their bodies in an isolated woodland grave near Talybont-on-Usk in the Black Mountains, many miles away from the farm. The German officers who would take the new identities were to arrive within the next few days, so stories were put about in the local area near the farm that Lieutenants Crawford and King were the new tenants of Llangellis Farm on the Gower Peninsula and would be arriving to take up residence within a few days.

*

After barely four hours' sleep, I was back at my desk and making my notes for the initial interviews with Schultz and I was expecting Alicia to join me at any moment. I already knew that Schultz was employed as one of the chauffeurs by Sir Wilhelm Branden but was in possession of some contradictory evidence that had come from Constable Evans, who had met Schultz at Llangellis Farm where he had introduced himself as Joe Schultz, a representative for the Branden Farm Machinery Company in Cardiff. I had decided to set Ivor the task of reconciling this anomaly by finding out all he could about the farm machinery company and whether Schultz worked for them or was simply a chauffeur. I suspected that the Branden Farm Machinery Company was another front company being used by the German spy ring and was probably registered to Sir Wilhelm Branden, and I would wager next week's wages that members of the Wurtenberg Holdings board were directors of this company too. I was going to ask Alicia to take the lead on the questioning of Schultz to emphasise that this was all about the rape case as I was sure that Kruger would recognise my name from the hit and run incident some months before, and I didn't want him to draw any conclusions that I was still working on the previous case.

Alicia arrived about seven-thirty and although she had managed barely a few minutes more than me in bed, she managed to look fresh and alert and ready to go. She was aware that cases involving husbands raping their wives were notoriously difficult to prosecute because the defence of conjugal rights was difficult to argue against in courts where the judge and jury were exclusively male, but she was optimistic that the physical evidence of the injuries to Heidi Weisse would make a significant impact in court if the case got that far. Alicia was going to press Schultz hard to get him to reveal why he had chosen to attack his estranged wife in such a violent way in a public park instead of visiting her at home. She was also going to focus on where he had been for the past six years since he was last resident in Cardiff, and when he entered employment as Sir Wilhelm's chauffeur why he did not seek an amicable reunion with his estranged wife. I agreed that this was a good strategy and may well lead us to information to do with the rape case that might have a bearing on the espionage activities more widely.

Kruger arrived at the front desk promptly at eight forty-five, but we kept him waiting for thirty minutes in the interview room before we brought Schultz up from the cells for a consultation with his lawyer. We were not allowed to be present at this interview, but we could tell from the raised voices and the glowering expressions on their faces when Alicia and I joined them at ten to begin the first interview that their legal consultation had not gone smoothly. Kruger changed his expression when he spoke to us in a businesslike manner, anxious to get proceedings dealt with quickly and his client released from custody as soon as possible. Alicia made it clear that we were dealing with a serious criminal charge involving grievous harm to the victim and the vicious forced rape in a public park of a respectable woman of good character. "The lady concerned has suffered severe mental harm as well as the physical injuries inflicted on her by your client and there is no way that this could be dismissed as something that could be dealt with quickly, like some petty crime."

Kruger interjected with, "But this was a husband exercising his right to have sex with his wife, and no criminal court will find him guilty of rape in these circumstances, I think you will find."

Alicia was not put off by this statement at all and replied, "If this incident had taken place at home in the privacy of their own bedroom and had not been attendant to such horrific violence resulting in grievous bodily harm visited upon the victim by your client then maybe there would be an argument to be put here. This attack took place in a public park and was perpetrated by a man who has not had any contact with his wife in over six years and who requested a meeting that evening to give some explanation for his absence, but he ended up assaulting her violently whilst raping her."

Alicia now turned to Schultz and addressed him directly. "What do you say, Mr Schultz, to the allegations sworn in a statement made to the police from her hospital bed by Heidi Schultz, née Weisse, that you viciously attacked and raped her in Cathays Park two days ago?"

Schultz shrugged his shoulders and said, "I didn't do it."

Alicia responded by asking him to explain what he meant by this, and he shrugged his shoulders again and said, "We had a few drinks in the Cross Keys and she was begging for it as we hadn't seen each other for a long time, so I gave her one in the park on the way home for old times' sake."

"You admit to having sexual intercourse with Heidi in the park?" Alicia immediately responded.

Schultz looked a bit confused and said, "Well, I just said so, didn't I?"

Alicia pressed him again. "But, Mr Schultz, you said in response to my first question that you didn't do it and now you are telling us that you did engage in sexual intercourse in a public park with Miss Weisse. So, which is it?"

Schultz looked sheepish and then admitted that he did have sex with Heidi in the park that night. So Alicia smiled and said, "I am glad we have cleared that up," and then proceeded to ask, "Can you explain how Miss Weisse came to be found unconscious in the park having sustained two black eyes, scratches to her face, a wound to the back of her head, likely to have been administered by a heavy punch that caused a severe concussion, and signs of violent entry to her vagina and bruising to her upper thighs? The police surgeon has also reported that there are bruises to her arms and hands where she had tried to defend herself against her assailant during the attack."

Schultz replied, "Heidi always likes it a bit rough, doesn't she?"

"I wouldn't know," Alicia retorted, "but am I to take it that Heidi wanted you to beat her severely during your lovemaking and you were pleased to satisfy her desires?"

"Yes, she always liked to be slapped around a bit when we were at it."

"So, Mr Schultz, you also admit that you administered the beating which caused the injuries to Heidi Weisse whilst you were having sex with her in the park. So, now we have come a long way from your initial statement that you didn't do it to an admission that you engaged in sex with Heidi and beat her up at the same time."

Kruger intervened at this point and said, "It is perfectly clear that Mr Schultz engaged in sexual intercourse with his wife in Cathays Park at the date and time mentioned and that he has admitted that Mrs Schultz likes to be treated roughly during the sex act and that he had obliged. At no time have you brought forward evidence that Mrs Schultz did not consent to these acts taking place and, on the contrary, according to my client, she positively encouraged them to take place and readily agreed to go into a dark and secluded part of the park for that express purpose. Mr Schultz is sorry that in the exuberance of their lovemaking, he might have been too heavy-handed, which he regrets now, but at no time was there any coercion or force used on his part. Mr Schultz has been married to Heidi for nearly ten years and was happy that they have affected a reconciliation after a long separation."

Alicia now placed the sworn statement of Heidi Weisse on the table in front of them in which Miss Weisse described exactly what happened to her on the night of the attack. "It it abundantly clear that she had no intention of affecting a reconciliation with Mr Schultz, nor did she enter Cathays Park with the intention of engaging in any sexual activity with him but only to take the short cut to the tram stop. She states clearly that she did not consent at any time to sexual intercourse or encourage him to beat her in this most violent matter. Heidi Weisse is a woman of good character and there is no reason to doubt her version of events."

Kruger interjected that there were no independent witnesses here and the case rested on the husband's word against his wife, and the balance of proof was heavily in favour of the husband in this matter. Alicia replied that the case revolved around who was the most believable witness and immediately switched track and asked Schultz if he was a trustworthy and honest man. Schultz looked confused and looked at his lawyer for guidance but then nodded, and Alicia asked him again that by nodding was he saying that he was an honest and truthful man? Schultz said that he was and had nothing to be ashamed of. Alicia immediately commented that being honest and truthful was not the same thing as having no shame over his actions and immediately placed on the table between them Joachim Schultz' police file from his time in Cardiff between 1906 and 1910, which documented numerous incidents in and around the city involving violent assault, affray, petty theft and heavy drinking, which had been dealt with by the stipendiary court. "At the time of your disappearance from the city there were several police warrants in existence for your arrest for outstanding crimes that were never served, and it was strongly suspected that you were tipped off and skipped the city and laid low to avoid arrest. Enquiries amongst your wife's family and the community where you lived during your married life show that you had a poor reputation as a liar and cheat with a violent temper amongst your neighbours and relations. There were strong suspicions that you beat your wife and that Heidi was afraid of you, but no charges were ever brought, but I suppose you are going to argue that this was acceptable as it was your right as a husband." Alicia concluded, "These records prove conclusively that you are neither honest nor truthful and readily turn to violence, especially when you have been drinking. By your own admission, you had been drinking in the Cross Keys Hotel bar that evening and decided that you would take the opportunity to take your violent sexual pleasures out on your estranged wife."

Schultz rose up out of his chair threateningly and shouted at Alicia that he would give her a sample of the same, and he may well have attempted to do so had not myself and the constable at the door restrained him and handcuffed him to the chair. Alicia remained cool and calmly remarked, "Your actions just prove our case for us and reinforce what we already know… that you are a man who has no morals, who just takes what he wants and is not afraid to use violence when its suits his purpose." Schultz shouted back that he loved Heidi and that they were reconciled and were getting back together. Alicia smiled and quietly intimated that a violent rape which left his loving wife unconscious with serious injuries in the park did not seem to back up his story of a loving reconciliation consummated by passionate sex. "If what you suggest is true, why did you run off and leave her lying in a pool of blood in the park? Did you try to get medical assistance? Why is it that you just returned to your accommodation at Craddock Park and carried on with your daily routine until we arrested you nearly forty-eight hours after the incident took place? And finally, why, if you are an honest and truthful man, did you try to escape through the rear window of your room when we came to arrest you?"

Alicia sat back and concluded by saying, "You have been charged with rape and assault and battery of Heidi Weisse and will be held in the cells at this police station until you can be arraigned before the magistrates for remand to the *assizes*," and she collected her files from the table and stood ready to leave the room. Kruger said that he would seek bail and she replied that he was entitled to ask but the police would object to bail on the grounds that Schultz was a dangerous and violent criminal and should be held in custody as there was a strong likelihood that he would disappear, as he had done previously in 1910, to escape arrest.

I followed Alicia out of the room and congratulated her on such a firm and measured performance and I was glad that I had selected her to lead the interrogation as she had produced the admissions from Schultz, and we were now certain that he was guilty. Back in our office, we were able to talk about the wider context of the case in regard to the espionage ring, and we were fairly certain that Schultz's actions would be considered by them dangerous to their clandestine activities and they would be faced with a huge dilemma of what to do about him. They would be desperate to release him from police custody as the longer we had to interrogate him, the greater the risk that he might let slip vital information about their spying activities but once they had secured his release on bail or acquittal from the charges, they were still faced with the problem of what to do with him. He could no longer continue as a member of their team because he was now too well known to the police, whereas they needed to remain invisible to be effective in their roles. Schultz had become a liability and maybe Kruger realised that he should have been more circumspect before accepting him back after his prolonged absence. It seemed most likely that Schultz would disappear once he was released from police custody, and we would not have a second chance with him. We resolved to prepare a strong justification for remanding him to prison until the *assize* court next month, giving us ample time to investigate where he had been for the past five years and why he had returned to Cardiff at this time.

Ivor had made a start on the background research on Schultz already and we knew that he wasn't listed on the 1911 Census as resident in the Weisse household, nor had he been able to find any references to Joachim Schultz in police files so far. The search of police files would be like searching for the proverbial needle in a haystack except that he had a distinctly German-sounding name, which would be more easily remembered by station sergeants with responsibility for record-keeping in the various police divisions. Ivor reckoned that if Schultz wished to keep a low profile, he would lose himself in a large city or town, so he sent his request to the largest towns and cities first and was disappointed that he got a negative response except for a phone call from the station sergeant from East India Docks in London, who said they were looking for a Swiss national, Joe Schultz, who had allegedly broken into a house with the intention of robbery and was disturbed by the householder and his wife in the act of burglary. Schultz beat the man seriously and left him unconscious and then tied up his wife and viciously raped her before making his escape with some jewellery and cash from the house. The victims were unable to give much of a description of their assailant, but enquiries in the neighbourhood brought up Schultz's names in three different places as the likely perpetrator who had been boasting in various dockside pubs and trying to sell items of jewellery. The offences took place about four weeks ago and although we searched for Schultz at his lodgings and at his regular haunts, he seemed to have disappeared from the district. They were excited to receive Ivor's request as the similarity of some aspects of the case made it likely that we were both dealing with the same suspect. We were elated because this information considerably strengthened our case to be put before the magistrates at the bail hearing.

I congratulated Ivor on his application and remarked that he may not be the best cross-country runner, but he was certainly an excellent investigator. He went on to say that he was following another lead concerning Schultz's nationality status and that he would be taking the train to London in the morning to visit the Swiss Embassy in Mayfair, where he had an appointment with the head of the consular department at 13:00. He explained that he had sent a written request to the Swiss Embassy regarding Schultz's passport and had received a reply that there was a passport issued to a Joachim Schultz, but they wished to discuss it with us in person. He did not know what they were going to tell him, but it seemed likely that they had some concerns that they wished to share discreetly with us. Again, this could be a step forward in discovering something further about the identity of Schultz and solving the mystery of where he had been over the past five years or so, and we wished Ivor every success on his trip to London. I decided that I would concentrate on fleshing out the detail on the information gathered by Constable Evans at Port Eynon, and Alicia would prepare our case for remanding Schultz in custody at the magistrates' court at the end of the week. Ivor then said that he had an appointment with the companies registrar the following morning to receive details of the search for the Branden Farm Machinery Company, which he could not make because of his trip to London. I volunteered to do this for him as I would need to make enquiries in the city the next day regarding Crawford and King.

EIGHT

The registry at Companies House had made copies of the relevant pages from the register concerning the Branden Farm Machinery Company and I was not too surprised to find that it was a business owned by Sir Wilhelm Branden and its registered business address was Craddock Park, which was Branden's country estate. It was not listed as a subsidiary or linked to Wurtenberg Holdings, but some of the directors were members of both boards, Anton Kruger was their legal representative and Pugh, Taylor and Sullivan were members. All the other directors listed were not known to us and would need to be investigated to see if they were part of the spy network or not. The directors who were unknown to us previously seemed as innocent as the original suspects at first glance, and I realised that we would be busy searching out their backgrounds to try to discover linkage to the fourteen or so individuals who we also suspected were German spies. There was Peter Martin, a tug master from Pembroke Dock, and Rhys Evans, who worked as a stevedore manager in Swansea Docks, who were both board members. Frederick Webb was from Barry Island and was listed as the company accountant and Helga Richards the company secretary. The company existed to provide the latest farming machinery for dairy and arable farmers in the South Wales region and according to records the company was solvent with significant assets in cash and stock and had been trading profitably for over eight years. There may be no connection between Wurtenberg Holdings and the farm machinery enterprise, but it was imperative that we investigate thoroughly to see if it was another shell company or a genuine business venture operated by Sir Wilhelm.

After leaving Companies House, I drove out to Llantwit Major, about twenty or so miles out of the city, to visit the Officers' Convalescent Hospital where Lieutenants Crawford and King had recovered from their wounds. It was a fine morning and the drive along the coastal road was enjoyable and relaxed my mind and gave a pleasant respite from all the thoughts whirling around inside my head. The hospital proved to be an imposing building that stood out on the hillside looking towards the coast but was, in fact, much closer to the village of St Athan than Llantwit Major. It had not been built as a hospital but had been the location of Llantwit College, a minor public school since 1875. The school had moved to temporary accommodation during the war and they had apparently loaned the building to the Army Medical Corps for the duration. I made my way to the hospital administration office and showed my warrant card and asked if there was someone I could talk to who would be able to give me information regarding two of their former patients, Lieutenants Henry Crawford of the Oxfordshire Regiment and Oliver King of the Welsh Fusiliers. The young female clerk said that would be easy because they were famous in the hospital because they were going to become farmers despite their injuries. She made a quick check through her file and said that the best person to speak with would be Sister Elizabeth Cummings, in charge of Glendower Ward, where both officers had been treated. She gave me directions on how to find my way to the ward and she said that she would telephone ahead so Sister Cummings would expect me.

The sister was a handsome woman in her mid-thirties who welcomed me warmly and said she was intrigued to know why the police were interested in two of her patients. I told her that I was investigating a matter of national security and we were concerned that her two young lieutenants may have become unwittingly involved in something that could be a danger to them and disastrous to our war effort. I asked her to tell me about these two wounded officers and how they became friends and decided to set up as farmers. She was very cooperative and talked fondly about Henry and Oliver, who were obviously popular characters in her ward and in the hospital more widely.

She explained that they were a convalescent hospital and specialised in the long-term recovery of the wounded, who were either returned to duty in the army or invalided out of military service because of the severity of their wounds. "Many soldiers who lose their limbs or eyesight are no longer able to perform their duty and our job is to help them recuperate and adjust to a civilian life where they can live as useful and as comfortable a life as is possible according to their wounds. We do not carry out a great deal of medical work here other than maintaining treatment programmes that were initiated elsewhere but focus on recuperation and adjustment to a life that might be very different than they were used to before the war." She glowed with pride when she told me about Henry Crawford and Oliver King, whom she considered to be two of their best success stories.

"Crawford arrived in the ward first and although he had made a miraculous recovery from most of his wounds and to the external eye would look to be as fit and healthy as the next man, he had, of course, lost his lower left leg and foot from mid-calf. The stump had healed well, and he came to us to be fitted with a false leg and foot and to learn to walk using this prosthetic aid. He was not particularly well adjusted to the course of treatment prescribed for him and suffered bouts of depression as he struggled psychologically to come to terms with his disability. He was reticent and grumpy and reluctant to mix with any of the other patients, and although we tried hard to encourage him that with the false leg he could go back to teaching and live an almost normal life despite his injuries, this did not seem to lighten his mood. He continued like this for several weeks until Oliver King was admitted to the ward and was allocated the bed next to his.

"Oliver King was physically fit but had suffered the shattering of both eardrums from the blast of an enemy shell exploding within the trench close to his position on the fire step. He was blown clear and suffered only superficial injuries physically, whereas the soldiers who were between him and the blast were killed or received serious injuries. He was knocked unconscious but when he came round, the damage to his eardrums became evident when he was unable to hear any sounds at all. He was like Crawford in that his injuries were not immediately obvious and there was a strong likelihood that he would be able to live as normal a life as possible in the future. He was more fortunate than those who were born profoundly deaf as he was already able to speak clearly, and the audiological specialist ordered that if he followed an intense course of learning to lip-read, he would be able to converse in one-to-one situations quite quickly." However, in the longer term, they would prescribe one of the latest electric hearing aids to amplify sounds in his ears and these machines were getting quite effective since the invention of the telephone had improved our understanding of the amplification of sound. He was like Crawford as he also struggled with coming to terms with his disability and was seemingly reluctant to engage in learning to lip-read beyond the thirty-minute daily sessions that were programmed with the audiologist. Sister Cummings explained that Crawford needed someone who would make him walk and King someone who would practise lip-reading with him, and she proposed they encourage them to help each other. "Slowly at first, they got to know each other, walking together in the grounds and talking endlessly so that Crawford began to feel comfortable walking with his false leg and King became proficient in lip-reading. They began to realise that they were coping well with their disabilities, and they began to think about their future together. Neither of them had close family connections and nobody from either family came to visit them whilst they were in hospital."

She had a notion that Crawford was from Banbury in Oxfordshire and his parents had passed away before the war, and although he had an older brother, they had not seen each other for many years, and King had been brought up by an aunt in Chepstow as his parents were Methodist missionaries in Africa, and as far as she knew they were still living there. He had no siblings, and his aunt was now quite frail and in failing health. Both of them were financially secure and there was no great imperative to return to their former civilian employment and so they searched for something that was within their new capabilities but different from their old lives. Crawford had enjoyed his few years in teaching but had no great desire to go back to it, and King had been bored to death training to be a chartered accountant and wanted something more challenging and physical for the future. Ironically, their service in the army had awoken a taste in them for the outdoor life and together they found themselves steered towards professions that might also meet that need. They looked at jobs at sea, including fishing, but quickly concluded that they were both interested in farming and they both considered that they were fit enough and financially able to take on the tenancy of a farm and to raise dairy cattle with some mixed arable crops. They spent hours every day reading all the books they could find about the rudiments of dairy farming and crop growing. It became their real passion and so great was their enthusiasm that almost every other patient and member of staff knew about their grand plans and could see how this joint motivation had truly recuperated these two wounded veterans so completely. They wrote dozens of letters to land agents around the country to secure a suitable property to lease, but by the time they were discharged, they had not found a suitable farm to rent. She finished by saying that it was strange that they had not heard a word from them at all since the day they left them. "We were sure that they would want to share with us all here their success on their new farm, but we haven't heard a thing." I asked whether she knew where they were going when they were discharged, and she thought for a minute and then said she thought they were going to

Tenby for a short holiday and then intensifying their search for a suitable acreage to rent.

When I got back in the car, I sat for a few minutes and mulled over the story that Sister Cummings had imparted over the past hour, and I too thought it was strange that they had not kept in touch with the nurses at Llantwit Major, especially as they had settled on a farm not too far away, near Swansea. The other thing that struck me was that these were two men who no one would particularly miss as they had no family to speak of and were financially secure so did not need to rely on anyone else. I didn't know at that time whether this was significant or not or indeed why the thought had occurred to me. These ideas were rolling over in my head as I drove back to Cardiff, eager to share what I had discovered with Alicia and Ivor later in the day.

Ivor had caught the 08:05 Red Dragon Express to London that morning and was in Paddington Station by 11:45 where he caught a horse-drawn cab to take him to the Swiss Embassy, which was in Mayfair in a side street behind Grosvenor Square. The cabbie dropped him outside the entrance to the consular section and Ivor approached the front door and rung the bell and waited for the door to be opened. A young lad dressed in a footman's uniform opened the door and enquired as to his business, and when he stated his business and showed his warrant card, he was admitted and shown to a waiting room to await the head of the consular section. He wasn't kept waiting very long before he was greeted by a rather avuncular-looking man of about fifty, wearing morning dress and pince-nez, who introduced himself as Herr Adolfus Liebnitz. He welcomed Ivor and said he was glad that he was able to come to London as the matters that he wished to discuss were sensitive, especially during wartime when his country was at great pains to preserve its neutral status. "We do not wish to take sides. Neither do we wish to give advantage to one side or another by not taking the appropriate action where necessary." Ivor was confused and felt that Herr Liebnitz's opening remarks were somewhat cryptic in the least and was about to ask for further clarification when he was shown into a private office and Liebnitz relaxed and said he could speak more clearly now that they were in private. He began by saying that the Swiss Government were grateful to Cardiff Police for bringing a serious matter to their attention when we made our enquiries about this passport holder. "The passport that you asked about is genuine, issued by the passport office in Geneva in 1906 in the name of Joachim Schultz, but it is with some sadness that I need to inform you that the holder of this passport disappeared whilst on a business trip to Germany shortly after and never returned to his family again. The family informed the police in Geneva immediately and a joint investigation was conducted with the police authorities in Berlin but to no avail, except that we knew that Schultz was not dead because his passport was used to enter Britain and Germany several times before and during the war. It is a mystery to us why a Swiss neutral has travelled between two countries at war but has not entered his home country once in this period or contacted his family at all. We understand that you have Joachim Schultz in your custody, and we would be grateful, if during your enquiries, you could establish, beyond doubt, the true identity of this man who is holding the Schultz passport."

He handed Ivor an envelope containing extracts from the Swiss file of personal details of Joachim Schultz for our information and which may assist us in establishing his genuine identity. "The Swiss security service suspect that Herr Schultz may have befallen some misfortune in Berlin and been replaced by a German imposter who now has the means to travel between two warring countries under the cover of his neutral passport. Herr Schultz, of course, may also be a traitor to his country and decided to work as a spy for the Germans, but either way it would be good to know the truth." Ivor asked a few more questions and established that Schultz had spent long periods in Germany during the past five years interspersed with shorter periods in Britain, and Swiss passport records showed this to be the case, although the stamps were not in the passport itself. "We can see that in June 1910 Schultz travelled by sea from Kingston upon Hull to Bremerhaven, and we have no record of a return trip until 1912 when we have evidence that he crossed the English Channel to Dover and stayed in Britain for five months before returning to the Continent later in the year. He disappears again until early 1914 when he is recorded as crossing the Dutch border at Brüggen on the 14th of January and is listed in the passenger manifest of the *SS Prince of Orange* bound for Ireland via London on the 17th of the same month. He is known to have left the ship at Tilbury Docks on the River Thames the next day, and there has been no knowledge of his whereabouts until you contacted me a few days ago, except for an entry into Germany in January 1915 through the docks at Hamburg and a return via the Channel ferry via Calais to Dover in April 1917, just three weeks ago."

Ivor was excited to read the contents of the file in detail on the train back to Cardiff and to have time to build the profile of this man calling himself

Joachim Schultz. The real Schultz was, of course, a Swiss national and as a neutral would be unlikely to be mixed up with German espionage, but if it was as Herr Liebnitz had intimated, that the current passport holder was a German spy substituted for the genuine Swiss businessman, then this was vital evidence which may contribute to bringing down the whole spy network in South Wales. He reckoned that if this was the case, the genuine Schultz had probably been murdered whilst on the trip to Berlin and an imposter put in his place. This was the most probable reason for his estrangement from his family and friends in Geneva, who would easily discover the perception. Meanwhile, all the time the passport was used to travel, it would indicate that Schultz was alive and well and detract from any suspicion that he had met his untimely end in Germany. Ivor was perplexed by the pattern of movements listed in the file and somewhat frustrated that the passport office records did not give a complete picture and that not all border crossings were necessarily recorded. Ivor couldn't remember the exact date of the marriage of Schultz and Heidi Weisse but he thought it must have been sometime in 1906 and if Schultz was an imposter, it must have been after the demise of the genuine Schultz. He made a note to check the date of the wedding and to enquire with the border control police whether there was any entry for Joachim Schultz landing in Britain in 1906 in their records. We knew that Schultz lived in East Street, Cardiff with Heidi between 1906 and 1910 when he mysteriously disappeared in early June that year, which corresponded with evidence that he had left the country on the Hull-Bremerhaven ferry and entered Germany a few days later. There were no records of his whereabouts for at least two years when he resurfaced crossing the Channel and entering Britain through the port of Dover in March 1912 and leaving again by the same route in early August. He appears to have stayed in Britain for over five months but there is no information about where he was staying or what he was doing during this time. He could see that Schultz had entered France but there was no indication where he had travelled on to after he had left the ferry. Did he return to Germany or stay in France? Ivor was not sure what to make of this, but it seemed likely that he did return to Germany because the next time he was recorded crossing a border was when he crossed from northern Germany into Holland at Brüggen in January 1914. This was just before the war started, and if this Schultz was an undercover German operative, he may well have been briefing sleeper cells and anti-government factions on their activities once war was declared. We had no information of where he went or who he met or indeed how long he stayed, but we do know that he left, presumably, to receive fresh orders or training in early 1915 when his records show him entering Germany through Hamburg Docks and leaving again nearly two years later. Ivor made a further note to find out which shipping line was operating into Hamburg at this time and how Schultz had managed to get a berth on this ship. He was almost certain that all travel connections between Britain and German ports had ceased on the outbreak of war, but it was still possible for neutrals to travel via non-combatant countries. The final piece of evidence was Schultz's re-entry into Britain through Dover about three weeks ago and his sudden reappearance in Cardiff and employment as a chauffeur for Sir Wilhelm Branden. Ivor knew that both of his colleagues would be interested in looking at the evidence he had uncovered, and he couldn't wait to share it with them later in the day. Alicia now had answers to some of the questions as to where Schultz had been during his five-year absence that she was investigating, and there was enough evidence to throw suspicion on his identity, and this leverage may prove useful in future interviews with the suspect in the next few days.

It was after six when we gathered in our small office at the station to share what we had discovered during our investigations over the past twenty-four hours. This was an important strategy for us because the combined strength of our three minds focusing on the evidence seemed to help us move forward together and keep the whole team up to speed. Ivor was bursting to tell us about his trip to London and what had transpired at the Swiss Embassy, so we were happy to let him go first and were not disappointed because the revelations about Schultz's movements verified by the documents provided by the Swiss passport office proved beyond doubt that Schultz had visited Germany at least three times in the years preceding the outbreak of war and had been in Germany in the last few months. It was perfectly possible that his business might have required him to travel between Britain and Germany and holding a passport from a neutral country, this was perfectly possible. However, we came up with numerous questions that made this seem improbable and we listed them in our central notepad for consideration. First, Schultz's business involved watches and clocks and he had built a reasonably successful business selling specialty Swiss watches and clocks in his home country and in Austria and Germany, where there appeared to be quite a healthy market for these products. There was no evidence suggesting that he had sold any of his merchandise outside these three countries, and secondly, after his disappearance in 1906, he had cut himself off from his family and all connections in Switzerland, which suggested that he no longer traded in these commodities. Thirdly, he had domiciled himself in Cardiff for five years immediately after his disappearance and married Heidi Weisse, possibly bigamously, having left a wife in Geneva. During this time, he did not seem to be running any kind of business to do with watches and clocks but was known to the police as a petty criminal. Fourth, he ran away when arrest warrants were issued for him for burglary in 1910 and we know that he went directly to Germany to escape those charges, reappearing two years later on entering Britain again and leaving some five months later. We had no idea where he went or what he was doing during this period, but we were sure that he did not come to Cardiff or contact his wife or her family. It appeared that he may have spent the next couple of years in Germany and the records showed him returning to Britain in early 1914 and then spending three months in Germany in the early part of this year before re-entering the country just three weeks ago. His Swiss passport guaranteed that he could travel and enter both warring nations even though the means of travel were much less regular during this time. He could be a legitimate Swiss businessman but on balance none of us believed this to be the case because we had all met Schultz and could see he lacked the bearing of a businessman or smooth tongue of the salesman as he was certainly a rather rough and ready individual, more used to using his fists than persuading rich watch and clock fanciers to buy his wares. We were all satisfied that we had enough evidence to pursue a line of questioning regarding his nationality and identity. It was vitally important that bail was refused when he appeared before the magistrates and that he was remanded in custody in prison to await the next sitting of the *assize* court in Cardiff early next month. Once he was safely behind bars, there would be ample opportunity for us to conduct a more thorough interrogation without his lawyer always being present.

*

Whilst they were busy at work, Dr Julius Matthias had also been active exerting pressure on Heidi Weisse under the pretext of a concerned employer calling to check up on her welfare. This guise was soon dropped once they were alone and he was able to reveal the true purpose of his call. Heidi was pleased to see him at first as the relationship with both Matthias doctors had always been warm and friendly and she was glad to see a friendly face. Julius expressed deep concern at what had happened to her and began probing to establish whether she was sure that it was Joachim Schultz who had attacked her that night. She was a little taken aback and couldn't understand why Dr Julius was questioning her in this way and then she started to get angry and shouted back at him that she had no trouble recognising her estranged husband even though it was nearly six years since she had last seen him. They had met by arrangement at the Cross Keys Hotel and had talked for nearly two hours and he had behaved amicably and treated her respectfully and indicated that he was looking for a reconciliation. She explained how she had made it abundantly clear that her priority was to understand where he had been for the past six years and why there had been no communication between them during this time. She was not interested in getting back together until she understood the reason for his sudden disappearance from Cardiff more fully. Julius thought for a few seconds and then changed tack and proceeded to ask whether, accepting that it was Joachim who had attacked her, she was aware of the implications of prosecuting this case against him and the threat that it posed to their operations here in Wales. "Everything we have worked for is at risk if we allow Joachim to go before the British courts as he is vital to our communication with the U-boats with his radio operator training, and if he inadvertently gives away some information about our group, we could all be vulnerable to arrest and capture. The British are quite gentlemanly about some things, but their good nature does not extend to enemy spies whom they almost always sentence to death by hanging," which he suggested was not a very pleasant end. "Even if Joachim is brought to trial for the attack against you, it is not certain that a jury of men would find a husband guilty of rape for having sexual intercourse with his wife even if it was a little rougher than usual. There are strong legal precedents from similar cases here in Wales, where the defence of conjugal rights has secured an acquittal. However, we cannot be sure that this defence will guarantee an acquittal in every case even with these precedents, as the physical injuries inflicted on you were serious and the attack took place in public, and so for the safety of us all, Oberst Kruger orders you to withdraw your allegations against Schultz and change the statement you made to the police identifying him as your attacker to persons unknown. You can say that Joachim accompanied you to the entrance of the park but left you at that point when you were a little worried about missing the tram at a short cut through Cathays Park where the attack took place. This will ensure that the case is dropped, and Schultz will be released from custody immediately and the colonel assures you that he will face German military justice for what he has done, so you can be sure that he will face severe punishment."

Heidi was confused and angry that her commanding officer was ordering her to withdraw her allegations and to say that an unknown person had attacked her in the park just a few minutes after she had left Joachim at the gates. She was devastated and with tears running down her cheeks she complained loudly that she had been brutally raped by Schultz and he needed to pay for what he had done to her. Matthias comforted her and put his arm around her shoulder and told her soothingly that she was right, but in wartime, they could not afford for this to happen for the security of the whole spy network. "But Schultz will face punishment for what he has done, and you will be rewarded for your loyalty." Matthias was convinced that Heidi would do as she was told and felt confident that he could report back to Kruger that she would obey his orders. Heidi was less than happy with what she was being ordered to do and was far less certain that she should forgo justice for the benefit of the others. All she could think of was that Schultz was getting away with the horrendous crime and there was no one who would make him pay, and this strong sense of hurt within her made her reluctant to comply, although she knew that if she didn't comply, she would face court martial for disobeying orders. She knew that she wasn't strong enough to go directly against the orders of her colonel but decided she would make them wait for twenty-four hours before she took the action they demanded.

*

I recounted the story of Crawford and King at the convalescent hospital and how they had become quite popular amongst staff and patients because of their enthusiasm for their chosen farming venture and how they had impressed everyone with the effectiveness of their recovery from their wounds once they settled on something worthwhile that they could do after their discharge from the army. They were held in a genuine respect and affection which still persisted today amongst those who knew them, but the most interesting question nagging in my head was why they had not had any communication with their many friends at the hospital since their discharge. They had not sent any messages to say how they were getting on or with their new address; it was as if they had disappeared completely. Added to that was the lack of friends or family who they were in close contact with or who they would return to after leaving the army. "The last sighting of this pair was on the day they were discharged from Llantwit Major together with the intention of spending a week's holiday in Tenby before intensifying their search for a farm property to lease in West Wales. There had been no sightings of either of them until Constable Evans met them in the company of Joachim Schultz at Llangellis Farm a week or so ago. There had been a ten-week gap between leaving the convalescence hospital and turning up at the farm, where there were no sightings of either of them that we are aware of. We do not know which hotel they had booked into in Tenby, but I am sure that a scrutiny of the registers of hotels in the resort will confirm their presence there. I know that both men were financially secure so would assume that they would stay at a more expensive hotel rather than a boarding house, plus we have a good line of enquiry if we contact the land agents in West Wales to see if Crawford and King had viewed any potential farm properties during this period. I will ask Constable Evans if he could enquire as to which company acted as agents for the lease of Llangellis Farm as this might be the best place to start our search." Alicia finished off our debriefing session with an account of her lack of progress in looking into Schultz's background but kindly thanked Ivor for discovering far more from his visit to the Swiss Embassy, which gave us fruitful ground to dig deeper the following day. We were elated at the real progress we had made over the last forty-eight hours and decided to celebrate by calling into the Royal Welsh Tavern just behind the police station for a drink before heading for home.

The pub was busy and the atmosphere hazy with smoke, which we hoped wouldn't set off Ivor's coughing too much, but we needn't have worried because judging by the friendly greetings and nods from other drinkers around the bar, I realised that he was well known in this establishment. We found a place to sit in an alcove and Ivor went to the bar to get the drinks and on looking round to see who our fellow drinkers were, I was surprised to see that there was a sprinkling of off-duty policemen wearing civilian jackets over their uniform tunics, which explained why Ivor had found his way here. I enjoyed an off-duty beer but had not been anywhere in Cardiff and restricted my drinking to an occasional pint when I was back home. Ivor bought two pints, and a gin for Alicia, and we started to relax and wind down from the case for a few short minutes. Ivor was good company and chatted enthusiastically but kept being drawn away into other conversations amongst other regular drinkers of the Royal Welsh so that Alicia and I were left alone, unable to join in the bonhomie enjoyed by Ivor and a little self-conscious about sitting so close together on the small bench seat. I could feel the warmth of Alicia through her skirt radiating into my trouser leg, and the more I enjoyed this sensation, the harder I found it to speak. I knew that faint heart never won fair lady, but I was overcome by a fear of rejection, nevertheless, so I stayed silent and gulped down my pint quickly and went to the bar to get refills. When I placed the drinks down on the table and sat down again, squeezing as far into the corner as possible, I could feel that I was still pressed against her leg. We tried to make light conversation but neither of us had that free communicative spirit that Ivor exuded, and I just felt gauche and stupid. After about ten minutes or so, I felt Alicia's hand grab mine gently and she squeezed it intently and leant towards me to speak into my ear. She said she was going to go after this drink and would be pleased if I would walk her back home. My heart jumped and I was elated, but I didn't want to appear too eager, so I just smiled and nodded my head and the next ten minutes or so were purgatory as I tried not to rush my drink so I could be alone with Alicia as I walked her home. I was not sure whether Alicia held any feelings for me or whether she considered me simply as a trusted colleague, but I had entertained amorous thoughts about her ever since we had started working closer together. It wasn't just that she was an attractive woman, but I respected her for the skills she brought to our team and her patience and calmness in difficult situations, and I had already seen these traits in action in this investigation.

Eventually, we both finished our drinks and got up and bade our farewells to Ivor, who was in a heated discussion with a group of drinkers in the other corner of the bar. He waved us goodbye and was back into his conversation before we had reached the door to the street. I felt as if I was ten feet tall when Alicia put her arm through mine, and we walked together through the dark streets towards her lodgings about a mile away. The gaze of others being no longer evident, I began to settle. My heart stopped thumping in my chest, and I began to gain confidence and chatter with Alicia more naturally and much less like a policeman interviewing a suspect. She leant in closer to me as we walked along, and I think we felt much more comfortable with each other than in the pub. The walk to the house where Alicia had a small apartment came to end remarkably quickly even though we had walked slowly without any great urgency in our steps. She lived on the first floor of a large double-fronted Victorian house in a one-bedroom flat rented by Cardiff Police for the accommodation of female officers. Males were banned from entering the property between the hours of eight in the evening to eight in the morning. Alicia explained that the propriety of the house was assiduously maintained by a wrinkled old dragon called Mrs Probert, a stalwart of the chapel and one of the first female officers in the Cardiff Police, who had retired after thirty years of service in 1910, when she had taken this job. She lived in the ground-floor flat and kept a detailed log of all the comings and goings of all the female officers who lived in the house. "And I'm sure she reports our movements to the female superintendent at headquarters." This news sent shivers up my spine, and I resolved never to cross the path of Mrs Probert if I could help it, and I could feel my short-lived confidence draining away when Alicia stopped about thirty yards shy of the front of the house and pulled me into the shadow of a large tree, which hid us from view, and planted her lips against mine. I was shocked by this unexpected turn of events, but I relaxed as my male hormones began to take over and I kissed her back as passionately as I knew how. The wonderful sensation of the first kiss made my knees weaken, but I succumbed to the moment and although there was a slight taste of gin on her mouth, she tasted sweet and wondrously pleasant. I was in heaven, and when our lips parted, Alicia confessed that she had been longing to do that for a long time, and I just looked sheepish because I had not been more forthright before. She said we must be careful because police regulations do not allow sexual relationships between officers working in the same team and if we became serious about our intentions in this respect, one of us would have to transfer to another team. For me, this would be a tragedy because Alicia and I worked so well together that I did not want to be separated from her, professionally or romantically. Then Alicia kissed me once more, this time on the cheek, and slipped away quickly towards her house, leaving me standing by the tree in a dream. I felt like going back to the Royal Welshman and celebrating with some more drinks with Ivor but knew that I couldn't breathe a word about what had transpired between Alicia and me that evening for fear of breaking police regulations. I had walked out with a few girls when I was in the pit but because of the strong chapel morality of the pit villages, I had never developed a full sexual relationship with any of them apart from some fumbling, touching and kissing for fear of being found out. I wondered if this was going to be the same but this time the chapel was replaced by police discipline that would keep us apart. By the time I reached my room in the section house, I was feeling quite morose because although there was a chance of an enticing new beginning with Alicia, we were destined only to meet in secret outside of work.

Alicia and I drove up to Tenby two days later to visit the expensive hotels and to check their registers for Crawford and King and on the way called into the police station at Port Eynon to ask Evans to find out the name of the agent who leased Llangellis Farm to Crawford and King. Evans was willing to do this and said he would make enquiries with the three land agents who were in business on the Gower, but he was not confident that it would be a local firm as many farms were marketed by firms in Swansea or Cardiff, but he would see what he could find out and he would telephone if he discovered anything of interest. Alicia and I enjoyed being together and talked about ourselves as we drove to Tenby, enjoying that feeling of discovering new things about each other that may help to lay a foundation for our relationship, but when we reached our destination, we switched back to professional mode to tackle the job to be done. Most of the decent hotels were in the same area to the west of the town centre towards an area called Westcliff, and this meant that we could park the car and walk easily to each hotel to make our enquiries. There were nine hotels in total on our list; eight were grouped together and one was overlooking the harbour to the east of the beach, so we took four each and would drive to the Harbour Hotel if necessary. Alicia took the Grand, Seaview, Tenby Heights and Queens Hotels, whilst my list included the Hutchins, Royal Tenby, Pembroke Manor and Golden Dragon Hotels. We decided we would meet back at the car as soon as we had visited all four on our lists and we set off. I drew a blank in all four of the hotels where I inspected the registers and found no entries for Henry Crawford or Oliver King, and I was disappointed for I was sure this was a good line of enquiry, but I hoped that Alicia had had more luck than me. I walked despondently back towards the car to see Alicia hurrying towards me waving the paper in her hand at me, and my heart lifted as I was sure she must have found something. The Tenby Heights Hotel had a reservation in the names of Crawford and King for the specific dates concerned, but they had not showed, so their rooms were let go. The manager was annoyed because he had received no message cancelling their booking in advance and had therefore been unable to let their rooms for the whole of the week they had reserved. We sat in the car and talked this over and it only served to deepen the mystery as to why two men, seemingly in excellent spirits, leaving the Llantwit Major hospital in the morning and telling everyone they were holidaying for a week in Tenby, fail to turn up at the hotel where they had booked their rooms. Why had they changed their minds at the last minute? Or perhaps their minds had been changed for them? We decided to complete the check of all the hotels on the list just to be doubly sure that they hadn't just chosen to switch to a different hotel for their holiday, but this proved a blank also.

Our last call at the Harbour Hotel was fruitless, but they were still serving lunch, so I decided to treat Alicia before our return journey to Cardiff. The dining room was pleasant, overlooking the busy harbour and the beach, and had the set three-course menu for that day, which looked appetising. Alicia and I were able to slip off our identities as detectives for a while and relax as an ordinary couple and enjoy each other's company and a meal together. The menu was golden vegetable soup followed by Welsh lamb with vegetables and roasted potatoes, and apple tart for dessert. As we enjoyed the food, we found that we were relaxing into each other's company well and talking freely about our pasts and our aspirations for the future. We seemed lucky to have a great deal in common and particularly shared a strong commitment to working as detectives, although Alicia regretted that there were fewer opportunities for female officers to advance in the CID. She hoped that the security branch might offer greater opportunities for her to advance in her career. We stretched out the meal and our conversation until we were the last in the dining room and I could feel that the waiters were willing us to stop chatting and leave them to clear up and lay up for dinner.

We climbed into the car and set off on our long journey back to Cardiff, which would probably take three hours if we were not held up by farm traffic in rural Pembrokeshire. We were lucky that the roads were largely clear, and we made it back to the station by six-thirty that evening, but we were both tired after a twelve-hour day and decided to meet up with Ivor in the morning. I walked Alicia back to her apartment then went straight back to the section house to sleep. I had enjoyed my day alone with Alicia and although we had kept our focus on the case, we had had the chance to step out for a couple of hours and enjoy lunch together in Tenby. We had established that Crawford and King had intended to spend a week in Tenby and had reserved two single rooms for the week but had failed to turn up. The big question was where did they go and why, after telling their nurses and fellow patients that they were off on holiday in Tenby, had they changed their minds? They had secured the rooms with a deposit paid by cheque, which was now forfeit because of their no-show without a cancellation. The mystery was where did they go and where had they been between the day that they left the convalescent hospital and were next seen at Llangellis Farm some two months later? Maybe the results of the letters we had sent out to the land agents in the region might throw some light on their search for a farm property to rent and give us some hints as to their whereabouts during this period. I also hoped that Evans would be able to make some progress with his enquiries about the leasing of Llangellis Farm, and there was a nagging question in my head which I was unable to answer which was why there appeared to be a connection between them and Joachim Schultz, who we now suspected to be living under a false identity as an employee of Sir Wilhelm Branden, who we suspected of connections to a German spy ring. Although I was tired, I was unable to sleep for some time as I wrestled with these ideas, which kept me wide awake for several hours. Eventually, I dropped off, more through mental exhaustion than having come up with any satisfactory explanations.

When I got to the station in the morning, Ivor told me that Alicia had just gone out in a great rush to visit Heidi Weisse, who had sent a note to the front desk of the police station during the night that she wished to speak to her urgently. There was no detail in the note about what she wished to talk about and why it was so urgent, but we were both thinking that Schultz's lawyer had got to her and persuaded her to drop the charges against her estranged husband. We both sincerely hoped that this was not the case but suspected that this would be the most likely outcome and the reason why Alicia had wasted no time in getting over to East Street to speak with Heidi. I was quite resigned to this outcome as I knew that the evidence was building up to be able to prove that Joachim Schultz was not who he said he was and was an imposter living under the false identity of a Swiss national in this country for many years. We had proof that he had been in Germany several times before and during hostilities with Germany, which if he was not a neutral meant he was a German spy. I knew that we could arrest him at any time on charges of espionage when we had resolved the issue of his nationality if we got the chance, because I knew that Schultz's arrest would have spooked the spy network greatly, for after over ten years of operating discreetly in South Wales without any threat of discovery, members of their network had been subject to police interest twice in as many months. Kruger and Sir Wilhelm Branden were astute enough to know that they must be rigorous in detracting police attention away from investigating their affairs in any greater detail. We were still certain that they only had a limited understanding of what we knew about them and were unaware that there was a special police security branch unit set up specifically to monitor their actions in greater detail. George Bennett had played a clever game in keeping what we were up to as low key as possible, and even officers in our own station had little knowledge or understanding of the cases we were working on, and we were very tight-lipped about what we were doing and had developed a false rumour that we were looking closely at corruption and theft from the docks because significant amounts of war supplies were being bought and sold on the black market. This story provided us with cover for our frequent comings and goings into the docks and the frequent requests for court warrants to look at financial records of suspected offenders. Ivor and I were also sure that if Schultz was released from custody, there would be a strong likelihood that he would disappear quite quickly as he had a proven track record for doing this. Ivor was sure that we ought to inform all ports to be vigilant and keep watch for his Swiss passport and arrest him before he boarded a ship to take him out of our reach. I said that was a great idea but if Schultz was a German spy, he could be lifted from an isolated beach by a U-boat's dinghy, and we would be none the wiser.

We were now quite despondent even though we had not heard from Alicia what the urgent meeting was about, so we tried to be patient and wait for her return to confirm our worst fears or cheer us up with some positive news. I concerned myself with writing up my reports on the enquiries in Tenby for adding to the case file, but time passed slowly and still Alicia had not returned, and Ivor and I were on edge waiting to hear from her. It was nearly eleven o'clock when the telephone rang and I leapt across the desk to answer it, expecting to hear Alicia's voice but was surprised that the cheery voice I heard was that of Constable Evans. I could hear the excitement in his voice as he had news that he was obviously eager to impart, so I asked him to slow down and speak a little slower so I could write down what he was trying to tell me. He said he had had a lucky breakthrough yesterday afternoon when he was in conversation with the chief clerk, Bryan Williams, of the branch of the South Wales Bank in Oystermouth Bay on another matter and had casually dropped into the conversation a remark about whether the new tenants of Llangellis Farm had opened accounts at his branch, which was the only bank on the peninsular until you got to the outskirts of Swansea. Most farmers on the Gower used this bank branch, which had long experience of agricultural finance and was trusted in the area. He said he knew that the two gentlemen who were living at the farm were not the leaseholders as they had handled the financial transaction and contract directly between the estate of the previous owner and the company that had taken out the lease on the farm about three months ago. Evans said he asked whether this was usual practice and Williams had intimated that it was unusual but not unheard-of and was not against the law. Evans said he would like to introduce himself to the leaseholders and would write to them offering his support and assistance if they needed it, being new to the area, if he could give him the company address. Williams replied that he couldn't give out the personal details of a client without a court order or warrant. "But I can tell you the company name, which is Wurtenberg Holdings, and you can look them up for yourself in the companies register in Cardiff." The only other unusual factor was that the two lessees were women, and he could remember that one had the same name as he did and the other had an unusual Christian name, which he was sure was Sabine, but he couldn't remember their full names without looking up the records. I thanked Evans for his prompt call and the information he had given me, which linked in well with other information from other sources, and I remarked that he had built such good relationships with the local people when he could rely on their help in an enquiry without recourse to court warrants, etc. I recounted the contents of the call to Ivor, and we realised that this was a startling discovery, and Ivor flipped open the Wurtenberg Holdings details from the companies register that we had accessed some eight weeks before and we could clearly see that the lessees could only have been Hilda Williams and Sabine Matthews or Matthias.

So now we had an intriguing circle of connections that linked Llangellis Farm clearly to the group we suspected to be members of a German spy network operating in South Wales. The circle appeared to have been completed by the installation of Crawford and King as occupants of Llangellis Farm, but try as we might, Ivor and I could not reconcile ourselves to the notion that two wounded British officers would be mixed up with German sympathisers. Neither Crawford nor King, to our knowledge, had ever expressed any pro-German feelings or criticised our prosecution of the war and had both served bravely in the front lines for over a year before they were wounded in action, and it seemed unlikely from what we knew from their background that they had German origins or relationships that might get them involved in such treasonous activity. Crawford's and King's names were not entered into the contract and if Evan's informant was right, the contract was signed a month before they were discharged from hospital ostensibly to search for a suitable property to lease. If they had already secured a farm to work on, why had they hidden this information from the staff and their friends and implied that they still had to find a suitable property? It just didn't add up and we were confused, especially when we considered how Wurtenberg Holdings got to know about Crawford and King and their desire to work a farm anyway. I did not believe that there was any intention to work the farm as a going concern but to operate it on the surface to appear as a working farm, but I was sure the real value of the farm was its isolated location and closeness to several secluded beaches, where contact could be made with U-boats and small boats could be rowed ashore. How could they operate it as a safe house with Crawford and King in residence unless they were part of the spy network too?

I knew that it was necessary to revisit Llantwit Major Convalescent Hospital and examine staff and visitor records to establish whether there was any possible way that the spy ring could have discovered the story of these two wounded soldiers taking up farming after leaving hospital. I reckoned that all three of us would need to do this, considering the large number of records we expected to be checked, and decided that this was a task we could put off until tomorrow when we could devote all day to it.

It was twelve-thirty before Alicia finally returned to the office. We could tell by the expression on her face that the news was not good and could hardly wait to hear the bad news confirmed. Heidi had withdrawn her allegations of rape and battery against Joachim Schultz. "When I questioned her closely about why she had changed her story, it became obvious that external pressure had been put on her by persons unknown, for she would not tell me who had persuaded her to change her mind. She has given me an alternative statement which now states that Schultz left her at the gates of Cathays Park, and it was her idea to take the short cut through the park, against Schultz's advice, because she was in danger of missing the last tram to East Street. She said he reluctantly agreed, and she ran into the park and took the left-hand perimeter path to bring her to the side gate by the tram stop when she was attacked by an unknown man, who was wearing a balaclava to disguise his face and who raped and assaulted her and left her unconscious in the park. She was certain that this man was not Schultz because his clothing was of a different style and colour and he spoke with a Welsh accent. This story was clearly contrived as she was careful not to give any significant information which might identify her mysterious attacker and had not retracted any of the detail of what happened to her but had simply removed Schultz from any part in it." Alicia had already discussed this with Inspector Bennett, who advised that Schultz should be freed from custody that afternoon but re-arrested as soon as we had more definite evidence concerning his nationality and passport. All three of us felt deflated but when we filled Alicia in with the details of what we had learnt that morning, we picked up our spirits a little as we had new lines of enquiry to pursue the next day, which might provide some of the answers we were seeking.

NINE

Anton Kruger was informed that his client would be released from police custody at two o'clock that afternoon and we switched our enquiries to the staffing and visitor records at Llantwit Major Convalescent Hospital. We knew we had our work cut out because the visitor records for the period in which Crawford and King were patients filled three large ledgers and the staffing records a whole filing cabinet. Ivor and I chose the visitors and Alicia selected the staff records, and I was glad she had chosen those files because I suspected that this was where we would find the connection we were looking for as I felt it was less likely that wounded British soldiers would have German sympathisers as friends or relatives. Alicia was far more exacting than Ivor or me, and I was sure she would identify potential links if they were there to be found. It was quite painstaking work and three hours went by without anything of any interest but in the afternoon, I came across an address that caught my attention because it was in Penlyn in Cardiff, and I was certain I had seen this address before. However, the name associated with this address in the register was not familiar at all and I was tempted to pass on, but something made me note it down to look at again later. The name was Nancy Prothero and she had signed into the visitors' book that she was visiting Alwyn Prothero, and this immediately struck me as strange as this was a male hospital for wounded officers and there were no female patients. I mentioned this to Sister Cummings, who suggested that she was probably visiting someone on the staff and filled in the wrong book on arrival. I asked her if she knew of anyone on the staff called Prothero. She was sure that she didn't but there were fourteen wards, and she didn't know everyone working at the hospital. I flagged up the name to Alicia, who said she would check in the staff records and let us know as soon as she found anything. Alicia asked to see the entry for Nancy Prothero, and she too had a faint recollection that this address was significant but couldn't remember clearly why but was sure that a review of the early files would turn up this address quite easily. She had a feeling that it was connected to Hilda Williams but could not swear to it. Ivor and I continued searching the visitor records and found that Nancy had visited Alwyn three times in the space of six weeks, which suggested that they must be good friends and quite close.

Alicia turned up the record for Alwyn Prothero later that afternoon and it transpired that she was a nursing orderly who worked on one of the wards treating soldiers with shellshock and other mental conditions resulting from their wartime experiences. She was only twenty years of age and had joined the hospital in 1914 with a view to training to become a nurse in time. Her work record was good, and she was highly thought of by her nursing sister in charge of the ward where she worked. Alwyn lived in the staff quarters so Alicia decided that she would interview her directly and she was sent for immediately by the matron's office. Alwyn was a slight, rather nervous girl who was clearly frightened that she had done something wrong but couldn't think what she had done so had taken on a slight air of belligerence in her demeanour. Alicia was calm and friendly in her approach and explained that she was investigating the disappearance of two former patients of the hospital, Lieutenants Crawford and King. She asked if Alwyn knew them, and she admitted that she knew of their reputation because their story was widely talked about in the wards by the staff and patients, but she had never met them. Alicia gently brought the conversation around to Nancy Prothero, who had visited her three times in six weeks during the time that these two officers were in the hospital but had not visited her again since they were discharged. Alwyn said that Nancy was her sister-in-law and was married to her brother and lived in Cardiff. She was surprised that Nancy had come to see her so frequently because she had not been before, and although they were in-laws, she had only seen her once or twice since the marriage to her brother eighteen months before. Alicia prodded gently about why Nancy had come to see her and what she talked about. Alwyn said, 'It was rather inconvenient with her just turning up during working hours and distracting me from my work on the ward, and she wasn't interested in me and only wanted to talk about Lieutenants Crawford and King anyway. It was like she was on a mission and she pumped me for all the details I had heard about these two officers and what they were going to do. I told her that I didn't know them and could only tell her what I had heard from the common gossip around the hospital, but she seemed satisfied with that." Alicia asked how Nancy knew about these two remarkable officers in the first place and she had the feeling that Nancy had heard about the two lieutenants from her mother, to whom she had told their story in one of her letters. Nancy had said that she was so inspired by their story that she wanted to know more so that more people could know about how two wounded veterans were making a new life for themselves. Alicia pressed her on whether she had any idea why Nancy intended to use this information to inform people in this way, and she seemed a little confused as to how she could do this because she had no journalistic training and worked as a chambermaid at one the big houses, which she thought was called Craddock Park. Alicia thanked her for her help and said that she didn't think they would need to talk to her again.

Alicia came through to Ivor and me and said we might as well stop trawling through the visitor ledgers as she was certain that she had established a link between the German spy ring and the convalescent hospital. She was absolutely convinced that Alwyn Prothero was a totally innocent party who had been used by the espionage ring without her knowledge to provide information about Crawford and King, unaware of who was asking and why they wanted the information in the first place. She had established probable links between Nancy and the spy ring, although she wasn't sure whether Nancy was a member of the ring or just being used as the conduit for information by them. Nancy worked at Craddock Park, which we already knew was the home of Sir Wilhelm Branden, and she wrote an address as one which bore a striking similarity to the address where Hilda and Mordred Williams were residents and Alicia was sure that five minutes back in their office, she would be able to confirm whether this was the case when she looked at their files. It seemed to fit together but was also confusing as to the reason why the Germans were interested in these two wounded veterans.

It didn't take Alicia more than a few minutes searching the files on Hilda Williams to confirm that the address was hers, and she decided to find the notes on the 1911 Census records that they had viewed in the early days of the investigation, but it took a little longer to discover that Nancy Prothero was néc Williams and was the middle daughter of the four children registered to the family at that address. It was not surprising that the daughter of Hilda Williams had found employment with the man she worked for at the Dock Company. Ivor confirmed that Schultz had been released at two that afternoon and had been collected by two men in a small van, who had signed the register as Crawford and King and given their address as Llangellis Farm. This was mysterious because this was the second time that these two were known by us to have associated with Schultz, who was supposedly only a representative of their farm machinery supplier. The fact that they had collected him from police custody suggested a closer relationship than a purely businesslike one with the farm supplies salesman. Again, the nagging questions persisted as to how these two had become embroiled with enemy agents so quickly after their invaliding out of the army, or were they imposters masquerading as these wounded officers as a cover for their real purpose? If this was the case, the big question was what had happened to the real Crawford and King?

I postulated a notion that I could not yet prove but strongly suggested could be true to my two colleagues, completely prepared to be shot down in flames, but was surprised when they largely agreed with my assertions. I believed that the spy ring had been looking for a safe house in a remote location close enough to isolated beaches for them to meet boats coming ashore from submarines without attracting too much attention from the local population. They had identified Llangellis Farm as a highly suitable location for their activities but were wary of just dropping two able-bodied male strangers in to apparently work the farm without attracting the attention of local people as to why young and apparently fit men were not serving King and country as members of the armed forces. They had already used the services of Dr Julius Matthias to falsify medical certificates to provide exemption from call-up on medical grounds for the Grubers and were probably quite wary of using this method again, and since the police had become interested in the medical records of Friedrich Gruber a couple of months before, they had become much more cautious as regards attracting any further attention to their activities. The general populace had become increasingly concerned about conscientious objectors and others who might be trying to dodge the call-up and were now openly questioning young men of military age who were not in uniform as to why that was. There was an acceptance that some people were in vital civilian occupations that needed to be done to support the war effort and that some people were medically unfit, but there was strong feeling that significant numbers were just cowards trying to dodge conscription. There was less reason for able-bodied men to be retained in the civilian workforce when more women and older men were able to take on many of the vital jobs, and the longer the casualty lists grew and the larger the number of families touched by tragedy, the greater the resentment felt. They were looking for a convenient cover to put German agents into Llangellis without attracting too much attention in the local area when by chance they heard through gossip within Hilda Williams' family of the remarkable story of the two badly wounded officers who were no longer fit for military service but who were determined to become farmers and continue to support the war effort despite their injuries. Hilda Williams was ordered, probably by her boss, to discover more about these two men, and she instructed her daughter to contact her sister-in-law who worked at the convalescent hospital and find out as much as she could about Crawford and King. This information was passed on by Hilda to her fellow conspirators at Wurtenberg Holdings, where I think a decision was made to kidnap the two of them and substitute two German agents in their place at Llangellis Farm. No one would question the bona fides of two young and reasonably fit men who, despite their injuries, were attempting to cope with farm work. The fact that Crawford and King disappeared so rapidly and with complete secrecy immediately on their discharge from the hospital and failed to turn up or even contact the hotel they had booked for their holiday added to the potency of this theory and when added to the fact that there had been no sightings of or contact with either of them since that day, further confirmed the idea that something drastic had happened to them.

Ivor suggested that they might be prisoners at the farm, and we could mount a raid on the farm to rescue them, and although this sounded an attractive proposition, it would be difficult to do with our limited resources and the lack of evidence in our possession to secure convictions. It would also blow cheaply the only real advantage that we had over the spy ring, which was that they were almost completely unaware of our investigation and how much we knew about their activities, and we should aim to keep it that way until we had sufficient evidence to arrest and charge all the known suspects in one coordinated swoop. I did not agree with Ivor that Crawford and King were prisoners of the Germans at the farm, for I was certain that they would have been murdered and their bodies disposed of for the security of the whole spy ring. They would have to expend resources in guarding and keeping them at the farm and if they escaped or were rescued by us, they would provide invaluable testimony against their captors and reveal our hand that we were on to them. In that case, I was certain that the suspected leaders of the spy ring, Sir Wilhelm and Anton Kruger and the Matthiases might slip through our fingers, and we would be left with only the bit-part players to mop up and arrest, leaving their leaders free to escape and set up elsewhere. I kept this to myself at this moment in time and suggested that we could task Constable Evans from Port Eynon to drop in at the farm in the next day or so to check that Schultz was still at the address registered with the custody sergeant on his release form. I knew that Evans was a clever and resourceful policeman and was blessed with extraordinary powers of observation, so I was sure that he wouldn't miss much if he got the chance to look around the farm and speak to Crawford and King. This was agreed as a useful strategy and I telephoned Evans to brief him on what we wanted to know, and he was most willing and eager to carry out his mission and would make a point of dropping into the farm when on his rounds the next day.

Ivor produced the report that he had received from the forensic department, who had scrutinised the medical record finally provided by Helmut Gruber for Freidrich Gruber as grounds for his medical exemption from military service. The conclusions drawn by the analyst were interesting, suggesting that they were satisfied that the document was a forgery and represented nothing more than a mock-up of an actual patient's medical record. The record purported to have covered a period of twenty-two years and contained entries completed by seven different doctors, who had apparently attended Friedrich during various epileptic episodes, but chemical analysis showed that each entry had been written in the same ink as was used for the last entry. Analysis of the paper showed that the age of the paper was relatively new and was probably made during the past two years when the quality of the consistency of writing paper had declined because of the war. Lastly, the handwriting expert was certain that the nib used for each entry was the same and little attempt had been made to disguise the handwriting. His conclusion was that each entry had been written by the same person and not by the different doctors to whom they were accredited. There were further comments regarding the lack of medical data and observations regarding the severity and frequency of the epileptic fits, nor was there any detail of the medicines or other treatments prescribed and their effects on the problem, which would have been expected in the record of a patient with a chronic condition such as epilepsy. The director of the forensic laboratory added a note that he would be able to testify as an expert witness in court if needed, and we were elated that we finally had evidence that could lead to the conviction of the Grubers and the Matthiases for fraud and deception, although we still had bigger fish to fry.

Evans made a point of approaching Llangellis Farm from the west so that his approach would not be apparent from the farmyard and had decided to make this slightly covert approach after observing the farm for about thirty minutes to try to establish where the inhabitants were situated. The only movement he had detected was near to the front of the farmhouse and he had managed to recognise both Crawford and King and again he was impressed by the speed and agility exhibited by Crawford, who you would never suspect was wearing a false left leg, so freely did he move about the farm. He also observed that he was able to converse freely with King despite his deafness and found this confusing because he did not think lip-reading was very effective unless both parties were reasonably close to each other, and he was certain that they seemed to be carrying on easy conversation when they were many yards apart and without looking at each other. He had no sightings of Schultz at all, but he could have been inside and out of view from his viewpoint. Finally, he mounted his bicycle and rode up the lane and turned into the farmyard and rode up to the front door and rang the bell. It seemed quite a few minutes before he heard the sound of someone approaching the door and the key turning, and Crawford was standing in front of him. He looked a bit surprised when he saw the uniformed constable standing on the doorstep but managed to smile with his lips but not with his eyes as he enquired as to what he could do to help the constable. Evans said that headquarters had sent him to ask Mr Schultz a couple of routine questions now that he had been released from custody so that they could close the files on his involvement in the case. Crawford tried to look perplexed and stammered a little, asking what case he was referring to. Evans explained that Mr Schultz had been arrested on suspicion of the rape and battery of Heidi Weisse and had been held in custody for nearly seventy-two hours until the victim withdrew the charges. He smiled now and relaxed and said that Schultz was not there, and now that they knew what he had been accused of, he would not be welcome there again. Evans sensed something was wrong here and asked them to confirm when they last saw Schultz, and Crawford was sure that the only time he met Schultz was when he came here with his farm machinery catalogues, but Evans knew that both Crawford and King had collected Schultz from Tiger Bay Police Station just a couple of days earlier and had signed the register to confirm doing so. Evans decided to keep quiet about this and asked whether he could speak to Mr King, just to confirm whether he may have seen Schultz. Crawford said that he was sure that he hadn't but could see that the constable would not be moved until he had spoken with King, so he said that King was profoundly deaf but did read lips, so he may be able to get an answer to his question and he invited the constable into the porch whilst he went to fetch Mr King. He watched him walk away down the passageway and now he was rising and falling in the classic limp of a man walking with a false leg, which was a movement totally absent from his movement when he was not aware of being observed a few minutes earlier. King came to the front porch and asked Evans what he wanted to know, and Evans made a conscious effort to look him full in the face and speak slowly and clearly in asking his questions, and he gave the same answers in almost the same exact words as Crawford a few minutes before. He thanked him for his cooperation and asked if he was wearing a hearing aid and he said that he wasn't but was lip-reading. Evans congratulated him on his expertise and skill and said that their conversation was very similar to a conversation with a person with perfect hearing and thanking him again, left the porch and mounted his bicycle and cycled away back to the station to call me.

When Evans telephoned Cardiff, he had to wait for a few minutes for me to be brought to the phone and then he recounted what had transpired that morning at Llangellis Farm. He described how he had covertly approached the farm and observed what was going on before he approached the farmhouse and how he had watched Crawford and King talking freely with each other and calling to each other over distances too far apart for lip-reading to be effective, which suggested that the King residing at the farm was certainly not deaf, and this feeling was backed up by his short conversation with him where he appeared to understand every word instantly and replied immediately. He believed that King had perfect hearing and was probably an imposter. He had also observed Crawford walking about the farmyard without any trace of a limp but later, when he was stood in the porchway, "Crawford walked with a very pronounced, almost theatrical limp, which suggested to me that he has two able-bodied legs and makes it probable that he is also an imposter. Both men deny any knowledge of Schultz and deny collecting him from the police station when he was released from custody, and I am certain that they are both lying. I was not able to search the house, but I observed no trace of a third person at the property during my observation, so I don't think Schultz is there." I thanked him for his report, which had given us more to think through, and I would keep him in contact as we investigated this further. The question was where was Schultz now that he was no longer safely in our cells? I decided a trip to Craddock Park was required to check whether he had returned to his old employment as a chauffeur. I called on Sir Wilhelm and asked if Schultz had returned to his apartment above the stables and Sir Wilhelm bristled and said that the villain was not welcome there and they hadn't seen him since the night of his arrest. I asked if he minded if I had a look at his old room and he said I was free to check but would not find any trace of him there. I did check out the room and it was exactly as we had left it on the night of his arrest, and I was certain that he had not returned there to collect any of his things. I was beginning to think that perhaps he had been spirited away by dinghy to a waiting U-boat from the beach near the farm and we wouldn't see him again, but I was about to be proved wrong.

Two days later in the week, I received a telegram from Colonel Stewart informing me that Brecon Police had been called to investigate what appeared to be a shallow grave that had been recently disturbed by animals and appeared to contain the bodies of at least three or four men that might prove to be of interest to my investigation as one of the bodies was missing a lower left leg that had been surgically removed, suggesting a war wound of some sort. He had arranged for me to meet with Inspector Aston of Brecon Police to share the details of the case as he felt that this might prove an interesting new development for us to follow. I tried not to be too excited that there was a definite connection with our investigation, but I was certainly keen to investigate this matter further. The grave was in thick woodland on the hillside above the River Usk near the village of Talybont, which was a remote and wild area, not much frequented unless you were a forester or a farmer who made your living in these hills. Alicia and I would make the trip to Brecon first thing next morning and I telephoned Inspector Aston to tell him we were coming, and he agreed he would meet us on the forecourt of the Talybont Inn at ten-thirty to take us up to the gravesite. He said it was a gruesome place situated some 200 yards from the nearest path in a dark and desolate clearing in the trees, and the police surgeon from Brecon was working slowly to discover how many bodies were buried there in total as they estimated at least four or possibly more. It was difficult to be certain because animals had uncovered some of the remains and limbs were missing, but by the following morning, the doctor hoped to have removed all the body parts to the mortuary for post-mortem examination.

Alicia and I left early next morning. We had both packed a small overnight bag so that we could stay in Brecon to hear the results of the police surgeon's examination. I had tasked Ivor with booking two rooms at the Coach House Hotel in the square at Brecon, close to the police station. I was excited on two fronts this morning, because this was my first murder case and I had an opportunity to spend some time away from Cardiff alone with Alicia. I expected Inspector Aston to be a middle-aged detective nearing his retirement and was surprised when he turned out to be a young inspector in his early thirties with a professional manner and a warm and friendly disposition. He did not know what our interest in his case was, but he knew that Alicia and I were with the security service, and I guessed that he had been briefed by senior officers to give us as much assistance as he could. I confessed to him that I was not at all sure what our interest might be in his case, but when we had had a chance to look at the site of the grave and the bodies themselves to ascertain their identities, I may be able to tell him something more. I was able to tell him that we were searching for several persons of interest to the security service who had disappeared recently and despite our best efforts, we had been unable to track them down. The discovery of a multi grave in a remote location sparked an interest in us. I assured him that we would not interfere in his handling of the case nor get in his way, and if we were unable to gain any positive identifications for the suspects we were looking for, we would return to our base in Cardiff immediately and leave him in peace. He climbed into our car and directed me to drive through the village towards the river and to park adjacent to the footbridge over the river about half a mile beyond the village, where we could walk across to the woods where the bodies were discovered. There was a rough track leading up the side of the hill on the other bank of the river, but it was not passable by ordinary cars and was only suitable for tractors. We walked across the footbridge, enjoying the view of the geese and ducks on the water, glad we had brought heavy coats and boots to wear as it was still quite cool that morning. The climb was steady but not too strenuous and after twenty minutes' brisk walk, Aston cut off into the undergrowth and we left the path and entered the dark forest canopy. As we drew nearer, I could see the police surgeon's team had erected some tents and screens to protect the view of the grave from passers-by, although we hadn't seen a single soul on our walk up there. Aston introduced us to Dr Llewellyn-Lewis, the local police surgeon, who said he had so far discovered two male bodies that would be removed within an hour to the mortuary in Brecon, as soon as the tractor and trailer got there. "Ironically, these bodies have been here the longest and were placed deeper in the ground but are complete, having been protected from the ravages of foxes and wild dogs that have been visited on the bodies deposited here more recently. There are at least two bodies here but because they have been partially dismembered by animal attention, I am unable to confirm whether there might be a fifth body, although I suspect that one of these bodies may be a female. We will need to search the surrounding area over the next couple of hours and will remove the remaining bodies to the mortuary later this afternoon." He explained that he would return to the mortuary to begin the post-mortem examination of the first two victims that afternoon and if we wished to observe the examination, we were welcome to attend.

There was not much to see around the graveside, and we did not wish to get in the way of the forensic team, so Alicia and I searched around the vicinity to see if there were any obvious signs of how the bodies had made the journey to their gruesome resting place. It was difficult to make out any clear tracks within a ring of one hundred yards from the grave and we were about to give up when Alicia noticed a patch of undergrowth flattened by what looked like a heavy vehicle of some sort. We reckoned that the tread marks from the tyre tread indicated that this was a bigger vehicle than a car but was not big enough to be a tractor and thought that this was most likely a van or small lorry that was powerful enough to make it up the forester's track without attracting too much attention. I reasoned that it was most likely a general-purpose van or truck used on many farms in the area that would easily blend in with other farm traffic. I alerted Inspector Aston, and he got his men to cordon off the tyre marks to make a plaster cast of the tracks for further investigation. The flattened grass and the indentations in the ground tended to suggest to me that this parking place had been used on several occasions and probably in different kinds of weather, for the ground must have been soft and wet to leave the tell-tale signs that the vehicle had been there at all. I was also thinking that this might suggest that the bodies had been dumped at different times, which backed up the police surgeon's theory because of the different depths that the bodies were buried in the mass grave. Alicia began poking around the area to see if we could establish the path taken by the killer's vehicle when it left the forester's roadway and entered the trees. At first, all we could see before our eyes was a wall of foliage and trees on all sides but gradually as we looked for the signs of the movement of a vehicle through the undergrowth, the indications were there of which way the vehicle had entered and left the wood. There were tyre tracks visible at several places and broken branches and twigs, which showed that a larger vehicle had passed this way and with a couple of hours of meticulous searching, Alicia and I had established the pathway from the road to the graveside with some certainty. We were feeling quite pleased with ourselves with the progress we had made and were making careful drawings and notes to share with Inspector Aston on our return to Brecon when Alicia was distracted by signs of another hidden pathway leading away from the entry point from the forester's road in a different direction. My mind was working at full speed as I considered all the possible options before us and wondered whether we were about to discover another multi-occupancy grave in these woods. Was there a prolific killer loose in South Wales with potentially as many victims as the mysterious Jack the Ripper?

I could hardly consider this thought but the tracks in the woods certainly looked very similar to the ones leading to the graveside we had already discovered, and the tyre tracks also looked very similar to those on the other pathway. It was nearly 300 yards before we came to the same kind of area of flattened grass where the vehicle had come to a rest. This time, we walked in circles at twenty feet and then thirty feet out from where the vehicle had stopped and quickly found a series of scuff marks on the grass, which suggested that a heavy load had been dragged across the ground in a particular direction. Alicia was first to spot an area of disturbed earth, a little larger than the size of a standard grave, that seemed to have been hidden from view with broken branches, bracken and ferns so that the casual passer-by would not see the disturbed earth unless they were looking for it. Again, we made notes and drawings and hurried back to the graveside to report what we had found to Inspector Aston but, unfortunately, he had already returned to Brecon with the first two bodies. It was urgent that the second site was secured and protected from interference before detectives had an opportunity to investigate it properly, so I ordered two of the uniformed constables to accompany me to the second site and guard it until the inspector returned. I felt satisfied that they would keep the scene clear of any potential disturbance until Aston returned later that day with extra men and resources. The drive back to Brecon took about forty minutes and we were able to find the mortuary quite easily behind the police station and found the inspector already there observing the first post-mortem. Interrupting the proceedings, I reported that Alicia and I had found, with a little searching of the woods, what we thought was probably a second grave in a location about

500 yards east of the grave they had found. The doctor was also interested in our discovery and suspended the post-mortem temporarily to arrange for a second forensic team to accompany Inspector Aston back to the site we had located earlier that day. The inspector suggested that the post-mortem should continue without him, but he was sure that Alicia and I would observe it on his behalf.

Doctor Llewellyn-Lewis had already made a good start on the first autopsy and had examined the body in some detail. He talked as he worked, and his assistant made detailed notes of everything he said for later reference. "The first body was that of a male, approximately late twenties in age, who was well nourished and in good shape physically, with a physique that suggested an active outdoor life, and I would surmise that he might have seen military service. However, the body was missing the lower left leg and foot, which initially gave rise to the notion that it might have been taken by foraging animals, but further examination has shown that it was a result of an expert amputation performed by a skilled surgeon sometime in the last five to six months. My conclusion would be that this was the body of a soldier wounded in action as there was evidence of secondary wounds around the amputation site caused by shrapnel and blast burns that were well healed but nevertheless easily visible on the body." The doctor said that there were scratches and small blisters around the stump, suggesting that the victim probably had a false leg that he wore to walk which probably chaffed the skin around the base of the remaining leg. The cause of death was one shot to the base of the skull at the back of the head, which suggested more of an execution than a murder in haste. He had already retrieved part of the bullet from the victim's skull for more detailed examination by the firearms experts, which may help to identify the weapon that had been used. He went on to say that the recovery from the amputation had been good and he would suggest that we were looking at a soldier who was wounded in action and had lost his lower left leg no more than six months ago and had spent at least three to four months in hospital and rehabilitation since then. I interrupted and asked whether he could estimate how long he had been dead and he said it was not an exact science, but he would estimate by the decomposition of the body no more than eight weeks, but it could be four to six weeks. Although he was unsure about a shorter timescale, he was absolutely certain that it was no more than eight weeks ago and I was intrigued to know how he could be so sure of this date, and he replied with a smile on his face that the victim had a letter in his inside jacket pocket from a land agent in Llanelli, Perry Shaw Limited, dated eight and a half weeks ago, offering an appointment to view a farm premises near Laugharne later that week. "The victim received and read this letter before he died and placed it into his pocket, which is why I am certain he was still alive eight weeks ago." The doctor asked if any of this was useful to our investigation and I said that much of what he had surmised aligned well with a person we were aware of who was last seen approximately eight weeks ago.

"He could well be a former lieutenant in the Oxfordshire Regiment, wounded in Belgium, who had a lower left leg amputation and was fitted with a false leg at a convalescent hospital near Cardiff, who seemed to disappear on the day he was released from the military hospital without a trace. We know that when he was discharged from hospital, he was in the company of another wounded officer from the Welsh Fusiliers who was also invalided out of the army because he was made profoundly deaf by a huge explosion that destroyed his eardrums completely. They had become close friends in hospital and had decided to attempt to build a new life for themselves as farmers. They left the hospital together and had booked a week's holiday at a hotel in Tenby but failed to turn up and have not been seen since."

The doctor indicated that it was difficult to tell whether someone was deaf after their death, but he would examine the inner ear and look for damage to the eardrums which might confirm his deafness, but he said he could confirm that the second victim had been shot in the same fashion as the first victim with one shot to the back of the head. He said that he would remove the bullet if it was lodged in the brain and compare it with the first bullet to see if it was fired from the same weapon. He continued with the examination of the second victim, and we listened as he talked us through the process and he came to largely the same conclusions as he had with the first victim, that he was in his late twenties, in good physical shape, well nourished and probably a soldier, with no immediate indication of any physical injuries that might render him unfit for military service. We could not see well from our vantage point as he cut into the skin at the back of the ear and peeled it back to expose the inner ear to view it more clearly and said he could see that the eardrum had been completely shattered by a massive shock which would have caused total deafness in this ear. He then repeated the operation on the other ear and found almost the same situation and felt it safe to suggest that this victim had been totally deaf at the time of his death. Alicia and I were satisfied that we knew why Crawford and King had disappeared on the day they were discharged and not seen again. The doctor then used a saw to cut into the back of the skull and when he lifted off the top of the cranium, he could see that there was considerable damage to the cerebellum, which had undergone severe shock consistent with the blast from an explosion large enough to burst both of his eardrums. He called us to come closer to the table so he could show us the damage to his brain and then showed us a healthy brain from one of his samples in the laboratory, and we could easily see that the shape and size of the brain had been impacted by some trauma. I asked if the damage to his brain would have manifested itself in the victim's behaviour and he replied that he could not be certain without looking at the medical notes of his treatment at the hospital which originally treated him. However, after the initial shock, he would have probably recovered enough brain function for near-normal cognitive powers to return, but he could not be sure what the longer-term effects would have been on his overall mental and physical health.

We left the mortuary a little after five and drove out to the gravesite again and linked up with Aston and his team, who were removing the other remains from the grave and preparing to transport them to the mortuary. He said that there were definitely three more bodies, two men and a woman, and Alicia asked if she could see them. We walked over to where three canvas-wrapped shapes lay in a row waiting to be tagged and loaded into the waiting van for the journey to the mortuary, and the first thing I noticed was that one of the corpses was much larger than the other two and I hoped that this might make identification a simpler process. I lifted the canvas covering the face and almost immediately Alicia and I recognised the features of Schultz, who we had had in custody a few short days ago. Alicia immediately went to the corpse that had been indicated as being female and I held my breath as she lifted the canvas to reveal the face of Heidi Weisse, who had paid a terrible price for being the unfortunate wife of Joachim Schultz. We called Aston to one side and explained to him that we could positively identify these two bodies as being husband and wife, Joachim Schultz and Heidi Schultz, née Weisse. I gave him a brief account of why we were certain that this was the case and told him about the rape allegation that we had investigated a few days before and how the case was dropped after Mrs Schultz withdrew the allegations and her husband was released. Aston understood but was confused as to why security police were interested in this case and how this couple ended up dead in this mass grave a few days later. I told him that I was not authorised to tell him any more about the case we were working on but could see that it would make working together more difficult if we couldn't share a little more of the details with the senior officer investigating the murders. I promised that I would telephone our boss when we reached Brecon and see how much of the detail of our case he would allow me to reveal to him to assist the smooth running of the overall investigation. He was grateful and realised the difficult operational conditions we were working under and said that he would not be back in Brecon before seven-thirty or so by the time he had finished there. I suggested he join Alicia and me for supper at the Coach House Hotel when we could discuss things further in more pleasant surroundings. He was happy to agree and doubted that Doctor Llewellyn-Lewis would be unlikely to begin the examination of these three corpses until the next morning at the earliest. The team working at the other site were still setting up and would probably dig all night to get the grave open before daylight if they could.

The Coach House Hotel was a comfortable coaching inn which had served travellers passing from England to Wales along the A40 London Road for almost one hundred years. There were two public bars fronting the street that seemed well frequented by local townspeople and a private dining room and residents' lounge behind. The rooms were not grand but were clean and comfortable and were certainly superior to my small room in the section house in Cardiff. I was looking forward to spending some time alone with Alicia and was glad when I discovered that she was in a room across the corridor from mine. The hotel was equipped with a telephone located in an enclosed booth in the corner of the lobby, and I booked a call through to Colonel Stewart for seven o'clock and I was lucky that I just managed to catch him before he left for dinner, but he listened to what we had discovered in Brecon, and I asked what I could tell Inspector Aston to ensure his continued cooperation. He agreed that we should divulge a little more of the overview of the case that we were working on but keep the details confidential. "I will send Major Harcourt-Evans to Brecon tomorrow to take overall command of the investigation and to brief Inspector Aston a little more fully." Before he finished the call, he expressed his satisfaction at the way that we had made the connections and drawn conclusions quickly, which he hoped would move our operations against the German spy ring forward immeasurably.

After changing our clothes, we were seated in the residents' lounge bar waiting for Aston to join us for supper and he arrived shortly after eight, apologising for being late and not having had time to change his clothes before eating. We reassured him that he was perfectly presentable and ordered a large whisky and soda and settled him in the third chair at our table. I wasted no time in explaining to him that we were not allowed to give him a detailed briefing of the details of our investigation, but I had been authorised to tell him that for several months we had been working on a case tracking the operations of a suspected German spy ring, whom we believed to be embedded at the docks at Newport, Swansea and Cardiff and passing vital intelligence about shipping movements to the German Navy. "This seems to have resulted in an increase in U-boat attacks against allied shipping in Welsh coastal waters and we have been tasked with bringing this to an end. We have so far identified at least fifteen suspects working within the spy network and have been building as much evidence as we can so that we can close them down and arrest all the leaders of the spy ring rather than just the small players. To give away our hand too early might make the leaders go to ground or escape the country by U-boat, leaving the network lying dormant but intact, to be resurrected again after the heat is off.

"The two bodies taken to the morgue this morning match the descriptions of two wounded British officers, Lieutenants Crawford and King, who were discharged from the army from their convalescent hospital with the intention of running a farm together but have never been seen again since their day of departure. However, two mysterious characters using their names appeared at a remote farm in West Wales soon after, purporting to be them. However, when the local constable met them at this farm when making a routine visit, he became suspicious that things were not quite as they should be and began to suspect that they were imposters masquerading as the two wounded veterans. He was aware that these two were wounded officers whose injuries were severe enough to have invalided them out of the army as unfit for military service, yet neither of them displayed any signs of their disabilities on the occasions he met them. We can also tell you that the two bodies we identified this evening were well known to us both, having dealt with a serious allegation made by the woman against her estranged husband only a few days ago, and we can attest that they were both alive on Tuesday last when the male was released from police custody. We can positively identify them as Joachim and Heidi Schultz, who are also suspected to be members of the spy ring. It can hardly be a coincidence that these bodies, each linked in some way to the spy network, could turn up in this remote grave, and this leads us to think that we need look no further than the members of the spy network as the perpetrators of these murders. We also surmise that the mode of killing, which was more akin to an execution, with just a single bullet to the back of the head, was not that of your more usual murder. The discovery of the bodies we suspect to be Crawford and King solves the mystery of where they have been for the past two months and answers the question, which has been nagging at us since we discovered the existence of two imposters on the farm, of who they were and why they were there. We are now sure that the imposters are German operatives brought into this country to prosecute further offensive actions against our homeland security. They are both able-bodied and mid-twenties and would need to have a convincing cover story as to why they were not serving in the army, and hence the murders of the real Crawford and King provided them with a convenient and credible identity.

"We also believe that Schultz and his wife were killed by the same people because of the increased risk they posed to the overall security of the group. Our enquiries have suggested that Schultz was travelling on a false Swiss identity that he has used to enter Germany several times in the past four years. We have discovered that he has a previous criminal record in Wales and London for forgery, violence, sexual offences and burglary and that he fled from arrest in Cardiff in 1910, only to reappear in Wales a couple of weeks ago. He raped and severely assaulted his estranged wife shortly after he had returned to Wales on the pretext of effecting a reunion with her. She was found in a public park unconscious and partially clothed, with serious injuries, and was taken to hospital, where she gave a statement to Alicia that her attacker was her husband, Schultz. He was arrested and charged with the rape and assault, but we believe pressure was put upon Heidi to withdraw the allegations by her superiors in the spy ring and the charges were subsequently dropped. Alicia and I are firmly convinced that Heidi Weisse was determined to see her husband pay for the rape and violence he had wrought on her and would never recant on her allegations of her own accord. The attention of the police to the Schultz case was a major threat to the security of the spy network and we suspect that the leaders of the ring would have removed Schultz and Heidi as threats to their security by murdering them to promptly get them out of the way. It is imperative that we do not reveal any details of what has been discovered to the newspapers and try to avoid too much gossip about the case with those not directly involved so that the German spies do not discover that we have found this grave. They will feel some confidence that this grave is in a remote enough location such that discovery by chance is highly unlikely, and they will feel secure to carry on their operations free from police interference. It will be important to make local enquiries in the vicinity of the forest because it is obvious that the spy assassins have visited this site on at least three occasions, and some local people may recollect seeing an unfamiliar vehicle in the area several times and give descriptions of the occupants. It would take a fair amount of time to dig and bury the bodies, and to avoid detection, the work would probably have been done during the hours of darkness."

TEN

Aston was taken aback by the complexity of the case but was anxious to cooperate with us and bring the network to justice as soon as possible. He agreed that no statements were to be made to the press and every effort would be made to keep the site free from unauthorised visitors as far as possible, but he was certain that villagers in the vicinity of Talybont would have noticed the police presence and continued interest in that area of the forest and would jump to conclusions themselves in the absence of any official explanation. We agreed that we would discuss this with Major Harcourt-Evans in the morning and decide then how best to keep the lid on the story. After this session, we ordered a very passable Welsh lamb casserole and a bottle of red wine and enjoyed the food and relaxed a little after the strains of the day. Aston left us just after ten o'clock and we agreed to meet at nine in the morning at the morgue. Alicia and I were both tired after our early start and very busy day and decided to take our wine upstairs and turn in for the night to be fresh for the morning. We parted in the corridor between our bedrooms with a hug and a quick kiss in case we were observed by other guests heading to bed. The events of the day were whizzing around my head, although I felt we were on the verge of breaking this case wide open and within sight of winding up the spy network very soon, and I drunk my wine and got ready for bed. It felt luxurious and soft in this large bed, which was so different from the hard trestle bed I slept on at the section house, and I could feel myself sinking further towards sleep when I thought I heard the creaking floorboards on the other side of the bed and the softest whisper of night clothes falling to the floor and felt the mattress sink as a warm, naked body slid under the covers next to me. Insistent lips pressed eagerly to mine and an urgent probing of a tongue pushed its way into my mouth so teasingly that I was now instantly awake and wrapped my arms around Alicia's naked form and pulled her closer to me. This was the surprise I had dared to imagine as possible and it was now happening right here and right now and I was filled with anticipation, excitement but also fear that I would not be able to perform and satisfy Alicia with my performance. Although many men of my age were married with children, I was still quite a novice when it came to sex because I had devoted more of my time to study and advancement rather than women. I was not like my brother Gwyn, who was well known in our village as a ladies' man and who chased any girl who gave him a smile, and I had always been reticent about approaching women for fear of rejection, until I met Alicia. I had experienced some fumbling and groping with village girls after a few drinks and a couple of times had engaged in a kind of intercourse, but it was never very satisfactory but tonight it was different. I had wanted Alicia from almost the first day and I couldn't believe my luck that she appeared to want me too. I could feel my excitement rising and my penis straining to be released from my underdrawers, and the swirling tension in my groin was almost impossible to bear for much longer and I was certain that I was going to ejaculate long before I could enter Alicia.

Alicia seemed to sense my discomfort and tension and immediately slid her hand down my stomach and pulled the drawstring of my drawers loose and gently nibbled at my nipples with her lips and teeth as she worked her fingers under the waistband and gently took hold of my erect member and pulled it free. I felt I was going to burst and shoot my semen all over the bedclothes and I imagined the shame of my failure if I did, but Alicia seemed to know exactly what to do to bring me back from the brink but keep me excited and primed to go. She threw back the eiderdown and for the first time I could see her marvellous nakedness in front of me as she climbed on top and sank herself slowly and gently down the length of my penis until I felt that I was touching the end of her vagina. I could gently feel the flexing of the walls gripping and rippling as she worked her pelvic muscles with such delicious effect, still managing to keep my tension at bay until she started to lift herself slowly at first, up and down, thrusting faster and faster, drawing the tension from deep inside me through my testicles and finally erupting into her with a mighty release. I think I cried out in exhilaration, but she did not stop and kept thrusting hard into my groin, causing such a delicious pain that I didn't want her to stop as I could see the look of ecstasy on her face as she moved with such intense purpose, her breasts swinging beautifully in front of my eyes. I was reaching that point when every drop had been drawn from my core and I was beginning to hope that she might stop soon when I realised from the changing expressions on her face and the low moaning from her lips that she was still building to her orgasm. I was already feeling moist and could hear the noise of our coupling slapping together wetly as we thrust into each other when Alicia arched her back and I felt the shudder pass through her body into mine, and an intense squirt of her orgasm erupted around my penis and leaked out over the bed sheets. I had never experienced a sexual experience to match this before, but I could feel that my penis had not lost much of its vibrant erection and was still hard, and this was unusual for me as I usually went limp immediately after ejaculation. Alicia had drawn much more from me and as she lifted herself off my penis, she knelt between my legs and flicked her tongue around the head of my member and kissed it all the way down to my testicles, which brought me smartly back to attention and ready for action. She then gently took all of my penis into her mouth and worked her head up and down, mimicking the action of my penis in her vagina, which set up such an exquisite sensation in my groin that I thought I was going to ejaculate again with even greater force than last time, but Alicia slid her lips back up my penis and rolled onto her back and said let's not waste your semen and pulled my member towards her vagina and lifted her legs up so I could penetrate deeper as I entered her from above. I found that this time there was less tension as my fear of a premature ejaculation had passed and I enjoyed thrusting hard until I felt Alicia shuddering her orgasm again and I released too as we climaxed together. Alicia pulled me down on top of her and continued to kiss me deeply as we both came down from the post-coital high and, eventually, we stopped kissing and began whispering softly to each other until we drifted off to sleep.

    I don't know for how long we slept that night, but I know I was in a deep dream of great satisfaction and pleasure when I was woken by a loud hammering on my bedroom door. Alicia stirred too and I told her to be quiet so that no one should know we had shared our bed together against police rules. I found my dressing gown and went to the door and opened it slightly so that anyone there could not see into the room. It was a uniformed constable from the police station with a message that I should come quickly as a discovery has been made at the second site in the forest that I should see. I thanked him and said I would get dressed and drive out to the site as soon as I could, and he saluted and disappeared down the corridor. I was excited to know what had been discovered at the second site but was also disappointed as I had dared to hope that I might make love with Alicia again before breakfast. I relayed the message to Alicia, and she immediately switched from the dreamy apparition in my bed to a professional detective in seconds and leapt out of bed, collecting her clothes and robe and slipping across the corridor to get ready to leave for the excavation site. I could hardly contain my pleasure at finally spending the night in bed with a woman I was falling in love with and who seemed to have the same feelings for me but also with the sense of expectation of what we might find in the forest that morning. Twenty minutes or so later, there was a knock on my door and Alicia slid into my room for the second time that night but this time she was dressed in her formal clothes and hat with a heavy overcoat and gloves over her arm. We found the car in the stables behind the hotel, and I swung the handle to start the engine. It was still half an hour before dawn and the air was freezing cold but after a few swings I could feel the compression building and she roared into life, puffing out grey smoke behind. Thankfully, the soft top was up and within a few minutes the heat from the engine would heat up the cabin of the car enough to take the chill out of the interior of the car. We set off through the deserted Brecon streets until we joined the A40 London Road and were able to head east at a reasonable speed because there were no other vehicles on the road, and in about thirty minutes we were able to turn off the main road and take to the lanes leading through Talybont to the forest track leading off the bridge over the River Usk. Dawn was just breaking, and the sky was lightening up from the east, which made driving on the country roads a little easier, and we passed through the apparently deserted village centre where just a few signs of life were visible in one or two cottages where people were up and getting ready to begin their day. At last, the bridge came into view, and we parked by the side of the road and began the hike across the river and up the forest track to the excavation site. We saw no one until we were almost at the cut-off into the trees we had identified the day before when we saw the familiar figure of Inspector Aston, who looked somewhat dishevelled, as if he hadn't been to bed at all. He was wearing the same clothes as yesterday and the stubble was showing grey on his chin; his eyes were wide and red as if he was fighting to keep awake. He greeted us warmly enough and thanked us for the supper last night and told us that he had not made it home last night as he was called up here before he had time to leave the station for bed. I was anxious to hear what they had found but I waited for him to tell it in his own time, and after a few minutes of chat about the cold weather and the difficulty of digging the frost-hardened ground he finally got round to telling us that they had not found another grave and there were no bodies and I thought that I was glad of that but why had he called us up here so urgently? He paused a little for dramatic effect and then continued. They had found a considerable haul of weapons, mostly of German or Swiss origin, and boxes of ammunition and explosives, mostly small bombs and grenades and some detonators. "I wanted you to see them before they are crated and transported to the army depot at Crickhowell for safe lodgement at their armoury because the weapon store at Brecon Police Station is not big enough to store this amount of weaponry securely." He led us over to the site and before us, laid out in neat rows, were twenty pistols, half a dozen rifles and some small machine pistols with magazines and boxes of ammunition for each. The pistols looked to be familiar, and I thought they were possibly Lugers but I wasn't sure and would have to wait for an assessment of what we had discovered from a weapons expert. There were also four small metal boxes containing stick grenades and small bombs and assorted detonators and wire. This was a considerable arms dump, and we were sure that these were consignments of weapons hidden by the German spies that were smuggled in by U-boat and were probably meant for use against targets in South Wales. He said that he wanted to get these weapons packed up and transported to the army base before it got too light and local people started getting curious about all the police activity on this hillside. "I will accompany the consignment and then join you in Brecon to meet with your major later this morning and perhaps we can go to Crickhowell Barracks in the afternoon to inspect the arms find and seek the advice of the sergeant major armourer as to their possible origin and any clues as to who might have put them there."

It was now just after six in the morning, and I suggested we head back to Brecon where we could enjoy breakfast at the hotel before meeting Major Harcourt-Evans later in the morning. We were seated in the dining room just after seven where I ordered the full Welsh breakfast, whilst Alicia ordered a lighter breakfast of fruit and boiled eggs. I was ravenous from my night exertions with Alicia and after we had eaten sufficient, we sat in the lounge with some hot coffee and mulled over what we had discovered in the last twenty-four hours and weighed up whether we had yet acquired enough evidence to move against the German suspects or not. Alicia and I felt particularly sad about the tragic end of Heidi Weisse, who we both felt was brave enough to pursue her allegations of rape and assault against her estranged spouse and did not deserve to end up on a frozen Welsh hillside alongside the savage brute who had used her so badly in life as well as in death. Of course, Crawford and King did not deserve their premature end either, and we resolved to double our efforts to seek out the clues that would lead us to the assassins. I had no doubt that we would find that the orders to commit these murders would have come directly from the senior board members of Wurtenberg Holdings, but I did not think that Anton Kruger or Sir Wilhelm Branden would dirty their hands with the actual killings themselves, so the mystery to solve was who would have carried out the murders at their behest? There were only a few likely suspects from those we had already uncovered as members of the spy ring to be considered, and we soon narrowed the shortlist to Manfred Gruber, Ernest Sullivan, Jonathan Pugh or David Taylor, who were all active members of the ring and on the board of Wurtenberg Holdings. We had eliminated both the Matthias doctors and Hilda Williams as they seemed to lack the physical strength required to carry out the killings, especially of such a strong and violent man as Joachim Schultz, and Kruger and Branden would have distanced themselves from the murders as far as possible. Sullivan, Pugh and Taylor did not operate in Cardiff, and we would need to liaise with our colleagues in Newport and Swansea for more detailed intelligence about these three. Although I was sure that it was Manfred Gruber who had tried to run me down in the side street, I felt that this was, purely, panic and not the action of a seasoned killer, and I was inclined to put him further down the list of suspects. Alicia reminded me that the two imposters at Llangellis Farm could also be likely suspects, and they had a clear motive to eliminate Crawford and King to take on their identities.

The young waitress, Eileen, came to clear our cups and saucers whilst we were talking and after she had removed the tray to the kitchen came back into the lounge and approached us rather sheepishly. She was lucky to have caught us as were just leaving for the morgue, but she rather shyly attracted my attention and was full of apologies that she had overheard our conversation, but she had heard us mention some names that she recognised as previous guests in the hotel. She stammered unsteadily that one of the men was an Irish gentleman, named Sullivan, who had stayed there lots of times over the past year since she had started working in the hotel. I asked her how many times he had stayed but she was unable to remember exactly how many days in total, but she was sure he had been a guest in the hotel during the past week. Alicia said, "What other names did you overhear that you recognised?" and she replied that there were two gentlemen who she thought were called Mr Crawley and Mr King, who also stayed last week for two days. I asked whether they were staying at the same time as Sullivan, and she nodded her head and said that she thought so. I would need to check the hotel register carefully to establish the accuracy of this information, but I thanked her for her courage in confiding in us what could prove to be vital information to our enquiry. She asked me not to tell the hotel manager, Mr Fairless, that she had been speaking to us, and I said I would keep her name out of the conversation with the manager but later we might need to take a statement from her for our records. She curtseyed and scuttled away to the kitchen whilst Alicia and I sat back in amazement at the impact of this simple piece of information that had dropped into our laps unexpectedly and as a result of a couple of names overheard from our conversation by the waitress, who had been moving around the lounge serving guests without either of us being aware of her presence.

The information she had given us narrowed our list of suspects to three, Sullivan, Crawford and King, who, if the hotel register backed up Eileen's evidence, would be pinpointed as our three prime suspects. Mr Fairless was a little reluctant to give us free run at the hotel registers, but I invited him to come back into his office away from the reception desk where I quietly explained to him that we were from the secret security branch and this was a matter concerning danger to our country, and we suspected that German agents had been regularly frequenting his premises over the past year or so. "I am sure that you would not want it to be known that you did not cooperate fully in the hunt for German spies who have been enjoying hospitality in your hotel for the past year whilst boys from the local regiments are dying on the Western Front." I hinted that if this ever got out in the town, it might damage his business substantially and reduce his personal standing in the town. His face turned pale and he went to the reception desk and brought the register through into his office, and I asked him to leave us whilst we examined the entries.

It did not take long to find the entries for Crawford and King for the Tuesday and Wednesday of the previous week, who had shared a twin room on the third floor for two nights, and the entries for Sullivan stretching back for over a year. He had indeed stayed at the hotel on the Monday and Tuesday of the previous week and his stay had overlapped with that of the other two suspects by one day and a night. He had also stayed in the hotel on seven previous occasions over the past fourteen months, but it was impossible to say whether he was alone or in company with other persons as none of the names listed were familiar to us. Crawford and King had travelled to Brecon in a van and a registration number was listed and their address was given as Llangellis Farm, but Sullivan had not recorded any motor vehicle alongside his details, although he had given an address as 37 Bargoed Villas, Newport. I glanced at the clock on the wall to see that we were already twenty minutes late for Dr Llewellyn-Lewis at the mortuary and suggested to Alicia that we should leave the register and come back later and scrutinise it in detail after lunch. She said we must split our resources and that I should go to the morgue and meet with the major and Inspector Aston whilst she gleaned as much information as she could from the hotel registers by copying out the names of other guests who had stayed in the hotel the same dates as Sullivan with their details for further enquiries. I agreed and rushed off to the mortuary in double-quick time. The doctor had only just begun to examine the subsequent bodies but was happy for me to sit in and listen as he worked, and although the detail of his examination was interesting, I was only really interested in the manner of their deaths, which were entirely similar to those of Crawford and King. He was unable to tell me what kind of weapon it was, other than it was a pistol that had been fired once from very close range at the back of the victims' skulls and that until he could examine the remains of the rounds themselves, he could not say whether they were from the same gun or not. The third body was of a small man with a physique similar to that of a jockey, and the doctor commented on the pronounced muscle growth in his inner thighs and arms, which was common in frequent horse riders such as cavalrymen or jockeys. This struck me as somewhat significant because I seemed to recollect from the back of my mind that Sullivan was involved in horse racing in Ireland before coming to Wales and I noted that this could be a connection. Whilst the doctor continued droning on, the rear door opened and Major Harcourt-Evans slipped in, tall and smart in his uniform. I was a bit surprised because I had always seen him in civilian clothes before, but I guess he was dressed to impress his authority on the team he was going to command in this case. We stepped outside into the corridor where we shook hands, and I gave him a quick briefing of where we had reached in the last few days. He was impressed that we had made such rapid progress in such a short time and doubted that he was needed to lead this investigation as I was doing very nicely as it was. Grateful though I was for praise, I thought that his presence would help us keep a blanket on the spread of any information that might warn the German agents that we were on to them and impress upon the local police how important this case was. I also made it known that I had not worked alone, and Alicia Bell had been invaluable in moving the case forward too.

The major summed up by saying, "We have five corpses all found in one mass grave, murdered by one pistol shot to the back of the head, which the police surgeon suspects was with the same gun. We can identify four of the victims positively as linked to the German spy ring and you have uncovered evidence in the hotel registers of the Coach House Hotel which puts three other suspected German agents in this hotel on a number of nights last week and one of them on six previous occasions. Tuesday last week was when Schultz was released from custody and collected by two men answering the description of Crawford and King from the police station and they both stayed here in that hotel that night. We also know that Tuesday was the last day that Heidi Weisse was seen by her family, and I believe that these events are not coincidental but clearly planned. Let us see what Miss Bell can dig up in her research of the hotel registers whilst we go over to the police station and meet with Inspector Aston." The meeting was scheduled for eleven o'clock and Aston was accompanied by Superintendent James and the Chief Constable of the Breconshire Force, Colonel Rawlinson, and took place in the boardroom. Superintendent James led the meeting by questioning why they should hand over control of the murder investigation to the security branch when it was clearly in their jurisdiction and was currently being led by a competent inspector with a proven record of solving murder cases. Major Harcourt-Evans was quite conciliatory in his opening remarks, explaining that there was no slight intended towards the effectiveness of the Breconshire force or the competence of Inspector Aston, but it was a vital necessity that this case be kept secret and no information be divulged beyond the small circle of officers involved in the investigation. Secrecy was paramount to prevent the discovery of these bodies becoming common knowledge whilst we were progressing with our ongoing investigation to uncover an active network of German agents and spies, who we believed to be operating in South Wales currently, and who we believed were responsible for these murders. He outlined our case so far without giving away details of specific suspects or events and made it clear that from the initial suspicion, significant intelligence about the movement of merchant ships entering and leaving Welsh ports was reaching German naval headquarters. In consequence of which, we had noticed an increase in the number of U-boat attacks in Welsh coastal waters that had become so frequent that the combined loss of ships and the tonnage of war supplies lost was serious enough to affect our ability to sustain our forces in battle. Not only were the attacks more frequent but they appeared increasingly to be directed against ships that were laden with valuable cargo, and the U-boats were working together to deliver the maximum impact against our merchant fleet. Ships unladen, sailing in ballast, were largely left alone, whilst heavily laden ships were always attacked first.

"Initially, we believed that there were a small number of people of German origin or associations responsible and began our investigation by looking for people who had access to regular shipping movements and were of German origin or had connections with Germany but did not make much headway because the vast majority of those with strong German or Austrian connections were already interned in camps with no chance of gaining access to the information required. We widened our search by looking at those with some German connections who had not been interned and discovered about six potential suspects who had the opportunity to observe, record and share the shipping information we believe was being passed to the enemy because they worked in or frequented the docks in Cardiff, Newport and Swansea.

"This was our starting point and we set up a specialist unit of security police detectives, of which Wesley Morgan is one of the leading officers, who have investigated the initial six suspects and expanded our list of suspects to over sixteen who we have established are linked inextricably together through their finances and activities. My officers have worked undercover and with considerable stealth to establish that a German network exists and operates within our midst without divulging to the suspects that we are watching them so closely. Four of the five bodies found are known to us. Two are unfortunate wounded British officers who lost their lives to provide cover for two people we believe to be German spies. The other two were junior members of the spy ring who have been murdered because they posed a risk of discovery for the rest of the network when their actions attracted police attention," and he briefly described the rape and assault of Heidi Weisse by Joachim Schultz. "The fifth body is unknown to us, but we hope that together we can establish this victim's connection also and bring these enemies of the state to justice. It is important to us to establish who the killers were but far more vital is to bring down all the spy network by rolling it up in one go. To enable us to do this, the security branch humbly requests support and the knowledge and experience of the Brecon Force to bring these enemy agents to trial. If we are successful in this enterprise, we will have performed a remarkable service to this country and helped to enhance our ability to win the war. It is highly unlikely that individual charges of murder will be brought against any of them, but you can rest assured that your murder cases will be solved, and the culprits will face the ultimate penalty for espionage or treason charges."

The major finished with another plea for their cooperation in this matter and requested that he take over overall operational control for the prosecution of the case, reporting jointly to Colonel Stewart, Head of the Security Branch, and Colonel Rawlinson, and that the senior investigating officers would be Inspector Aston and Detective Morgan, who would take their orders from me. The colonel requested that we withdraw whilst they discussed the proposition in private, and we sat in the anteroom for the next hour whilst they discussed how much cooperation they were or were not willing to give. Finally, Aston came out and ushered us back in and we retook our seats and, looking around the table, I could not tell from their faces what their decision had been until the chief constable smiled and indicated that although they did not like this digression from normal police procedures, they were convinced that only by working together were the chances of capturing all the German spies operating in this part of Wales probable. He had decided to work on a joint investigation with us and agreed to the command structure proposed but had one request: that the headquarters for this investigation should move from Tiger Bay Police Station in Cardiff to the Brecon police station and that Morgan and his staff could work from here. I was elated when I heard this as I could see greater opportunity to spend time alone with Alicia, but I could also see that there were advantages to building a joint team with the Brecon officers and it would also be much easier to operate in secret without the Germans getting wind of our activities. Major Harcourt-Evans said he was delighted and would confirm these arrangements by the end of the day after he had conferred with Colonel Stewart on basing the investigating team in Brecon.

Aston and myself were dismissed from the meeting and I heard Rawlinson inviting the major to stay for lunch as we got up to leave the room. We made our way downstairs and crossed the square to the Coach House Hotel to see what progress Alicia had made with the registers during our absence. She had done what she does best and meticulously cross-referenced all the other guests who had stayed at the hotel at the same time as Sullivan or Crawford and King. She had made up a grid of names and addresses and dates and had highlighted one name that had appeared twice in the register on the same days as when Sullivan was also in residence. This was a Thomas O'Malley, who also had an address near to the docks in Newport and although this might be just a coincidence, it was certainly worth following up fully. She said that her initial look at the names had not suggested any other links that she thought worth following up. She was just finishing up with the hotel register, so we waited and then walked together to see whether the police surgeon had made any further discoveries of significance. The post-mortems were now completed, and he had not been able to find much more evidence that might lead to the identity of the fifth victim, but he did have something interesting to say regarding the shattered pieces of the bullets found in three of the corpses. Crawford, King and Schultz had bullets or fragments of bullets still within their skulls, whilst with the female and the unknown man the exit wounds suggested that the bullets had passed right through their skulls and come out the other side. The doctor said they were now sure that the ammunition used was parabellum .30, which was used, commonly, in the German Luger 1900, and from the size of the entry and exit wounds on the other two victims, he would be prepared to say that the same kind of ammunition was used, which also suggests that the killer had probably used the same weapon for each killing, suggesting a possible single assassin. It could be possible that the same gun was used by multiple shooters, but this would be unusual.

Our appointment at Crickhowell Barracks was at two in the afternoon so after leaving the mortuary we drove the half-hour journey to the army camp situated on the outskirts of the town near to the Heads of the Valleys Road. We were meeting with Sergeant Major Pugh at the armoury, where he had laid out and labelled on trestle tables each of the weapons that had been found in the underground cache and took us into the room to inspect them closely. There were twenty Luger model 1900 pistols which he said were highly accurate and much prized because they fired over longer ranges than most other pistols of the same size and had a magazine which held eight rounds, and there was a quantity of ammunition sufficient for eighty rounds for each pistol. He commented that these pistols were only manufactured in Germany or Switzerland and were popular with several European armies and were standard issue to officers in the German Army. On the next table was laid out a variant of the Luger pistol known as the Artillery Luger, which he explained was known as the Lange Pistole 08 and modelled on the Luger pistol but had been amended with a longer barrel about eight inches long and equipped with a folding stock so that it could be used as a carbine in place of a rifle. The standard issue Mauser rifles used by the German forces were much longer and difficult to conceal for covert work, but this variant with its folding stock could be easily concealed under a coat or jacket. The weapon was equipped with a 32-round magazine which made it a very useful weapon in close combat situations. There was also a similar quantity of ammunition for these weapons too, alongside an array of stick grenades and small bombs, explosives and detonators. Pugh was certain that these weapons were new and had never been fired as far as he could tell as they were well coated in oil and grease to preserve them whilst buried underground, and he could be certain that weapons of this type could not be obtained within this country. As they appeared to be new, it was likely they had been sourced directly from the manufacturer and at present there were only two factories making these weapons, one in Germany and one in Switzerland. It would not be illegal to purchase a single pistol but in times of war extremely difficult to do so given their origin. He was certain that this consignment had originated from Germany and had somehow been smuggled into this country and buried on this remote hillside to avoid detection. I asked if he could surmise how long they had been buried and he was unable to be certain but by the condition of the weapons he would suggest no more than three months underground. I asked if they could be fired in the condition they were in when they were taken out of the box, and he confirmed that they would need to be stripped and thoroughly cleaned and then the sights zeroed before they could be used and that this would be a task for a trained military man used to handling these weapons. I was sure that the cache of weapons had been brought in via U-boat landings on the remote beaches in West Wales and hidden here for future use. The sheer volume of weapons and ammunition plus grenades and other explosives suggested more than one delivery by submarine, which also meant several visits to the remote hillside which could easily have been observed by local people. I reckoned that focusing on the dates around the time that Sullivan and O'Malley were known to have been in the area from the hotel guest register, we might be lucky enough to find a witness or two who remembered them.

The Coach House Hotel was willing and able to secure the two rooms that Alicia and I occupied for the next couple of weeks but had more trouble finding a vacant room for Ivor but with a little rescheduling of bookings found him a room in an annexe to the hotel across the rear yard above the stables. We decided to spend that night in Brecon and drive back to Cardiff in the morning to brief Inspector Bennett and collect Ivor and move the investigation headquarters to Brecon Police Station. We were hoping to enjoy an undisturbed night together of passionate lovemaking before the need for discretion became even more important with the arrival of Ivor in the same hotel. Police regulations expressly forbade male and female police officers from working together on the same investigation and if Alicia and I disclosed our relationship publicly, we would be separated and placed in different teams. We had both put a great deal of energy into breaking the German spy ring and wished to see it through to the end and had resolved that once they were safely in custody, we would announce that we were a couple and accept that we would not work together in future. I had already admitted to myself privately that I was being supremely selfish, whilst recognising that any responsible officer would have already informed his superiors of a budding relationship, but I wasn't prepared to lose my close contact with Alicia so soon after finding her. I knew that our future together would not be like that of many couples who would marry and settle with children, because I knew that we were both dedicated police officers, enjoyed working for the secret security branch and were very ambitious in our own right. I was determined to become a detective and to rise through the ranks as far as I could rise and saw the security service work as a conduit for fast promotion for an able investigator. The thrill of sifting through the evidence to reveal the truth was my adrenalin and the reason that I had joined the police force in the first place. Alicia, I knew, enjoyed police work as much as I did, and whilst I thought I was a good detective, I recognised that Alicia was exceptional because of her meticulous attention to detail and application of logic in solving a case. She always managed to remain calm and focused when under pressure and felt that she had to work harder than her male colleagues to gain recognition for her work. She was one of very few female officers who were progressing to become detectives and she felt that she was every bit as good as her male colleagues in this respect and was determined to prove it. There were many in the police force who thought that female officers were a necessary evil to deal with female offenders and children and do some paperwork behind the scenes but should be kept away from real police work, and it was fortunate for us that Inspector Bennett was more forward-looking and pleased to get Alicia into our team. The security service would help me gain promotion and I felt that it would provide a similar lift to Alicia in her ambitions too.

We were tired after our interrupted sleep the night before and retired to bed after an early supper around eight and Alicia left it for an hour before she slipped across the corridor and into my room where we enjoyed a whisky nightcap before she stunned me by performing a lascivious and erotic striptease dance routine right in front of my eyes. I had never seen anything quite so tantalisingly sexual before, and her performance far surpassed any of the racy end-of-the-pier machines with their fuzzy naked images that I queued up to view on the pier as a young boy at Porthcawl on trips to the seaside. This was a beautiful woman revealing her deliciously gorgeous flesh to excite the man she wanted to make love to her when her full nakedness was revealed, and it was quite genuine and totally effective. I realised that she had no embarrassment or reticence about showing her body to me because she was confident in her beauty, and she could plainly see that I was struggling to contain myself. I wanted to rush forward and join in tearing the last few clothes from her body and revealing her completely to me, but the power of her entrancement of me just held me in suspense until she brought her erotic dance to a wonderful conclusion. I was glad that I had removed my jacket, waistcoat and collar before she had entered my room; otherwise, I would have been overheating, for sure. She came to me and rubbed her naked body against mine and my excitement nearly burst through my undergarments, but I just about managed to hold off my climax as she gently kissed my neck and removed my clothes slowly, one by one. As soon we were both naked, she opened her lips and her tongue streaked into the back of my throat as she pulled me down on top of her onto my bed, where I was delighted to find how excited she was and open and ready to accept me immediately. I was almost too eager to enter her and fumbled a little trying to find my way in and was beginning to panic a little until the end of my penis connected with her wetness and smoothly slipped deeply into her with one delicious thrust and we were as one body. I had never enjoyed such pleasure before and lifted her legs up towards her shoulders so I could penetrate her further, and I could see from her face and feel through her pelvic thrusting in concert with mine how much she was enjoying our union. My initial excitement and teetering on the brink of ejaculation had subsided sufficiently for me to sustain forceful and deep thrusting at a fast enough pace to induce little moans from Alicia with each successive deep push within her. The walls of her vagina began to grip and snatch at the thickness of me inside her and her contractions increased the faster I plunged into her. Finally, a deep moan began deep inside her and rose up through her body and escaped as a massive sigh as she climaxed as I felt the gushing wetness squirting out of her. I knew that I could now ejaculate but decided to keep her tingling on the edge of ecstasy a little longer and increased my thrusts again until she screamed as she climaxed a second time and I released my semen with great relish. I rolled onto my back, temporarily spent, with a tingling sensation running through my groin and my testicles shrunk to half their normal size. Closing my eyes, I was beginning to wind down from such bliss when Alicia's lips kissed my penis, and she began to clean up the mix of semen and her juices which coated my penis and groin with her tongue. This was the most lascivious experience I had ever felt and was effectively reawakening my member from its apparent decline to stand erect for further action once more, which prompted Alicia to mount me again as if she was getting into the saddle and riding me with as much force as I had thrust into her. This time, she was the one who held back and brought me tantalisingly near to a second ejaculation several times before I could not hold back any longer. This time, she pulled out just in time for me to shoot my semen over her flat stomach and I realised that she hadn't climaxed this time and I began to feel that I had failed her somewhat. Alicia wasn't dissatisfied because she wriggled up my torso and sat across my chest bone and thrust her vulva into my face and asked me to caress her with my tongue. I had never done this before but pushed my tongue out as far as I could into her labia and worked it gently around her clitoris and as far into her vagina as possible. This was a new experience for me, but it was not unpleasant and surprisingly enjoyable as I had never explored a woman's genital area as closely before, and I was beginning to enjoy the voyage of discovery when Alicia admonished me to be a bit more vigorous and started pushing her vulva into me with greater force and I began to get the message. I had heard talk about oral sex but did not believe that people did it and now that I had tried it for the first time, I could see why they did. I had also never met a woman like Alicia, who initiated sex and prompted her partner to do what she liked as well as simply fulfil his pleasures. In the chapel valleys of Wales, sex was considered a necessary evil for the procreation of children and wasn't something to be enjoyed, and even beyond the constraints of the chapel the popular perception held was that sex was for men to enjoy and women to endure. I was delighted that I had found in Alicia a woman who enjoyed sexual intercourse as much as me and was not ashamed to show how much she enjoyed the mutual pleasure of making love together. I felt blessed that we were sexually compatible but also glad that we shared so much more than just carnal knowledge together. Eventually, after about an hour of lovemaking, we both curled up with our arms around each other and fell into a deep and satisfying sleep.

ELEVEN

We made an early start back to Cardiff to brief Inspector Bennett on the investigation so far and to collect Ivor and move our headquarters to Brecon Police Station by the end of the day. The inspector had already received a signal from Major Harcourt-Evans on the terms of the agreement with the Breconshire chief constable as to the price for their cooperation and was excited to hear how much progress had been made in the past few days. He agreed that our priorities were to follow up on Sullivan and O'Malley in Newport and to plan an operation with Brecon police to arrest Crawford and King at Llangellis Farm if we were able to confirm their involvement in the five murders. He felt that they could be apprehended at Llangellis without the knowledge of their arrests reaching the rest of the spy ring in Cardiff, especially if they were removed to Brecon Police Station for interrogation. It could be more difficult to detain Sullivan in Newport because he would likely be in contact with the other members of the Newport cell and his absence quickly noticed, whereas it might take a few days before the absence of the pair from the farm might be missed. We discussed the weapons cache found near to the mass grave and would further our enquiries as to how they made their journey to the remote Welsh hillside when they seemed to have come from Germany, and we were sure that the size of the consignment would have been noticed by witnesses along the way. We would increase our efforts to interview local people in the Talybont area and along the likely route that would have been taken, assuming the weapons had been landed from U-boats in Rhossili Bay, to establish whether there were witnesses who had noticed the movement of this consignment, which would have been large and may have been moved at night or early in the morning or late in the evening when there were fewer potential witnesses around. We were unsure how long it would take to complete our work in

Brecon, but we all felt that we were close to rounding up the German spy ring within a few weeks.

Ivor was delighted to be escaping from Tiger Bay Police Station, although we guessed he would miss his jolly nights in the pub. He was not too downhearted when he realised he would be staying in a hotel with a large public bar in Brecon. He asked for half an hour or so to pack a few things together whilst we loaded our files into the trunk box at the rear of the car and by mid-afternoon we were back on the road to Brecon. Our plan was to move into the office provided for us at the Brecon station and then introduce Ivor to Inspector Aston and his team and then plan our moves together so that we could make immediate progress in the morning. Aston was in complete agreement that we should follow up on Sullivan and O'Malley and suggested that Alicia and I should go to Newport whilst Ivor took over the role of running the Brecon office and collating the evidence that came in from all sources. Sergeant Townley and two constables from Brecon would travel to Port Eynon to liaise with Constable Evans to set up a discreet surveillance on Llangellis Farm and keep track of the movement of Messrs Crawford and King. Aston and his team would continue to investigate the murder scene and the weapons dump and the search for witnesses. By eight that evening, we were back at the Coach House where we enjoyed a quick supper and a few drinks with Ivor before we left him making new friends in the bar whilst Alicia and I slipped upstairs. We had decided to be more cautious now that Ivor was in the hotel and Alicia said that although she would love to spend every night sleeping in my bed, it would be more prudent to spend most of the night sleeping in her room to avoid suspicion. I agreed, although I was disappointed at having to sleep alone again but knew it was for the best and so we parted in the hallway, but Alicia whispered that she would come to me when the hotel was quiet. It was a long wait before she came, and I was anxious not to fall into a deep sleep before she came just before midnight. We made love and cuddled for a little while and then she slipped quietly back to her room for the rest of the night.

We had an address for Sullivan as Bargoed Street, Newport, which we could see from the map was in a busy working-class area close to Newport Docks and it was quite difficult to find as the whole area was a rabbit warren of terraced streets, alleys and yards. We abandoned the car a little distance from the docks and caught a tram towards the dock gates and walked around the area, keeping our eyes open for Bargoed Street. We did not want to attract too much attention to ourselves, so we split up and agreed to rendezvous at the tram stop in one hour and set off to search different sectors of the area. Alicia had put a shabby coat on over her clothes and tied her hair up in a scarf and carried a shopping bag, and I certainly thought that she blended in with all the other housewives going about their usual business. I left my jacket and tie in the car and put on an old flat cap and tied a muffler at my neck, just like the itinerant stevedores who lounged at open doorways if they had not been picked to work that day. I was aware that both Alicia and I would easily be recognised as strangers in this close-knit dockland area, but I hoped that our disguises would be sufficient to enable us to make a quick check of the area before we withdrew. Alicia found that Bargoed Street was a terrace of mean back-to-back houses just one hundred yards or so from the dock walls and she had identified the address that Sullivan had used at the Coach House Hotel on several occasions. The house was nondescript with no distinguishing features to mark it as different from all the others in the surrounding streets but joining in conversation at the grocer's on the corner, she was able to ascertain that Bargoed Street and Magor Street were much favoured by Irish people judging by the accents she heard in the shop, which were certainly not Welsh. She hung back, pretending to take time over her shopping, and when she took her few purchases to the counter remarked to the jolly Welsh woman behind the counter that she thought she was across the water in Ireland, not in Newport at all. The shopkeeper replied that most of her customers were Irish because those who had escaped from the troubles to Newport seemed to have settled in these streets. Alicia replied that this was interesting and that she was new to the area, but she had an uncle from Ireland who lived somewhere in Newport and she was hoping to look him up sometime. The lady behind the counter asked for his name and said if he was living in Newport, he would probably live within a couple of hundred yards of her shop and come in there regularly. Alicia said he was Ernest Sullivan and came from Dublin and the shop lady scratched her head and said that she did not know him personally, but she thought he was the single gentleman who lived about halfway down Bargoed Street who kept himself to himself. Alicia thanked her for the information and paid for her few pieces of shopping and left the shop and hurried away in the direction of Bargoed Street but did not stop, continuing directly towards the tram stop to meet up with me.

Having identified where Sullivan lived and established that he was still living there, we now decided to see what we could find out about Thomas

O'Malley and we decided to return to the car and change our clothes back to our normal police attire before approaching the local church, police station and his ex-employer. The coroner at Brecon was sure that O' Malley was probably killed sometime after Crawford and King, judging by the position his body was found in the grave and the extent to which decomposition of the body had set in, which meant he had been absent from Newport for at least six to eight weeks all told. Somebody in the local area must have missed him in that time and Alicia and I were determined to find out what we could before we headed back to Brecon. Most southern Irishmen were followers of Roman Catholicism and we felt that the local parish priest may have knowledge of O' Malley and his whereabouts. St Saviour's Church served the dock community and would be where the Irish community would worship, and although it was a long shot that O'Malley was a member of the congregation here, there was a chance that the parish priest might know of him.

The church was a large and imposing stone structure built at the end of the last century by a subscription of local Catholics, according to the plaque at the front of the church, and situated only three streets away from Bargoed Street and the dock gates. The priest was Father Murphy and he was a garrulous Irishman of about sixty with grey hair and bright, twinkling eyes and seemed happy to have someone to chat to even if it was only the police in the absence of more stimulating conversation. He struck me as the kind of man who would engage you in pleasant conversation in a pub just for the pleasure of enjoying the intercourse with like-minded individuals over a pint or a glass of whisky. We asked him if he had a parishioner called Thomas O'Malley in his congregation and he replied almost without hesitation that he did, but that he hadn't seen him in the church for some time. I explained to him that we were investigating the discovery of a body in a remote grave in the Black Mountains, which we thought might be the remains of Thomas O'Malley, but we hadn't been able to make a definite identification yet. "Anything you can tell us about Mr O'Malley might assist us in solving the mystery and would be helpful even if it turns out not to be him." He crossed himself and then thought for a few seconds, but then his demeanour changed and he seemed to clam up and indicated that there was not much he could tell us. Alicia asked how long he had been coming to this church and the priest thought and said for at least three years as he was sure that he was here before the outbreak of the war. She asked if he knew where he came from and he said that he was not sure but felt it was from somewhere near to Dublin judging by his accent.

I was pretty sure that Father Murphy could tell us much more, but I felt he chose to say as little as possible at this time. I asked if he had any idea why he had left Ireland and come to Newport and he shrugged his shoulders and said that it was to find work most probably, but he thought there might have been some trouble back home, which underlined his removal to Wales at that time. We asked him to be more specific about this, but he was reluctant to say more but suggested that the regular drinkers at the dockers' pub opposite the main gate of the docks could probably help us with more information.

Thanking him for his help, I made as if to go as Alicia asked one final question about some of the entries we had found in a hotel register close to where the body was found when a Thomas O'Malley had stayed in the hotel on two separate occasions at the same time as another man with an address in Bargoed Street. If this had been on only one occasion, it could have been dismissed as a coincidence, but two occasions several months apart seemed to suggest something more than that. "We believe that they travelled together for some common purpose, and it would be beneficial to our enquiry to be able to interview this man about the case." Alicia continued that perhaps the priest would know him too and mentioned the name Ernest Sullivan. Was he also a member of the church?

The priest's face clouded over and he seemed to be annoyed that he was being asked these awkward questions when all he wanted was a pleasant and light-hearted chat. Finally, he replied that Sullivan was not a member of his church and would not be welcome if he chose to enter these doors, and we were taken aback by the vehemence of his hatred for Sullivan. He said, "You will not find anyone here who will have a word to say in favour of Mr Sullivan because he is a man of violence, an enforcer and informer. Many people believe he is possibly a killer too. There are many people who are aware of Sullivan's activities back in the old country, but you will find them too frightened to break their silence about him. He worked for the Irish rebels fighting against British rule in Ireland but had to flee when a job he was on went wrong and a prominent leader of one of the home rule factions was murdered by mistake." He was now almost shooing us out of the door and was in a fluster and said, "Do not mention me or this church as I don't want Sullivan to know I have been talking to you."

As we came out into the sunlight from the dimly lit interior of the church, it was difficult to adjust our eyes immediately but as we walked back to the car, I had a strange feeling that there were eyes on us, although I couldn't make out anyone particularly watching us. I now reckoned that the presence of the car in these streets was a mistake, and we would have been better served to remain on foot in our disguises from earlier in the day. I hoped that there would not be repercussions for Father Murphy if it became known that he had been talking to the police that afternoon. Our next call was to the police station where we received a more friendly welcome than at the church but didn't learn a great deal more that we hadn't already guessed or discovered about Sullivan or O'Malley. The station sergeant filled us in with what they knew, which wasn't much more than confirming what Father Murphy had told us, but he did offer some interesting gossip which he said could not be corroborated but everyone we would talk to in the Irish community would say it was true. Apparently, Sullivan was a kind of bodyguard and muscleman used by the leaders of the Irish rebel movement against British rule. He was the enforcer ensuring that people kept their mouths shut and continued to provide financial support to the rebels to buy weapons and explosives to sustain their campaign against the British. In the years immediately before the war, Sullivan accompanied one of the leaders of the movement to Germany on several occasions to purchase the arms and ammunition they needed. On the final buying trip, so the story goes, they were ambushed by British agents and only Sullivan escaped with his life, and that was when he escaped to Wales to avoid retribution from his rebel friends. There was much gossip that Sullivan had done a deal with the Germans, who were happy to supply the weapons free of charge, and Sullivan pocketed the money. "Sullivan appears to have lived quietly since he has lived here, and we are not aware of any of his activities that might attract our attention."

We asked about O'Malley, and he was known to the sergeant because he too was a regular drinker at the Earl of Monmouth pub by the dock gates and he knew him by sight and that he had a job in the shipping office. Alicia asked whether Sullivan ever drank in this pub and the sergeant said that he did but not as regularly as O'Malley, and Alicia followed up with whether O'Malley had anyone in particular who he drank with on a regular basis, and the sergeant scratched his head and said that he thought that there were two particular men that he drank with three or four times a week, but he couldn't remember their names offhand. I jumped straight in and said, "Do the names Jonathan Pugh or David Taylor ring any bells?" and he broke into a broad grin and said how did I know that because he thought that might be their names. We were now certain that O'Malley had connections to the spy ring because he associated in the Earl of Monmouth with Sullivan, Pugh and Taylor, who were all board members of Wurtenberg Holdings. When we came out of the police station, we were sure that a visit to the Earl of Monmouth would offer very little of use to us since we had been spotted as police officers and had been snooping in the streets around the Irish quarter and been to the police station. The drinkers in the pub would have been forewarned and would certainly close ranks, so we decided to head back to Brecon after what had been a very fruitful day.

Later that evening, we recounted our experiences in Newport and what we had managed to find out about Sullivan and O'Malley, with the bonus that we were able to link them with Pugh and Taylor, who we also suspected were members of the spy network. We needed to know more about Sullivan's past life and especially his involvement with the rebels in Ireland and his break with them over the German arms deals. It seemed to be common knowledge that Sullivan had acted as the hard man for the rebel leaders in southern Ireland and had been used to violently suppress any dissension or opposition to their political ambitions. The mystery over his break with them and involvement with the German arms deals needed to be unravelled enough to understand whether he was committed to the German cause or not. He could be a violent criminal plying his trade as an enforcer for the Germans for hire. It seemed certain that the spy ring leaders were willing to use violence to keep their people in line and to protect the security of the network. They had no conscience about murdering Crawford and King to substitute their operatives in their place, and Schultz and Heidi appeared to have been dispatched promptly the instant that the spy masters felt under threat by their presence. I thought that I could telephone Colonel Stewart in the morning and enquire as to whether he had any contacts with specialised knowledge about the rebel Irish groups operating in the Dublin area. Aston's officers had been continuing the questioning of local inhabitants near to the Talybont forest and had found a couple of potential useful leads who remembered seeing a general-purpose van in the area on several occasions in the general vicinity of the forest road. The van was plain with no company name on the side and very similar to vehicles used by the foresters and farmers in the local area, but there was no positive description of the driver or the passenger from any of the sources. However, he said the local bobby from a village near Brynmawr had contacted the office and thought he might have seen our suspects one night about ten days ago and would be happy to tell us what he had seen. Aston had driven to Brynmawr and interviewed the constable that afternoon at the police station and had discovered what he believed was the first positive sighting of our suspects. He described being on cycle patrol around the outskirts of Brynmawr, around midnight, ensuring that all was secure, when he noticed a dark-coloured van parked by the side of the main road from Merthyr. He thought it strange that a van would be parked on the open road at this time of night so cycled closer to give it a quick check. He noted down the registration number in his notebook and when he moved to the front of the van, he was surprised to see three men squashed into the front cab, so he approached them to enquire whether they needed any assistance. They seemed alarmed when they saw him and almost jumped out of their skins when he tapped on the side window strut. They were a strange crew because two of them were English and were very jumpy, but the third man sounded Irish and was quicker to regain his composure and took charge and answered the constable's questions. They identified themselves as working for the Branden Farm Machinery Supplies company from Cardiff but had broken down on the road and had been delayed for four hours whilst repairs were carried out. They were able to produce proof of their identities, which he copied down as Crawford and King for the Englishmen, and the Irishman said he was Thomas O'Malley and produced an identity paper to that effect. Aston had remembered to take the photographs of Crawford, King and O'Malley from the morgue and showed them to the constable. I explained that these were pictures of Crawford, King and O'Malley taken by the coroner in Brecon the day before and asked if he recognised any of them, and he was sure that none of these men were in the van that night. The only other tidbit of information he gave me was that he heard one of the Englishmen call the Irishman Ernest, which he thought was a bit strange at the time since the Irishman said he was Thomas O'Malley. He said that he had checked the registration number of the van and it was registered to the farm machinery company as they had indicated. "I was not entirely happy with the situation but being outnumbered three to one decided to let them go on their way and check up on them once I was back at the station." Aston was glad that he had driven down to Brynmawr as he was sure that we now had a firm sighting of the murderer and his accomplices. The first two men using the names of Crawford and King would probably be the German imposters masquerading as the British veterans, and the Irishman calling himself O'Malley was almost certainly not him. The description given by the constable was a close enough match to the description of Sullivan, but Aston didn't have a photograph of him to confirm it but would try to get the necessary confirmation from him in the next couple of days.

Alicia and I already knew that the Branden Farm Machinery company was owned by Sir Wilhelm Branden and its name had been used already by Joachim Schultz to provide cover for his visit to Crawford and King at the farm safe house that had been observed by Evans from Port Eynon. Every way one turned in this investigation, the web of connections all led back to the German spy ring, and we were very close to rolling them all up into custody very soon. The surveillance team led by Sergeant Townley and his team were already in place on the Gower and were keeping watch on Llangellis Farm and the movements of Crawford and King and any other comings and goings at the farm. They had already confirmed that there was a brown van parked in the farmyard but from their vantage point were unable to see the registration number clearly but after dark one of them would creep forward and note its number down. The two subjects did not actually attend to much farming and spent most of their time indoors and seemed to have a secret storeroom camouflaged by shrubs and bushes that concealed some steps leading to a door, where they made frequent visits, sometimes singly but other times together. They couldn't tell from their vantage point what was of such interest to them but had counted eight visits alone in a single day, so there must be something significant there. They did not seem to have a dog so they would try to venture closer after dark to have a look and report back in the following day's update. It was good thinking by Aston to send this team to the Gower because they had settled right away into the hard discipline of thorough surveillance very quickly and knew what to look for. Ivor had been busy collating all the information into our files and cross-referencing what we had discovered into the wider picture. Everything we brought together today would keep him busy tomorrow, and we relied on his good sense as an investigator to highlight things that we had missed or failed to make a connection with.

Colonel Stewart was very quick to respond to my request and introduced me to a colleague from the Foreign Office who was an expert on Irish affairs and suggested I go to London to consult him about Sullivan's involvement with the Irish rebels and had arranged an appointment with Sir Vernon Miles in Whitehall for midday the following day. I arranged to drive to Newport and pick up the Red Dragon express to London the following morning and I was walking out of Paddington Station at just before eleven in the morning. The short tube ride brought me to the front entrance of the Foreign Office in good time for my appointment with Sir Vernon Miles. I was slightly overawed as the portico and entrance were so grand and the staircase magnificent and there was a massive sense of purpose in the hustle and bustle of clerks and officials going about their daily business. I was accosted politely by a top-hatted commissionaire in red coat and gold buttons who doffed his hat and asked what my business was, and when I stated my appointment was with Sir Vernon Miles, he called for one of the runners, who were young boys about fourteen sitting on a bench behind his desk. A smart young lad in the runners' livery stepped forward and was instructed to take me to Sir Vernon's room on the third floor and he saluted and guided me up the stairs at such a pace that even as a fit man I had difficulty keeping up with him. Finally, we came to a large oak door with a name plaque with Sir Vernon's name inscribed on it. The boy knocked and a deep voice from within shouted to come in and he swept open the door and ushered me into a large and well-furnished private office where a rather imposing man with long grey whiskers, which were fashionable twenty or so years before, stared at me from behind a large oak desk. He boomed at me to sit and then asked if I was Detective Constable Welsey Morgan from the secret service. I replied that I was, and he relaxed and reduced the level of his voice to a more usual conversational level and indicated that he knew I was interested in Ernest Patrick Sullivan, the Irish rebel terrorist. He asked me to explain what my interest might be, and he would try to see how he could help me. I explained how Sullivan had cropped up as part of our investigation into a possible German spy ring operating in South and West Wales, who we were certain were feeding top secret information about allied shipping movements to the German U-boat command. He listened intently as I gave some details of how Sullivan was involved in the spy ring and his possible involvement in the murder of five people and then held up his hand to stop me and asked whether we were sure that we had the right Ernest Sullivan. I could not be certain, which was why I was seeking his help, but we were sure that Sullivan was an Irishman originating from the Dublin area and had some involvement in one of the leading Irish rebel groups fighting for freedom from British rule. Sir Vernon stopped me again and smiled and then said that he was not trying to be awkward, but he needed to be sure that we were both talking about the same person before he revealed sensitive information from their files. Ernest Sullivan was well known to the Irish Division of the security service and was wanted for the murders of General Anders Stephens, military governor at Dublin Castle; Sir Jolyon Pearce QC, High Court Judge sitting at Dublin; Majors Peters, Always and Lawson, shot whilst having dinner in a restaurant close to Leopardstown Barracks, and many more serious acts of violence against Irish folk who chose to go against the wishes of his rebel leadership. Sullivan served in the British Army for seventeen years and rose to the rank of sergeant and saw active service in South Africa but was dishonourably discharged in 1902 for striking an officer and sentenced to twelve months in military hard labour. He seriously beat Lt. William Hawtrey, pulling him from his horse and beating him severely with his own horsewhip after he had slashed a child begging in the street around her face, almost taking out her eye. Sullivan showed no remorse for what he had done and said he had acted as he did to teach the lieutenant a lesson he should have already known. The court martial found him guilty and he was reduced to the ranks and sent to the military compound at the Verne Citadel, where he broke rocks for twelve months' hard labour. After release from prison, he returned to Ireland and found it difficult to find work and settle down until he met Rory McCloud O'Hare, who was a rising young star in the founding and moulding of the political movement for home rule. O'Hare was a violent man and had always made his way in life with his fists and other heavy-handed methods, but when he decided to stand for election as an official of the organisation and to represent them publicly, he put away his violent ways but engaged Ernest Sullivan to work covertly behind the scenes and force his way to the top of the organisation. Sullivan played a very low-key role in the organisation as a runner and general dogsbody, but this was only a ruse because it enabled him to have an ear to what the rank and file supporters were saying and thinking and secretly report this back to O'Hare, who directed whatever action needed to be taken. As the Irish rebellion grew stronger, it drew more and more supporters to the cause but also increased the fractious nature of their cause, and increasingly splinter groups and factions broke away from the main home rule organisation. This led to much more work for Ernest Sullivan, who could be relied on to deliver a beating, a knee capping or a killing with cool efficiency and secrecy. However, during the latter months of 1913 and into 1914, when tensions were rising between Britain and Kaiser's Germany, the Irish Home Rule movement courted support from the Germans in terms of arms and ammunition plus funding in return for guaranteed neutrality in the event of war from a free Irish government.

The Germans were interested in this agreement and entered negotiations with the Irish rebel movement and although O'Hare volunteered to act as their representative in these talks, the high council selected a prominent Dublin lawyer, Fergus O'Hanlon, to conduct the talks in Germany, but O'Hare managed to persuade his fellow board members that Fergus would need the protection that could only be provided by someone like Sullivan, and they agreed. "To our knowledge, O'Hanlon and Sullivan went to Germany twice before the war began and a third time after hostilities had commenced, travelling via Spain. We have not been able to discover the exact terms agreed with the Germans at these meetings, but we are certain that arms, ammunition and war supplies plus gold bullion was shipped to Ireland on nine occasions, either using neutral ships or covert delivery by U-boats at night to deserted beaches. The tenth delivery, however, became a problem, and we strongly suspect that Sullivan was a prime mover in it. An urgent meeting had been called because Germany wished to increase the benefits it was getting from the agreement by increasing its embassy staff in Dublin and bunkering facilities for German ships in Dun Laoghaire Harbour. Sullivan knew that Fergus O'Hanlon would oppose this vehemently but that O' Hare would welcome increased presence of German support on Irish soil. We believe that Sullivan connived with the Germans to have O'Hanlon murdered in a supposed ambush and Sullivan was able to redirect the arms and gold to a secret location by U-boat in Wales. We believe that Sullivan sold the first arms cache to a German spy network who were operating undercover in Wales through a company called Wurtenberg Holdings and that Sullivan remained in Wales and offered his services to the German spies. We are unaware where the gold has ended up, but I am sure that it has been converted into cash and found its way into a secret bank account in Sullivan's name." I was able to tell Sir Vernon that Sullivan was residing at 26 Bargoed Street, Newport and that the information he had imparted just then filled in many of the gaps in our knowledge about Sullivan. I assured him that when in the next few days warrants were issued for the arrest of Ernest Sullivan for the Brecon murders, I would ask Colonel Stewart to liaise with his office so that he could charge him with the outstanding Irish murders also. Sir Vernon was grateful for our cooperation and wished us well in our attempt to bring the German spies to justice.

Another few of the jigsaw pieces had dropped into place and I was now sure that Sullivan was the assassin used by the German spies to dispose of inconvenient people, and of the five bodies I knew how four of them came to be in the mass grave. It was still a mystery why the fifth body, that of Thomas O'Malley, was there at all, although we knew that he and Sullivan were acquainted and that he drank with Pugh and Taylor, who were also directors of Wurtenberg Holdings, in the same pub. As yet, we hadn't discovered why he should end up dead in a remote grave in mid-Wales. I wrestled with these ideas all the way back to Newport on the train but was still no nearer to an answer when I alighted at Newport station. As I drove up the Heads of the Valleys Road, a small suggestion was growing in my head that if O'Malley was a member of the German spy ring, why hadn't we heard anything about him until we discovered his body at Talybont? He was obviously trying to get close to the German agents operating in Newport, but it did not appear to me like he was one of them and I was wondering whether O'Malley was working for the Irish rebels to locate Sullivan or whether he was maybe an undercover policeman. I would run these thoughts past Alicia, Ivor and Aston when I got back, and they would probably tell me I was being stupid. However, I was wrong as they all thought that it was a perfectly legitimate angle to take and encouraged me to seek out further information about O'Malley in the morning. So, I had reconciled myself to several days of desk work and telephone calls as I tried to delve into the real identity of O'Malley. Many ideas were floating around in my head and maybe he had served with Sullivan in the army in South Africa or he was a boyhood friend from their hometown; a fellow member of the Irish rebel cause or something else, and I did not really know where to start. I decided to sleep on it and make my decision in the morning, provided I was not too preoccupied with Alicia during the night.

The decision was made for itself when in the morning Aston suggested that the museum at Brecon Barracks contained a huge archive of army service records which might prove a good place to start. I wandered down Military Road towards the barracks, which was the home of the South Wales Borderers, and was easily directed to the museum entrance by the sentry at the main gate. The museum had only been open about fifteen minutes and visitors had not seemed to start arriving, so I had the place much to myself. The layout and displays of uniforms and weapons and medals from campaigns stretching back several hundred years were impressive, but I was not there to enjoy the museum but to seek information. The main noticeboard showed that the curator was a Major Goddard MC and a white arrow pointed towards his office to the left of the main entrance. I knocked at his door and a voice called for me to enter and I pushed open the door and stepped inside to be confronted by a small man with only one arm but a ready smile, who asked how he could help. I introduced myself and asked whether his archives might help me locate the service records of two persons of interest to us who might have served together in South Africa. He was non-committal because his records were far from complete, but he would be willing to conduct a search, although it might take a little time. When I gave him the names, Ernest Sullivan and Thomas O'Malley, he asked if they were in Irish regiments, which would help narrow the search down. I was not sure whether they had served in Irish regiments or not but knew for definite that Sullivan had fought in the Second Boer War and reached the rank of sergeant but was court martialled and dishonourably discharged from the army in 1902 for assaulting Lieutenant Hawtrey. Goddard thanked me for these details and said that this information should enable him to track Sullivan down reasonably quickly, but even so it might take a few days and he would send a note to the police station when he had some results to share with me. I was grateful for his help and thanked him, but he didn't seem to notice that I was leaving as he was already planning how he was going to start this search. Confident that this was a positive beginning that morning, my step was considerably lighter as I made my way back up the hill to the town square and my desk at the police station to start searching Irish census records for the 1861 and 1871 Censuses. I thought this might be easy because at least they were public documents and available for inspection by members of the public on demand. The problem was that the census archives were huge, and whilst local records were kept in the council offices and public libraries, copies of the complete records were only retained in major cities, university libraries and central government offices. My chances of discovering much from the records held in Brecon were slim, to say the least. It looked like I would need to make a trip to the University of Cardiff library to view the census records for the area of Dublin that Sullivan came from sometime in the next couple of days, although I did discover that I needed to submit a written request for the persons I wished to locate and the area, ward, district or town and for which census, and that the archives officer would call me to the library when the information was available for collection. This was good news because I hated the thought of the hours I would have to spend trawling through hundreds of pages of the archive to try to catch a glimpse of Sullivan or O'Malley and here it was being done for me. This was easy street for an investigator and all I had to do was wait for the results to fall into my lap. Alicia and Ivor teased me terribly that I was now superfluous to requirements as they could get information direct from public officials without the need of their lead detective and that I would be of better use if I made a pot of tea for the office since I had no work to do.

Aston called us to gather round as he had received the latest twenty-four-hour report from Townley at Llangellis Farm, and he had something to report. Around two in the morning, dim lights had come on inside the farmhouse and a short time after both figures could be seen approaching the secret room beneath the slurry pit. They had a high-powered torch with them, and they were able to see them move the camouflage away from the steps and descend and enter the secret room. Emerging a few minutes later, both men were armed with what looked like small machine guns, but it was too dark to identify the make or model clearly. Townley designated one of his constables to remain on watch at the farmhouse whilst he and the other constable followed Crawford and King at a safe distance, making sure that they were not discovered. The two men walked in the direction of the clifftop directly towards the spot where the steps led down to the beach. It was difficult to keep track of them because they were both dressed completely in black and had turned off their torch as they seemed to know the way. Townley thought they may have lost them in the dark when he saw a flash of their torch from the top of the cliff steps which flashed on and off as if signalling to a vessel out at sea. Even though Townley had a small telescope with him, he was unable to detect any vessel lying offshore until he thought he saw a pinprick of light on the horizon answering the signal from the clifftop, but still could not make out any vessel. They were tempted to follow their suspects down the steps to the beach but thought that the beach was too open and too small to afford them any place of concealment and they would be easily discovered. He decided to search for a place to hide and a vantage point overlooking the beach where they could watch what was going on. The night was cold but overcast and visibility was moderate, and nothing much seemed to be happening on the beach for a long time until there were three flashes much closer inshore answered from the beach and a naval whaler-type boat was clearly visible crashing through the surf, making straight for the shore. The whaler was crewed by an officer and four sailors all in the uniform of the German Navy, and they had a passenger who was dressed in dark civilian clothing and was clutching a holdall tightly to his chest. Two seamen jumped ashore and pulled the boat prow onto the beach whilst the other two leapt onto the sand holding machine pistols in case of an ambush, and they could see the passenger step ashore, shake hands with Crawford and King, wave farewell to the boat coxswain and start to head for the steps. The German sailors' feet were on Welsh soil for only a few brief seconds as they had delivered their passenger and were pulling hard through the surf back to their vessel out at sea in less than a minute. The German ship had not been identified but it was most probably a U-boat trimmed down so only the conning tower showed above the water to make discovery more difficult. Our two men remained in their hiding place until the three suspects passed them by and after a few minutes they followed them from a safe distance. "We don't know who the new arrival was, but Constable Lewis thought he could hear them speaking in a foreign tongue, which sounded a bit like German to him."

Townley's latest report increased the imperative to raid Llangellis Farm as soon as we could to secure the arrest of all three of the occupants of the farm as soon as possible. I had a feeling that the new arrival would be a replacement for Schultz, and I wondered whether he would take the identity of murdered O'Malley, although I had no evidence to this effect. Aston agreed and had already issued a warning to Sergeant Townley to fall back and keep out of sight and to take no action until we arrived to support him, as the Germans were heavily armed. We would arm ourselves in case they put up a fight, but the objective was to take them prisoner as stealthily as possible. Aston went upstairs to speak with the superintendent to get his approval for the resources for the raid and we began to plan the operation in more detail. We set the deadline for hitting the farmhouse as ten that evening and we had a busy day of preparation ahead of us before we needed to set off for the Gower Peninsular around six. Alicia, Ivor and I studied the OS maps of the area and sketches of the layout of the farm drawn by Sergeant Townley to see the best approaches and how we could be sure of restraining all three without them escaping as it was vital to take all three into custody without any hint reaching the spy ring in Cardiff. Our plan was to involve about eight officers armed with pistols to approach the farmhouse across the fields and not the road and to secure all possible escape routes before smashing a window and throwing in a couple of smoke bombs to flush the inhabitants out into the open where we would be waiting for them. The last thing we wanted was a gunfight at the farm, which would attract the attention of people as to something going on at the farm and for that news to travel fast to members of the spy network. We also wanted to arrest all three suspects uninjured so that they could be interrogated immediately without any delay for any medical treatment.

Our plan was to advance towards the farmhouse under the cover of hedgerows and trees behind the farm until we had secured a cordon around the building, and the ruse was to get Constable Evans from Port Eynon to drop in on a supposedly routine call whilst he was passing and whilst they were distracted to smash the windows at the rear and throw in two smoke bombs to force the occupants out into the open, where they would find all chances of escape cut off by our men. Immediately upon arrest, they would be handcuffed and put into three separate closed vans for a fast journey, through the night, where Inspector Bennett would be ready with a team to begin the interrogation at Tiger Bay Police Station. Alicia, Ivor and I would drive back to Cardiff as well to be ready to join the interrogation team, whilst Aston and the Brecon men would search the farm thoroughly before withdrawing to Brecon. Our plan was to establish whether these three were foreign agents and to get them to break their silence on the leaders of the spy ring in return for not invoking a capital sentence, which was usual in such cases. We reckoned that the Crawford and King imposters would be easily exposed as frauds when we found that Crawford had two good legs and King could hear perfectly well, and we were hoping that the newcomer just arrived from the U-boat would not yet be so comfortable with his cover story that we could not easily break him. The whole operation was to be conducted in total secrecy so as not to alert the other members of the network that we were on to them so that we could round up all the suspects we had already identified, which might also lead us to other members or sympathisers that were unknown to us. If things went well for us tonight, I was confident that we would roll up the whole spy network in Wales within a few days.

The whole team was briefed at 17:00 hours by Inspector Bennett and myself and then we loaded up and left for the Gower by 18:00 and I knew that we would rendezvous at Port Eynon Police Station by 21:00 at the latest. Townley and his men would remain on watch at the farm until we moved in to join them by 22:00. At 22:30, Constable Evans would approach the front of the farmhouse on his bicycle and knock on the front door and alert the occupants that some of their sheep had strayed from the field and were in the road. This message was designed to induce them to leave the house and come out in the open to assist Evans in rounding up the sheep but if it didn't manage to get them to move, the smoke bombs would be thrown in through the rear windows and we would enter through the smoke, wearing smoke masks, to arrest the occupants of the house before they had time to realise who we were and pick up their weapons to defend themselves. Our men had been briefed that we were not to fire our weapons in any circumstances unless we were fired on first as we didn't wish to alert the local community that a police raid had taken place. The rendezvous with Townley and his men went as planned and we moved covertly to within a short distance of the rear of the house and waited for the flashlight signal from Evans that he was about to approach the front of the farmhouse. We waited another sixty seconds and then heard the knocking on the front door and Evans calling out that their sheep had got loose and were running away down the road. This did not seem to invoke much of a response from inside, so Evans renewed his efforts, banging on the door with greater force. Finally, we heard a muffled response from inside the house which sounded as if the occupants were reluctant to come out and I gave the signal for the smoke bombs to be deployed immediately. Two pistol butts smashed the glass in the windows and the smoke grenades were let off inside the downstairs of the house and a hefty police shoulder smashed into the back door and we piled into the kitchen with our pistols cocked and ready for use. We were easily able to identify the occupants because they were coughing and guttering as they tried to cope with the smoke hitting their lungs and making their eyes smart, whilst each member of my team had protection from a gas mask. Within two minutes, all three of them were restrained and handcuffed and placed in separate vans. Townley went immediately to the secret room he had observed over the past few days and on breaking open the door found a cache of weapons and explosives and a wireless transmitter with German Army labels on the casing. This discovery of German weapons was positive proof of enemy involvement and probably enough to secure a conviction for spying in court even without any of the other evidence, and I was certain of solving the mystery of the murders of the real Crawford and King and the involvement of the imposters in these killings.

 The vans set off for the long journey back to Cardiff, which would probably see them arrive at Tiger Bay Station by three in the morning and Bennett and his team would be ready to begin the interrogation immediately. Alicia and I drove back shortly after the vans had left but as our vehicle was faster than the vans, we should be in the police station with enough time to spare to brief the others before the interrogation began. The three suspects had been kept separate with no opportunity to communicate at all and had been given no information by us as to who we were and why they had been arrested. They were brought out of the vans singly and with blankets over their heads, so they were quite disorientated when they were booked in at the custody desk and placed in cold, damp cells within minutes of leaving the van.

TWELVE

The interrogation began in three separate interview rooms within fifteen minutes of their arrival in the station to allow them no chance to settle, orientate themselves or sleep. They were brought to the interview rooms singly with no chance of knowing whether their fellow suspects were even in the same police station or not. Alicia and I were to begin the examination of the third suspect, who we believed to have newly arrived by U-boat within the last twenty-four hours, whilst Inspector Bennett was taking Crawford and Detective Sergeant Powell was leading on King. Our suspect looked like a frightened rabbit and was pale and his eyes were roving around looking everywhere, attempting to gauge some idea of where he was and what was facing him. He was surprised to be faced with a man and a woman across the table who did not identify themselves and we were dressed in plainclothes and not military uniform, as he had probably expected. I led with the initial questions and Alicia sat back quietly making notes of what he said, and we hoped that our simple open questions would be enough to trip him up and give the game away. If he had arrived within the last thirty-six hours by U-boat, he would probably still be unsure about his cover story and know little of his location or compatriots, and we were sure that this provided us with the most leverage to get to the truth of his real identity. I opened the questioning by telling him that we were police detectives investigating the deaths of five people whose bodies had been recently discovered in a mass grave in a remote forest in the mountains near to Cardiff. I explained that the two men who he was staying with had come up in our enquiries as people we should speak to and who may have knowledge about some or all of these murders. Our interest was only in talking to these two men who lived at the farm, and we were surprised to find him staying there as well. "This was unexpected and we now have to conduct this straightforward interview to establish your identity and your connection to the other two men and eliminate you from our enquiries, which I hope we can do quite quickly and you will be free to go." This opening gambit seemed to be effective as we could see that he physically relaxed and became much less tense in his whole demeanour as a result. He seemed to have settled and, sighing a little, he looked confidently into my smiling face and I could see a growing sense of relief reflected in him as I looked back, and I was pleased because this relaxed air was exactly what I hoped to establish in him before we started the interrogation proper.

My first questions were purely straightforward and designed to put him at ease and I placed the statement form on the desk between us and asked him for his name to put at the head of the sheet. He answered immediately and confidently that he was Thomas O'Malley and I followed up by asking if he had any middle names and he shook his head. We knew now for definite that he was not O'Malley as he had been positively identified as one of the victims found in that hillside grave, and we knew from our records that O'Malley had two middle names, Edward and Francis. I pressed on by asking for his date of birth and for his home address, which he gave as 56 Bargoed Street, Newport, which we knew was the house where Ernest Sullivan lived and as far as we could ascertain O'Malley had never been a resident at this address. I thanked him for his personal details and casually dropped into my conversation that his name sounded Irish, but his accent didn't sound Irish at all. He said that he travelled a great deal with his work and had lost the Celtic lilt from his aspiration and his accent had become flattened out and sounded more English than anything. I asked what he did for a living, and he said he was a bookkeeper and helped small businesses keep their accounts in order. I followed on by asking him how he came to be at Llangellis Farm, not at home in Newport, when we came calling. He said that he had come to sort out the farm accounts at Mr Crawford's request but because of the distance from Newport, the job could not be completed in just one day. "So, you were unlucky to be staying over on the night we arrested Mr Crawford and his associate, Mr King." I asked him how Crawford had known about the accounting service he offered because Newport to the Gower Peninsular was hardly local and there may be similar services operating in the Swansea area which might have been more convenient for them. He looked a little confused and said he was recommended to them, and they had subsequently written to him asking for him to call at the farm and sort out the annual book returns. I remarked that he was lucky to have satisfied customers who would recommend him by word of mouth and that this sounded a great way to build his business. I asked if he knew who had recommended him and he said he thought that it was through Joachim Schultz, who worked for Sir Wilhelm Branden. Schultz could not have recommended anybody as he was, of course, another corpse in the mass grave at Talybont, but Sir Wilhelm's name had cropped up yet again at the heart of this affair. "So, you had never met Mr Crawford or King before yesterday when you travelled up from Newport. I suppose it must have been a long and tedious journey by train with all the connections that needed to be made to reach the Gower." He nodded his assent and we realised that he had no idea that the Red Dragon Express from London ran directly from Newport to Swansea. O'Malley was spinning us a pack of lies.

At this point, I indicated that I needed to leave the room for a few minutes and nodded to Alicia and went out into the corridor and closed the door behind me, but I didn't go anywhere but just waited in the passage whilst Alicia worked some magic with the suspect. As I left the room, O'Malley relaxed as if he was glad to have survived the questioning thus far when Alicia spoke softly to him in German suggesting that he was lucky that Detective Morgan was a fool who could not yet see the massive holes in the cover story they had given him. "O'Malley is lying on a slab in the mortuary in Brecon alongside the body of Joachim Schultz and it won't take the detective that long to work this out for himself." He replied in German and asked how she knew all this, and she said because she had been embedded within Cardiff Police for many years and reported back to Berlin. He asked what he had to do to get out of there and she moved closer to him and, speaking almost in a whisper, made it clear that the only way to make things go better for himself was to cooperate with the detective and tell him who he was and what he knew. "I am certain they will be lenient with you and make you a prisoner of war. If you are not cooperative, then they will almost certainly hang you as a spy before the end of this month." He was frightened now and stuttered that he couldn't betray his comrades and she reassured him that they would remain safe as she would warn them and tell them of his noble action of sacrificing himself so they could succeed with their mission. I showed my face at the window and Alicia knew to revert to her previous role and switched back to English and sat back in her chair.

Frantic thoughts were revolving in O'Malley's head, and he was totally confused about how he should proceed. She said, "What is your real name so I can report your brave actions back to our masters in Berlin?" and he whispered back that he was Leutnant Dieter Smitt of the Imperial Navy and had been sent here as a wireless specialist and asked that a message be sent to his parents that he was alive and well. Alicia smiled and switched back to English and expressed her thanks to Leutnant Smitt for giving her his real identity and she apologised for the little ruse that she was certainly not a German undercover agent but a British security police officer on the trail of enemy operatives in Britain and he had been most helpful. When I saw the suspect slump down with his head in his hands, I assumed that Alicia had got the vital information she was after so I re-entered the interview room. Alicia passed me a sheet of notepaper with his name and rank in the German Imperial Navy and without speaking his name out loud I went straight into the next line of questioning about how he had entered the country and made it to Llangellis Farm. I pressed him hard on his method of entry and after much probing he admitted that he had been landed by small boat from a German submarine at a beach near to the farm where he was apprehended. I pressed him harder on his relationship with the two men he was staying with at the farm but other than admitting that they were the two men who had guided him from the beach the night he was landed in Rhossili Bay, he said he had never met them before but assumed they were Germans as they both spoke the language like natives, but he only knew them by their code names of Crawford and King.

Alicia and I decided to take a short break and to leave him for thirty minutes or so to reflect on his situation as we checked the progress of the other two interviews. Inspector Bennett had ordered Crawford to remove his trousers so he could inspect his false leg and immediately discovered that he had two perfectly good legs, which blew his cover story completely and enabled him to move the questioning beyond that of his false identity. He quite clearly was not Crawford so who was he, where was the real Mr Crawford and why had he taken his identity? The suspect stubbornly declined to answer his questions until Bennett slapped down onto the desk between them photographs of the gravesite in Talybont and the bodies of Crawford and King lying on the slab in Brecon and Bennett asked if he recognised either of these two men. The suspect shook his head but looked shocked and pale when Bennett pointed out that the body on the left was Lieutenant Crawford, who he claimed to be, and that on the right was Lieutenant King, who his accomplice claimed to be. He went on to tell him that he had witnesses who would swear that the genuine Crawford and King were picked up outside the hospital, when they were discharged, by two men matching their descriptions. "Further to this we have evidence that two men claiming to be Crawford and King stayed at a hotel in Brecon near to the site where the bodies were discovered and that a vehicle matching the one that you have been driving was witnessed several times in the vicinity of the gravesite. You can also be linked to one of the other victims, Schultz, who was collected by two men calling themselves Crawford and King when he was released from police custody. All three of these men simply disappeared into thin air after contact with you and your friend." Bennett thumped the table and loudly stated that there was sufficient evidence to charge him and his associate with the murders of Crawford and King and he was satisfied that the court would find him guilty and the hangman's noose would be placed around his neck within a few short weeks.

Bryn Howells had used much the same technique when he interviewed the final suspect and began the interview with the report of the examination of the suspect by an ear, nose and throat specialist from the General Hospital to establish if he was deaf or not. Of course, the examination showed conclusively that there was little wrong with this man's hearing apart from a little earwax and that he was an imposter too. As pre-rehearsed, he followed the same line of questioning as the inspector, showing the gravesite and the bodies on the slab and reviewing how this powerful evidence would certainly lead to the gallows and a murderer's death at the end of the hangman's rope. We had all taken a break from the interrogations at the same time to give them a few moments to ponder on their situation now they were in the hands of the British police. Alicia explained how she had used her fluency in German to lull her suspect into relaxing his guard and revealing his true name and rank in the German Navy and confirmed that he was met by the two other suspects on the beach when he was brought ashore by small boat from a German submarine about thirty-six hours ago. He only knew the two others by their code names, Otto and Heinrich, and the adopted names they had been using whilst at the farm. Alicia was certain that because Otto and Heinrich were far more experienced, they would be unlikely to fall for the same ruse as Smitt but she was sure that with a little more pressure, Dieter Smitt would probably reveal all that he knew but indicated that the farm was not his final destination as he would only be staying at the farm until collected by his contact, known only as Oberst. We all agreed that it was clear that we had pulled off a major coup in arresting three German agents operating undercover and illegally in Wales, but this was not the time for celebration because we needed to break them as swiftly as possible before word of their arrest leaked out to the ears of the spy ring before we were ready to take decisive action against them.

On our return to the interview room, I had decided to treat Smitt with the respect due to an enemy officer and spoke politely to him but was also sure to remind him that he was facing not only charges relating to espionage and being an enemy spy, but he was also guilty of murder or at the very least of being an accomplice in the murders of five people, three of whom were members of his own network. I put it to him that if he cooperated with us in the matter of the murders and who his contacts were to be in the spy network, he would be treated as a prisoner of war and confined in a prisoner of war camp for German officers for the duration of the war. He looked crestfallen as the realisation hit him that he was dammed whichever way he went, so he chose to give up what he knew in the hope of favourable treatment from the British. He reckoned that the experience of studying for a course in naval signalling at Greenwich Naval College before the war had taught him that the British put great store by their sense of fair play and would probably treat him less severely if he gave them what they wanted. The change in him was miraculous as soon as he made his decision to make saving his own skin his priority, and he spilled out the whole story without too much prompting from us. He explained that he was a trained wireless expert and had been serving as a signals officer on a German battle cruiser until two weeks ago when he was ordered to attend a briefing and training at the Imperial Navy Intelligence School in Bremerhaven, where he was told that there was an urgent need to replace an undercover field operative working in Wales with a trained wireless and signals specialist who was also fluent in the use of English. He was briefed that there was a network of German agents working throughout all the seaports around the coast of Britain sending back vital information about the movement of ships to and from the major seaports, which provided valuable intelligence for the U-boat command to attack these ships and inflict considerable damage on the British war effort. He said he had been given few details about who he would be working with other than he would be met on the beach by Otto and Heinrich, who would hide him on their farm until he was collected by his contact, code-named Oberst, within a day or two of landing. He was given a passport in the name of Thomas O'Malley from the Irish Free State who had an address in Bargoed Street in a place called Newport, but he was always sceptical that this cover story would stand up to any real scrutiny. He believed that his English was good enough to pass himself off as English because he was fluent in the language and was such a good mimic of English pronunciation that he had been able to flatten his natural accent almost completely. He had had hardly any time to familiarise himself with the life of O'Malley before he was boarding U-467 in Bremerhaven to set off on his journey to the Welsh coast. He told us that he didn't know the real identities of Otto and Heinrich, but he believed that they were both from the German Army and that he should not worry about his cover identity because he would be working undercover and would not be mixing with British people outside of the network. I was satisfied that Dieter had told us everything that he knew and had only arrived in the country such a short time ago that he could not be complicit in the murders either. He had confirmed for us some useful pieces of information, though, which could prove to be useful tools to lever information from the other two suspects. We knew that they'd collected him from the beach and accommodated him at the farm and they had code names and were bi-lingual in German and English. Smitt suspected that they were from the German Army but was not certain, but we could be certain that they were a part of the German spy network, but also there was mounting evidence of their involvement in the actual murders or assisting in the murders of the five victims discovered at Talybont Forest just recently. Finally, we knew that there was a code name, Oberst, being used within the spy network, and it was vital to discover who this was and perhaps we would be able to squeeze a name out of Otto or Heinrich in the subsequent interrogations.

Otto was the first to be interviewed for a second time and straight away it was put to him that as we now knew that he was masquerading as a wounded British veteran whose body we had discovered in a mass grave on a remote Welsh hillside, we had no option but to charge him with the wilful murders of Lieutenant Crawford and Lieutenant King within the past nine weeks or so and he was probably involved in the murders of the three other victims found in the same grave. Inspector Bennett continued by saying that he had thought that Otto was probably a German officer bound by the kind of code of honour that decried common criminal activity such as these vicious murders, but he had assumed wrong. There was now little option for them but to be tried by military court at the earliest possible juncture and be put to death by the hangman's noose and buried in unconsecrated ground within the prison walls, which would be a dishonourable death for a German officer. Bennett then started to read out the charges but before he had got through even the first sentence Otto was protesting his innocence and, with tears in his eyes, he admitted that he was a German officer who would not stoop to murder or bring dishonour on his regiment or family in this way. Bennett stopped reading the charges and asked directly for his name, rank and number and received without hesitation the reply that he was Hauptmann Otto Ludwig von Aldmann and gave his service number. He said that he was a regular soldier and had been serving in a light cavalry regiment for six years until he was seconded to the Army Intelligence Corps at the beginning of the war. He was chosen for this work because he was fluent in English having spent many summers holidaying in England with his mother's relatives every year. He was prepared to admit that he was on active service in Wales as a German officer but was not prepared to answer any further questions about his current mission. However hard he was pressed, he would not even reveal the name of his compatriot Heinrich. He was fully prepared to accept whatever fate was coming to him now that he had admitted to being a German spy working undercover in Britain, but he would not accept the blame for murder. Bennett was not satisfied and pressed on, saying that even acknowledging that his code of honour precluded his involvement in vicious murder, there was enough compelling evidence of his involvement, even if he didn't perform the actual deed himself, to show that he was involved as an accessory to the five murders and that he would need to hear more from him before he could discount his liability in these killings. "If you didn't carry out the killings, then you must tell us who pulled the trigger because we know that you were there at the gravesite and were most probably present when the murders took place. Four names, including yours, linked to the German spy ring can be placed at the murder site at the date and times that the crimes were perpetuated, and if you want us to believe that you are innocent, you need to tell us who fired the fatal shots."

Bennett took a step back and left Hauptmann Aldmann to think over what he had said and then he pressed forward again with a theory of his own. Inspector Bennett extrapolated that he was certain as to what had happened in all five cases and that he had four names already in the frame and that he was one of them. There was, of course, King, O'Malley and a mysterious Irishman called Sullivan, who had a long track record of violence and was the probable murderer. "I believe that all four of you worked together under the direction of Sullivan to carry out these murders." Aldmann looked completely deflated and all trace of the confidence he had earlier displayed vanished completely and he placed his head in his hands and mumbled in German to himself. Bennett turned the screw further and pressed him even harder and said that he should not take us for fools. We could work out exactly what had transpired and his involvement as an enemy agent operating secretly in Britain in the spying activity had led to the loss of British merchant ships and the deaths of merchant sailors as well as the murder of five victims, two of whom were wounded British veterans who had served with distinction in the trenches. He challenged, as a cowardly defence, his assertion that common murder was against his code of honour as a German officer when he had already broken that code by serving as a spy. Bennett stood up and walked to the door and threw a last remark back at Aldmann that he would be glad to see him dangling at the end of the hangman's rope within a few days for the crimes he had committed. As he passed through the door, and in a loud voice, he instructed the constable to return the prisoner to his cell to await his appearance before the military court in a couple of days. The interview had not delivered the full results that he had been expecting and he was surprised that Aldmann had not revealed that Sullivan was the assassin even though all the evidence pointed directly to him as the most likely culprit.

Bryn Howells was using similar tactics with Heinrich but was content to be less aggressive and more amenable in his approach to the suspect than his boss had been with Otto. He started gently by making a retrospect of what we had already clearly established as the truth. First, we were certain that he was not Lieutenant King but an imposter masquerading as the unfortunate British officer who lay dead in the morgue at Brecon. In addition, the medical examination of his eardrums showed that his hearing was perfect, and this was the second convincing proof that he was not who he claimed to be. Finally, his compatriots, in whose company he was arrested, had both admitted to being German officers working as spies in this country. Howells continued in a friendly manner that there was little point in denying that he was also a German spy, and he would be obliged if he would give his name, rank and number. Howells further pointed out that enemy spies were usually shot by firing squad but those who cooperated and told us what we wished to know could be sentenced to imprisonment as prisoners of war and sent to an officers' camp where the likelihood was that they would be repatriated at the end of the war. "Your comrades have chosen the path of cooperation so there is little point in holding out alone and facing the hangman whilst your friends enjoy the prospect of a return to their homes and family after hostilities cease." Howells pretended to shuffle through his papers and the ensuing silence gave Heinrich a few moments to reflect on what he had just said until Bryn started to lay on the table photographs of the corpses recovered from the gravesite at Talybont Forest and swivelled them round so that the prisoner could see them clearly. Howells went silent again for twenty seconds or so before asking what he could tell us about these murder victims and how they came to their end on the remote wooded hillside in Talybont Forest. Before Heinrich could deny any knowledge of the murders, Bryn reminded him that he was in possession of compelling evidence that linked Heinrich directly to these murder victims and he pointed to each photograph as he named the victims. "The first two are Crawford and King, the wounded officers whose identities you have stolen and who disappeared the day they left hospital and were seen in the company of two men answering the descriptions of you and your comrade. The third photograph is of Joachim Schultz, and we have a report from the local constable from Port Eynon that Mr Schultz was visiting your farm on the same day as Constable Evans paid you a welcome call. The constable will swear that the man he met at your farm is the one shown in this photograph and coincidently when Schultz was released from police custody after the charge of rape against him was withdrawn by Heidi, the man who signed the release paper was you. The fourth victim is Heidi Schultz, his wife, and we are certain that they were both members of the spy network that you are part of. The fifth victim is Thomas O'Malley, who can be linked to you through a random road check carried out by the night watch constable on the high road close to the forest where the bodies were discovered when your van was parked late at night by the side of the main road, and you were inside in the company of O'Malley and another man called Sullivan. We also have evidence that you and Sullivan stayed at the same hotel in Brecon on several occasions and once when O'Malley was there too."

Bryn Howells leant back in his chair and then continued in the same pleasant tone that he was now left in a quandary because his lack of willingness to cooperate and identify himself left him with no alternative but to prosecute him as a common murderer as there was a mountain of evidence to secure a guilty verdict from the court and a date with the executioner. "If you are open with me and admit that you are a German officer and a spy like your comrades then I can deal with you on the charge of espionage, and if you cooperate fully, we are willing to be lenient with those who help us put the real culprits out of action, but if you persist with silence then you will be tried for the five murders within a matter of days." King jumped up out of his chair in loud protest that we couldn't do this to him as he was a German officer and bound by the highest code of military behaviour, and he was still shouting and protesting his innocence when Bryn and the guard constable forced him to sit back down in his chair. Bryn warned him that if there was any further outburst, he would be handcuffed to the chair, and he subsided to silence again. Bryn acknowledged that they were now making progress and the biggest hurdle, the admission that he was a German officer and obviously a spy, was now over so there was no obstacle to answering his questions further, starting with his name, rank, etc. He then reluctantly admitted that he was a *hauptmann* engineer, and his name was Berthold von Passman and he was a member of military intelligence. Howells immediately sprang back at him, "But why did you murder Lieutenants Crawford and King? You should be careful how you reply because there is more than enough evidence to secure your conviction for these murders." He bridled again but remained seated and raised his voice, saying that he was a military officer with expertise with explosives and sabotage and had been sent to Wales to conduct attacks against military targets as a legitimate wartime activity and not to murder innocent people. Howells replied quietly that he could only accept that as an answer if it was backed up with definite confirmation as to who did commit the murders. "We know that all five victims had been shot in the back of the head, execution style, and forensic analysis of the bullets suggested that they were all fired from the same weapon, which was a German Luger pistol. We have evidence which places you at or near the gravesite and the site of the hidden arms cache at the same time as O' Malley and Sullivan, so if you wish to prove your innocence, you must tell us more or we shall be unable to help you." I could see Passman working out in his head the risks he faced by cooperating or not and then he slowly revealed that the orders for the killings came from the colonel, who always made use of the Irishman, Sullivan, as his proxy assassin.

"Sullivan was a rough and violent man who would shoot anyone if he was paid for it and was completely without honour. We hated having to work with him, but we had little choice because he and the colonel had a close relationship stretching back over many years and it was well known they had worked together to steal arms shipments destined for Irish rebels from the German military and had secretly become very rich."

Howells knew that this confirmed the rumours we had already heard about how Sullivan had defrauded his old comrades in the Irish Freedom Movement, but had no idea who this German accomplice was as he quietly slipped in the question, "Did this person have the code name Oberst?" Passman could not control the surprise in his face and although he denied knowing anything about code names, Howells knew he was lying and went on to ask for the name that his colonel used and how he kept in contact with him. He clammed up immediately and I thought he was not going to say anything further but after thirty seconds or so he said that he did not know his name but only knew that he was a lawyer and we could contact him via a PO box for a holding company in Cardiff. However hard Bryn tried, he was unable to get Passman to say any more. Howells was delighted because resulting from this interview he was now certain that Oberst was probably the lawyer, Kruger, and the holding company was Wurtenberg Holdings, and he was anxious to return Passman to his cell as soon as possible so that he could share what he had discovered with the rest of the team.

Our team briefing was lively and exciting as we felt that we had cracked this case wide open and would be ready to pounce on the members of the spy ring and bring them into custody almost immediately. We had three German officers in custody who had admitted spying for our enemy and clear information that the leader of the spy ring was another German officer, Oberst, who was most likely Kruger, and Sullivan was now the prime suspect for the murders of all five victims. All the suspects had been linked via Wurtenberg Holdings, which appeared to be the likely vehicle used for managing the work of the spy ring in open sight. Bennett was satisfied that we had progressed far enough to begin planning a coordinated arrest operation to bring all the suspects into police custody in one smooth operation. He stressed that the manpower requirements alone made this a mammoth operation and it was imperative that we acted in a totally coordinated manner so that none of the spy ring network were able to escape. The resources required to do this were greater than he could muster on his own authority so he had decided to contact Colonel Stewart, Major Harcourt-Evans and the Brecon chief constable as well as Admiral Hastings to discuss thoroughly how we could work together to pull this off secretly in one smooth operation. We were certain that the spy ring leadership were still unaware that Otto and Heinrich and the new arrival were already in police custody, and we decided to alert Constable Evans at Port Eynon to stake out the farm in the likelihood that

Oberst or his representative appeared at the farm to collect Dieter Smitt. If such a person arrived at Llangellis Farm, he was to be quickly apprehended and placed in custody to prevent him sending any messages back to the spy ring leadership. We doubted that Kruger himself would perform this task but expected he would send someone of much lower status who would not attract too much attention. Meanwhile, the Brecon contingent were ordered to redouble their efforts to locate and detain Sullivan as quickly as possible. Colonel Stewart gave his approval for the planning of codename "Operation Wurtenberg", to be launched within twenty-four hours, and the Brecon force allocated twenty officers led by Aston, and the navy directed a company of marines to be placed under Colonel Stewart's command in case there was a need for military force to secure the arrests. We were aware that this spy ring had not been averse to using violence to protect themselves in the past and were well equipped with arms and explosives, so the likelihood of armed resistance was quite high.

Bryn Howells was to lead a team of ten police constables from Cardiff to raid Sullivan's address in Bargoed Street, Newport, although we were not in possession of any firm knowledge that he would be there, and then to arrest David Taylor and Jonathan Pugh, who were also residents of Newport. Inspector Aston was to link up with the officers from Port Eynon and secure the site at Llangellis Farm and take into custody any courier sent to collect Smitt if he or she arrived at the farm at all. In addition, it was vital to thoroughly search the farm and surrounding land for any intelligence which might lead to the arrest of hitherto unknown members of the spy ring and reveal further information about German codes and communications with U-boats operating in Welsh waters. Alicia was to lead another ten officers to raid the registered offices of Wurtenberg Holdings and arrest the Matthiases and anyone else found there. Again, these premises were to be thoroughly searched for incriminating evidence against the members of the board of the holding company and their employees. Ivor was given the task of arresting the Grubers at their father's tailor's shop, although it was expected that Manfred Gruber would not be there and would probably be arrested alongside Hilda Williams and Sir Wilhelm Branden at the Dock Company offices. Inspector Bennett would lead the marines into the docks to throw a security cordon around the Dock Company headquarters, where he could arrest the three suspects without any chance of their escape. I was given the task of bringing in Oberst, or Anton Kruger as he was known to us, and we expected to find him at his law office in central Cardiff, although a back-up team would stake out his home address in the case that we did not find him at his offices. I selected four burly constables from the Tiger Bay station who I knew were expert in the use of firearms as I felt that there was a good chance of some resistance from Kruger. The operation was planned to be launched at 08:00 the following morning and the raids were timed to be coordinated at 09:00 exactly, which would give time for them all to have reached work or started their day's business before we struck. Colonel Stewart said that all the suspects arrested were to be held at Llanthony House, where there were sufficient cells available in the basement to hold them securely and adequate interview rooms and accommodation for the interrogation team to be housed. Sergeant Major Martin would head the security team and Major Harcourt-Evans and Inspector Bennett would lead the questioning.

The prospect of decisive action on our part in the morning excited me greatly and I was also happy because I managed to get a spare hour to spend alone with Alicia as the pressure of work over the past couple of days had kept us apart. We were unable to slope off to some private place to make love as too many of our colleagues were around, but we managed to find a quiet corner to sit and drink some tea together and talk quietly. She was excited because she had a major role in tomorrow's operation too and we discussed how this was the first time, since the team was formed, that we had taken major action singly instead of in a team effort. We knew that this was a kind of test or opportunity for us to show Colonel Stewart what we were capable of achieving and we both sincerely hoped that we could do well, rise to the occasion and show what we had learnt. We were coming to the end of our first big operation, the success of which we hoped might have a significant impact on the progress of the war and provide a stepping stone for better things for both of us in our careers. Our hearts were racing as we turned in for an early night as we needed to be on the move by 05:30 and at allocated start points by 08:00. There was a lot to do in the morning including the issuing of arms and ammunition to be ready to go on time. As I climbed the stairs to my room, I saw the headlines on a discarded newspaper which heralded the start of a great battle on the Somme in Belgium, and I realised that so much of my time had been taken up with this case that I had completely lost track of what was happened more generally in the war. I read the story of the commencement of the allied attack along the Somme with interest and sadly reflected that my brothers Cliff and Dylan would be there with their regiment, the South Wales

Borderers, who would almost certainly be playing a major part in the battle. I read through the analysis of the strategy employed by the British Second Army and prayed inwardly that they would be safe and survive the battle without major injury and come home safely to Mum and Dad. I thought too of many other boys and men who came from the valleys who were serving in this Brecon-based regiment and prayed that the loss of life would not be too catastrophic in the home villages.

THIRTEEN

I didn't sleep well because the level of excitement was too great, and I only managed an interrupted and fitful night's sleep but after a hot breakfast and a mug of tea I was feeling wide awake and ready for the day's action. I signed out a Webley Mark VI pistol from the armoury and five magazines which contained thirty rounds all told and my four compatriots withdrew the same weapons and ammunition but, in addition, I also took some small explosive charges and two smoke grenades in case we needed to make a forced entry into Kruger's premises. I hoped that we would be able to arrest Kruger without the use of violence, but we knew that Kruger was a trained soldier and may well be prepared to resist arrest violently. We made a careful approach towards Kruger's law offices so as not to attract too much attention and managed to park the unmarked vehicles within a hundred yards of his premises in a location that enabled us to maintain a good view of the front entrance to the building. We knew that his offices occupied the ground floor of the three-storey building which had been converted from a large family residence into business premises sometime in the past, and I reckoned that there would be a rear exit from his premises leading into an alleyway between the adjoining buildings from the next street. I sent Constable Howe to place himself in the alleyway behind Kruger's offices to prevent the rear exit being used as a possible escape route. We settled down to watch the front of the building and waited patiently for the appointed time to move in and arrest Kruger at the exact same time as the other arrests were taking place by the other teams. I knew that Howe was a strong and reliable officer who would stand his ground but would not do anything rash if faced with Kruger fleeing through the back gate. He would alert us by blowing his whistle three times and would follow the suspect at a discreet distance until we arrived to back him up. The hands of my pocket watch were moving so slowly, and I had slipped it out of my waistcoat pocket three times already and it was not yet twenty past eight. I wondered whether I could contain my impatience for a further forty minutes when Jones, who was driving that day, nudged me and pointed to a taxicab pulling up at the front of the building and Kruger got out and climbed the steps and entered the double front doors. This brought me back to reality for I realised that if I had allowed my impatience to take over, I could have led a raid on the offices before the target had even arrived in the building and I would have messed up the whole operation before it had even begun. I wondered if Alicia and Ivor were feeling the same way but realised that they would both be cool and calm and obey the orders as given.

Several other people entered the building after Kruger but none of them looked familiar to me as members of the Wurtenberg group and we had no way of knowing whether they were entering Kruger's premises or the other businesses operating on the upper floors. I was concerned to know how many, if any, innocent people were in the building and especially in Kruger's offices as I was aware that we needed to protect lives in the event of a firefight breaking out. My plan was to affect the arrest of Kruger without the use of force and to remove him from the premises and into our enclosed van as quickly as possible to be driven away on his journey to Llanthony House with the minimum of fuss. We waited for the hands of my watch to click round to nine o'clock and we quickly made our move and three of us deployed up the steps and into the front entrance, leaving Jones to cover our backs outside the front door and Howe at the back of the premises. We had all checked our pistols were loaded and ready to fire but kept them concealed under our coats when we entered the reception area of the law firm. A pleasant young woman greeted us and asked if we had an appointment and I replied that I was Detective Wesley Morgan and I wished to see Anton Kruger and she replied that Mr Kruger was busy with a client but if we would like to wait, she would see if he could fit us in after he had finished his consultation with Mr Sullivan. My ears pricked up when I heard this name and I hoped that this was not just a coincidence and this Sullivan was just a legitimate client, so I asked the receptionist whether this client was Mr Ernest Sullivan from Newport and she confirmed that it was and now I was worried whether we had enough of us to arrest them both together that morning. I was in a quandary as to whether to make a call to the station for back-up or to strike whilst the iron was hot and attempt to arrest them both immediately. I made my decision quickly and we drew our weapons and removed the safety catches and told the receptionist to take herself out of the front of the building and down the steps and to wait there until we had completed our work. We advanced to the heavy wooden door marked with Anton Kruger's nameplate and I hammered on the front panel and shouted that it was the police, and they should come out with their hands up, which was immediately answered by two shots that punched holes in the sturdy woodwork of the door. It would have been close if we had not moved to the sides of the door immediately after hammering and the bullets passed harmlessly in front of us. I kicked at the door with all the force I could muster, and it immediately sprang open, and I was glad that it was not locked and so offered little resistance. In a split second, I took in the scene before me as the two occupants of the room clambered out of the window into the garden with as great a speed as they could manage in such a confined space. I did not recognise the first man, who was already three-quarters of the way through the window and was holding a Luger pistol in his right hand, but I assumed that he was Sullivan, but I had no doubts about the second man, who was wearing the formal morning dress of a lawyer and whom I clearly recognised as Kruger who I had met when he had represented Schultz on the rape charges a few weeks earlier. Sullivan tried to fire off another shot at the three of us as we burst through the door, but Constable Hughes returned a single shot which hit Kruger in the back of his left leg and prevented him from making good his escape. Sullivan was now free of the window and leapt over the wall into the garden and hurried towards the back gate, where I knew Constable Howe was posted. I left Constable Lewis to administer first aid to Kruger after securing him with handcuffs and Hughes and I went out of the window in pursuit of Sullivan, feeling there was still a good chance that we would be able to apprehend him before he could get away. The bolts on the back gate only held up Sullivan's flight by a few seconds and he was out into the back alley, and we immediately heard Howe's brisk and confident challenge for Sullivan to stop and lay down his weapon followed by an exchange of shots. I feared the worst as Sullivan was a practised killer and we came through the door cautiously with our weapons ready to fire and my heart sank when I saw Howe slumped on the floor and Sullivan running hard and about to turn out of the alley and out of view about one hundred yards ahead. I knew that there was little chance of pursuing him from this far behind because he would soon be lost in the warren of back alleys that afforded access to the tradesman's entrances of the grand houses in this district. We turned our attention to Constable Howe, who was by now clambering to his feet apologising for not stopping the fugitive, but I told him he had done well and I could see he had taken a bullet in his left shoulder, which needed some treatment. Thankfully, it was only a flesh wound and although he would be sore for a few days there would be no permanent damage, and I cheered him up when I told him that our operation was completely successful as we had our target in custody.

Kruger was sat behind his desk looking somewhat dejected and sorry for himself as his hands were securely manacled and a tourniquet had been applied to his leg to stop the blood flowing from the gunshot wound he had received in the fleshy part of his left calf, which had bled profusely on the carpet. I addressed him formally and told him he was being arrested under suspicion of espionage and murder under the terms of the Defence of the Realm Act and would be held in custody until he could be tried by military court. He said he was a respectable member of the Cardiff legal profession and was innocent of all charges and protested his innocence and was still complaining loudly about being shot and treated so badly by the police, who acted without evidence as we escorted him out into the street and locked him into the rear of the Black Maria van. Hughes and Lewis got into the cab of the van and would convey the prisoner to Llanthony House whilst Jones and I dropped Howe at the General Hospital and then followed on behind them. The escape of Sullivan preyed on my mind and the disappointment of being unable to arrest him as well struck me as a failure but when I mentioned this to Jones, he said I was being too hard on myself. We did not expect Sullivan to be there and if we had expected to find him at that location, we would have come with more men and secured a greater perimeter before entering the building. I knew that his opinion was right, but I still subsided into silence and went over it all again in my mind as we travelled the valley road to the Black Mountains, and I was only shaken out of my reverie when we pulled into the driveway leading up to Llanthony House and stopped at a newly erected checkpoint manned by soldiers in uniform under the command of Sgt. Major Martin, who checked us off his list and directed us to the rear of the house where we could book our prisoner into the custody suite in the basement of the main house.

It appeared that we were the first to arrive with our prisoner and I hoped that this was not a sign of a lack of success with the other operations but purely a coincidence, but I did manage to feel a little more positive because we had the probable leader of the spy network in custody and whatever happened with the arrest of the remainder of his team, it was a major blow to the German undercover operations in Wales. Kruger was brought from the van and booked into the facility and once he had been thoroughly searched and his wound tended to by the doctor, he would be stripped and given a prison smock to wear and placed in an isolation cell. All the prisoners would be treated the same way and they would be held in isolation for the whole time they were in custody to avoid any chance of communication between them. It was a deliberate policy to keep them isolated and disorientated with no knowledge of who from their network had been arrested and who had got away. As soon as Kruger was dealt with and securely locked in his cell, a convoy of three vans arrived at the basement entrance and Ivor came through the door with a beaming smile on his face and confirmed that he had Helmut, Friedrich and Joachim Gruber in the vans outside, and the custody sergeant requested that he would deal with each singly. Helmut was brought out of the first van looking a sorry and disheartened figure, still dressed in his tailor's apron with tape measure around his neck and black sleeves over his shirt and as he looked up, he saw me and stumbled and let out a stifled cry as he recognised his original tormentor from months ago. His facial expression now changed to one of complete despair as if he realised that there was no way out of the situation that he now found himself in. Whilst Helmut was being processed, Ivor told me how smoothly his operation had gone as he had split his team to enter through the shop and from the rear courtyard behind the stables to ensure all inhabitants of the premises were caught. The Grubers' security was risible and they were taken completely by surprise and were hustled out and into the vans within a couple of minutes, leaving a small team to search the premises thoroughly for further evidence of their collusion and involvement in spying. I briefly told Ivor about the firefight and wounding of Kruger as he tried to escape and our surprise at finding Sullivan at the same premises and how he had fired three shots at us and exchanged fire with Howe, wounding him slightly, and got away. The two Gruber brothers were brought out individually and booked in after their father had been locked in his cell and, within twenty minutes, they were locked down too and they awaited the arrival of the next set of prisoners, which turned out to be both Matthias doctors, Sabine and Julius, who were booked in separately, fitted out in prison uniforms and locked in their solitary cells. Alicia had led her team well and managed to take the Matthias doctors completely by surprise and she too had left officers searching the Matthias house and the Wurtenberg Holdings documents for further intelligence of the German spying activities.

I was pleased to see Alicia had suffered no setbacks, but she was concerned when she heard that my team had come under fire from Sullivan when arresting Kruger.

Over an hour later, two naval trucks arrived containing Sir Wilhelm Branden and Hilda Williams, guarded by a platoon of marines and accompanied by Inspector Bennett, who was extremely annoyed that Manfred Gruber had slipped from their grasp. He was apparently out of the office delivering his daily shipping schedules to the various departments when the raid had started and had appeared to realise quickly that he was under threat of arrest and had used his familiarity with the layout of the docks to evade capture and had slipped away unseen. Despite thorough searches by the marines, he could not be found anywhere in the dock area and Bennett had already issued his description to all South Wales police stations to be on the lookout for him. He was even angrier when he heard that Sullivan was also on the loose and hoped that they would not be able to link up and continue to run the spying operations in secret. Branden was processed first and protested loudly that he was a knight of the realm and a man of some standing in Wales, but this cut no ice with the sergeant booking him in, who gave him a cuff around the ear and told him to shut up his noise and begin to cooperate. Branden quietened down a little after the ringing in his ears subsided as he began to realise that his protests meant nothing to these ruffians in uniform and withstood the indignity of the stripping of his fine clothes and putting on the rough prison attire and he was escorted to his solitary confinement. Hilda, on the contrary, carried herself with dignity and confidence throughout, which showed the strength of her character compared to that of her boss. She was resigned to the treatment that would be meted out to her by the British authorities but was, in no measure, ashamed of her role as a German spy and was proud of her part in working against her enemies for the good of her motherland.

Bryn Howells' team had yet to report in, but they had to effect the arrests of three suspects at different locations which would take more time, and we knew that the arrest of their principal target would be abortive because we now knew that he was not in Newport but in Cardiff that morning. However, we expected that they would be arriving soon with Pugh and Taylor in their custody and Inspector Bennett suggested that the interrogators should see the housekeeper and get the keys for their rooms and relax for a few hours until all suspects were safely locked up, when he would call a briefing after dinner to plan our strategy for the initial questioning which would begin that night. I was given the same room that I had occupied during training, and it felt a bit like coming home as it was certainly more luxuriously appointed than my room in the section house. I threw myself onto the bed and was asleep within minutes as all the tension of the day drained away as I sunk into the soft warmth of the mattress.

When I woke, it was well over two hours since I had lay down and I felt as if my batteries were recharged enough to be able to face the rest of the day and I made my way downstairs to find out what was happening. Bryn Howells was the first person I met on the stairs, and he confirmed that Taylor and Pugh had been safely apprehended and he had left half his team to search the three addresses in Newport thoroughly whilst he had brought his prisoners to Llanthony. He was just going to his room to freshen up before dinner at seven and the inspector would brief us in the main library at eight-thirty. I found Ivor and Alicia already in the lounge and I was happy to talk over the events of the day with them and enjoy a pot of tea as we waited for dinner. They said that there was still no word from Aston, who was at Llangellis, but it was expected that he would report in later that evening. I was glad of a good hot meal as I didn't realise until I sat down how hungry I was, and the meal passed off with everyone in high spirits as we had pulled off a major strike against the enemy spy ring that day. Inspector Bennett was accompanied by the colonel, Admiral Hastings and a marine major when he called the briefing meeting to order, and he began by giving a brief account of results of the operations carried out. We had achieved nearly all of our targets and apprehended everyone except for Sullivan and Manfred Gruber, and he indicated that there was already a massive manhunt underway to secure their arrests as soon as possible. He said he was proud to say that the day had provided a blueprint for successful combined operations between the secret security service, the police and the Royal Navy, which enabled us to put enough resources in the field at one time to mount such a large operation. He thanked all who took part for a professional job that was well done and hoped that this would prove to be a successful model for future cooperation. The police were engaged in detailed searches at all the premises raided that day and we expected to find further evidence of the operations carried out by German spies in our region. "We have yet to hear from the team led by Inspector Aston, who are searching Llangellis Farm, but I am sure we will hear from them as soon as they discover anything of significance for us."

He then went on to set out the methodology for the questioning of the prisoners and allocated pairs to conduct the interrogations. "It is important to disorientate the prisoners as much as possible and to that end their cells have no natural lighting, and the electricity is controlled by us to give them a false sense of time. They will have no idea how long they will have been in custody and will lose track of what day it is very quickly. This will take its toll on us as well as we will be interrogating our prisoners at all times of the day and night, so we must rest between questioning sessions and always appear fresh and smart in direct contrast to their increasing debilitation. The cells are bare of any comforts or furniture and there will be no heating provided, although they will receive food and water every day. Do not feel sorry for them and always remember that these people are our enemies, who have contributed to the deaths of many merchant seamen and at least five murder victims too. We have already discovered that the sleepers are of German origin, and we need to establish that they are living under their real names, which I think is probably true in most cases. However, those of you assigned to the leaders, Kruger and Branden, will need to attempt to break them to gain further knowledge of the extent of the German spy network in Wales. Although we may think we have achieved a major success in arresting this large group of enemy agents, we must not be too optimistic as they may only represent one cell and we may be able to secure information which will lead to the discovery of other spies operating in Wales that we are not yet aware of." He concluded by saying that Inspector Aston had reported in during the late afternoon and had discovered significant intelligence that required our urgent action and this development had caused us to delay the questioning of Kruger and Branden for twenty-four hours, although all of the interrogations of the other prisoners could begin immediately after this briefing. "Aston has uncovered a secret radio and German naval code books which contain details of the next U-boat landing in Rhossili Bay for 23:30 tomorrow night. It is our intention, with the help of the Royal Navy, to apprehend the German agent as he comes ashore and capture the U-boat and crew whilst they are vulnerable in the shallow waters of the bay. Wesley, Alicia and Bryn will accompany me on this operation and Ivor Bethal will take charge of the questioning in our absence."

After the briefing was complete, the team split into their pairs to begin the interrogations of their allotted prisoners and a precise operation coordinated by the sergeant major swung into operation to deliver the selected prisoners to the right interview room without them having any contact with any of their fellow prisoners. Meanwhile, Inspector Bennett gathered the three of us in a corner of the sitting room to tell us what little he knew about the action the following night in Rhossili Bay and suggested we get a good night's sleep as we would leave for Cardiff at 06:00 to rendezvous with the Trafalgar Company, Royal Marines and Colonel Stewart for a full briefing at naval headquarters at 10:00. The decoded radio messages indicated the arrival of another German agent, code-named Timo, who would be brought ashore from U-65 as near to 23:30 as was possible. The U-boat commander would signal the letter M three times at intervals of ten seconds and wait for the acknowledgment signal T five times before sending the boat onto the shore. Our plan would be to acknowledge from the beach and be ready to receive Timo when he stepped ashore and for the navy to station two frigates close by to block the U-boat's escape into deeper water and to attempt to capture the submarine and her crew intact.

Even though it was now moving from spring towards summer, the early morning temperatures in the Black Mountains were cold and damp and I made sure that I was well wrapped up and had eaten a hot breakfast with two mugs of tea before setting off for Cardiff. Luckily, all four of us were able to get into Inspector Bennett's police car and we were soon asleep as his driver took us down the windy lane from Llanthony to Abergavenny seventeen miles away and then via Crickhowell to join the Heads of the Valleys Road to take us to the capital. The body heat of five of us in the cab of the car soon warmed us through and the journey passed pleasantly enough, and I was pleased that Alicia sat between the inspector and I and when she fell asleep, she leant close into me, and I enjoyed the feel and smell of her all the way. The driver was very good at his job and handled the car so well that we arrived at naval headquarters safely and in good time, refreshed and ready for the briefing. Colonel Stewart opened the briefing with an overview of what we intended to achieve and then invited Admiral Hastings and Inspector Bennett to fill in the details of their respective parts of the operation. The marine company was going to split into two parts of two platoons each under the command of a lieutenant. The first two platoons were going to support Inspector Bennett and his team on the ground to secure Llangellis Farm and the coastline either side of the target landing beach, whilst the other two platoons would embark on the frigates to provide possible boarding parties to capture the U-boat before it could make an escape or scuttling charges set off to destroy the submarine. It was imperative to capture the U-boat in one piece if we could as we were certain there was much to learn from what we would find inside. The captain must be prevented from jettisoning the ship's log and code books, etc., in the weighted bag as these documents could be vital to discovering how the U-boats maintained contact with their agents ashore and assist us in discovering the disposition of the U-boat fleet around our shores. *HMS Welshpool* and *HMS Porthcawl* would be on station on either side of Rhossili Bay ready to move in fast once the U-boat was stopped on the surface with a small boat in the water. The marine wireless operator attached to Inspector Bennett's team would signal the frigates once the U-boat's acknowledgment signal had been received and replied to from the beach, and the frigates would race in at full speed to block any attempt at escape by the U-boat, and it was hoped that a boarding party of marines would be put aboard the submarine to secure her crew as prisoners of war and bring her into the nearest naval port. If the U-boat managed to reach water deep enough to dive, both frigates were armed with depth charge bombs and were authorised to attack and sink the submarine to prevent its escape to the open sea. The admiral stressed that this would be a fine conclusion to their involvement in this joint operation led by the security police against enemy agents operating in Wales and wished us all luck.

Inspector Bennett went through our part next, which was to secure the capture of agent Timo and the boat crew from the U-boat and to extract them from the beach to the security of Llangellis Farm as quickly as possible. The inspector warned us of complacency and reminded us that although we had ten German spies in custody and under interrogation, we could be sure that we had not yet arrested every German agent working in our area. "We know for sure that Ernest Sullivan and Manfred Gruber are still free, and we have no intelligence as to their whereabouts, but we do know for certain that they are both men capable of violence, including the murder of innocent people, to secure their safety. They have managed to remain at large since the arrest of the remainder of their network which possibly suggests that there may be others, agents or sympathisers, who they are able to turn to for help to hide them safely from capture until things quieten down."

We were dismissed to share an excellent lunch in the naval mess and at 14:00 our team left Cardiff for Llangellis Farm. I collected our car from the Tiger Bay police station and Alicia and I travelled up together, whilst the Inspector and Bryn travelled in their car. It would only be a short detour to collect our car and I reckoned that we would arrive at the farm only ten minutes or so after them. It was great to be able to be alone together as the hectic pace of the last week or so had necessarily kept us apart and I was missing the lovely sensual nights we had spent together in Brecon and longed for them to return. We talked a lot as I drove, and I was sure that Alicia was missing our intimacy too and we started making plans how we could be together without attracting the attention of our colleagues and breaching police regulations. The simple solution could be that one or both of us left the police service and then we would be free to pursue our romantic relationship as we pleased, but we both felt fully committed to a career in police work and felt that there was a bright future for both of us as detectives. To stay in the police and to remain lovers or develop beyond the simple sexual aspect would mean no longer working together on the same team and maybe that might prove a suitable solution. Neither of us really wanted to give up working together because we felt we were a good team who brought different strengths to our working partnership, which had been proven to achieve positive results already, but we realised that this would be the only likely remedy for our present situation unless the police changed their regulations, which we didn't think would happen in the foreseeable future. It was a refreshing change to talk about ourselves rather than the case and it lightened our mood considerably to be thinking about our future, and I felt glad that Alicia thought that we did have a future together.

Aston and his team were still pulling Llangellis Farm apart inch by inch in their search for more evidence of enemy activity when we arrived and had uncovered more weapons of German origin and a large stock of explosives and detonators in the secret room behind the slurry pit. The local vet had been called in to foster out the animals on the farm to local farmers and he was loading a dozen sheep and four goats into a truck in the farmyard when we arrived and had already rehomed two pigs and four cows earlier in the day. Aston greeted us warmly and I realised how much I had come to like him from the short time we had worked together on this case, and he filled us in on everything they had discovered at the farm. As he showed us around, I noticed four trucks with naval markings parked at the rear of the farmhouse and could see that they had already set up a field kitchen and were busy preparing a hot meal for us all before our nighttime operations. Most of the marines were gathered in a semicircle around a large board and easel and a young lieutenant was talking them through their positions, which were marked on a large military map displayed on the board. He was taking questions from the men gathered around him and was illustrating his answers on the map, and I was reassured that they seemed to know exactly what to do. I was impressed with their professionalism and knew that the chances of a successful outcome that night had been increased significantly by their support. Our final stop was the farmhouse itself and the main living room had been thoroughly searched so was now being used by the police team as the command hub, and we were able to find a small space to sit down and collect our thoughts quietly before the evening meal.

After a hearty meal of beef stew and vegetables, I certainly felt that the lining of my stomach was full and radiating warmth throughout my whole body and I had enough fuel in me to cope with that night's operation. At 22:00, we went through a weapon's check to ensure that the firing mechanisms were working freely and were fully loaded and that we had spare magazines in our pockets and at 22:30 we moved out of the farm across the fields towards the cliff edge to take up our positions on the beach. The marines moved into their perimeter positions at the same time and were all in position and ready by 23:15. We were poised for the arrival of agent Timo, and I reflected that he would be surprised by the strength of his welcoming committee when his feet touched the beach. We waited in silence as the minutes ticked by, our eyes scanning the horizon for the flashing signal from the U-boat, but nothing came. I was beginning to get anxious, as the watch hands edged on and then moved past the thirty-minute marker, that the U-boat was not coming and that all this was for nothing. Five minutes had now crept past and still no signal when suddenly a series of bright flashes shot across the bay in front of us and the wireless operator whispered that this was the signal that we were waiting for, and the inspector gave the order for the acknowledgement to be sent and the reply "T" from our hand-held light. I looked out to sea, trying to make out the shape of the submarine lying on the surface, but all in front of my eyes was black, although it was softening to grey nearer the shore, and I was unable to detect any movement. The night was cloudy with a light wind coming off the sea and blowing across the land, and I fancied I smelt a hint of diesel engine fumes in the air that could be from a submarine but could not be sure that it was not my imagination. The wireless operator called out to the inspector that something was happening above us on the clifftop and passed the headphones to Bennett so he could listen to the report from 2nd Lt Ennis, who reported that the western perimeter had been breached by a man who had reached the cliff edge and who was shouting in German and waving a scarf above his head, attempting to communicate to the submarine out at sea. He had been rendered unconscious by a blow to the head with a rifle butt from one of my men and had been escorted back to the farm in handcuffs. He was not sure whether the man could have been seen from a vessel out at sea, but they certainly could not have heard what he was shouting and he was dressed in dark clothing and was waving a light-coloured scarf so he thought it was unlikely that he could have been spotted. This was worrying and again I was thinking what a waste of valuable resources it was if we were to fail at this late stage.

A few more minutes ticked by and then Alicia, who had always been credited with sharp eyesight, let out a cry that there was a small boat just beyond the surf about one hundred yards out, and she could see six sailors in uniform rowing steadily towards the shore with their backs to us and a petty officer armed with a machine pistol in the stern alongside a figure in civilian clothes carrying a suitcase. We immediately deployed towards the shoreline but kept our weapons hidden so as not to give the game away before they had reached the beach. The sailors knew their business and handled the boat well as they made it through the surf and touched the bow gently into the sand as two of the oarsmen jumped over the side and secured the boat, whilst the passenger climbed over the freeboard agilely and came ashore. Alicia stepped forward and spoke in German to welcome Timo ashore and he was immediately suspicious as he was expecting to be met by Heinrich and Otto, but Alicia, as cool as ever, continued to talk to him in German, saying that they had been otherwise detained and she had been sent to meet them instead. All the time she was talking she was gently leading him away from the shoreline towards the base of the steps and began the climb to the top of the cliff, which prevented him from seeing the smooth actions of the marines, who overwhelmed the German sailors and took them into custody. Alicia kept up the pretence as they climbed and said that he would be reunited with Otto and Heinrich very shortly, until the silence was broken by the sound of naval guns firing as the frigates closed in on the submarine, still lying on the surface waiting for the return of its boat's crew. Timo was startled by the noise and was slowly coming to realise that he might be in trouble and was struggling to unfasten his coat to draw out his Luger when Alicia, switching to English, told him to put his hands up as she was pointing her pistol at his head. "Timo, I am a British detective, and we know that you are a German spy who has just been landed from an enemy warship and I am arresting you for espionage." Timo looked aghast and then threw down his suitcase and attempted to rush back down the steps towards the beach but immediately fell into Bryn's arms and was covered by my pistol whilst the handcuffs were fastened securely, and he was led away. I rushed over to Alicia to make sure she was uninjured and was relieved to find that she was okay and we made our way back up to the top together. The marines had captured all seven of the German sailors and disarmed them and marched them across the fields to the farm for processing and transport to the prisoner of war camp at Sennybridge. There was one more surprise when we reached the farmhouse when we found Manfred Gruber being attended to by a marine medic, who was bandaging the wound he had received from the marine rifle butt, and it became clear to me that he was the man trying to warn the submarine from the clifftop. I was immediately aware that Gruber was far more important in the network than I had first thought, for he had certainly known about the safe house and the imminent arrival of the new agent by submarine and was prepared to take individual action to attempt to warn the submarine of the trap we had set. Gruber's eyes opened wide with surprise when he saw me, and he looked daggers of hatred at me as I greeted him and said that he should have done a better job with the horse and cart as I was now arresting him on the charge of espionage. As soon as the marine medic was finished, he would be handcuffed again and transported to Llanthony House to join the interrogation with the other members of his spy network.

All the time we were talking there was a background of explosions and shellfire as the two anti-submarine frigates harried the surfaced U-boat and prevented it from diving. The German skipper deployed his casing gun party and attempted to beat off the frigates with gunfire and he might have been successful had he been facing a single frigate, but with two assailants splitting his fire and denying him the deeper water, his chances of escape were slipping away fast. He attempted to concentrate his fire on *HMS Welshpool* and although he managed some near misses, which drenched the decks of the frigate completely, he scored no hits. This strategy allowed *Porthcawl* to move in much closer and to open fire from almost point-blank range. The first salvo from the *Porthcawl* was slightly over but with a small adjustment in the range the second salvo hit the conning tower and started a fire and the flying pieces of hot metal swiped two of the gun crew off the deck over the side. Thirty seconds later, a further salvo struck the deck gun and put it out of action, killing the remaining gun crew. The submarine was now defenceless unless they could reach water deep enough to dive where they could release their torpedoes at the frigates, which were giving no ground and pressing home their attacks. *Porthcawl* laid off about two cables to the starboard of the submarine with all her guns swung out to target the drifting U-boat, and her machine guns were mounted along the rails to cover any hostile movement from the German crew. *Welshpool* had launched a whaler which was pulling steadily towards the submarine carrying the Royal Marine boarding party when a figure wearing a peaked cap, observing their approach, climbed into view at the top of the conning tower and then climbed over the deck rail and onto the ladder to take him down to the deck. As he climbed down, the lookouts on the bridge of the *Porthcawl* reported that it looked as if he was carrying a heavy bag and the skipper immediately knew that this was the weighted bag for the disposal of the ship's documents and code books to stop them falling into enemy hands, and he immediately ordered the machine gunners to sweep the submarine's deck with machine gun fire to stop him throwing the bag into the sea. All the gunners opened fire together and laid down a blistering cascade of fire across the open U-boat deck, but still the German skipper persisted in climbing down and managed to get his two feet firmly onto the steel decking and stretched up and swung his arm back to throw the bag over the saddle tanks into the sea. The gunners increased their rate of fire, and the multiple hits were seen to strike the upper torso of the brave German captain, who jerked and staggered as each round struck home and then plunged headfirst over the side and into the sea, and it looked as if he had taken the bag with him. *Porthcawl*'s skipper was disappointed but could not but admire the bravery and devotion to duty of his opposing commander. The boarding party were now scrambling onto the main deck and fast heading up the ladder to enter the control room and capture the submarine intact. The marines faced a little resistance from the engineering officer who was trying to set the scuttling charges but was captured before he could set the last detonator and the submarine was ours. The German first lieutenant was ordered at gunpoint to sail the submarine into Swansea Port, where they would be landed and taken to the prisoner of war camp in Sennybridge. He was a little surly but the armed presence of twenty fully burly marines gave him little choice in the matter and he reluctantly agreed. There was one stroke of luck, however, when it was discovered that the weighted bag had not gone into the sea and had been caught on one of the twisted pieces of rail damaged by one of the *Porthcawl*'s hits and remained dry and in one piece. The bag was retrieved safely by one of the marines and would be conveyed to naval intelligence as soon as they reached port. It had been an exemplary operation all round and although there were a few harrowing moments when things could have gone wrong, good luck ensured that things went our way. We had captured a newly arrived German spy and secured the arrest of Manfred Gruber, with only Ernest Sullivan still on the run, and the navy had captured a U-boat and her crew intact and were now in possession of the secret code books used by the Imperial Navy and the decoding books used by their agents behind enemy lines. This should enable us to read the messages that passed between the spies and their masters more easily and make it harder for them to operate secretly from us. We were in good spirits as we returned to Llanthony House in the middle of the night, leaving Aston and his men to continue the clear-up work at Llangellis Farm.

FOURTEEN

A search of Timo's clothing and suitcase revealed that he was carrying another wireless transmitter hidden behind a false bottom of his large suitcase, which suggested that there was an intention to boost the communication capacity of the network or that it was destined for another new spy network that we were unaware of at the present time. In either case, we had struck a significant blow to the enemy's intentions by closing the Wurtenberg network that night and should focus the interrogation of the leading figures on breaking them down and revealing what we wished to know. I had a suspicion that gentle police questioning might not exert the kind of pressure necessary on the likes of Kruger or Branden to make them give us the kind of breakthrough we were looking for. We tended to be too polite and obeyed the rules pretty much as we allowed their lawyers to be present throughout the questioning and we recorded everything they said in a formal statement to be presented as evidence in court. I concluded that we needed recourse to additional questioning techniques that were not so hamstrung by the legalities of normal police procedure to get answers fast. I was shocked and rather ashamed of myself for what I was dreading to suggest, that we should use violence and torture to get answers quickly. I was a policeman dedicated to upholding the law, not breaking it by disregarding the rights of the prisoner, and I was about to dismiss the thoughts from my head when I thought I would share my thoughts with Alicia. She listened to what I was thinking and then replied firmly that although what we were proposing was far beyond normal police procedure, it was probably the only way to get answers quickly. She reminded me that these prisoners were enemy spies who had lived amongst us, spied on us and passed information back to Germany, which had led directly to the deaths of many of our own people. The moment they took off their uniforms and hid themselves from us, they forfeited their rights to be treated as enemy soldiers and to be treated fairly by the police and judicial system. They were enemies of the state, and we needed to deal with them as harshly as possible to extract the information they possessed. We agreed to raise this with Colonel Stewart and Inspector Bennett on our arrival at Llanthony House and the rest of the drive passed peacefully.

Alicia braced the subject of more aggressive questioning with the colonel and inspector and they both agreed that we needed to have some stronger measures available to us and to that end had taken the precaution of drafting in two specialist interrogators from the army who were expert at using more robust techniques to extract the information we required as quickly as we needed it. However, we would start with normal police procedure first and ascertain how cooperative they might be prepared to be before we resorted to the more extreme measures. A little later in the day, we were introduced to Sergeants Finlay Causwell and Angus Bellamy, who had been seconded from the military police where they specialised in hunting down and interrogating enemy prisoners. They were both rather large and taciturn and would be classified by Alicia and me as persons we would not wish to meet in a dark alley at night. However, they both spoke fluent German and seemed to know their business well. They were busy setting up a special room at the other side of the basement away from the cells and interview rooms, where they could work on their prisoners with a degree of privacy. The colonel noticed my expression when I was introduced to them and pulled me aside a little later to say that there was no need to be squeamish because it might well be necessary to inflict a little pain to get a prisoner to crack and tell us what we needed to know. I was quick to try to convince him that although I had doubts about using torture, I realised that it might prove necessary as I didn't want the colonel to think I was out of step with what the team were doing. The questioning of the lesser players was proving reasonably positive, as if the sleepers with only small parts to play were willing to give up what little they knew for more favourable treatment, and all, except Hilda Williams, gave very similar justifications for their actions. They suggested they had settled in South Wales for genuine reasons and had lived respectable and useful lives but as relations between Britain and Germany had declined in the years before the outbreak of war, pressure had been exerted from Berlin for them to work against their new country. They were forced to make a choice between supporting their new home or remaining loyal to their kith and kin, which was usually backed up with threats of violence towards their families who remained in Germany. In these circumstances, they felt they had little choice but to agree to work for them but denied having any detailed knowledge of how the spy ring was led and operated on a wider basis. We suspected that this story was partly true but only gave us half of the story and that once they had become involved, they became willing participants and had received more than adequate payment for their services. None of these prisoners admitted to having knowledge of similar spy networks operating in Wales or to being more widely involved in violence or murder on behalf of the spy ring. However, we were able to confirm that the code name Oberst referred to Anton Kruger and that Branden acted as his second-in-command. We also discovered that Hilda Williams and Manfred Gruber were able lieutenants to the two leaders and Ernest Sullivan was universally disliked by all of them because he was the enforcer used by Kruger to ensure total obedience within the spy ring. It was interesting for us to note that the leading players in this spy ring were long-term residents of South Wales and had lived as sleepers for many years before they became active as spies. Although the prisoners tried strenuously to convince us that they had been coerced into acting as spies for their mother country because of threats to their families and relations in Germany, it was difficult to accept this as true. It appeared far more likely that the German Intelligence Service had placed key people into sleeper positions as part of a coordinated plan to have resources in place in the event of conflict between the British and German empires so that vital information could be gathered about British shipping and for acts of sabotage to be undertaken. The coincidence of this many German nationals coming together as the board of Wurtenberg Holdings was too difficult to accept and whilst we were prepared to accept that some had lesser roles than others, they were all guilty of the crime of espionage and would pay the price for their actions in time of war.

It was agreed that Causwell and Bellamy would begin with Sir Wilhelm Branden, who was brought from his cell to the furthest room along the basement corridor where the two sergeants were waiting. Branden was making a show of confidence trying to demonstrate how untouchable he was as a knight of the realm, but his expression changed when he entered the threshold of the room where the sergeants were stripped down to their vests and all the tools of their trade were laid out on a table to the side of a large chair in the middle of the room. He turned immediately white and tried to struggle against his escort and resist being taken into the room. I had unfortunately drawn the short straw and had been detailed to record everything that

Branden revealed under interrogation, so I observed all that took place that morning. The escort conveyed him bodily across the room and secured him to the chair with large straps for his forearms, ankles and forehead so that he was now unable to move. The chair was made of heavy wood and was secured to the floor by steel bolts, so he was completely immobile, however hard he attempted to struggle. Causwell took the lead as questioner whilst Bellamy remained silent, in charge of the considerable number of tools that they had laid out for their use. Branden's face now showed his fright and surprise that the British police would dare to treat someone of his standing in such a torrid manner. He had thought of himself as untouchable and beyond the reach of the law and was supremely confident that whichever side won the war, he would benefit because of his status and fortune. His shock was all the greater because he was about to find out how mistaken he was, and this was doubly underlined when Sergeant Causwell started to say in a quiet but measured way that it would be a pleasure to ask the questions that needed to be answered about the activities of the German spy ring of which he was a leading member. He strongly recommended that Sir Wilhelm take the road of cooperation and answer all the questions put to him honestly and truthfully, in which case he could promise that the use of the tools of the trade laid out before him would not be necessary and he would be treated with the respect that went with his status. He warned Branden against pretending he could hold out against the pain that would be inflicted if he did not cooperate fully. "Every man has his limit, and it is impossible to resist the extremes of pain and it is better to tell us what we want to know before these measures become necessary." He explained that he and his colleague had no personal issue in this interrogation, and it was of no consequence to them whether he cooperated or not, for their only task was to obtain the answers that were required. "Do not be tempted to lie because the investigating team have gathered masses of information on the activities of your group over the past few months and will know when you are not being truthful."

 Sergeant Causwell stepped back and took a glass of water from the table and drank slowly and rather theatrically as he left Branden to reflect on what he had just said and get clear in his mind whether he wished to cooperate or not. After what seemed an age but was probably only ninety seconds or so, he turned back to the prisoner and began the questioning with a nice easy question, asking him to state his full name for the record. The prisoner replied that he was Sir Wilhelm Branden, and I thought I could see a kind of wry smile cross his lips as if he felt he could endure this kind of questioning forever when Sgt Bellamy stepped forward and smashed him in the face with what looked like a cloth truncheon, which I later found out was a sock filled with sand. This weapon was as hard as a wooden truncheon and the impact was just as great when wielded by a fourteen-stone man, but the sand ensured that it left no marks or broke the skin. The prisoner's head was knocked backwards against the padded headrest of the chair, and he was disorientated for a moment but when he opened his eyes, he found Sgt Causwell staring at him and saying quietly that if he lied to us, this is what would happen every time. The sergeant asked him again for his full name and again he replied with the same answer and again received several blows from the sand-stuffed sock, which set his head reeling. Causwell's quiet voice again persisted with the same question, adding that if he couldn't answer the first question truthfully it was going to be a long and difficult session which would not end until he had given us what we wanted to know. "Let me help you by amending the wording of the question a little, and state for the record the full name that you were born with."

He mumbled that he had changed his name by deed poll in 1906 to Sir Wilhelm Branden and that was his legal name now. Causwell quietly restated that he wanted the full name that he was given at birth by his parents, not the name he had adopted as a deception in 1906. Bellamy stepped forward and hit him twice more with the sock, leaving the prisoner gasping for breath after the impact of these blows. From my vantage point at the desk at the side of the room, I could see that Branden was suffering after six of these pile-driving blows to the head from Bellamy and seemed confused about what to say but finally he managed to whisper, "Wilhelm Otto Conrad von Brandenburg," in a voice that could just about be heard by Causwell, who repeated the names in a clear voice for the record.

Causwell now thanked the prisoner for his cooperation and offered him a sip of water as a reward and then followed up with the supplementary question, "And where were you born?"

The prisoner looked up and replied in a cracked voice, "Craddock Park near Cardiff," and Causwell pressed on directly by asking, "What is your nationality?" Branden replied that he was Welsh, and Causwell stepped back again and then in a kind of personal conversation with himself started debating the important question as to whether if he was a Welshman, was he guilty of treason, or if he was a German national, was he only guilty of espionage? But he concluded that either way he was a rat and deserved what was coming to him. Causwell turned back towards the prisoner and said that Wilhelm Otto Conrad did not sound like Welsh names at all and sounded very German to him, and he rather cleverly switched to German as he said this, and the prisoner replied also in the same tongue that his family were a proud and noble German family who had settled in Britain after the marriage of Queen Victoria to Prince Albert and had grown rich from their royal patronage and that they had never envisaged that they would have to choose which country to pledge their allegiance to in time of war. He had been happy to be Welsh and German at the same time until the war came along, and he was forced to choose one side or the other. Causwell switched back to English and asked him if he was still being totally truthful here, and Bellamy swooped in and threw a bucket of ice-cold water into the prisoner's face, which came as a huge shock to him as he had been expecting a couple of blows from the sock. The prisoner was further disorientated and soaking wet and shivering as Causwell upped the pace of questioning and began by asking if he was a member of the board of Wurtenberg Holdings, and it took two more icy bucketfuls before he would admit that he was a member of the board of this company and another blow with the sock for him to admit that he was actually the chairman of the board. Causwell drilled deeper and pressed the prisoner to describe the operations of this holding company, which appeared to have assets and resources considerably in excess of the total revenue of the subsidiary companies which it controlled, but he was unable to do so satisfactorily. Causwell went even deeper and asked the prisoner to explain why a successful businessman, who was owner of the Cardiff Dock Company and several profitable agricultural businesses, was involved with this highly questionable holding company, but he gave no answer. Three buckets of water went into his face in quick succession, and he was now completely drenched and shivering, and his prison uniform was stuck to his body.

Everything I had observed so far, although beyond what we would do in a normal police interview, did not seem too extreme or to have caused the prisoner more than discomfort and some minor injury, and I began to feel less reticent about the methods being used, although when I looked at the new information we had gleaned so far, it was striking by its paucity. When Causwell stepped back and came over to my desk I said as much, but he smiled and said we are doing fine, and we were just softening him up and getting him used to answering truthfully before we moved to more intensive questioning designed to extract the things we didn't already know. He then turned back to the prisoner and said, "You must be very uncomfortable and cold and it would be best if we got those wet clothes off you before you catch your death." He indicated to Bellamy to come across to the chair and unstrapped Branden and helped him to stand up whilst they stripped off his wet clothes and threw them in the corner. I expected, and I imagine so did the prisoner, I suspect, that he would be given fresh dry clothes to put on, but he was just left standing, shivering, looking a very pathetic figure already. I could see that the stripping of his clothes had robbed Branden of his dignity, and his confident bluster was now totally dissipated as he hunched over, using his clenched hands to cover his flabby abdomen and genitalia. Causwell was in no hurry to rush on with the questions and just left him standing in the middle of the room whilst he and Bellamy discussed quietly how best to proceed. The prisoner of an hour before would have complained loudly at being ignored but now he pathetically waited for the next part of the nightmare to continue, hanging his head in silence.

Finally, Causwell ordered Bellamy to handcuff the prisoner and to hook the chain which joined the two cuffs together over a hook on the ceiling above the prisoner's head. Branden was quite a tall man at around six foot and he now stood with his arms firmly pinioned above his head and his body at full stretch so that he could only touch the ground on tiptoes, which must have exerted extreme pressure on his arms and legs as he stood almost suspended in the middle of the room. Causwell explained the rules again; that cooperation would be rewarded but failure to answer would receive further punishment. They then proceeded to ask a set of questions regarding the other members of the board, their names, background, recruitment, etc., which slowly revealed the names of all the board members that we already knew from the information held at Companies House. However, when the questions went on to how people became members of the board and why, he was much less forthcoming and received repeated blows to the body, particularly to his back around the kidneys from the sand-filled sock, until he began to be more voluble. The Matthias doctors had been recruited at the university in Wurtenberg when they were studying for their medical degrees as potential agents for the German secret service because they planned to practise medicine overseas. They had lived and worked in Cardiff for over twenty years and had built a respectable and profitable practice and had established themselves in local society and they were selected by Berlin to join Wurtenberg when it was set up. Similar stories were trotted out for the others. Hilda Williams was recommended by family in Germany before he hired her as his secretary at the Dock Company and was a natural to join the board of the holding company. Kruger was a well-respected local lawyer, the Grubers were German ex-pats who had built a small but successful business in Cardiff and performed small duties for the company, Pugh and Taylor were similar stories, but none of it rang very true because they were a disparate band of people with little to offer the holding company business except that they were of German origin and connected in some way to shipping. Causwell took a step back and then swung his leg in a mighty kick that swept Branden's legs out from under him and left him suspended and swinging from the hook in the ceiling, squealing and crying like a stuck pig. "Tell me what it is that links all of you together, because we are sure that you are all German spies working together to pass shipping movements to the German Navy through the Cardiff Dock Company." Branden kept silent and wept but gradually managed to rebalance himself on his toes and regain a little composure, but Causwell knew that they were making progress and that the prisoner wouldn't hold out for too much longer if they kept up the pressure. Causwell continued the questions and said, "We know that one of the board members has the code name Oberst and we suspect that you are Oberst. One of the German officers we have apprehended at Llangellis Farm admitted that his contact was Oberst and he would be collected from the farm by him. He was unable to tell us who Oberst was because he did not know, but he indicated that it was someone from Cardiff and a leader of the group, which seems to point to you."

Branden vehemently denied it was him but said he did not know who this Oberst was and Causwell said he was very disappointed that Branden had chosen denial as the best course of action as he was now forced to take actions that he had hoped to avoid, and he nodded at Bellamy, who came forward with a large pair of bolt cutters. Causwell said, "I will ask you again who Oberst is, and if you fail to give a satisfactory answer, Mr Bellamy will remove the little toe on your left foot as a little inducement to encourage the truth to come out." Branden looked horror-struck but also realised that his interrogators were deadly serious and would stop at nothing to get the information they required, so when they asked again, he gave a name immediately but as Causwell turned away and smiled, Bellamy lopped off his little toe with the cutters amidst screams of pain and blood spattering from the amputation. Branden was crying out now and the tears were streaming down his face, and he pleaded with Causwell to stop what he was doing as he had told the truth. Causwell retorted sharply, "We are certain that Manfred Gruber is far too young and inexperienced to be Oberst as the code name suggests an experienced military man and translates into English as the colonel. We believe that Gruber was a willing lieutenant but nothing more. Think again carefully because I am willing to ask Mr Bellamy to remove all of your toes if you fail to give us the identity of the agent named Oberst. Branden begged and pleaded that he didn't know who Oberst was but it was not him, and Bellamy removed a second toe on his left foot and then a third before he finally broke down and told us that Kruger was a colonel in the German Army and the commander of the Wurtenberg group.

Causwell thanked Branden for finally telling us what we wanted to know and apologised for having to resort to these methods to get him to cooperate. "But we will take a short break and then we will resume talking in what we hope will be a more cooperative manner," and he and Bellamy left the room. Branden was left suspended, naked from the ceiling, in considerable pain, and my natural instinct was to render him some aid but knew I could not and even when he pleaded with me that as a British policeman I could not allow this to continue, I replied that he should have thought of that before he decided to commit treason for he was a traitor to the country and the people who had enabled him to become rich and prosperous, and I too left the room where I found Causwell and Bellamy relaxing and enjoying a smoke in the corridor and exhibiting no remorse for what they had just done to their prisoner over the last couple of hours.

Bellamy offered me a cigarette, which I refused, and then he said that police detectives always take it hard when they observe their first robust interrogation, but it was necessary to break enemy agents who had been trained to resist and would never give up the answers we required with normal interview procedures. "In a few minutes, we will go back in, and he will spill everything he knows, which should enable you to interview the others with an upper hand and without the need to resort to our methods. We do not like what we have to do but we are military policemen in time of war, and the work we do is as vital to defeating the enemy as that of the infantryman in the trenches, and we are sure that the work we do ultimately saves lives."

I acknowledged what he said as genuine and then asked, "If Branden had not given up Kruger, how many toes would you have cut off?" and he said all of them, of course, and if that hadn't worked, they would have linked up the small electric generator to his testicles and torched him until he did. I gulped and was glad that we hadn't had to go that far and went back into the room, where the combined smell of blood, sweat and evacuated bowels hit me in the back of the throat and almost made me gag, and I was glad that Causwell and Bellamy did not see my reaction.

The final session was far less brutal for although the pain had subsided from the peak, he was still totally compliant and spilled out all he knew in answer to their questioning. He revealed that Kruger and Sullivan were the real power behind the running of the Wurtenberg spy ring and that the colonel used Sullivan to suppress dissent and ensure maximum obedience amongst its members. Kruger was a fanatic who relished inflicting defeat after defeat on his enemies, and it was common knowledge that he and Sullivan had defrauded the Irish rebels out of large sums of money for the supply of weapons which did not arrive in Ireland and was diverted to Wales. He had arranged for the murder of the Irish negotiator of the deal to shift suspicion away from himself. Branden suspected that Kruger had commissioned Sullivan to murder the two British officers, Crawford and King, and was certain that he had ordered the killings of Schultz and his wife and O'Malley when they became a threat to the security of the network. He revealed that they were in the process of planning a series of sabotage operations against military and communications targets in and around Wales, and this was the main reason why specialists were sent from Germany by U-boat, to assist in these raids. He revealed that attacks were planned against the mainline railway junction at Newport and at the entrance to the Severn Tunnel, the Royal Engineers' barracks at Chepstow and the admiralty supplies depot at Caerwent as well as the headquarters of Cardiff police. The latest arrival was brought in at the last minute to replace Schultz, who had become a liability when he was arrested by the police for the attack on his ex-wife and they both had to be dealt with quickly to avoid further police interest. However hard Branden was pressed about Sullivan and where he would hide out to avoid arrest, he was unable to answer and Causwell was inclined to believe him and changed the tack of his questioning and probed into whether there were other German agents operating in South Wales that they were in touch with, and he indicated that the main focus of spying revolved around shipping movements and the spy networks were set up around major ports and he was unaware of any other groups in Wales. However, he did reveal that he and

Kruger had travelled into England on a couple of occasions and met, in the city of Bath, with the leaders of a similar group. He was at great pains to make us understand that he was unable to give the names of the men they met as they were known only by the code names Dimitri and Dieter for security reasons, but he suspected that they operated a group working in the Bristol and Avon docks but was not certain. "We sometimes arranged to transport packages for them that came by U-boat because they found it more difficult to enter the shallow waters of the Severn Estuary without detection." Branden had been under interrogation for over six hours but had revealed a mine of information which would be very useful to us for winding up the operations of the Wurtenberg group and possibly those in Bristol too. Unfortunately, he had not been able to reveal anything useful about the possible whereabouts of Sullivan, which was a major disappointment.

Bellamy and Causwell gently lifted Branden down from the hook in the ceiling and seated him back in the chair and removed the manacles from his wrists. Bellamy brought a bowl of warm water and washed the dried blood away from Branden's feet and applied antiseptic cream to stem the chance of infection and bound the damaged toe stubs with bandages and helped him to redress in a dry prison uniform. Causwell apologised to the prisoner for the necessity of having to inflict some pain and discomfort to convince him to tell us what we wanted to know. He concluded by saying that there was no dishonour in breaking under robust interrogation as he knew for sure that every single member of his spy ring would break under the same circumstances, and some would withstand more before they broke but some would withstand much less. They then escorted Branden back to his cell and I could hear him sobbing as he left the room and hobbled away along the corridor. I was not proud to have been party to the breaking of Sir Wilhelm Branden, but the intelligence gained was tangible proof that these methods worked when applied in the right circumstances. The selection of Branden as the first to withstand this kind of interrogation had been the right choice as it had revealed much additional information and opened up new lines for our investigation. There would be little need to apply such robust methods against the other prisoners as we had an almost complete picture of the Wurtenberg operation already. I found myself wondering what would happen to Branden now and I guessed that being a British national he would be charged with treason rather than espionage, although his ultimate fate would be the same. I felt physically and mentally drained even though I was just observing this interrogation but went first to make my report to Colonel Stewart and Inspector Bennett before seeking some solace by taking a walk in the fresh air. I realised that I could not excuse myself as just an observer as I had given my tacit approval as I stayed in the room whilst the two interrogators tortured a prisoner. I had always thought I would maintain the highest standards and would not resort to violence in my dealings with prisoners, but I was ashamed at how quickly this veneer of abiding by the rules had just fallen away and I became a willing party to what went on. I realised that there was no turning back, that I had crossed the divide and accepted that the end justified the means and that there could be no retaking the high moral ground under any circumstances.

I wandered into the fields behind the house and climbed the slope towards the ridge that overlooked the valley, and I knew I would not be disturbed as I walked there. I was scheduled to assist Alicia in the morning with the interrogation of Hilda Williams and was stood down for the rest of the day and I knew that Hilda would not be an easy nut to crack, and I wondered what success we would have with her. As I crested the ridge, my heart sank as I could see the outline of a figure resting against a tree with their back to me. I could not see who it was and thought I would turn away and walk across the open moorland when a voice I recognised called out to me and I knew it was Alicia. I was elated and made my way across to the little sheltered spot where she had settled, and she smiled and took my hand and guided me down to sit beside her and explained that she knew that I would be upset to be witness to the interrogation of Branden by the two sergeants and that I would seek to be alone afterwards, and she had guessed I would climb up to the moor. I was so glad to find her here and her presence just calmed me down but also awakened my desire for her. Alicia rolled over and lifted her skirts to straddle my midriff like riding a horse and I could feel her fingers working quickly to undo my trouser buttons and release my penis with an upward force as I wriggled my bottom to push my trousers and underwear down my buttocks to give me some greater movement. Alicia lifted herself up and slid herself gently down the length of my member until I could feel her cervix whilst she spread her skirt over the top of my middle section, and she rode me at first at a gallop and then at a gentler canter until I climaxed as she arched her back in orgasm. I lay back, spent, and realised that Alicia had planned this carefully in advance and had come prepared as she was not wearing anything underneath her skirt, to enable my ease of entry. We lay there, side by side, slowly subsiding from our passion and I knew that I was falling deeply in love with this extraordinary woman and as I dreamed of spending my life with her, I gently worked my fingers around her labia and kissed her deeply on the lips, pushing my tongue into her mouth. After twenty or so minutes of quiet intimacy, we knew it was time to return to our duties and returned to plan the interrogation of Hilda Williams.

When Hilda was brought into the interview room, she displayed a haughty and superior look on her face that tried to convince us that she was not going to cooperate with us at any price. I hoped that this was only a show of strength and merely bravado on her part. I reasoned that she must have realised by now that we had arrested almost all of the spy network and that we were in possession of hard evidence against all of them, which would send them to the gallows. I also hoped that she would answer our questions because I knew the likely fate that awaited her at the hands of Causwell and Bellamy should she choose to be uncooperative. Alicia led the questioning and quickly established a fellow woman-to-woman relationship, which seemed to calm Hilda down somewhat and most of the early questions were designed to put Hilda at ease rather than put pressure on her. She established that Hilda had settled in Cardiff in 1896 but was born in a small village near Brüggen on the German and Dutch border where she grew up to be bi-lingual in Dutch and German, which allowed her to pretend that she was Dutch when she came to live in Wales. She had studied English at Frankfurt University and qualified as a licensed translator and came to Britain where she felt there was a good career. In 1900, she married Mordred Williams and became a housewife until Sir Wilhelm Branden offered her a job as his personal assistant in 1906 after he had received a recommendation from one of his German relatives as to Hilda's ability as a translator and secretary. Alicia encouraged Hilda to speak more about this and her job at the Dock Company, feigning real interest, which lulled Hilda's caution and she talked freely. Hilda described how Mordred's salary as a haberdasher and draper was insufficient for their needs and it was necessary for her to return to work to make ends meet. When Alicia felt that Hilda had become more relaxed and her defences were coming down, she changed the tack of her questioning and said, "This must have been an excellent decision on your part because your fortunes seem to have improved greatly since starting to work for Sir Wilhelm Branden. You have been able to move to a better class area of Cardiff where the rent alone must use up all of Mordred's earnings, but you have still managed to save and have a healthy balance in the bank so you must be an excellent manager of your finances, or you live extremely frugally." Hilda plumped herself up with pride and said that it was, of course, a bit of both as Alicia leant forward and shouted directly in her face that she should stop lying. "Even with your combined earnings, you and Mordred could not afford to live in the style you have become used to, and our examination of your bank accounts shows clearly that you are in receipt of sundry regular payments to the value of three or four times your monthly income from Wurtenberg Holdings and that the house you live in is owned by a fellow director of the same company, Dr Sabine Matthias, who charges you no rent to live in her house. Dr Sabine and her husband, Dr Julius, are coincidently also German ex-pats who, like you, have lived in Wales for over twenty years, and it is even more unusual that all the directors of this company are of German origin, except for Ernest Sullivan, who is Irish. You are also listed as a director of this holding company with the role of company secretary, so perhaps you can tell us how this holding company can be so profitable as to be able to make such generous payments to its directors when there is little evidence of much commercial activity by the holding company or its subsidiaries." Alicia ploughed on and asked for an explanation as to why there was an additional two hundred pounds a month paid into her account every month in addition to her salary from the Dock Company and what tasks she had to complete to earn this money. Hilda bridled and said she was the company secretary and was paid well to keep the company's administration organised and efficient and that she earned every penny. Alicia replied that she was sure that she did but had no doubt that if she had not performed well, she would have been dealt with severely by Herr Oberst, like Joachim Schultz and Heidi Weisse. Hilda replied without thinking, blurting out that Schultz and Weisse were traitors and had attracted the attention of the police to their activities, so they deserved to be dealt with by the colonel. She realised the admission she had made and tried to retract some of what she had said.

Alicia would not slacken her grip and pressed on that she had now admitted that Herr Oberst Kruger arranged to have Schultz and Weisse murdered because they were a threat to the security of the company. She wanted to know why a respectable business was murdering its employees because they became involved in a police case. If Wurtenberg Holdings was a legitimate company, why was it resorting to this behaviour unless, of course, it was a criminal organisation? "Several of your fellow directors have already admitted that they were enemy agents or spies and because they have cooperated will probably escape execution. We have also captured three German army officers who are in military custody who will be dealt with as prisoners of war, but German nationals guilty of spying and failing to admit their guilt or assist us in our enquiries will almost certainly be hanged." Alicia asked again whether Kruger had murdered Schultz and Weisse and she retorted angrily that he was an honourable German officer and would not stoop so low. The killings would have been carried out by Sullivan, who was a desperately violent killer and totally untrustworthy. Alicia remarked that however honourable Kruger may be, he was not averse to issuing the orders for the murder of the five victims we had discovered in the remote grave in the Black Mountains, and she replied that this was Sullivan. Alicia drew breath and then continued to ask whether Hilda was really trying to persuade us that Sullivan had committed these murders of his own volition, which was rather far-fetched even though we could fully accept that Sullivan had a record as a proven killer.

I interjected at this point and asked Hilda to explain to us why she was so certain that Sullivan was the killer and had acted alone in the murders when our evidence pointed to Sullivan carrying out the orders of someone else, most probably Anton Kruger. Hilda immediately went into a rant about what a despicable character Ernest Sullivan was and how he did not hold the same loyalty to the company as the rest of them. "You mean he wasn't a German but was just a gun for hire?" and she nodded her head and said that was exactly it.

"He is a revolutionary and lends his special skills of violence and assassination to whichever group will pay him and advance his career as an enforcer. He had no honour and did not believe in the cause but was perfectly happy to administer a beating or a murder provided the price was right. He kept himself separate from the rest of us and took his orders direct from Herr Oberst. I feel that he despised the rest of us, and we all knew that he would kill us as easily as look at us."

I pointed out that it was ironic that he was the only member of the Wurtenberg group to remain at large and he seemed to have completely disappeared without a trace despite every policeman in Wales looking for him. "Perhaps you have some ideas where he might be hiding out and who might be assisting him to evade capture." She shrugged, intimating that men in Sullivan's line of work did not cultivate too many friends, but he would naturally gravitate to other groups that might have use for a man of his talents and that is where I should focus my attention if I was looking for him and with that she sat back in her chair and refused to answer any more questions. Alicia and I were satisfied that we had adequate evidence to charge Hilda with espionage and as she was not a serving member of the German armed forces, she would be dealt with as a spy, and it was inevitable that she would meet her end at the end of the hangman's rope.

FIFTEEN

We were puzzled over what Hilda Williams had meant by her cryptic remark about where to look for Sullivan and even though we tried to work it out, we seemed at a loss to understand where she meant for us to look. I had always been convinced that there was another spy ring operating in South Wales and he would have sought refuge amongst their number even though despite our best efforts we had not succeeded in discovering any further evidence of other enemy groups operating in Wales at that time. The only hard piece of evidence we had was the fact that enemy spy groups had been set up to monitor allied shipping from all the major British seaports and Branden indicated that the nearest group to us was based in and around Bristol Docks. I also thought that we should maintain a close watch on the Irish ferry service to Cork from Fishguard in West Wales in case Sullivan attempted to return to Ireland for a while. Alicia thought that this would be unlikely as Sullivan was still wanted by the Irish Freedom Movement, whom he had double-crossed and swindled out of their weapons and money only a short time ago. She seemed to be coming round to an idea that was forming in her mind from the remarks Hilda had made that Sullivan was a revolutionary and would work for whoever would pay him to use his special skills, and she thought we should focus our attention on the increasing number of left-wing revolutionary or anarchist groups that had sprung up in Britain during the past few years. We knew that before the German spy group Sullivan worked for the Irish rebels and only left them for a better offer working alongside Kruger. Now that he had left Kruger, he would make himself very scarce to avoid the same fate as the German spies and she was sure he would have found a revolutionary group to infiltrate and help him keep a low profile for the next couple of months. She was quite despondent about our chances of arresting him anytime soon. However, Mr

Sullivan would resurface in the future when he would be required to put his special skills to work for his new masters and we would be ready for him as we knew enough about his methods of operation to recognise his calling card when we started to find his new victims.

By the end of the week, all the interrogations had been completed and a couple of additional names had been extracted under questioning of associates who worked alongside Wurtenberg Holdings but who were not full members of the spy ring, and warrants had been issued for their arrest. Two were members of Sir Wilhelm's staff who were party to some of his illegal activities, but the others were little more than hangers-on, but they would be arrested and questioned as a matter of course. We had yet to establish whether any other members of Branden's family were involved or knew of his anti-British activities, but it was planned to interview his wife and adult children during the next week. The German officers arrested at Llangellis Farm were handed over to the War Office and were to be incarcerated at SennyBridge Prisoner of War Camp for the duration of the war, but Kruger, the Matthiases and Grubers were charged with espionage and would be tried by military tribunal in the following week, whilst Sir Wilhelm Branden, Jonathan Pugh, Mordred Williams and David Taylor, as British nationals, were all charged with treason and would be tried in the Cardiff Assizes Court next month. It was a kind of anti-climax for us because the frenetic activity of the past months as we tracked this spy ring down and brought them to justice was suddenly over. We knew that we had some work to do to submit the evidence to the court and some of us may be called to give evidence in person, especially in the *assizes*, but we still felt a kind of deflation. Colonel Stewart expressed his satisfaction with the work of the team and looked forward to new investigations that would inevitably come our way in the next few days but suggested we all take a few days off to relax and recharge our batteries ready for the next challenges that would be thrown at us.

Alicia and I decided that we would take a few days off together whilst we had the chance and managed to secure three days at a small cottage on the West Wales coast near Barmouth that belonged to a relative of Alicia who was away serving in France. This was a godsend for us as we were able to get right away from everyone who knew us and be together all alone without fear of discovery by our police colleagues.

The countryside around Barmouth is mostly lush green and rolling hills leading down to the deserted beaches that skirt the estuary with a spectacular view across the Irish Sea towards the Llŷn Peninsula and the seaside town of Pwllheli. The cottage was small and basic but comfortable enough for a short stay and Alicia and I enjoyed the opportunity to enjoy being alone, walking the coastal paths and taking picnics to the beach and swimming in the cold sea. Alicia surprised me with her abilities as a cook, serving each evening an excellent dinner made from local produce purchased from the nearby village and vegetables and herbs from the kitchen garden. After our meal, we would snuggle together in front of the logs in the fire grate and enjoy the peace and quiet of our company together. The bed was rather old and the mattress lumpy but after frenetic bouts of lovemaking, combined with the tiredness from all the unaccustomed fresh air and exercise, we slept soundly for most of the night wrapped in each other's arms. Our short holiday passed quickly enough, and we were ready to be back on duty the day after travelling back to Cardiff, but we both felt that our commitment to each other was stronger than ever and that we were ready to work at our relationship more seriously. We were not to know what lay ahead of us as we signed on for duty that morning and that our lives were about to change in ways that we had not expected. I was summoned to the inspector's office within ten minutes of arriving at the station and as I climbed the stairs, I was wondering what our next assignment might be. I knocked on the door and waited to be called in and was surprised to see Bryn Howells sitting at the inspector's desk and George Bennett sitting in the soft chair to the side of the desk. I was wondering what was going on but waited for some words of explanation. George Bennett introduced me to Inspector Howells, who had just been promoted and would take over his post in Cardiff whilst he went on to tell me that he had been promoted to chief inspector and would set up a new security team investigating anarchist and revolutionary groups operating in Wales to be based at Swansea police headquarters. I congratulated them both and said that I would be looking forward to working in Bryn's team. Bryn thanked me profusely but then told me that I was being posted from his team to other work. He could tell from my face that I was disappointed until the chief inspector said, "You are coming with me as my number two, Detective Sergeant Morgan." I couldn't believe what I had just heard because although I was qualified to be a sergeant, I had nowhere near the length of service to be promoted that soon. Bennett continued that he needed someone he could rely on to help him put the new team together and although I was still young in the service I had more than proved myself capable of the job and ready for the responsibility. He then winked and said, "If I did not move you away to Swansea, there would be a great danger that you and Miss Bell would have landed yourselves in hot water together." I went bright red and was shocked that he knew about Alicia and I, but I could also see that he and Bryn were smiling. "Alicia Bell is being promoted to detective constable and she will be Bryn's second-in-command and the pair of you can carry on your romantic shenanigans without being in breach of police regulations," he said lightheartedly. I was in disbelief at what I had heard but also extremely pleased that we had both taken another step up the ladder and would no longer have to keep up the subterfuge about our relationship, which could be in the open.

Two days later, I was moved to Swansea with George Bennett, and we took up residence in our new suite of rooms on the top floor of the police divisional headquarters in the centre of Swansea. We got to work trawling through personnel records to select some suitable candidates to recruit into our team. George left the initial trawl to me but had tasked me with finding a mix of experienced and novice policemen that we could scrutinise further and then interview to select six or so to join our team. I was looking for those who were already detectives or constables who had shown the potential to go into plainclothes. I was also looking for candidates with a decent level of education and who would likely be good readers and would be able to understand the different political ideologies that underpinned many of these revolutionary groups. An ability to drive and familiarity with the use of firearms was also preferable. The chief inspector had booked four weeks' training at Llanthony House for the end of the month when Colonel Stewart's team would deliver a similar training programme to the one that had been provided for our original team. I knew that my first choice without looking through the personnel files would be Constable Evans from Port Eynon, who had proved himself to be a resourceful and observant officer and played an active part in capturing the two German spies on the Gower. I had been impressed by him and was sure that his ambitions lay in preparing to become a detective in the future. It proved arduous and time-consuming poring through the personnel files of suitable officers in the South Wales Force, and it was five days before I had drawn up a long list for a sifting discussion with the chief inspector. Even then it took us nearly a whole working day to reduce the list from twenty to a dozen, who we would interview in the middle of the following week over two days. Inspector Howells joined us to make up the interview team and we were able to give each candidate an hour to impress us that they were of the right calibre to join our new project. I was anxious to appoint another female officer in the team but was depressed to find so few candidates to choose from, but we included two young female officers in the final shortlist for interview. We had hoped to recruit eight new officers for training but struggled to find six men and one woman after two gruelling days of interviews. I was confident that the seven we had selected would rise to the challenge of the training and I would be able to mould them into a strong investigative unit able to work singly or in groups when we started work investigating in earnest. the revolutionaries and anarchist groups.

I managed to catch a quick weekend with Alicia in Cardiff before moving back into Llanthony House for the training of our new team, and Alicia and I made the most of being together because we would have to endure an enforced parting for at least four weeks whilst the training was on. As I was now a detective sergeant, I no longer had to live in the section house and could buy or rent a house or flat of my own, which meant that Alicia could stay with me discreetly when she visited Swansea, although there would still be difficulties over accommodation in Cardiff. I had managed to secure a ground-floor apartment with two bedrooms in a large house within walking distance of the station and was confident that this would meet my needs for the immediate future, for I knew that if I were to be promoted to inspector, I would probably have to move again. It was ironic, however, that I had hardly moved in when I was away for the whole of the next month. Only two of the new team were known to me already: Constable Evans from Port Eynon, who had impressed me so much in the capture and arrest of the German agents at Llangellis Farm, and Richard Simmons, who was one of Sergeant Tower's surveillance team sent from Brecon to watch Otto and Heinrich. All the other recruits were unknown but had come highly recommended and had passed the interview successfully.

Albert Prothero was older than most, being thirty-two, and had been a successful village bobby in an area close to Ammanford in West Wales for over six years. He had studied at Swansea University and started his working life as a teacher but found that he did not enjoy teaching as much as he had thought and had given it up after three years to train as a policeman. He enjoyed village life and played rugby and cricket in the village sides and had become a popular and respected figure in the area, but as the war dragged into its third year, his frustration increased that he needed to do more to contribute to the war effort. He had tried twice to volunteer for the army but was rejected because of his reserved occupation, but when he heard about the recruitment for our security team he volunteered immediately.

John Parry was from Cardiff and was the son of a Welsh father and Russian mother and was tri-lingual in English, Welsh and Russian and during his childhood had spent many holidays in Russia and could speak like a native Russian. This was an attribute that might prove useful to us if we required translation of documents or undercover work with some of the eastern European groups, and he was twenty-six and a keen sportsman and winner of the South Wales Police marksman competition with a rifle in 1914 and 1916, which might also prove useful to us operationally.

Dai Humphreys from Merthyr Tydfil and Joshua Matthews from Port Talbot were both experienced beat bobbies and had excellent records of service. The final member of the team, Bronwen Phillips, was the only female to get through the selection but had impressed all very much with her precise way of thinking and expressing herself and the speed of her thinking. She had worked in a city bank for five years before joining the fraud squad in 1914, where her analytical skills had proven invaluable in tracking misappropriated funds and fraudulent transactions. When I renewed my acquaintance with them on the first day at Llanthony House, I realised how excited I was to be working with this completely new team and relished the challenge of welding them into an effective unit to carry out the tasks we had been assigned to.

Colonel Stewart's opening address was lengthy and quite general as he talked about the security situation faced in our homeland from enemy infiltration, sabotage and spying and described the success of the first team in securing the discovery and arrest of fourteen German agents and spies operating in South Wales. He warned against complacency, however, for although we had enjoyed one massive success, the threats to our country and our ability to win the war were not only threatened by the enemy but also by extremist groups, anarchists and revolutionaries, who were becoming prevalent within our society and would destroy the values we held dear to achieve their objectives. He particularly drew our attention to the leftist revolutionary groups that appeared in considerable numbers amongst refugee groups from central Europe, Ireland and Russia, where the tzarist regime was under mounting pressure from the Bolsheviks. He explained that these groups relied upon support from the refugee community but needed British support for fundraising and influence. Working men and trade unionists were being targeted as prospects for membership because of their frustration at the lack of progress in the war and their search for a better world after the war was over. The rise of the Bolsheviks in Russia had encouraged many civilian workers and soldiers to believe that the traditional order of things could be turned over and the power to manage Britain taken away from the elite into their hands. He emphasised that we must stop this at all costs and stressed that as well as winning the war at the front, security police like us must win the peace so that our gallant troops could return to a settled world free from the upheaval of revolution. "Industrial unrest has been creeping up throughout the year and the setting-up of a Bolshevik state in Russia has given rise to a genuine fear that the old order could be overturned by the actions of these revolutionary groups stirring up greater discontent. There appears to be a real prospect of a worker-led revolution in Britain or at the very least a serious undermining of the established order of our society. The major hotspots for our attention are the munitions factories, shipbuilding and the coalmines, particularly in the central belt of Scotland around the Clyde and in the South Wales coalfield, where much of the discontent has become most evident. The government has decided to take action to preserve stability in the country with a two-pronged campaign involving increased propaganda by launching a national effort to present idealistic war aims and targets for domestic reconstruction after the war, backed up by the creation of surveillance teams like this one to seek out socialist plots and arrest the ring leaders."

We all listened carefully to the colonel's speech, but I wondered how many of us in that room believed the basis upon which he justified spying upon our own people. Most of us knew well enough how hard life was for industrial workers in wartime Britain but also how vital their work was in enabling us to continue to fight this war successfully. I knew that there had been strikes and many trade unions campaigned for changing working practices and better wages and conditions for their members. The strike weapons had proved extremely effective as employers seeking to meet wartime targets were willing to settle disputes far more rapidly than in peacetime. I was an ex-miner, born and brought up in a pit village, and I knew that these men were not unpatriotic and whilst they wanted a better life for themselves and their families, it was not at the price of the collapse of our country into a bloody revolution or defeat at the hands of the enemy. I felt a little unsettled about this in a similar way to how I felt about the torture of Branden in the basement of that building a few weeks before but resolved as I did then that it was necessary for the greater good, and the number of working men whose civil liberty and freedom was affected by this would be infinitely small.

George Bennett took over after the colonel had sat down and my interest was rekindled as he began to talk about the actual policing methodology we would employ and how we would deploy to achieve it. He stressed that much of our work would be passive, involving long-term surveillance of individuals and their institutions, which would mean a lot of good old-fashioned police work which could be little more than logging movements, accessing accounts, monitoring publications and public speeches. On the other hand, we may attempt to infiltrate some organisations which intelligence suggested posed significant threats. This would involve us in more proactive actions and maybe some members of our team working undercover secretly to gather the vital evidence to eradicate their threat. He mentioned several organisations which were high on the list for investigation, including the "Welsh Miners' Alliance", "Workers Against Conscription", the "Irish Freedom Union" and the "Workers Revolutionary Party of Britain". "These will be our initial targets and Detective Sergeant Morgan will allocate each of you to one or more of these organisations as your primary task." The Welsh Miners' Alliance was not a trade union but was a powerful political grouping funded by the Bolsheviks from Russia which attempted to encourage the promotion of socialist thinking and revolution amongst its members. It published a weekly political news-sheet distributed free within the coalfield, published pamphlets and propaganda films extolling the virtues of the October Revolution and the Bolshevik vision for a worker-led state in Russia and held public meetings in every coalfield town and village to persuade miners away from the miners' union branches, who they accused of being in the mine owners' pockets. I was too far detached from the miners' union now to be able to make any proper judgement on this, but I was aware from my days down the pit that there was huge resentment felt by colliers against their employers who they believed profiteered and made huge profits from the hard graft of the miners underground. I was sure that the increased pressure of the war would not have lessened this feeling in any material way.

The chief inspector went on to highlight several suspects who were to be our initial targets and revealed their pictures one by one and what information we knew about them. Donal O' Casey was the first name revealed and he was the leading member of the Irish Freedom Movement operating in Wales with the task of raising support for the new Irish free state and to encourage

Welshmen and women in their own quest for freedom from the dictates of London and to set up Welsh nationalist groups to resist English domination. The Irish freedom fighters believed that strong nationalist movements in Scotland and Wales would break up the Union and lead to the creation of independent states. This group were willing to use armed insurrection and civil war to achieve their aims, and their threat to the stability of the nation was considered significant. And they were suspected of carrying out a series of bombings against English targets in several parts of Wales.

Billy Williams was the leader of the Welsh Miners' Alliance but had no mandate for his position for he was self-appointed and had not been elected in any free ballot as trade union leaders were. He claimed to represent the best interests of the Welsh colliers but wished to shut the coalfield down with a total strike, which would bring the mine owners to their knees and bring the government running to negotiate with the miners as the supplies of coal for the war effort ran out. The real threat of the alliance was that it would destroy the influence of the elected union officials and bring about chaos in the collieries. Coal was vital to the war effort and interruptions in supply must be kept to the absolute minimum. Although there had been several strikes in individual pits, the disputes had been local and resolved quickly because the existing relationship between coal owners and the colliers generally facilitated agreement relatively quickly. The Miners' Union were willing to use the strike weapon frequently because it was proven to work and guaranteed to bring employers to the negotiating table quickly to resolve disputes as speedily as possible.

Workers Against Conscription were included in the list of top threats not because they were sworn to violent struggle but because they were borne out of the frustration and resentment felt by working men but more significantly felt by their wives and mothers at the massive loss of life; the maiming and serious injury affecting hundreds of thousands more young men who seemed to have little or no future after the war was over. This would be the hardest group to challenge and detract from imposing their will upon the thinking of the silent majority in this country as they worked almost completely by word of mouth and the solidarity of their joint loss, ensuring the ending of conscription and saving the next generation of young men from slaughter before the war was concluded. This movement was even harder to target because it had no national leaders, no newspaper or news-sheets, no meetings, but was a national movement organised almost exclusively on a local basis by people who felt the pain of loss in their families and communities, personally.

The final group was the Workers' Revolutionary Party of Britain which was well funded through generous financial support from the Bolsheviks in Russia and whose sole purpose was the total disruption of Britain and its empire as a credible entity. The organisation was run by Rory McCloud O'Hare, who cut his revolutionary teeth as a freedom fighter in Ireland before launching the workers' party in Wales. "O'Hare has a considerable reputation as a man of violence with a ruthless streak in the pursuit of his goals and is a known associate of another Irish revolutionary, Ernest Sullivan, who we know to have been a member of the German spy ring recently captured in this part of Wales. Sullivan was the only member of the spy network to evade arrest and he remains on the run. Despite extensive searches for his whereabouts, no sightings have been reported and it is suspected that he has gone to ground amidst the Workers Revolutionary Party and will remain hidden for some time to come and will only emerge when his specialist skills as an assassin are in demand again."

Whilst the daily training routine went ahead as planned, I spent most of my time researching all the background information I could amass on each of the target individuals and their organisations and putting it together into dossiers that could be referred to easily by the allocated pairs assigned to each group. There was a great deal of available knowledge about the operations and membership of the Irish Freedom Union and the Welsh Miners' Alliance, but Workers Against Conscription lacked the administrative infrastructure of the more formal organisations and had used their ad hoc word-of-mouth associations to spread their message very effectively without the need to write anything down that would give the government authorities the ability to lessen the impact of their campaign. However, what little I managed to find out about them did not raise any cause for concern other than this was a genuine grassroots movement of law-abiding people pressuring for change and seeking an end to the slaughter of the war. My biggest concern was the Workers Revolutionary Party, who shrouded the whole operation of their organisation in a secure cloak of secrecy. They pretended to be a political party with a genuine respect for the parliamentary process but the more I investigated their aims, objectives, political pamphlets and propaganda, the more it became increasingly clear that they were a violent group dedicated to overcoming the democratic process of British politics and replacing it with their own brand of revolutionary diktat in direct opposition to the socialist revolutionaries of Bolshevik Russia. I realised that if I were Sullivan, this would be the group that I would gravitate towards because of its secrecy and adherence to the kind of violence that he was most expert at. I had the strong feeling that this was where I would find leads to the whereabouts of Ernest Sullivan and decided that I would take the lead on the investigation of this group myself and elicit the support of Bronwen Phillips for this task. Rory McCloud and Sullivan were both men of violence who came together before in the Irish Freedom struggles before the war and who now found themselves divorced from their nationalist countrymen and involved in wider international revolutionary activities.

During the third week of the training course, I was called away to Cardiff to give evidence in the trials of Anton Von Kruger, Julius Matthias, Sabine Matthias, Hilda Williams and Manfred, Helmut, Friedrich and Joachim Gruber before the special military tribunal set up to assess the guilt of suspected spies. The trial was being held in the officers' mess of Cardiff Central Barracks and the tribunal was made up of six military officers from the South Wales Command and the case presided over by Lord Alwyn Reynolds KC, an experienced high court judge. All the accused were charged with espionage and much of the first day of the trial was taken up with legal arguments concerning whether Anton Kruger, a serving colonel in the Imperial Army, should be dealt with by this court or dealt with as a prisoner of war, but after lengthy arguments the judge ruled that the legal basis for the application was specious as Kruger had lived undercover, purporting to be a Polish national for many years before the outbreak of war. He went on to add that he did not doubt that Kruger had served as a colonel in the German Army many years before, but he had been wholly engaged in Wales for nearly a decade in the business of espionage and not as a military officer and he dismissed the application. This was a considerable blow to Kruger's defence because they believed they could secure the same treatment as the three German officers arrested at Llangellis Farm, who had cooperated with the police on capture and were now detained in the German officer prisoner of war camp at Sennybridge for the duration of the war, after which they would be repatriated. After the judge's ruling, they knew that they faced a difficult task in securing any lighter sentence for Kruger before this court. The prosecution was led by Lt. Col. Erskine of the Army Provost Department at the War Office, and he skillfully presented the case against all of them as a group rather than individual cases against each of them. He wished to establish their collective guilt and show that they were equally guilty of espionage even though some were leaders and others were led. He showed the collective accountability of all who served as a lesser or greater member of the Wurtenberg Holdings spy ring. He built a compelling case against them by using selected evidence presented by Alicia, Ivor, Chief Inspector Bennett and myself but was careful not to weigh the case heavily with too much detail, concentrating on showing that the actions of this group had cost the lives of innocent merchant seamen off the Welsh coast, the loss of valuable war cargoes and ships, an attempt to kill a police officer in pursuit of his duty, the murder of two wounded British officers and three members of their own group who they had considered to be a threat to their security. He concluded that each one of the defendants had deliberately infiltrated this country many years before the outbreak of war and lived respectable lives, waiting for the day when they could strike back against the country in which they lived and enjoyed a comfortable life. The defence was weak and consisted of a rather vain attempt to show that the accused were all employees of a respectable holding company trading through the docks in South Wales and their connections with Germany were tenuous and that they were honest and decent citizens. We were surprised that the case was strung out over five days but were not surprised when all eight of them were found guilty as charged. Lord Reynolds remanded them all to the military prison for five days whilst he considered the sentences he would impose, although we were certain that there was little doubt what the sentences would be. However, we were to be proved quite wrong because when the judge passed sentence the following week, he was at pains to show that although the prosecution had made a strong case for collective accountability, he believed that Kruger and Manfred Gruber deserved a harsher penalty because of their willingness to use violence and murder to pursue their aims. Whilst accepting that all the accused were German spies, he sentenced Kruger and Manfred Gruber to death and the others to twenty-five years' imprisonment with hard labour. As this was a time of war, there would be no appeal against the sentence and the executions were set to be carried out by hanging at Cardiff Jail one week hence. The other prisoners would be dispersed to jails throughout Wales, and I could not help feeling that hard labour could be a death sentence too for the Matthiases and Grubers.

Branden, Pugh, Mordred Williams and Taylor, as British nationals, were charged with treason and would be tried at the earliest opportunity in the Central Criminal Courts in Cardiff within the next month. Three days before the trial was set to start, the warders opening Sir Wilhelm Branden's cell that morning found him hanging from the top of the window bars with a rudely fashioned rope made from his bed sheet around his neck and looped through the window bars. He was still alive when they cut him down, although it was clear from his bloated face and protruding eyes that he had suffered considerably as the breath was choked out of him so that he was only barely alive. He was rushed to the infirmary but despite the efforts of the prison doctor, he did not last more than forty minutes before he drew his last breath. I felt a little of my former guilt at the rough handling of Branden's interrogation at the hands of the two military policemen in the basement of Llanthony House. That day would probably haunt me forever more throughout my police career and I hoped that I would never come to accept what was done to Branden as justifiable and right, for I resolved that the day I accepted this behaviour as right was the day that I gave up being a policeman.

I received a letter from home that day which told me that my younger brother Derfal had transferred to the Royal Flying Corp and was going to train as a pilot, which my parents thought was good news because he was removed from the danger of the trenches. I was not so sure as I had always thought that flying was quite a dangerous occupation, but I was sure it was more fun than squatting in the cold and wet trenches for months on end. Derfal was going to train at an airfield near Salisbury and I hoped that I might get to see him whilst he was home from France. The news about my other brother, Gwyn, was not so good, however, as he seemed to have gone off the rails a bit and offended the chapel sexual taboos by getting involved with a married woman. It was made even worse because his lover was an extremely attractive woman who had had affairs before whilst her husband was away at sea with the Royal Navy. Gwyn had always been one to chase after the girls and it was no surprise to me that he had fallen for this girl, but he was extremely reckless because messing with a married woman whose husband was away on war service was guaranteed to cause trouble in a tight-knit chapel community like ours. Dad had indicated in his letter that Gwyn had already received threats of violence from other men down the pit who were friends or relations of the wronged husband and had been forced to transfer to another pit to avoid them. I hoped that I might get a few hours to spare in the coming weeks to drive home and reassure Mum and Dad and have a word with Gwyn before the trouble got any more serious.

SIXTEEN

After the sentences were passed and the executions carried out, it was tempting to consider that the Wurtenberg affair was now over and that the security branch could turn their attentions elsewhere, but I found it difficult to close this chapter quite so easily as I had a nagging feeling of unfinished business. Sullivan remained free and although we were hearing whispers from our informants that he was active again amongst the anarchist groups operating in Wales, we were unable to pinpoint his whereabouts other than vaguely, although there were several incidents reported that may have the hallmarks of his handiwork. Constable Bronwen Phillips and I spent much of our time probing these rumours to find anything definitive that might lead to Sullivan and his associates without any real progress. We must have sifted through dozens of reports of small and more significant incidents and snippets of information from all over Wales and there was never a mention of Sullivan's name in any of the information that crossed our desks, but we were beginning to see mentions of activities in which a Workers Revolutionary Party involvement was suggested, and this caught our attention. Again, there was little specific detail, but it seemed that the increasing public approval amongst the working class of the activities of the Bolsheviks in Russia had acted as a catalyst for greater public interest in the ideas and activities of the revolutionary left. Many ordinary British folk were sympathetic to the revolutionary cause in Russia and were beginning to hope that this sort of overthrow of the entrenched elite could also be achieved in Britain. Public meetings, the publication of news-sheets and pamphlets, rallies and marches were becoming commonplace and were often organised by several revolutionary groups working together. This strategy was designed to maximise the impact and reach of their material but also served to obscure who the actual major players were and made the work of investigative policemen much harder. However, the WRP name kept popping up as being associated with events centred around the market town of Newcastle Emlyn in a less populated area in mid-Wales. There was no evidence that the leadership of the WRP were operating within this area, but it seemed to us that they were engaging in activities in an area stretching as far as Cardigan to Fishguard in the west and Milford Haven and Carmarthen to the south-east. O'Hare's name appeared several times as being involved in the disrupting of political meetings of local council and other civic authorities and with the assistance of an acolyte named O'Mahoney, he had broken up peaceful protest rallies and demonstrations by instigating violence against local constables and civic leaders.

O' Hare had been near the top of our list of persons of interest for a long time and was a well-known agitator with a reputation for violence, but the name O'Mahoney was new, and this name appeared nowhere in our files. The most probable explanations for this were that he could be a recent recruit to the revolutionary party with no previous record or that the name he was using was a false identity to hide his real name. It would be far too easy to plump for the false identity option and assume that this was really Ernest Sullivan doing what he did best, but we had not a shred of evidence that this was so. As always with police work, there was no substitute for solid hard work sifting through all potential leads until we could discount one or other of these theories. If it turned out to be Sullivan using a false identity, I must be careful not to allow myself to get too close to Sullivan as he would surely remember me from our last encounter in Kruger's law office when I so nearly put him under arrest. He would certainly be aware of the fates of his former German colleagues and would wish to keep well out of our way. The area of mid- and West Wales where they were operating was massive and it was almost impossible that two officers working alone could keep a focus on the search for this one man. I reckoned that Sullivan would not have a natural tendency to hide himself away from public view as he was confident and not afraid to work out in the open. I remembered the wise strategy of George Bennett immediately after I was run down and nearly killed by the horse and cart driven by Manfred Gruber, where George resisted the temptation to swoop on the Grubers but deliberately gave a false impression that the incident had been an unfortunate accident and that the police were not investigating any further. His intention was to play the long game and lull them into a false sense of security, allowing us the time to identify nearly all the members of the network before we acted.

He was certain that arresting just a few suspects now would only scare the others to go into hiding, to reappear when the heat had died down to carry on their spying activities. I decided that I would follow a similar plan and act as if Sullivan and the WRP were not central to my investigation whilst maintaining low-key surveillance and looking out for any definitive leads that might pinpoint where Sullivan was based. I knew that this would be a waiting game but had little other option due to the lack of evidence at my disposal.

Bronwen and I examined the reports where there was any mention or suggestion of WRP involvement and focused on the incidents where disruption or violence was reported. Bronwen managed to reduce the long list down to seven occasions where members of the WRP were the main perpetrators of the trouble in each case, according to witnesses. She reduced the list further to just four incidents for closer inspection because they included reference to the names O'Hare and O'Mahoney as being involved in the disruption. She marked the location of all the incidents on the map with yellow flags and then the seven where violence occurred in blue and finally the four where O'Hare or O'Mahoney were present in green. The map display was interesting in that it showed that all the incidents where disruptive and violent behaviour had occurred were clustered in quite a tight geographical area and the four where our suspects were named was even tighter, whilst the yellow flags were stretched all over mid- and West Wales, highlighting at least twenty other incidents where the WRP were not mentioned as being present. The four incidents that mentioned O'Hare or O'Mahoney were listed by Bronwen and included a Workers Against Conscription rally held in St David's Park, Cardigan, where a protest meeting of 200 or so people was broken up by a group of a dozen or more men wielding sticks and beating the anti-war protestors as they listened to the speakers. I was confused because I had mistakenly thought the interests of WAC would coincide with those of the WRP, but Bronwen pointed out that the WAC believed in non-violence and only engaged in peaceful protesting, whereas the WRP believed in violent struggle to achieve their aims.

The second incident was the following day and was also held in Cardigan when several leading delegates attending a conference of the Welsh Miners' Alliance were attacked in the street and beaten so severely that they were unable to make their speeches during the conference. The third incident was at Aberporth, where a mob led by O'Mahoney broke into the offices of the district council, smashed the office furniture and blew open the safe with explosives and stole the money collected that day in local rates and taxes. This incident was more severe than the others because the nightwatchman was hit so hard with a wooden club or metal bar that he had not yet gained consciousness. The fourth was an unsuccessful bomb attack on the police station in Newcastle Emlyn, where the bombers were discovered in the act of laying the explosive charges by a watchful constable who caught them in the act. The bombers were so startled that they ran off without setting the detonators, although they did fire several shots at the pursuing policeman. Luckily, the bombs were not made live and were easily dismantled and made safe at the scene, and the constable who had discovered them at work was sure that one of them was O'Hare. There were two other violent incidents outside of the tight inner ring, one at New Inn and another at Cross Key, but no mention of either suspect was made. This information suggested to me that O'Hare and O'Mahoney were settled somewhere within this cordon, in the Cardigan to Newcastle Emlyn area, and I was encouraged to narrow my investigation to this area more closely. I did not want to draw attention to myself in this area but thought that Bronwen could make enquiries discreetly in the local area as she was not known to be associated with the police. I knew that I would need to speak to her first before putting my proposal before the chief inspector for his approval before we could go ahead. I knew also that our two suspects were violent men with no scruples about hurting a woman, especially a policewoman, so I knew I had to play this very carefully to ensure Bronwen's safety. I shuddered at the thought of what O'Hare or Sullivan would do if they discovered she was watching them, so I thought long and hard overnight about what I would propose to the chief inspector the next day.

Although the disruptive activities were taking place all over mid- and West Wales, the evidence clearly showed that the WRP were largely confining their activities to within ten miles or so of Cardigan and were limiting their operations in this area almost exclusively. This suggested to me that they did not yet have the funds or resources to extend themselves beyond this area and indicated that they were probably based somewhere within the area or very close by. The use of violence had a clear objective, which was to disorientate the other protest groups and render them less effective in their campaigns or were deliberate acts of terror designed to attack forces of law and order and governance as demonstrated by the attempted bombing of the police station at Newcastle Emlyn and the ransacking and robbery from the district council offices. The use of firearms and explosives raised the threat from this group far beyond the other groups on our list, who restricted their activities largely to heckling at meetings and a bit of pushing and shoving against police. The presence of O'Hare and possibly Sullivan amongst the leadership of this WRP cell was the strongest evidence of the threat they posed to the lives and property of people in this area. Chief Inspector Bennett accepted my reasoning and agreed that we should concentrate all our efforts on tracking down this cell but was less comfortable with placing Bronwen Phillips undercover in Cardigan or Newcastle Emlyn to watch for the WRP and carry out surveillance. He felt that the risks were so high that a lone officer would not make much difference unless supported by other officers in the vicinity but also recognised that the greater the manpower, the greater the risk of discovery by the WRP. The operation must be as covert as possible, although I felt the best way to hide our intentions was to do so in plain sight, so he suggested that Bronwen be placed in a job in Cardigan or Newcastle as a cover for her being there and she should join at least one of the protest groups in the area and he suggested that Workers Against Conscription might offer the best opportunity to see the WRP at work because they had targeted their meetings before. He concluded by saying that he wasn't happy about Bronwen operating alone and suggested I second one of our colleagues from another team temporarily, to provide her with some security. I was grateful for his approval, although the constraints he had insisted on would make it more difficult to set up in the shorter term. I needed to find a suitable cover role for Bronwen that would provide a compelling reason for her to have moved to the area and I also had to find a colleague to work with her to watch her back and assist with the surveillance work.

*

Sullivan and O'Hare had established themselves in a run-down smallholding on the hillside above the village of Ponthirwaun located six miles from Cardigan and four miles from Newcastle Emlyn. The smallholding used to run large flocks of sheep and grow vegetables in the plots around the house, but the current owner had let it all lapse in recent years and now only grew enough produce for his own table and kept a dozen chickens. Rhodri Owen had once been a keen farmer but the loss of his two sons to the war followed by the death of his wife had led him to drink too much and let things go. He had become an angry and aggressive man, banned from most of the public houses in the area for fighting, and he would support any cause that would enable him to strike back and take revenge for his loss. He started reading the revolutionary pamphlets that circulated in the village and in town and found himself drawn towards the WRP. In time, his regular attendance and militant support for the party increased the trust they had in him and when O'Hare came to this region with his associate, O'Mahoney, and was looking for somewhere discreet to stay, Owen freely offered his place as a remote and secure place for his leader to stay whilst he was in the area, and although he thought this would only be a temporary arrangement they had lodged with him for nearly three months so far and there was no sign that they were going to move on just yet. Trust had built between the three of them and Owen had been brought into their confidence and assisted in planning each of their operations. O' Hare and O'Mahoney rarely left the farm and were certainly never seen in the nearest village, although Owen was at pains to keep up his usual routine to allay any suspicions that things were not as usual at the farm. He still bought his supplies and sold some eggs in the village and occasionally visited the pub for a drink but kept his ear to the ground in case any chatter or rumours about his guests should emerge. Owen owned a small van which they used for transport for any operations they embarked on but otherwise it was parked out of sight in the barn and Rhodri still rode his old mule to and from the village as usual. When the van was used to leave the farm, they took great pains to take the single track which led away from the village so as not to be seen or recognised in the village.

Rhodri had dug out a large dry pit for the storage of arms and ammunition and another for explosives and kept watch for anything unusual or people he didn't recognise passing the farm entrance or taking any interest in the property. Since the deaths of his family, there had been no visitors to the farm and Rhodri had no friends to speak of, so apart from the occasional letter no one came to the farm. He had found contentment in working with Rory and Ernest and devoted himself fully to the cause by providing the local knowledge needed for the successful planning of each new operation. Neither Rory nor Ernest were hotheads and were content to think things through carefully and plan meticulously to ensure success and avoid arrest. They liked operations to go smoothly, like the robbery from the district council, but were extremely upset that their attempt to bomb the police station had been thwarted and the operation failed. They spent hours analysing what had happened and why they had failed to detonate the bombs successfully and although some would put it down to misfortune that a sharp-eyed constable had spotted them in the act of laying the explosives, they were not prepared to accept that this was their bad luck but was a result of their inadequate planning. For days after this operation, they wrestled with what needed to be done better and came up with a plan for more efficient lookouts, to identify potential witnesses and to eradicate them before they could raise the alarm. Rhodri had counted the money stolen from the council and it had amounted to nearly five hundred pounds in mixed notes, copper and silver, which would be extremely useful for funding future operations in the area.

That morning, the three of them had been considering which objective should be their next target and there was a debate as to whether they should blow up the railway bridge which carried the mainline into Cardigan to disrupt trains across the region, although Rory argued that destroying the signal box at Newcastle junction would have the same effect and was closer. The third alternative was the assassination of Sir Walter Wynn-Jones, the chairman of the magistrates' court at Cardigan, who was well known as a hardliner who passed the harshest sentences on activists when they were brought before his court. Arguments were eloquently made for all three targets, and it was finally agreed that they would plan for all three in the next month. O'Mahoney swayed their thinking by pointing out that opportunity was what governed their choice here as the railway targets were fixed and could be attacked on any cloudy moonless night, whereas to get close enough to Sir Walter an opportunity needed to present itself for them to be able to get near enough to kill him and still make their escape. They considered shooting him with pistols or a rifle but decided that the shooter could stand a high risk of being captured so it was finally decided that they would plan to use explosives. Rhodri was tasked with reconnoitering the target's house and route to the magistrates' court and the courthouse itself as likely locations for the attack.

Sir Walter lived in a medium-sized estate near Llandygwydd about three miles outside of Cardigan and travelled to the court in a large enclosed car at nine in the morning, driven by his chauffeur. Rhodri had noted that the car had to stop at the main gate to the property whilst the chauffeur got out and opened the gates, drove the car through and then closed them again before they set off on their journey to Cardigan. The car stopped for approximately two and a half minutes and the target was most vulnerable to attack at this point. He had also noticed that there was a culvert which ran under the roadway about six feet before the gates to ensure the efficient drainage of excess water from the carriage driveway, and this could be a suitable location for planting the bombs the night before. However, he concluded that to do this would require the bomb layer to visit the site twice, to lay the bomb under the cover of darkness and to set off the charge whilst the car was stopped in the morning, which seemed a higher risk than at first anticipated. He also suggested that they could not be sure that the chauffeur stopped the car at the same point every time, which could mean a variance of the distance of the seat of the explosion from the target, so they couldn't be sure whether the target would be killed or just injured by the blast. There was much heated discussion about this but finally they agreed that the best option would be to shoot the magistrate as he waited in his car at the gates. This would require two of them, one as the driver of the van ready for a quick getaway and a shooter. They were all convinced that this was the best tactic to ensure that the victim was dead when they left. There was further disagreement about whether they should shoot the chauffeur as well, with Rory and Rhodri arguing that if they wore masks there was little chance of being recognised, whilst Sullivan was certain that the chauffeur should be killed alongside his master. Rhodri was tasked with getting a copy of the schedule of court sittings for the next month so that they could see on what days the court would be sitting so that they could plan the operation in more detail. Rhodri was nervous as this was the first time that he had seen O'Hare and O'Mahoney disagree seriously on a matter of policy and was afraid that this might be the first crack in their solidarity and may prove to be a weakness going forward.

The attack on the magistrate was fixed for Wednesday morning the next week, which would allow enough time to source a suitable weapon and ammunition and to carry out the necessary surveillance of the morning gate routine with accurate timings to prepare the shooter to make the killing shot as quickly as possible. They were certain that the best chance of success was with complete surprise and speed of execution and planned that the target would be shot within sixty seconds of stopping at the gate and that the shooter would be driven away within ninety seconds. Speed and efficiency would be crucial to their success; both attackers would wear dark clothing and pull a balaclava over their heads so that no one could identify hair colour or facial features. They would remain silent throughout so there were no audible clues either, for both O'Hare and O'Mahoney had strong southern Irish accents, too easy to recognise in this rural Welsh district. Sullivan was anxious to be the shooter and was prepared to source the weapon, which he said could not be traced back to them because it came from the German Army and had never been fired in Britain before. He had the weapon hidden in his bag and it was a Luger automatic pistol, which was highly accurate in the hands of a skilled shooter. They did not know that Sullivan had lied and that this pistol had been used many times and would be easily identified by the police as the weapon used to murder five people in Wales in the past year. Rory O'Hare reluctantly accepted Sullivan's suggestion to use this weapon but decided that he would be the shooter and Sullivan would be the driver. The plan would be to drive the van to a location approximately one hundred yards from the gates and for the shooter to climb over the wall and make his way through the trees towards the gates out of sight from the carriage driveway and wait for Sir Walter's car to stop in front of the gates. The van would move slowly down the road and pull in to block the exit as the chauffeur was returning to the car.

That Wednesday morning was bright and clear with hardly a cloud in the sky and although it made concealment more difficult, it also gave Rory excellent visual of the approach of the car towards the gates. As the chauffeur got out of the car and strode towards the gate, pulling a ring of keys from his pocket, he did not see the black-clad figure step out of the bushes and stretch to open the rear door of the car. Sir Walter was reading court papers from a bundle on the seat and, momentarily deep in concentration, did not notice the attacker for a brief second but he became aware that something out of the ordinary was happening as he caught a glimpse of the long barrel of the machine pistol coming through the door of the car and pointing directly at him. His instinct for survival was strong enough to make him dive for the floor, instantly throwing up his leather attaché case in front of his body. The first shot smashed into the leather of the case and the second was deflected but hit his left shoulder a glancing blow, which was not enough to prevent him gripping hold of his army service revolver which he always carried in his case for protection in case of attacks like this since magistrates had become regular targets of revolutionary anarchists during the latter years of the war. He managed to get a shot off but in his upended position he was unable to take a careful aim, but he was lucky to hit his attacker in the upper chest, knocking him to the ground on his back. The black-clad figure did not appear to be dead but had certainly been wounded seriously so Sir Walter felt he had the time to climb out of the car and take the decisive final shot to finish him off where he lay. He extricated himself from the opposite side of the car rearwards in a mix of case and papers and strode around the back of the car with his gun in his hand. Rory O'Hare was seriously wounded and could not summon the strength to force himself up onto his feet and take the third shot and just lay helplessly awaiting his fate, cursing that he would end his days at the hands of a middle-aged English gentleman from the class he hated most in the world. He reasoned how things could have gone so wrong so quickly after all their careful planning as he stared at the barrel of the army revolver pointing straight at his head; he knew his time was up. A sudden burst of shouting followed by two shots in quick succession, and he passed out at this moment and was unaware that Sullivan had run from the seat of the van, shouted at the chauffeur and then shot him in the forehead between the eyes and fired a second shot into the back of Sir Walter's head and ran to his accomplice lying before him. A quick examination satisfied him that Rory was still alive so he grabbed him unceremoniously into a fireman's lift and staggered to the rear of the van and threw him inside and covered him over with some sacks, ran back to the driving seat and drove off as fast as he could. He reckoned that the number of shots may have been noticed by anyone close by and the alarm raised already, so he thought it was essential to put some distance between him and the scene as quickly as possible. He was driven by the conflicting actions of driving away from the scene in a different direction to the farm to mislead any pursuers or heading straight there so that they could administer first aid as soon as possible. He decided to compromise and headed west towards Aberporth, intending to take the mountain tracks over the hill back to Rhodri's farm. He hoped that he could get there undiscovered in approximately thirty minutes and that Rory would survive long enough to make the journey. He had two imperatives at the front of his mind: one to get the van undercover and out of sight as quickly as possible and secondly to see if anything could be done to see to Rory's wounds.

Luckily for them, even though five shots had been fired in quick succession, it was nearly six minutes before the first person arrived to see what had happened and why there had been firing, and Sullivan had already driven nearly two and a half miles from the scene in this time. The first on the scene was Llewellyn, the gamekeeper, on his bicycle, followed by the under-butler and footman from the house running after him. Their sense of shock at the bloody scene before their eyes and the corpses of their master and his chauffeur lying in the road was a massive shock to them and threw them into some confusion. The young footman knew that they should raise the alarm and ran back to the house to use the telephone to call the local police, which meant it was eighteen minutes before the call was placed to Newcastle Emlyn Police Station, by which time the trail was pretty much dead. The duty sergeant promised to get someone out to them immediately and alerted the coroner's office in Cardigan, but it was after eleven before the first policemen arrived and twelve-thirty before a detective arrived on the scene. Detective Constable Grantley had never attended a murder enquiry before and was already out of his depth in securing the scene and looking for initial clues, and he knew that he did not have the skill or experience to handle a case of this importance and would ask the inspector to hand the case over to a more experienced officer. The police surgeon and his team were investigating the scene for any clues and liaising with the coroner's office for the removal of the bodies to the morgue. It was well into the afternoon before the wheels of police bureaucracy were fully turning and a murder investigation fully underway.

The delay in setting up the police response gave Sullivan ample time to make his way surreptitiously back to the farm without attracting any attention, and by ten o'clock that morning the van was hidden away out of sight in the barn and Rory was lying on the kitchen table with Rhodri examining his wounds. There was a lot of blood but when it was washed away, he could see only one entry wound high up on the chest wall which suggested that the bullet had missed his heart and lungs but was still lodged between the rib cage and the bottom of the shoulder blade. Rhodri had little medical knowledge but years of looking after animals had given him a rudimentary understanding of anatomy and he had listened to Rory's breathing and felt his pulse and was sure that the main objective should be to remove the bullet and then close the wound securely and let Rory rest and recuperate. With ample time, he should recover his full strength. He figured that the bullet would be more easily removed from his back and said that he would try to locate it by touch and cut it out with a sharp knife. He was sure that a failure to remove the bullet would lead to the flare-up of infection and possible blood poisoning, which if left alone, untreated, would cause long-term complications for Rory and possibly his death. He was sure that Rory really needed to be in hospital and to be operated on by a proper surgeon but this was not possible in the circumstances so he would have to do it here on the kitchen table. His biggest problem was that he did not have any anesthetic or painkillers that he could use so he reckoned that he would have to use alcoholic spirit to sterilise the wound and to numb the pain for his patient. He found two bottles of whisky in the cupboard and half a bottle of brandy and decided that this would have to do, and he instructed Sullivan to start making Rory drink down as many brandies as he could stomach to dull the pain whilst he sterilised his sharpest knives in the fire and scrubbed his hands and arms with soap and hot water. It took six large brandies to put Rory into a comatose state and they turned him over so he was face down and tied him down firmly on the table so he could not make any sudden movements whilst Rhodri was probing for the bullet. He reckoned that he could dig for the bullet and cut it out and flood the wound with alcohol to kill off the germs and then stitch the wound in his back and then the entry wound on his chest, smother both with honey from the jar from his hive and then bind his torso tight with bandages and get Rory into bed. He understood clearly that the first forty-eight hours would be crucial to Rory's recovery and hoped the cleansing effect of the alcohol would kill off the germs in the wound sufficiently and the natural healing of the honey would help him to regain his strength quickly. However, his biggest concern was that he had no access to penicillin to fight the infection if a fever started in the next couple of days or anything to regulate the pain in both wounds, which he knew would be extremely uncomfortable and difficult to bear without medication. Even though Rory had passed out through the amount of brandy he had consumed, he still flinched and jerked around on the table as the knife blade probed into his back. There was so much blood seeping from the wound that Rhodri could hardly see what he was doing and just had to proceed by touch, but found it difficult to push the knife blade too hard as Rory cried out with every prod of the blade. It seemed a long time but was probably only thirty seconds before he could feel something hard, which he knew could not be a bone by its position, and cleaned away the excess blood to get a closer look. He tried to work around the object with the tip of the knife, but this caused more intense pain for Rory, so he pushed his finger into the hole instead and immediately felt the rounded tip of a round from a revolver and managed to move it slightly. He had found a pair of tweezers that had belonged to his wife and used them to grab the top of the bullet and slowly and as gently as he could draw it out of his back and put it into the dish on the table. Immediately, he set about staunching the bleeding, washed out the wound with the whisky and smeared honey over the wound and put a small dressing over the wound. He untied Rory from the table and got Sullivan to help him turn Rory over so he could dress the wound to his chest the same way. Sullivan had examined the bullet and was certain it was a .45 from a British army service revolver that had been fired at the target whilst he was on the ground, judging by the angle at which the bullet had struck Rory high up on the chest. This is what saved his life for if the shooter had been upright, he would have surely killed Rory at such a close range.

With the operation over, Rhodri cleaned up as best he could and bound Rory's torso tight with a bandage he had cut into strips from a flat sheet in the cupboard and he and Sullivan together managed to carry Rory upstairs and put him into his bed, where he quickly descended into a deep, drunken sleep. Rhodri was certain that this respite was only temporary and within twelve hours or so Rory would be awake and feeling hungover and in excruciating pain. It was essential that he had something more to administer to his patient tonight; otherwise, all this work to remove the bullet would be to no avail. He poured two fingers of the remaining whisky into a couple of glasses and gave one to Sullivan and asked him to explain what had happened. "We had planned it so carefully so nothing could go wrong. You were certain that it would be a simple in and out and all over within two minutes." Ernest said that it did go almost to plan but they had not reckoned on the old boy carrying his old service revolver, fully loaded in his briefcase, and that he would be quick to react when Rory opened the door to take the killing shot. He said that he was unable to see what happened in the cabin of the saloon car, but he heard Rory's shot from the Luger, followed almost immediately by a second shot from a different weapon which severely wounded Rory and he fell to the ground. He could see that he would have to clear up the mess and leapt out of the van and shot the chauffeur and put a bullet into the back of the target's head. He had carried Rory to the van and put him in the back and covered him over with sacks, checked that they had not left anything that would give away their identity and drove away in just over the time they had allowed themselves for the attack. Sullivan was sure that they must learn the lesson of being too confident and not being prepared enough for every eventuality. Sullivan and Rhodri had never talked much since he had been living in Rhodri's house, but he seemed genuinely pleased with Rhodri's work treating Rory's wounds today and was about to start considering him as an equal partner with him and Rory and not just as the support player. Rhodri suggested that it was essential to go out that night after dark and rob a dispensing chemist's shop to get some penicillin and morphine to quell the pain and some more bandages. He said it was not possible to buy these items without a doctor's prescription but he would be unable to ask a doctor to sign one as he would want to see the patient before he issued such a prescription for these drugs. Their only hope was to break into the back of a chemist's shop that night and take what was needed. They decided to pay a visit to the pharmacy on the Newcastle Road in Cardigan around midnight that night.

It was important to be careful driving around late at night because very few vehicles were on the road after dark. Rhodri drove the van and, he being familiar with local roads and tracks, they managed to make their way to Cardigan without attracting any attention. The most vulnerable time was entering the outskirts of the town, although they knew that they would reach the chemist's shop within a minute and that there was an alley big enough to hide the van to the right of the shop premises. They pulled up in a dark patch and switched off the engine and waited for ten minutes or so to see if they had disturbed any prowling dogs or awakened any residents. It was soon apparent that all remained quiet, and Sullivan told Rhodri to wait in the van whilst he made a quick reconnaissance to discover the best way to enter the premises. He was back within fifteen minutes and said that they should be able to enter from the back of the shop and reminded him to be quick once he was inside the shop even though he thought the premises were empty. The rear door was made of steel, making it difficult to force, but was fastened with a heavy-duty padlock, which Sullivan snapped off with a large pair of bolt cutters they had brought from the barn. Sullivan entered first to check all was clear and Rhodri closed the rear door gently to avoid making any additional noise. Sullivan said they only had five minutes to get what was needed and make good their escape. There was little light in the storeroom, but Rhodri had brought three candles which were lit up and gave a soft glow in the room, enough to see by for a quick search without showing much light outside which might give them away. As Rhodri had suspected, the drugs were in a locked cabinet but with Sullivan's crowbar the door was soon open. Rhodri didn't really have much idea about how much of each drug they needed so just grabbed a large bottle of each and as many bandages as he could find, and they were out of the shop within the allotted time limit. Rhodri was loading the haul into the back of the van when a voice challenged him sternly and asked him what he thought he was doing. Rhodri spun round and came face to face with a constable shining his lantern into his face and asking what he was doing coming from the rear of the chemist's shop. Rhodri was quite flummoxed and almost panicked but was saved when Sullivan grabbed the policeman and with one deft movement slit his throat. The blood spurted out and the policeman collapsed to the floor without another sound. Rhodri was rooted to the spot, but Sullivan grabbed him and pushed him towards the driving seat, and they drove off as fast as they could.

SEVENTEEN

The murder of Sir Walter Wynn-Jones and his chauffeur had caused quite a stir and Inspector Hughes, in charge of the local station, had quickly realised that he did not have the manpower, resources or experience to handle such a high-profile case successfully, and immediately requested outside assistance from force headquarters. The detective superintendent at headquarters telephoned George Bennett and ordered him to send his best men over to Newcastle Emlyn and to take over the lead in this enquiry. Within an hour, Chief Inspector Bennett had appointed Detective Sergeant Wesley Morgan as the senior investigating officer and instructed him to select his team and to get to the area as quickly as possible. Wesley was grateful to be given this opportunity to lead another major enquiry so soon after the Wurtenberg investigation and was quick to select Bronwen Phillips, Constables Rhys Evans and Ivor Bethal.

*

I looked forward to working with Evans and Bethal again and I knew that they would warm to Bronwen Phillips as quickly as I had because she had a quick mind and plenty of common sense. She was also a fluent Welsh speaker, whilst the rest of us had only a rudimentary understanding of our native language. I requisitioned a second vehicle for us to take with us and we collected our personal things and had left for Newcastle Emlyn by mid-afternoon. Bronwen had been busy before we left and had found suitable accommodation for the team. We were all to be accommodated at the Castle Inn, where Ivor and Rhys were sharing a room and Bronwen and I had a room each to ourselves. The drive from Swansea took us about two hours through Carmarthen and up into mid-Wales and we reported to the police station and met Inspector Hughes by five-thirty just before he went off duty, but he gave me a brief overview of where the investigation was at this stage and said the police surgeon was carrying out the post-mortem that afternoon and would be ready to discuss his findings in the morning. I felt there was little we could do until we had heard from the coroner, so I took the case notes and we headed for the hotel to get booked in.

The Castle Inn was a cross between a coaching inn and a local pub and had a bright and lively public bar, which I knew would please Ivor, but I had a feeling that Rhys Evans was chapel and did not approve of drinking that much. I suggested we all meet in the lounge for half an hour before our dinner to go over the case notes so far and to plan our first moves in the morning. The rooms were quite spacious and clean, and my room had a large bay window overlooking the market square and a large double bed. I was pleased that there was a public bar for I knew that Ivor would become quickly and easily assimilated with the locals and would pick up lots of useful local gossip that the rest of us would struggle to find otherwise. There wasn't very much in the case notes as there were no eyewitnesses to the murders, only the statements of those who had discovered the bodies after the event. I realised that the findings of the police surgeon and his team would be the real starting point, but I decided that I would send Evans and Bethal to the scene in the morning to see what a couple of fresh pairs of more experienced eyes could make of it and to also examine the magistrate's car, which was still at the scene. Bronwen and I would meet with the police surgeon at the morgue and see what he could tell us about the murders after the post-mortem examination. I asked Ivor to keep his ears open when he was drinking in the bar for any suggestion in the local gossip about anyone who particularly had a grudge against the magistrate or any other background information that might give us some hints towards establishing useful lines of enquiry.

Bronwen and I arrived at the morgue at a quarter past eight to find the police surgeon and his team had already left to attend the scene of another murder a few minutes before. I was wondering what sort of place we had come to with two murders in twenty-four hours, and I wondered if they were in any way connected because I was sure that this part of Wales was normally quiet and peaceful. The young man manning the desk told us that a body had been discovered in an alleyway behind Baldwin's chemist's shop on the Newcastle Road in Cardigan. The body was that of the local beat bobby, Matthew Richards, who was on night duty last night and it appeared that he discovered a robbery taking place at the chemist's shop and had his throat cut. He told us that if we followed the road outside the morgue west for four miles or so we should see the chemist's shop on the left-hand side just after entering the town limits of Cardigan. Two officers of the law in this district killed violently in one day seemed too much of a coincidence and we set off as fast as we could to find this location and in about fifteen minutes, we could see the cluster of police vehicles and an ambulance in front of the shop on the left side of the road. We parked up and walked up to the shop where we bumped into Inspector Hughes, whose face immediately took on a look of relief when we walked in. He was glad we had arrived so promptly, and he was happy to hand everything over to me after briefly telling us that a robbery had taken place on this premises in the night and controlled drugs and some bandages stolen. We knew that the burglars had come in and left via the rear door and must have made their escape through the alleyway. The body of Constable Richards was found in the alleyway and his throat had been cut by a very sharp knife and I could see that there were tears forming at the corner of his eyes as he was telling us this. "The police surgeon is examining the body now in the alley before removing it to the morgue, if you want to catch him before he leaves." I thanked him and we made our way through the shop and out into the alley, which was completely cordoned off, and I could see that the body was already in the back of the ambulance to be removed to the morgue, but my attention was drawn to a large patch of blood on the ground where the unfortunate constable had bled to death and there was a man on all fours with a magnifying glass held up to his face who I suspected was the police surgeon. He stood up and called his assistant to make a plaster cast of tyre tracks that he had just been examining and then turned to me and asked if I was Detective Sergeant Morgan and introduced himself as Dr James Roberts, the police surgeon and coroner. I asked for his initial assessment of what had happened here, and he was reluctant to say too much but said he had some interesting findings in the case of Sir Walter Wynn-Jones and would say more then. Just to whet my appetite, he said that there had been a robbery at the chemist's shop last night and that he may be able to be more specific about time after he had examined the body in the morgue. The robbers could have taken a lot more drugs than was taken but only took two bottles, one of penicillin and one of morphine, which suggested to him that they wanted these drugs for a specific purpose, which could be treating a gunshot or knife wound. They could have taken many more bottles of these drugs if they had wished, which could have fetched a good price on the black market, but they left them behind. This suggested that these were not criminal burglars but were nevertheless outside of the law in that they wished to treat someone with serious injuries without going to a local doctor or hospital. He felt that this would give me something to think about during the morning and he would be happy to discuss my conclusions around twelve noon at the morgue.

Bronwen and I returned to the car and talked over what we had seen and heard that morning and then decided we would find our way to the scene of the murder of Sir Walter before making our way to the morgue again for noon. We found Evans and Bethal making a thorough search of the scene of the murder and were quite excited with what they had to impart after their thorough search of the inside of the car and the area immediately around it. They were both certain that there were two attackers and pointed to four sets of footprints clearly visible in the area within fifteen feet of the gate itself. One set indicated a good-quality dress shoe with a leather sole and heel, and they were only found close to the right rear door of the car and around the back of the car, which suggested that the wearer had exited the car and come round the back of the car to the nearside. They surmised that these were most likely to be the prints made by Sir Walter. The second set of prints were made by a heavy pair of work boots of the type worn by labourers or tradesmen, and they showed that the wearer had approached from the woods to the left of the gate and approached as far as the left rear door then fallen back a little, but there were no footprints indicating that he had run away. The chauffeur's uniform boots were easily identified as were his movements to open the gates and there was a second set of workman's boots, a larger size than the first pair, which approached from outside of the gates, probably running by the depth of the indentation in the gravel. It was easy to see that he had run towards the chauffeur and then behind the car towards where Sir Walter was standing, indicating that he was a second shooter. The confused footmarks suggested that the second shooter had lifted a heavy load and carried it some thirty feet to some kind of vehicle waiting in the road outside the gates. Evans interrupted Bethal at this point to suggest that the blood patterns added greater significance to the evidence of the relative movements of the attackers and the victims. He posed a theory that attacker one had climbed over the perimeter wall and made his way stealthily through the woods and approached the left rear door without being seen, attempting to get his shot at Sir Walter in complete surprise. However, the evidence in the car suggested that things hadn't quite gone to plan for although there were some blood spatters evident, they suggested that they came from a superficial wound, and Sir Walter's leather briefcase on the seat was stuffed full of papers and I was sure that Sir Walter threw it at his assailant to disturb his aim. It appeared that the first shot was deflected by the edge of the heavy bag. The footmarks around the rear of the car suggested that Sir Walter bravely came around the back of the car to tackle his assailant armed with his Webley service revolver, which we knew from the constable at the scene was found lying on the ground where he lay. There were two large pools of blood evident on the left side of the car about six feet apart. The bloodstains closest to the car were from the shot to the back of the head administered by the second attacker, whereas the bloodstains further away were more extensive and probably came from a gunshot wound to the body of the first attacker, which would have bled profusely. I surmised that Sir Walter got a clean shot at the first attacker and hit him in the torso, which brought him to the ground severely injured. The second attacker saw all this happening and ran from the vehicle to kill the chauffeur and Sir Walter with only two shots and to rescue his wounded comrade and get him away to safety.

Ivor continued their analysis and indicated that the tyre tracks in the road suggested a small vehicle, like a light van or car, and he showed me a drawing of some distinctive marks on the offside rear tyre which would make it easy to identify this vehicle if we saw these strange nicks in the solid tyre. The tread had been cut by something sharp that had left a distinctive v-shaped nick. I was reminded that I saw the police surgeon paying special interest to the tyre track outside the rear of the chemist's shop where drugs and bandages to treat a gunshot had been stolen the night before and a policeman murdered. Perhaps there could be a link between these two murders, and I was rapidly concluding that we were looking for two men, one of whom could be seriously wounded, which meant that their ability to escape from the area was seriously hampered by their wounded comrade. I was sure that they were likely to be hiding within a few miles of the scene of both murders. Attempting to escape from a murder scene with a badly wounded accomplice on board was high risk, and I was sure that they would have a hideout close by where they could wait out their time until the intensity of the police investigation began to wind down. The distance between the scene of Sir Walter's murder and the robbery and murder at Baldwin's chemist's shop was scarcely two miles, so I took out the local OS map and placed a cross midway between the two murder locations and then traced a three-mile circle and the another at five miles out for closer analysis when we returned to the station. I asked Ivor to make quick sketches of the footprints around Sir Walter's car and to draw a sketch map of the movements of the attackers and their victims as they had described to me earlier. It was still only eleven and I felt that we had made some big strides already so leaving Rhys and Ivor to finish their investigation at Sir Walter's house, Bronwen and I set off to the morgue to meet with Doctor Roberts.

I was anxious to hear what he had to say and to share with him my theory that the two cases were linked but knew that as a scientist he would only be directed by the evidence and would not be willing to follow fancy theories without hard facts to back them up. Bronwen and I settled down in his office to wait for him to come from the laboratory to give us his report on the murders of Sir Walter Wynn-Jones and his chauffeur. The doctor launched straight into his post-mortem report, talking ad lib directly from his notes as he had not yet had enough time to write up the report. He confirmed that both Sir Walter and the chauffeur had probably been shot with the same gun and he had sent the rounds he had taken from their bodies and the casings picked up from the ground around the car for further analysis by a weapons expert at Sennybridge Camp and he would expect confirmation within twenty-four hours. He was sure that it was a high-velocity weapon judging by the extent of the wounds to both men and the fact that they were both killed with just one shot to the head. This suggested that the shooter was an experienced shot and had executed them with the precision of an experienced assassin. However, Sir Walter had two bullets in him, the one lodged in the back of his brain which killed him instantly and a second round lodged in his right shoulder in the flesh below his collarbone. He could tell from the blood analysis that the shot to the shoulder occurred first and that this could not have been fired from shooter two's gun because the killing shot came from immediately behind the victim, whereas the first shot was fired from Sir Walter's front. "The tests on the blood found in the car and around the body of Sir Walter are consistent with his blood type, which was O negative, but the large pool of blood approximately six feet in front of where Sir Walter lay was found to be of blood type A. We also found a Webley army service revolver dating from the South African Wars which we believe belonged to Sir Walter who had served as a major in the South African campaign. This evidence suggests, although we have no body, that the blood came from the first attacker, who made the shoulder shot to Sir Walter, who then managed to draw his revolver and shoot him in return. The amount of blood on the ground suggests that he was hit in the main part of the body but the fact that his body is missing suggests that he was not dead, and the second attacker had probably removed him from the scene, and this is borne out by the disturbed marks and deeper indentations in the ground suggesting he was carried to a vehicle to make good their escape. People close by have indicated that they heard five shots in quick succession, although I have only been able to find three inside the bodies at the scene, which suggests that Sir Walter could have fired the other shots from his revolver, and we may be looking for a wounded attacker with two rounds inside him. The Webley is not a very accurate weapon except at close quarters, when it really packs a punch, so if this man has been hit twice at a range of six feet or so he could be in very serious danger of death."

I thanked the doctor for his report and described to him the evidence we had found at the scene and the theories that my team were developing from them. He was more than interested to share with us and to look at the sketches of the footprints and Ivor's sketch map and was particularly interested in the description of the unusual cuts on the tyre tread because he had made a plaster cast of the tyre track of the vehicle at the chemist's shop murder because he had noticed some unusual marks from the tyre tread too. We arranged to compare the two later that afternoon but before we left I suggested to him that maybe the two murders were linked and perhaps the tyre tread would prove it if they were identical, but also I liked the idea that one of the shooters had been seriously wounded during the attack and would need to be treated for these wounds with an antibiotic drug to stop the spread of infection and a strong painkiller to subdue the pain. The robbery at the chemist's suggested that they were taking what they needed to treat the gunshot wound effectively, which suggested that someone in the gang had some medical knowledge to even know what to steal from the shop. I asked the police surgeon whether this meant that we were looking for a rogue surgeon or an experienced nurse, but he shook his head and suggested that in this area lots of farmers and their workers had a rudimentary understanding of anatomy and basic medicine from the treatment of their sick animals and from dealing with accidents that can occur on the farm involving serious injury, especially in remote upland areas a long way from specialised medical help. In these circumstances, many farmers just performed medical procedures themselves without calling for medical aid. He said his guess would be that it was a farmer who would perform the operations to remove the bullets and apply first aid and his advice would be to look at some of the isolated and remote farms as likely hideouts for the perpetrators. He went on to say that even if the farmer concerned was quite able, the difficulty of setting up the sterile conditions to perform invasive surgery without the proper tools and no anesthetic would be very high risk indeed. The medications stolen in the Baldwin robbery and murder would only provide antibiotic treatment and pain relief for a relatively short time, and he would suspect that further raids on chemists' premises would occur within five to seven days.

I then asked the doctor for any initial thoughts on the murder of PC Richards in the alley outside Baldwin's chemist's shop and he said it would be difficult to give too much detail as he had yet to examine the body more closely, but he was able to say that there was evidence of a vehicle being parked in the alleyway during the night and he was waiting for the plaster cast to set to confirm this. There were plenty of footprints in the dust which suggested that at least three people had been present in the alley at the time of the murder and he could clearly identify three different kinds of footwear as having made the marks. The constable's standard police boot was the easiest to recognise and one of the other footprints was similar to the heavy-duty workboots worn by the shooters at the earlier murder scene. The third boot was of a better-quality leather boot popular with farmers who preferred a design which was a cross between a work boot and a riding boot so that they could ride horses around the farm or work on foot without changing their footwear. He cautioned me that these were only theories until he had compared the footprints from both scenes more closely and looked at the cast of the vehicle tyres and compared it with my officer's sketch of the tyre track at Sir Walter's gate, but we might have a firm conclusion by mid-afternoon. "The most significant inference we can probably draw from this information is that we could be looking for three perpetrators, the two shooters and the farmer, as there is no evidence of the farmer being present at the murder of Sir Walter, but he was certainly present in the alleyway outside the chemist's shop last night."

He concluded from his initial examination of the body that Constable Richards had died from a single cut to his throat which severed his carotid artery and jugular and he died from severe bleeding within several minutes, although the severity of the trauma would have rendered him almost lifeless on the floor from the initial shock. "The attack came from behind and the cut was a single stroke from left to right across the throat and from the depth of the cut I would surmise that the blade was very sharp indeed and was probably a specially sharpened domestic razor of the folding type that could be carried safely in the pocket or baggage without arousing suspicion and used as a normal domestic razor if required. The attacker was several inches taller than Richards, judging by the angle of the cut in his neck, and he had deliberately chosen to take this weapon because the discharging of firearms at this time of night would have immediately raised the alarm." In his opinion, this person was a skilled killer and knew that his single stroke of the razor would render Constable Richards lifeless on the ground, whereas a less experienced assailant would have taken several strokes to achieve the same impact, suggesting that in both cases there appeared to be one attacker who was a more skilled assassin than the other.

"When he was attacked, Richards had his back to the gate in the perimeter wall of the chemist's premises and this is obvious from the blood pattern and the position of the body on the ground. He would have been taken by surprise and I guess this would be because his attention was focused on the second man, probably the farmer, who was being questioned by Richards about his presence in the alley at this time of night. We found his notebook and pencil on the ground about two feet from his body and there is the beginning of some notes on the page, but it is too cryptic to give us much of a clue. I looked at the pad and could see he had started to write something, but with the blood and the dust from the alley staining the page all I could make out were the letters "R" and "H", the possible meaning of which was not immediately obvious to me."

After the morgue, my team met together at the police station and Inspector Hughes had found a large room which they had used as a furniture store in the attic for our use. It was a bit dusty and untidy, and the skylights needed to be opened to let in some fresh air, but within an hour the room was spick and span and we had settled into our temporary base. There were five cells in the basement that we could use if required and two interview rooms on the same floor also, and Hughes had arranged for a post office engineer to install a telephone in our office with a direct line to the local telephone exchange. Housekeeping completed, we settled down for our first serious review of the evidence so far and Ivor set up a huge board where we could write up the key issues so far and the checklist of things that we must do with a scale of urgency alongside each issue. It did not take long for the board to get filled and I called a halt and tried to get the team to focus on the highest priorities on our list.

First, we spread out an unmarked copy of the local ordnance survey sheet for this area and using a large compass fixed one point on the midpoint between the two murder scenes and opened it to three miles on the scale of the map and described a circle and repeated the operation again at three miles. We now had a credible starting point, and I had a strong feeling that we would find them within the inner circle, and I tasked Rhys and Ivor with a detailed examination of both circles which I had noticed covered quite a large area, although much of it was extremely hilly, rough country and the farms and hamlets quite sparse. I asked them to list all the farms, smallholdings and isolated dwellings that we would search in the next couple of days, ignoring the villages where we would be able to perform house-to-house enquiries in the next couple of days and where concerned citizens would report anything they considered out of the usual when asked by the police. I wanted Bronwen to lead this activity with the help of some constables from Newcastle police station because she was a fluent Welsh speaker and although the questions would be conducted in English, I asked her to conceal the fact that she spoke Welsh so that she could eavesdrop on any side comments in Welsh that were different from the answers given in English.

We then settled to tackle the question of what the R and H in Constable Richards' notebook might mean and brainstormed some random ideas to try to focus our thinking more purposefully. We came up with several possibilities that bore further thinking, starting with the most obvious and working outwards. Firstly, we had to consider that this had no bearing on the events at the chemist's that night and was perhaps a note to jog his memory about something that had happened earlier. Secondly, it might be a reference to a person he recognised from a previous case, and these might be his initials, and Bronwen suggested she would look at all the cases that Richards had dealt with since he joined this police station to see if there was a person with the initials RH in his case files. Thirdly, we thought he might have jotted down a place name where he had seen this person before and I said that I would search the map for any places, house names or physical features with RH in their name. Bronwen disappeared downstairs to investigate Constable Richards' case files whilst I looked for RH places on the map. After an hour of checking the map with a magnifying glass, I had only found one place with RH, which was a small village called Rhyd situated just south of the main road to Cardigan and certainly within the target area. I hoped that Bronwen had better luck, but it was several hours before she reported back that she was glad that Richards had only been at Newcastle Emlyn for eighteen months for he had over fifty cases that he had dealt with in that time, and it seemed that he was a very conscientious young policeman. She had read through his files to cull out the names of suspects, victims and those convicted or receiving warnings or fines but had found only one RH, which referred to a Roland Hughes who was a sheep farmer who had died last winter when he fell and broke his leg one winter's night and froze to death before he was discovered two days later. She had made two lists: the first listing all those with names beginning with R and the second surnames beginning with H….

Ralph Jones   (drunk and disorderly)   Morgan Howells (poaching)
Ronald Evans   (theft from employer)   Wynn Howells (fraud)
Roger Price   (burglary)   Ivor Herbert (petty larceny)
Rhodri Owen   (threatening behaviour, ABH)   Joshua Hughes (vagrancy)
Rhys Williams   (stealing a bicycle)
Randolph Thomas (deception)

The list did not help us much and I thought perhaps we were looking in the wrong place and decided that we would concentrate on the villages highlighted on our map for the house-to-house questioning and see if any likely names popped up there.

Bronwen lead a team of six local constables to the largest village, Llandygwydd, which was in the centre of the circle we had drawn on the map. This was quite a thriving village with some local shops and three public houses and the sort of place where local people from the more remote farms and small holdings came for their supplies. Bronwen decided to start with the pubs because at this time of day they would not be too busy as most men would still be at work, but the bar flies who did not work would be there and the publicans may have a little more time to answer questions. The Llandygwydd Arms was open but there were only four customers and we started asking them about any strangers seen in the village or local people who were violent and caused trouble in the vicinity, but nobody could tell us much. We moved on to the Shepherd's Rest on the other side of the road where there were even fewer customers, but the landlord knew Matthew Richards and was sorry for his murder, but he couldn't think of anyone in the area who would do such a thing, but when I asked him whether he had seen any strangers in the pub he said that two Irishmen came into the bar one night about six weeks ago but they kept themselves to themselves and left without causing any trouble. Descriptions were taken but the descriptions were too vague to be certain, but they could have possibly fitted O'Hare and O'Mahoney but were not definitive enough to be taken as evidence. We already knew that they had been operating in this area for some time so it was likely it could have been them. The third pub was the Golden Dragon at the end of the village which was empty of customers but the landlord was a voluble fellow and chatted away freely to Bronwen but wasn't really able to tell her anything of any substance except that he suggested a call on Granny Hawkins, who lived in the white cottage opposite the pub and who was a noted gossip and village watcher and could tell us everything that went on in these parts.

Granny Hawkins was reluctant to talk at first but when Bronwen said that people in the village had said that she was the person to talk to if we wanted to know anything important about what went on there, this appealed to her vanity, and she puffed herself up and said that she might be able to help. She lived alone so watching the comings and goings of the villagers provided her with some innocent amusement and living right at the entrance of the village she was in a prime position to identify strangers when they came into the village. She confirmed that there were two Irishmen living on one of the remote farms, but she did not know which one and she had only seen them a couple of times in the village itself, but she saw them once in Cardigan and she was able to give a far more detailed description than the pub landlord. I asked if there were any troublemakers in the village and she said that there were a few drunks and some young lads who were always ready for a fight but otherwise it was very peaceful. She thought for a minute and then said that one of the local farmers had gone off the rails since the death of his two sons fighting in France and his wife shortly after. "And I think it has gone to his head a bit because he has been banned from all the pubs in this village and in other villages too so he doesn't come into the village that often, although I have seen him once or twice riding his mule to get supplies from time to time, which is strange because I know that he has a small van. Since he lost all his family, he blames the government for the death of his sons on the Western Front and is convinced that his wife died of a broken heart as a result. People say that he goes to those public meetings that are held against the continuation of the war, but I don't know if that is true." Bronwen asked whether she knew the name of this unfortunate man and she said his name was Owen and she knew his wife, Elizabeth, and his first name was Rhodri. Bronwen asked whether she knew where he lived, and she was uncharacteristically vague, saying that she had never been to the area where his farm was situated but she thought it was a hill farm above the village of Pontnewydd about five miles from there.

Bronwen suspected others in the village would probably know his address so she would ask at the butcher's, grocer's or seed merchant's, where he might order his supplies, to get a more accurate idea of his location. The first shop she came to was Mog Edwards and Son, Seed Merchants and Farm Supplies, and Bronwen enquired as to whether Rhodri Owen was a customer of theirs and they confirmed that he had been for twenty years or more, but his account was much smaller now that he lived on his own. They were unable to give an exact postal address for his farm as all the invoices were sent direct to his bank in Cardigan and were always settled promptly each month. However, Mr Edwards said the farm was called Cwm Farm and was found by taking the mountain track out of Pontnewydd to the north-west, following the road as it climbed the side of the mountain until you came to a fork in the track after about one and a half miles. "The right-hand fork leads directly to Mr Owen's small farm and there is a signboard on the gate, but you can't get lost because the track only goes for about a hundred yards or so past the house. It is a steep climb and quite narrow in places, but most small motor vehicles or light vans should make it easily enough." Bronwen was delighted with what she had discovered that afternoon and was anxious to get back to the station to let me into what she had found out.

I had spent the afternoon back at the morgue with Dr Roberts, who had examined the plaster cast of the tyre tracks he had taken outside the chemist's and compared it with the sketches Ivor had made of the tyre tracks outside Sir Walter's front gates. The similarities were not immediately obvious but careful inspection with his magnifying glass brought the images into sharper focus and he pointed out to me that the unusual marks on the rear nearside tyre were identical, which proved categorically that this vehicle was present at both murder scenes as it was almost impossible to conceive that there would be two vehicles in the area with the same unique notches cut out of the tyre tread in the whole of Wales. He congratulated me for my earlier suspicion that these two cases were linked as this had now been proved to be so without a shadow of a doubt. He had also received the report from the army firearms expert at Sennybridge Camp, which was very interesting also. From the examination of the spent rounds removed from the victims' bodies at the autopsy and the cases collected from the scene he was certain that we were looking at two different weapons of the same type. They were unusual because they were German manufactured weapons and he identified them both as being Luger machine pistols, which were not legally available in this country and the small number in use in Wales had all been smuggled in by enemy agents or German sympathisers. The warrant officer armourer commented that he had looked at similar rounds from Luger machine pistols several months earlier when he was assisting the Brecon police with the murder enquiry into five bodies that were found in a mass grave in the forest above Talybont reservoir. He told us that he had looked at the file and photographs from that investigation and was certain that the rounds which were removed from the backs of the heads of Sir Walter and his chauffeur were fired from the same Luger machine pistol as in the murders of the five victims from the Talybont grave. I was delighted to hear this because we were certain that the assassin who had killed the two British officers, Crawford and King; Joachim Schultz and Heidi Weiss; and Thomas O'Malley was Ernest Sullivan, and I was desperately looking for the evidence that would link O'Mahoney to Sullivan and it seemed that his fondness for his favourite weapon may have just given me that vital piece of evidence I needed. The other weapon used in the attack was also most likely a similar model, a Luger machine pistol, but there was no evidence that it had been used before in committing a crime. I thanked the doctor profusely and told him that I had been working on the investigation into a German spy ring operating out of Cardiff and they had ordered the assassin, Ernest Sullivan, former Irish rebel and a proven killer, to commit the five murders that the report referred to. I told him that Sullivan was the only member of the spy ring to escape justice and I now believed that he was the killer of Sir Walter and his chauffeur and Constable Richards and was masquerading in this area using the name O'Mahoney. I also suspected that the wounded assailant was Rory McCloud O'Hare, who was a well-known and violent bullyboy and leader of the Workers' Revolutionary Party. We knew that he had been active in these parts for a couple of months and had participated in several acts of violence and robberies, but had little idea where his hideout was located.

 On the journey back to the police station, Bronwen was running over in her mind what she thought she had discovered that afternoon and her initial exuberance at making a breakthrough as she began to have second thoughts. She could not even remember if this man Rhodri Owen was on her list or not and what she had learnt about him from Mrs Hawkins was very sad, the fact that he had lost his wife and two sons, resulting in convictions for drunk and disorderly behaviour, but did it suggest that he was involved with the WRP? Even attending anti-war meetings was not particularly damning because half of the mothers in Wales belonged to this extremely popular protest group at that time in the war. It would take a big leap of imagination for this to add up to a man who was likely to become actively involved in armed robbery and murder, especially when he dealt with his business affairs through his bank and was considered a model customer who paid his bills promptly. When she entered the incident room later that afternoon, I could see immediately that her face showed that she was quite perplexed and less sure of herself than her usual confident manner. I knew that she must have suffered a setback or disappointment of some kind during her afternoon house-to-house enquiries which had brought on this uncharacteristic mood, but I was anxious not to make things worse, so I held back from asking her what was wrong. I launched into a description of the significant new clues which had proved categorically that the three murders were linked because the tyre track cast and Ivor's sketches were identical, proving that the same vehicle was present at both sites. The weapons expert's examination had identified that two Luger machine pistols were used in the attack on Sir Walter but that the weapon that delivered the fatal shots was known to police already as it was the weapon used by Ernest Sullivan in the five murders carried out on the orders of the Wurtenberg spy ring. This gave us our first positive link to Ernest Sullivan as we knew already that this was his weapon of choice. The doctor's team were continuing to look at the footprints to ascertain whether they could say if the wearers were at one or both of the crime scenes. Bronwen still remained quiet, so I coaxed her into giving us an account of what she had found from the house-to-house enquiries, and she said she was despondent because she had learnt very little of any value from a wasted afternoon. I tried to be as reassuring as I could and said that house-to-house was sometimes like that but was also very necessary because it was sometimes possible to pick up that nugget of information that makes everything drop into place. I told her that there was no reason to be downhearted after one frustrating day, but she burst into tears and through the sobs said she was so stupid and had jumped to conclusions too quickly just because an old lady had spun her a plausible tale.

EIGHTEEN

Eventually, she dried her tears and apologised to the team for being upset but we all encouraged her to tell us how she thought she had been taken in and gradually the story came out about the farmer who had lost his two sons and then his wife in the past year and had gone off the rails a bit, drinking too much and being ejected from pubs, attending anti-war protest group meetings but at the same time continuing to farm his land and pay his bills on time. She said that she found herself convicting this man on pure hearsay without any real evidence that he was our man. I asked her whether this farmer had a name and she said he was Rhodri Owen, and it was Rhys Evans who pointed out straight away that this name was on her list as one of the cases dealt with by Constable Richards, so they would have recognised each other if they met in the alley outside the chemist's. Bronwen immediately perked up but then subsided again as she realised that it didn't fit the RH profile from the notebook, but it was Ivor this time who said that it did because Richards was writing the name Rhodri in his book but only got as far as the second letter when his throat was cut. It now seemed so obvious that RH were the first two letters of his first name and Richards was noting down the name as he recognised him from their previous encounter. Bronwen explained that she had spoken with the seed merchants in Llandygwydd village, and they had confirmed that Rhodri Owen was a long-term customer but were unable to give her a postal address because the farm was in a remote position and he received his post via his bank but they were able to describe to her the directions of how to get there. I opened the map again and placed it on the table and asked Bronwen if she could trace the directions on the map. She followed the directions easily and took the north-west road out of Pontnewydd, which we could see from the map was little more than a farm track that climbed the side of the hill quite steeply. Mr Edwards had suggested that the fork in the road with the right-hand turn-off was about one and a half miles up this track but when we looked at the map it looked to be significantly further. The left-hand fork continued to the summit of the hill but then descended towards Aberporth about five miles further, but we assumed that as this was a narrow single-track road, it was very much a by-way and most traffic towards the coast would take the main road via Cardigan, which would be much quicker. The track leading to Cwm Farm seemed to be just under a mile long but was a dead end and only seemed to run for a short distance past the entrance to the farmyard. Cwm Farm was the only dwelling marked on this side of the hill, with the nearest neighbouring farm situated at least two miles away over the ridge on the road to the coast. The farm was secluded and hidden by a stand of trees along the path of the coastal road, and it would be very difficult to approach the farm buildings without being observed but I knew that we had to find a way to observe who was residing at the farm as guests of Rhodri Owen.

We racked our brains to find a way that we could mount a surveillance of Cwm Farm without the occupants being aware that they were being watched but every suggestion from around the table seemed impossible. We tried to think of ways to get near to the farm that would appear bona fide, but Bronwen said that Owen rode into the village on his mule to collect supplies himself and once or twice a year Edwards Farm Suppliers would deliver a bulk order by light van, and this would be arranged in advance. Since his wife and boys were gone, he had apparently discouraged visitors to the farm, preferring very much to keep his own company. Bronwen said that she had just remembered something that Granny Hawkins had said when she had remarked that it was strange that Owen rode his mule to collect supplies when she knew he owned a small van for use on the farm. He had rarely been seen in the villages of Pontnewydd and Llandygwydd driving the van, whereas he had often been seen riding his mule. However, it was common knowledge that Rhodri had started attending political meetings, especially those of groups opposed to the war, and went to their evening meetings as far afield as Aberporth and Cardigan, which were probably too far to journey to by mule at night, so we surmised that he probably made use of his van and travelled by the back roads to avoid being seen. I began working out how far the farm was from the two murder scenes and calculating how long it would take to reach the safety of the farm from either location. The distance, in both cases, was quite small, less than five miles, but given the remoteness of the farm and the narrow roads I estimated approximately thirty minutes in each case. The fact that the villagers in the nearest villages only remembered Owen on his mule and never driving a van suggested to me that when he was using the van, he avoided driving through the villages, where he was well known, and probably used the remoter road over the summit towards Aberporth, where there was less chance of being recognised. Ideally, we needed to get access to the farm to ascertain who was living there and whether there was a motor vehicle hidden in one of the outbuildings and, if so, did it have the same distinctive pattern on the rear offside tyre tread we had already discovered from the plaster cast and sketches? But I was unable to see how we could do this unless we had a miraculous stroke of luck.

Bronwen suggested that as she was an accomplished cross-country rider, she could ride over the hillside from the coastal side of the hill and get as close to the farm as possible and note what she could see, which would at least give us an idea of the layout, which would be vital when we were able to raid the farm. I reckoned if we had to go in, it would have to be under cover of darkness so that having a clear idea of the farm layout would be imperative to avoid casualties if Sullivan started firing. I was reluctant to agree at first even though I had been prepared to send her into this area undercover a few days before, but now I felt that the risks had grown significantly because of the three murders in less than twenty-four hours which we attributed to the residents of this farm. I had the additional worry that if we sent Bronwen in to reconnoitre Cwm Farm, she would have to be completely on her own as we could not get close enough to render her support or assistance without being seen by the farm's occupants if she were to arouse their suspicions and get into trouble. Bronwen said that she understood the risks perfectly well and was still willing to undertake the mission with her eyes open as to what she might face. The weather forecast was poor for the next twenty-four hours but then there was a period of reasonably fine weather and good visibility, so we planned to go ahead with the closer look at the farm on the morning of the day after next. This gave Bronwen time to organise borrowing a horse and getting her gear together so that she could pass herself off as a wealthy lady enjoying a cross-country ride in the vicinity if she was challenged. Luckily, Bronwen had been a keen equestrian during her teenage years, and she knew of a couple who kept horses from her days taking part in cross-country riding events who kept a stud farm near Lampeter, which was less than twenty miles from our present location. Bronwen left the meeting to speak with her friends and to arrange the details and necessary preparations for her mission.

Two mornings later, we were ready to put our plans into action and Michael Flint and his wife had proved to be very willing in assisting Bronwen with her request and had allowed her the pick of their best cross-country horses and loaned her all the clothing and gear she would need to establish her identity as a wealthy lady enjoying riding on the mountainside. They even brought the horse to a secluded location less than two miles from Cwm Farm but hidden behind the brow of the hill, where they would wait for her to do the recce and then return the horse to its owners. It was a bright and clear morning when we all assembled in a small copse which allowed us to remain out of sight from any casual passersby on the road. Bronwen was ready to set off just before nine, which would give her time to gently wend her way down the hillside without attracting too much attention but also to get a good view of the farm layout from above. As she rode out of the copse and headed for the brow of the hill, I began to feel considerable forebodings that she was heading into real danger, and I was strongly tempted to call her back and think of a safer strategy to achieve our objective. I wondered if I would have thought the same way if it was Rhys or Ivor riding over the hill or it was because Bronwen was female. Anyway, it was now too late to stop her as she was already several hundred yards beyond the summit, and I could not have called her back even if I'd wanted to and things would have to run their course whatever the outcome. I moved to the edge of the wood where I could look over the summit with my binoculars and keep track of her movements as the horse made its way downhill under the control of Bronwen. She appeared to have a clear view across the whole valley where the farm was situated, and I was sure that she would be able to see the layout and prospect of the farmhouse and the various outbuildings spread around it. I had briefed her to look for possible approaches to the farmhouse that would offer the most cover for us and to ascertain how close we could get to the house without being seen. I watched her through the glasses for twenty minutes until she disappeared into the dip behind the rear of the farm and was lost from view.

*

Sullivan had not slept well that night and was sleepy and bad-tempered that morning and was at the back of the farmhouse smoking when he caught a glimpse of a rider coming down the hill about five hundred yards away. He was immediately suspicious because during the eight weeks or so he had lived at the farm he had seen no other riders, except for crazy Rhodri on his mule. He fetched his telescope from his bag and brought the image of the rider into focus and was surprised to see that it was a young woman. He wondered what she was doing there and checked all around to see if she was alone and thought he would keep an eye on her to make sure that she was just a passing rider who would be gone in a few minutes. As the seconds passed, Sullivan kept his telescope trained closely on the female rider and he was becoming increasingly aware that she was not riding aimlessly but was purposefully marking out the layout of the land and the possible approaches to the farm. He ducked his head inside the back door and called Rhodri and told him to get on the mule and carefully ride to cut off the rider's escape as he retrieved his machine pistol from his bag and slipped off the safety catch to be ready for action. He told Rhodri to be ready to act as soon as Sullivan approached her as his suspicions that she was a police agent were growing fast and they needed to know for sure. If she was genuinely a random rider then she was of low threat but if she was police, then they would have to act fast and move locations before the inevitable police raid was upon them. He had been beginning to think that the eight weeks they had remained static might prove to be a weakness and he knew that the secret for any outlaw staying free to act remained in keeping mobile and not allowing the authorities to get a fix on where you were situated. Even without the enforced need to stay at Rhodri's farm after the last operation because of the wounds to Rory, they would have been wise to move on to another safe house. However, the assassination of Sir Walter represented a considerable escalation in scale compared to their previous operations and it was almost inevitable that it would concentrate police activity more thoroughly to track them down. Sullivan could see that the rider was indeed a professional and was engaged in a detailed reconnaissance of the farm, possibly as part of pre-raid planning by the police, and it was imperative she be apprehended so that the intelligence she had gained did not make it back to her commanders. The raid would come whatever happened next, but he reckoned that if they caught her now, she could be interrogated and dealt with quickly enough so they could make good their escape in the van. He assumed that the police commander was reluctant to raid the farm without more detailed knowledge of the layout and approaches to the farm, and equally he needed to know what the police already knew about them and their involvement in the recent murders so that he could use that information to ensure he made good his escape. He would prefer to continue in partnership with Rory but would not hesitate to leave him behind if he felt he would slow them down. Similarly, Rhodri Owen had been useful in providing this safe house for a couple of months and had the local knowledge that he lacked, but if for a moment he thought his usefulness was over, he would not hesitate to put a bullet into the back of his head to save himself.

By this time, the rider had approached to within two hundred yards of the rear of the farmhouse and it was apparent that she was not aware that she was under observation as Sullivan remained out of sight behind some bales of hay in the farmyard. He caught a glimpse of Rhodri mounting the mule and riding to the downhill side of the farm to circle round behind the rider without being seen. Sullivan waited for a minute or so and then stood up from behind the bales and walked out into the open, calling out in a friendly manner as to whether he could help her. Bronwen was almost taken by surprise by the sudden appearance of this man speaking in a warm and friendly way, but she knew that it was not Rhodri Owen because of his broad Irish accent, and she suspected that this was either O'Hare or Sullivan, aka O'Mahoney. She was immediately on her guard as she knew that she could be outnumbered at least three to one and hoped that she wouldn't regret leaving her police pistol behind if she had to defend herself. The Irishman kept coming towards her with a smiling face and friendly tone until she was close enough to see that the smile did not extend beyond his lips to his eyes, and it was purely an act to get close enough to her to draw his Luger and order her to dismount. Bronwen was not about to comply and immediately tensed herself and was tightening her grip on the reins ready to dash for safety when she became aware of a second rider sitting just twenty yards behind her on a mule with a double-barrelled shotgun aimed directly at her. In a split second, she had weighed her chances of escape as negligible and although she thought she could move quickly enough to avoid the first shot from the Luger, the shotgun blast from both barrels would seriously wound her and the horse at this range and bring her down. She decided to comply and loosened her grip on the reins and stepped down from the saddle. Immediately, the large Irishman grabbed her roughly by the arm and forced it behind her back very painfully towards the house whilst the mule rider collected the reins of her mount and headed towards the barn. When

Rhodri came into the farm kitchen, Sullivan had already tied the rider's arms and legs to the chair and he noticed a redness on her face where he must have struck her a few times already. The Irishman growled at Owen and asked him what he had done with the horse, which he replied was safely out of sight in the barn. Sullivan thought for a minute and then said that it might prove a better solution if he were to take the horse further down the valley at least a mile or two from the farm and let it go. "Wherever she has come from will be searching for her when she does not arrive at her destination on time. They will probably search for her before it gets dark. When they find her horse loose some distance away from the farm, it may well detract suspicion from us for enough time to get away from here safely."

Rhodri saw the sense in this and went back out to the barn to resaddle his mule and Bronwen's horse and set off to lead her horse at least several miles away from the farm. He went a little further than he intended but decided that this was better for the deception of the searchers and left the horse in a grassy glade near to a fast-running stream about halfway towards the nearest village. Once he had left the horse happily grazing, he rode away as quickly as he could but taking care to take a roundabout route back to Cwm Farm. He didn't see anyone out on the hillside, and he hoped he had not been detected by some unseen person whilst on this mission. Sullivan was glad to have got rid of Rhodri for at least a couple of hours, which would give him enough time to have some fun with this young woman, who was passably attractive and completely in his power. Sullivan had always found it difficult to engage in any kind of emotional relationship with women unless he was in complete control, and he derived his sexual arousal from that control and the pain he could inflict whilst taking his pleasure. He relished the opportunity to be alone with the female rider and knew that she would tell him everything he wanted to know without the intervention and objections of Rhodri Owen, who he guessed would not have the stomach for a rough interrogation. Bronwen was still groggy from the several hard slaps and blows to the head that had been administered by the tall Irishman, but she could hear what was said between him and the Welshman, who he had sent away to hide her horse some distance away from their present location. She was increasingly afraid that he intended to be left alone with her and was going to hurt her in the process. He had tied her so tightly to the arms and legs of the chair that she was unable to move a fraction of an inch, and all she could do was wiggle her toes to keep the circulation flowing and move her head to watch what was going on in the room. She had taken in that she was in the simple farmhouse parlour and she already knew from the lay of the land outside that she could shout and scream as much as she wanted and no one would hear her cries. The Irishman was not within her view, but she thought she could hear him talking to someone in another room and knew for definite that it was not the farmer as he had been sent to dispose of her horse, so she reckoned that the wounded attacker from the Sir Walter murder was still alive and in the other room.

Sullivan approached Bronwen tied to the chair and slapped her around the face several times with the flat of his right hand and ripped the front of her blouse open, tearing away the buttons, and thrust his hand under her shirt and sought out her left nipple, which he caressed gently between his finger and thumb until he felt it stiffen and stand firm when he suddenly squeezed and twisted it as hard as he could as she let out a scream of sheer agony. In between each application of pressure on her nipple, he asked her where she had come from and what she was doing riding so close to their farm. At first, she tried to answer keeping to the cover story she had agreed with Wesley before she had set off, although it was soon obvious that her tormentor did not seem to believe her as, by now, he had stripped her to the waist and cut off her underwear to expose her to the waist. This was the first time she had ever been naked in front of any man and she was distressed and sobbing because she could not move her arms to cover her modesty. Sullivan now began to work on the right nipple, this time making use of a small set of pincers instead of his fingers. The pain was excruciating for Bronwen, coupled with the degradation of her nakedness, and she began to deviate from the rehearsed story and to admit that she had been sent to reconnoitre the layout of the farm and that she was a police agent. Bronwen was unable to tell him any details about the proposed raid on the farm, despite the pain he inflicted on her, because she simply did not know anything about the raid to tell him. He seemed pleased and called her a good girl and said he was going to reward her for her co-operation, and he bent down and untied the ropes holding her legs to the chair, undid her arms and pulled her onto her feet, where he used his knife to cut away her riding skirt until she was completely naked. He grabbed her hair and pulled her to the sofa and bent her forward over the back, loosened his leather belt and dropped his trousers and entered her roughly from behind. Bronwen cried with pain and anguish and the complete humiliation of the violation at the hands of this man, who ejaculated loudly into her vagina and slapped her hard on the buttocks in triumph. He stepped back and wiped himself on the tail of his shirt and pulled his trousers up and resecured them with his belt. He was pleased with himself having discovered what he wanted to know and used this girl as he wished, and with a clean sweep of his switchblade, he cut her throat as smoothly as he had done for the police constable a couple of nights before. He watched her dispassionately as she bled her lifeblood across the rug behind the sofa and reconciled himself to the fact that at least she had died happy as he had taken her virginity just a few minutes before and her usefulness was over.

Sullivan spent the next five minutes collecting his things together and throwing them into his bag and loading his Luger machine pistols. He had reckoned that if Rory was fit and well and he could trust Rhodri, he would have been prepared to wait for the police raid to come and take the risk of getting the better of them in the ensuing firefight. However, although Rory was on the mend, he was not yet strong enough for a fight for survival with the police, and Rhodri could only be trusted to fire a shotgun and probably didn't have the guts to fight off the police attack anyway. He had concluded that they were both liabilities and, like the girl, were no longer of any use to him and that he would need to dispose of both before he made good his escape in Owen's van. He was sorry that his partnership with Rory O'Hare was to end here as they had been through scrapes together before and had made a good team, but Rory had brought about his own demise when he failed to kill the magistrate with his first shot and allowed the old boy to wound him so badly that he was no longer able to function properly. As he entered the bedroom, Rory looked up and half smiled and asked what the noise was from the parlour and Sullivan shrugged and said it was nothing and then brought his machine pistol out from behind his back and shot Rory once through the middle of the forehead. As he turned away, he whispered to himself that he was sorry that it had to end this way and closed the door behind him. He checked the parlour one last time and made his way out to the barn where the van was parked and caught a glimpse of Owen and his mule coming up the rise about half a mile from the farm. He had time to hide himself in the barn and wait for Rhodri to bring the mule into his stall, and whilst he was preoccupied with tending to the mule, he would dispatch Owen with a fatal shot and be on his way. Rhodri rode into the farmyard but didn't go into the barn with the mule as Sullivan had expected but went into the farmhouse where the bloody corpse of the naked female rider spread over his sofa confronted him and he knew in an instant why Sullivan had sent him away. Rhodri was not a sentimental man, but his sense of fair play and justice had been violated by Sullivan's atrocious actions and he went to the gun cupboard and loaded his best shotgun and stuffed his pockets with a dozen shotgun cartridges. He knew that he wasn't a dead shot but knew that the spread of the shot from his shotgun was enough to knock over and disable a man from a short distance. He also guessed that Sullivan was still on the farm so he set about searching through the other rooms, keeping his shotgun loaded and ready to fire should he find him. When he discovered the body of O'Hare shot in the forehead as he lay in his bed, he knew for sure that Sullivan would be waiting somewhere on the farm to kill him also as he would not wish to leave any witnesses alive to testify against him.

Rhodri had lived on this farm all his life and if it was intended that his life would end here, he was contented, but he was determined that he would make amends first by taking the life of Sullivan for the crimes he had committed and if successful he would turn the shotgun on himself. He slipped out of the back window of the scullery, which allowed him to skirt along the back of the house and cross the gap between the house and the rear of the barn without being seen. He knew there was a loose board in the far corner of the barn that he could easily remove and he could crawl into the barn without Sullivan knowing he was there. Sullivan would expect him to enter through the front door and would be lying in wait to pounce as soon as he came through the door, so he ought to be taken completely by surprise when he was challenged from behind. It was dark inside the barn although it was still daylight outside, but the lack of windows kept the barn dark most of the day so Rhodri knew that he would have to get quite close to his target if he was to get in a good shot at the target. He had already decided that he would give a full broadside of both barrels and had calculated anything under ten feet would have the maximum impact. However, approaching to within ten feet of Sullivan without making him aware that he was there was going to be difficult. Rhodri inched forward very slowly, placing his feet gently with each step, his eyes peering through the murky twilight and his ears pricked up to hear any movement from his target. He estimated that he had come thirty feet from the back wall of the barn but as yet had not managed to locate Sullivan's hiding place and was beginning to think he had been wrong all along, and that Sullivan had already fled the scene, when he could just make out the silhouette of the top of the van and was sure that Sullivan must be still there at the farm. His mind was still full of doubts as he continued to creep forward when, at last, he picked up a sound and thought he could pick out the outline of a big man making for the door and he let blast with both barrels and he heard a shout and saw the body go down with a heavy thump and rushed forward but in his eagerness to see what damage he had wrought on Sullivan he did not reload his shotgun. He bent over the shape on the floor and saw Sullivan's face smiling up at him with a machine pistol in his hand pointing straight at his chest. The machine pistol spat twice, and Rhodri felt the jolts as each round penetrated his chest and destroyed his heart as he was thrown backwards onto the ground behind him with a searing pain stabbing through to his core. It seemed to him to be taking ages to die but Rhodri Owen was dead within fifteen seconds of the shots penetrating his chest, and Sullivan was up and dusting himself down and checking for any buckshot wounds within twenty seconds, reloading his pistol and making his way to the van to make good his escape.

Sullivan had no qualms about leaving a trail of destruction in his wake and gave no thought at all for the three lives he had just ruthlessly cut short. O'Hare had been his friend for many years, but he had killed him in the blink of an eye when he thought he would hamper his chances of escape because of his injuries. Owen had given him shelter for the past two months and had aided him in his criminal ventures but had been dispatched with equal alacrity. His only regret was that he could not have kept the female rider alive so he could have taken his pleasure again with her body, but he was sure there would be other women he could rape in the future. Sullivan's whole purpose now was to get as far away from the farm as he could before the police realised something was wrong and brought forward the raid on the farm. He was satisfied that he could make use of the van to drive away from the farm, but he did not know yet what his destination might be. He knew there were small groups of WRP members and supporters dotted around mid-Wales and had met them from time to time on operations with Rory. These people had accepted him because he was a close associate of O'Hare, their chosen leader, but he was far from certain that they would accept him as their leader in Rory's place or even take him in and provide refuge because he was, after all, just a newcomer. He had been twice with Rory to the group based near Lampeter and stayed overnight whilst they planned and executed a raid to break up a public meeting held by the Welsh Miners' Alliance in Lampeter Town Hall. He remembered that the group was led by a man called Jenkins and his wife and they lived in a pleasant cottage about three miles from the town in quite an isolated position. Jenkins was a rough character and O'Hare had confided that Jenkins wasn't his real name and that he used a false name because he was a deserter from the army and did not wish to attract too much attention to himself. Sullivan decided that he would drive to Jenkins' place and if they took him in, he would have a place to lay low until the police search died down but if they didn't want to take him in, he had his sharp knife and machine pistols and he was perfectly willing to dispatch Jenkins and his woman and stay in their cottage for a few days without their permission. He backed the van out of the barn and headed down the valley towards the village where he knew Rhodri's van would be recognised so he pulled a cap down so that the peak covered his face and hoped that anyone who saw him pass would assume it was Rhodri. Sullivan had a passing thought that he might set the farm and barn alight and destroy all the evidence but realised that the flames and smoke would alert the police and bring them at great speed, so he decided against torching Cwm Farm.

The road to Lampeter was almost deserted and he wasn't aware of any other vehicles on the road ahead or behind him, so he was able to make fast progress and within an hour and a half he was parked in an opening in the trees about four hundred yards from Jenkins' cottage. As always, Sullivan played it safe and made his way through the trees stealthily until he found a vantage point where he could observe the cottage without being seen himself. He watched from this vantage point for over an hour, but it was imperative that he was able to get off the road as quickly as possible so could not afford to wait any longer. He had not observed any visitors and was sure that the cottage was only occupied by Jenkins and his wife, so he decided that he had no choice but to take a risk. Retracing his steps to the van, he checked his machine pistol was cocked and ready and his knife was easy to hand and drove slowly down the hill and pulled in and parked at the side of the house where the van could not be seen from the road and climbed out and waited for Jenkins to come out into the front garden. After a minute, the curtain tweaked and then he heard the lock being turned and the door opened just wide enough for him to see the barrels of a shotgun sticking out. Jenkins called out, asking what he wanted, and Sullivan said that he was running for his life and that the police had raided Cwm Farm and had killed O'Hare and Rhodri Owen this afternoon but that he had been lucky to have been in the village when the raid occurred and had been able to escape. Jenkins was still guarded and asked how he knew that O'Hare and Owen were killed, and Sullivan told them that he heard the shooting as he drove back up the hill and knew that something was happening. He described how he crept closer to the farm through the bushes and saw the bodies of Rory and Rhodri laid out on the ground alongside those of three policemen, which indicated that they had put up a fight. Sullivan had managed to creep back to the van and drive away before the police knew he had even been there. He said that he had to warn others in the group and came here first. Jenkins lowered his shotgun and opened the door and came out into the open and said that they would sheet over the van with a tarpaulin so that it would not be spotted by passersby and then he could come in and tell them all about it.

Sullivan spun a good story and Jenkins seemed to accept it without any question and was even less than cautious when Sullivan probed to find the locations of others in the Lampeter area who would need to be warned of the loss of O'Hare and the police offensive against the WRP. Jenkins agreed that Sullivan could stay for a couple of days until the initial heat had died down and then he would have to move on and find somewhere more permanent to stay. He was relieved to have secured this temporary respite and settled to a surprisingly pleasant evening. After a good meal and a few drinks, he was feeling remarkably mellow and satisfied with himself. He was almost tempted to do away with Jenkins with his knife and then bed Josie, his wife, rounding off his day nicely. However, the more drinks he consumed, the less he favoured the idea and the more he realised that Jenkins may prove useful yet. He already knew that he could have Josie any time he wanted once her husband was no longer of any use to him. Although Jenkins was not a prime mover in the organisation, he did have knowledge of the members of the WRP group in his area and Sullivan probed him for the names and locations of those who lived alone or without immediate family in places a little off the beaten track and now had three likely possibilities to consider. He knew that he would try to scout out each of the locations as far as he could before he moved on from the Jenkinses' cottage because he knew it was wise to be cautious as he was certain that the police would be not far behind him. He did not have a high regard for the constabulary, in general, but knew that the specially trained detectives in the security branch were a cut above the normal policeman and had demonstrated their abilities well enough in the closing-down of the Wurtenberg network and tracking Rory and him to Cwm Farm despite their best efforts to be extra careful to conceal their whereabouts after the murder of Sir Walter and the policeman in Cardigan. He reckoned that when the police team tracking the female rider became aware that she wasn't coming back and raided the farm, they would quickly work out that he had survived and got away. He was sure that they would have little idea where he might have gone, although they would know that he didn't take the road to Aberporth, which was the direction from where the rider had come and where he assumed the police team would be waiting. He thought he may have been seen in the village as he passed through, but it would take time to discover any witnesses and they would not be able to give any specific details as to which direction he had taken. He was sure that he had a breathing space of at least thirty-six to forty-eight hours before they extended their search and worked out where he was likely to be hiding. Firstly, he must keep the van out of sight because the police would have its registration details and although small vans were quite popular as general-purpose vehicles on farms, the total number of motor vehicles on the roads in this area was relatively few, making the task of surveillance a little easier. He was not certain whether the police team after him had any details of the local membership of the WRP but if they gained access to this information, they would soon start visiting known agitators in the party who might be providing a haven for him. What had seemed a clever ruse when he was escaping from the farm now, with the benefit of hindsight, was shown to be a flawed strategy and he knew he would have to think carefully about his next move if he was to evade capture. Jenkins had been drinking local Welsh cider all evening and was now slurring his words as he poured more flagons of cider down his throat. Sullivan drank a couple of mugfuls of the deliciously potent brew but kept his drinking moderate as he wished to keep a clear head for the morning. Jenkins had become more voluble as his capacity increased until eventually he lapsed into a kind of stupor and then a deep sleep. Josie struggled to get him up from his chair to get him to his bed, but his legs had gone wobbly and lacked control and he was soon collapsed in a heap on the floor under the table and she had no chance of lifting him. She looked at Sullivan for help and he suggested she leave him where he was and fetch a blanket and cover him over so he could sleep it off until the morning. Josie went into the bedroom and returned with a knitted blanket and spread it over her husband and then asked Sullivan if there was anything else he needed before she turned in. He thanked her and said a glass of water would be fine and she went to the scullery to pour the water and brought it to him in the parlour and placed it on the table.

Mrs Jenkins was not a great beauty in the accepted sense, nor was she petite and pretty like the young policewoman, but she was a comely country lass, strong and used to hard work, with a curvy and not unattractive body and as he looked at her, he felt a stirring of desire and knew that this was the opportunity he had waited for. He was patient and did not rush things and just sat back and drank his cool water and watched her finish her tidying-up and then wish him goodnight and head for the bedroom. He heard her close the door but there was no sound of a lock or bolt sliding into place, so he left it a couple of minutes before he made his move. Moving slowly and quietly across the parlour, he gently pushed against the bedroom door and it swung open a little way and he was able to slip into the room without distracting Josie from unpinning her hair before retiring for the night. He stood just inside the doorway, transfixed as she removed her blouse and let her hair hang down her back and with each stroke of the brush he could see her ample breasts, milky white, swinging with each arm movement. He must have let out an audible sigh as she suddenly became distracted and looked up and saw him standing there watching her with the grin of a hungry wolf all over his face. She did not seem afraid but just challenged him with a look that said what do you want and if you are man enough come and take it. Sullivan realised that there was more to this woman than he had first thought, and he moved forward until he was stood behind her and placed his hands around her neck and massaged down to her breasts and felt his hands sinking into their silky loveliness. He worked his fingers over the whole area of the right breast, a hard and erect nipple poking back hard against his fingers, and he could not resist the temptation to squeeze it as hard as he could. Josie squealed as he applied the pressure, but he felt that it was more a squeal of pleasure than of pain as she also gave a sigh of satisfaction and pushed her breasts forward against his hands for more attention. Sullivan lifted her up and turned her to face him and with a sudden movement ripped her thin shift apart so that her breasts were free as he grabbed her long hair and crushed his mouth against hers and pushed his tongue deep into her mouth. He knew he was on the right track because she kissed him back and thrust her tongue deep into his throat and squirmed with delight at the same time. Sullivan had never been a considerate lover as he had always taken what he wanted by force and enjoyed his sex as roughly as possible but when he went to rip her skirts away with his knife, Josie stopped him and stepped out of her clothes herself and was soon standing naked in front of him as he loosened his belt and dropped his trousers and threw her on the bed face down and immediately mounted her from behind. He felt some resistance in her vagina as he pushed his penis in without any foreplay but as soon as he started to thrust his buttocks in and out with some vigour he felt a warm wetness engulfing his member and Josie began giving little squeals and shouts the faster he went. He got faster and faster and Josie kept crying out for more and Sullivan hoped that she would not wake up her husband asleep in the next room, she was getting so loud. This was proving an unusual experience for Sullivan because normally he only felt resistance from those he was raping, but Josie had a rare appetite for what he was doing and did not seem to want him to stop but wanted him to give her more. He grabbed a large clump of her hair hanging down her back and pulled it sharply towards him to make her arch her back so he could penetrate her more deeply and she responded with screams of delight and wriggled her bottom to enjoy every nuance of his movement inside her. Finally, he could feel the pleasure advancing immeasurably up his penis and he knew he would ejaculate within a few seconds and there was a great relief and the hot white sperm sprayed into her with such force and his testicles shrunk to a quarter of their normal size and he pulled out of her, spent. Josie was quick off the bed and down onto her knees to suck the sperm from the penis and encourage his member to swell again to full size. She stripped his remaining clothes from his body and pulled him onto the bed and this time she was taking the lead because even though he might have enjoyed his climax, she was nowhere near reaching satisfaction. This time, she straddled him like she was riding a horse and simply took her pleasure by riding his penis until she enjoyed her first orgasm, which whetted her appetite for more and she reversed herself over his midriff again and sat on his member again and rode him to climax yet again. Sullivan was ready to sleep but Josie had other ideas and slid down the bed and took his member deep into her mouth and sucked him until he ejaculated with such force that his sperm was all over her face, and she finally consented to let him drift off to sleep.

From long experience of her husband's drinking bouts and comatose sleeping she was certain that he wouldn't come round until at least eight in the morning so she figured that she would let Sullivan sleep until six and then wake him for some more sex before breakfast. Jenkins had seemed an exciting prospect when he first came to the area but his recent heavy drinking and inactivity as he lay low from the military police after his desertion from the army had made her hate him. They never went anywhere together; all he ever talked about was revolution, and his drinking had made him impotent so he could not satisfy her needs in the bedroom anymore. She had spent most of the night working out her plan to free herself from her bondage with Jenkins. She hoped to give Sullivan such a good time in her bed that he would help her get rid of her husband once and for all with the promise of more sexual favours. She knew Sullivan was a violent and dangerous man and that he was on the run from the police and would not stay with her for too long but she hoped he would have no qualms about helping her dispose of Jenkins. She woke Sullivan around six and soon had his penis standing erect as she masturbated him to full alertness and, this time, he mounted her from above, pushing her legs back with his arms and entering her deeply. Josie had mastered the art of using compressions of the vagina wall to bring him just to climax and then to draw back so that he didn't quite ejaculate each time, which prolonged the art of their lovemaking for such a long time that they did not hear the stirring of Jenkins waking up on the parlour floor and calling out for Josie. They only became aware of him when he was standing at the end of the bed watching Sullivan cuckolding him in his own bed. He seemed frozen and unable to move as he looked in shock at the scene playing out in front of his eyes, tears cascading down his face. Sullivan tried to uncouple from Josie, but she held him in tighter and moved her bottom so that he would keep going, as if she wanted to degrade and humiliate her husband completely. After thirty or more seconds, Jenkins let out a shriek of pure anguish and rushed from the room and Sullivan jumped out of bed and, still naked, followed Jenkins into the parlour where he found Jenkins in the process of loading his shotgun, rambling that his wife was a slut and a whore and would open her legs for any man who came passing by and he would put a stop to her wanton behavior once and for all. He snapped the barrels shut and made as if to go back into the bedroom but before he could take a step forward, Sullivan had reached into his bag and pulled out his Luger and placed one shot in between Jenkins' eyes and he dropped dead instantly where he stood. Sullivan unloaded the shotgun and put it away in the cupboard and then rolled the body in the rug on the floor to contain any blood spillage, returned to the bedroom and climbed back into bed with Josie. She asked if it was done, he nodded his head, and she was so happy that she rewarded him with another session of sex for another hour or so. After breakfast, they would carry Jenkins' body to the pigsty in the next field and feed him to the pigs, who would very effectively dispose of any evidence that Jenkins had ever existed.

NINETEEN

Wesley was becoming increasingly tense by early afternoon when over three hours had gone by since Bronwen had ridden over the brow of the hill and disappeared from their view, but he knew that there was nothing he could do but wait as he did not wish to alert the occupants of the farm that they were so close by. The success of Bronwen's mission laid in her observing the farm without being discovered and bringing that intelligence back to the raiding party, who were ready to go in dependent on what information she brought back. He was tempted to send Ivor to survey the ground with his binoculars from a vantage point a little closer to the farm, which would give him a broad view of the valley but was hidden from the farm itself, but he held back because he did not wish to endanger Bronwen's safety with any rash action on his part. By three in the afternoon, Wesley could wait no longer and decided to send Ivor forward and nervously waited whilst he worked his way to a suitable viewing point to look over the valley. It seemed to take an age for Ivor to scan the valley thoroughly but after twenty minutes Ivor was up and running back towards their hiding place and Wesley knew that the news would not be good. He had scanned the valley below in sections and had not seen anything untoward in the area closest to the farm but at the extreme range of his binoculars he was sure that he could make out Bronwen's horse untethered, standing by a stream without its rider. He could not be certain, but the horse looked familiar even at this distance and he thought it would be coincidence that there were two horses and riders on this hillside today. Wesley followed him back to the viewpoint and looked through the glasses and agreed that this was Bronwen's horse all right, but what had happened to her? If she had fallen, they ought to be able to find her close to where the horse was standing and sent Ivor and Rhys in one of the cars to drive down the road towards the village and find their way to secure the horse and search the vicinity for Bronwen, who may have been injured if she fell.

*

My tension was rubbing off on the members of the raiding party and I called them together and briefed them on the situation and instructed them to check their weapons and be prepared for a move on the farm within the hour, dependent on what Ivor and Rhys found in the valley when they recovered Bronwen's horse. "If they find Bronwen, she may still be able to tell us what she saw but if not, we will have to go in blind and be prepared for a strong resistance from those inside the farm. We think there are only three of them, but remember that they are desperate men with violent antecedents and we are sure that they have killed three people in the past couple of days alone. It will be difficult to get close to the farmhouse without being seen and there is little or no cover across the farmyard itself for a frontal assault on the house." I could tell that everyone was concerned for Bronwen's safety for she was a popular and brave member of the team. One of the local constables called me to the edge of the ridge and pointed to where a light was flashing, and I could see immediately that a message was being sent by Morse code from Rhys or Ivor. Sadly, they reported that the search of an area several hundred yards around where the horse was grazing had not found Bronwen or any sign of her. The examination of the horse had not rendered any evidence of what had befallen her rider as the horse was not injured as if from a fall and all her tack was in good order. I knew that the answer must lie at the farm, although I had no evidence for that assertion, but the threat to one of our team was enough motivation for us to move on to the farm with great determination. I signalled with my torch that Ivor and Rhys were to secure the horse for collection later and then approach the farm from the downhill side and we would rendezvous with them at the fork in the mountain road where the spur led off to the entrance of the farm. Thirty minutes later, we were assembled out of view from the farm, hidden behind the hedgerow, which marked the property line of Cwm Farm, and I briefed my forces. Ivor was to work his way behind the barn and approach the rear of the farmhouse with three local constables whilst Rhys and I would approach the front of the farm accompanied by the other three locals. We were all armed with pistols and two of the constables carried shotguns also. We were not going to open fire unless they did first because our objective was to capture these suspects alive and bring them into custody to face justice in the local courts. I had a nagging feeling in the pit of my stomach that we would find Bronwen inside the farm and I hoped that she would be safe and well, but I was terrified that if they discovered she was a policewoman she would not have been treated kindly, but I kept these thoughts to myself. The frontal assault party crouched down and out of sight for five minutes to allow Ivor and his men to get into position and waited for their signal that they were in place and ready to go.

It was nearly seven minutes before the flashed signal to move was observed and our assault on the farm began quite gingerly at first as I had warned against being too eager and that we should approach cautiously and only return fire if we were fired upon. I suspected that we would find Bronwen in the farmhouse and did not wish to take any rash actions which might endanger her further and I had stressed how important it was to take Sullivan, O'Hare and Owen alive if possible. My group broke from cover and advanced across the farmyard at a steady pace and I had expected that we would have been spotted and that the firing would have started by now, but all remained quiet. Something didn't feel right so I speeded up and reached the front door in six or seven quick strides, but there was still no response from inside the building, only a forlorn sense of emptiness. Making sure that my pistol was cocked and loaded, I gestured to the constable at my left shoulder to kick the door down, which he did with ease. The door was not of a robust construction for it only took a couple of hefty kicks to detach it from its hinges and we were through into the entrance hall which led to the parlour in an instant. I knew immediately that the house was empty and that we were too late to apprehend the wanted men and was overcome with a powerful sense of foreboding that we were going to discover what we worst feared from the cloying smell of fresh blood in the atmosphere. Two steps further brought me to the parlour door and glancing round the room quickly, my eyes were drawn to the naked and bound body of Bronwen bent over the back of the sofa and the widening pool of blood beneath her behind the sofa where her blood had soaked through the carpet. I felt tears well up and run down my face and I let out a sob as I grabbed the blanket that was thrown over the back of one of the armchairs and placed it gently over Bronwen's body to preserve her modesty even though she was dead. Apart from the tears, anger rose in me too and I swept through into the bedroom with my pistol ready and I certainly would have shot any one of the three suspects dead had I found them. Instead, I was greeted by a body shot through the forehead by one clean shot and judging by the bandages around his shoulder and torso, he was probably one of the gunmen at the murder of Sir Walter. I was certain that this was O'Hare and I called out to my men to search for the third suspect, who should be either in the house or barn. My attention was attracted to some shouting and noises outside in the farmyard when Ivor came rushing in shouting that they had found another body in the barn, and he could see from the boots he was wearing that they were the same as the sketches he had made of the boot prints at the chemist's shop murder scene. There were also tyre tracks and oil drips on the floor of the barn which showed that a vehicle had been parked there and not too long ago judging by the wetness of the oil droppings and the slight smell of engine exhaust still lingering in the air. Ivor and I went to the barn to look at the third body and whilst I didn't recognise the victim, I was sure that it was not Ernest Sullivan, who I believed was the prime mover in these crimes. Ivor looked at the tyre tracks and quickly identified the peculiar knick in the tread of the rear offside tyre which matched the plaster cast of the vehicle that was present at both murder scenes, which we believed belonged to Rhodri Owen. I sent Rhys to the village to find a telephone to call the police surgeon and his team to get to Cwm Farm as quickly as possible, stressing that Constable Bronwen Phillips had been tortured and killed in the line of duty and we needed to apprehend her killer as quickly as possible.

Ivor and I returned to Newcastle Emlyn Police Station where I was able to call Chief Inspector Bennett with the terrible news of the death of Bronwen Phillips, probably at the hands of Ernest Sullivan, prompting him to seek additional forces from the local police stations to support our manhunt over the next couple of days at least. Bennett was shocked when I described what I had seen had been done to Bronwen and assured me of all the additional help he could lay his hands on and said that he would ensure that Bronwen's parents were informed of her demise. I stressed how upset we all were, especially as she had bravely volunteered to put herself at risk in seeking to gather vital information about the layout of the farm. I was feeling somewhat ashamed that I did not go myself, but Bennett snapped back at me that if I wanted to go further in the police service, I needed to assume greater qualities of command and a vital part of that was sending people out to do dangerous things for the greater good even when you knew they would be in perilous situations. "Bronwen volunteered with an open mind and knew what she was doing because she was a capable and brave young woman who displayed many of the positive qualities we have been looking for in police officers for our line of work." He hoped that her bravery and example would serve as a great motivator for even more capable young people to join the police service in future. Bennett's words gave me some temporary reassurance and made it possible for me to continue to focus on the task before us rather than sink into a pit of misery over the loss of such a valued colleague. There would come a proper time for us to mourn and grieve but not until Ernest Sullivan was safely behind bars, awaiting his appointment with the hangman's noose. Our most important task was to figure out where Sullivan could have run to when he made his escape from Cwm Farm. The information at our disposal was very limited but Ivor and I put our heads together and analysed the little we did know as a starting point. We knew he was driving a light van that we could identify by its registration number and by the distinctive tyre tread marks left by its left offside wheel, which made this vehicle unique. We could place this vehicle at the scene of two murders, which made it a legitimate subject for increased police surveillance to identify where it had been and where it was now and I issued a bulletin to all police stations within a thirty-mile radius with the details of the van and a request to stop and search and apprehend the driver if possible, with a suitable warning that the driver was dangerous and probably armed and should be approached with caution. We did not have a photograph of Sullivan to circulate but I had seen him several times and described his features to Ivor, who made a quick sketch of Sullivan's face from the description I had given him that looked passably like him, especially when attached to the further details of his height, build, hair colour and distinctive Irish accent. Ivor went to the local printer's to get his drawing photographed so that twenty copies could be made and quickly circulated with the van details to local police stations. Getting actively involved in this took our minds off the horror we had discovered at Cwm Farm and enabled us to wait patiently for the police surgeon to do his work and report back to us in good time. I already knew that Dr Roberts was thorough and would work as fast as he could to discover the details that would aid my investigation and was confident that I did not need to harass him to work faster.

I was certain that Sullivan had not turned right out of the farm because he would have been observed by our team, who were hidden in the copse to the side of the Aberporth road with a clear view of what passed either way so there was no likelihood of missing the van if it passed their way. The conclusion was that he must have turned left out of the farm gate onto the road which only led to the village of Pontnewydd about three and a half miles down the valley, and they studied the map to see what options or routes were open to him then. I also dispatched two constables to take the motorcycle and ride out to the village and question locals, starting with Granny Hawkins, to see if anyone had seen the van and what direction it had taken. We could see from the map that there were four different roads out of the village of Pontnewydd and little indication as to which he might have taken earlier that day, except that Ivor suggested he probably did not take the road to Llanbydder because he would have to drive right through the centre of the village to take that road with a far higher risk of being recognised by the locals. I agreed that this line of reasoning was probably correct and discounted this option and Ivor went on to say that although the road to Aberaeron did not require him to enter the village proper, it was also a less likely choice as it was the furthest destination and passed through hilly and remote landscapes with little or no habitation until it reached the coast. It would take at least two hours' driving to reach the Aberaeron area, which Ivor reckoned would be too much of a risk for a fugitive to take. He considered that Sullivan's priority would be to find a safe house for the night within an hour's driving, no more, and go to ground before the police search had a chance to get going. I was happy to accept Ivor's line of thought and deleted this option as well, which left us with two to consider.

    Lampeter was a reasonable-sized market town famous for its religious college and surrounded by rich farmland and could be, just about, reached in one hour from Cwm Farm, whereas Llanbydder was much smaller, offering less opportunity for hiding than the larger town. Following Ivor's line of thought, I began to think that although Sullivan had proved himself to be resourceful and capable of thinking quickly in a tight situation, he always liked to have a safe location to fall back on. All the time he worked with the Wurtenberg network, he had kept his safe house in Newport and when he was so nearly arrested in Kruger's law office, he had not run aimlessly searching for a hideout but went to a friend he could rely on to shield him until the heat was off. He had run directly to Rory O'Hare, whom he had worked with before in the Irish Rebellion and whom he knew he could trust, and the more I thought about this, the more a funny feeling was building in my stomach; would he do the same thing again, but the question was, whom did he know in this region whom he could trust to hide him for a few days?

I wrestled with this notion for several hours until I was so tired that I was falling asleep at my desk and decided to call it a day and return to the hotel to get some sleep so I could be fresh for the new day with renewed vigour. Ivor and I walked together across the main market square to the hotel and although I was hungry, I could not face food and went straight to my room, although Ivor popped into the bar for a couple of pints of the local ale before he turned in. I remembered nothing about getting undressed and into bed but awoke fresh and raring to go and knew that I would do justice to the full Welsh breakfast that morning. My mind was now clear and what had seemed a fog last night had now dispersed, and it was obvious to me that the only people that Sullivan could run to were either German spies or members of the Workers Revolutionary Party. I was sure that we had captured the players in the German spy network, which only left the members of the WRP, whom Sullivan could have met whilst engaged in their activities in this part of the world. I knew immediately that I needed to speak to Major Harcourt-Evans about what we know about WRP membership in this part of Wales and would telephone him as soon as I got to the station.

I had a reply from the major within three hours, which he sent urgently by motorcycle dispatch rider from his headquarters in Cardiff to deliver the list of known WRP members or sympathisers in this part of Wales to me personally at Newcastle Emlyn Police Station. He had attached a short note with the list, apologising that the list was not as extensive as he would have liked but stressing that the WRP operated as a secretive organisation who did not publicise their membership widely and often wore masks when involved in public displays or disruption of other political groups and meetings to keep their identities secret. However, surveillance had enabled the security service to identify approximately twenty names within a thirty-mile radius of Newcastle Emlyn and he hoped that this might give us the start we were looking for in our search for Sullivan. He also offered us extra manpower if required in the form of the latest batch of trainees at Llanthony House, who were in the final week of their course and ready for deployment and who could be placed at my disposal at short notice. This was good news which meant that we would be able to raid most of the addresses simultaneously which might prevent warnings being transmitted to other WRP members that we were targeting then in this area. Ivor and I started sifting through the list and marking their locations on the large map and began to consider the priority for each location. We decided to organise the list into three categories depending on whether they were high, medium or low priority and spent half an hour or so arguing about the criteria we would use to make our decisions sensibly. It was agreed that it would be unlikely that Sullivan would be hiding in a town or larger village as it would be difficult to keep the knowledge that there was an extra person living in the house a secret from friends and neighbours over a period of time, and the problem of hiding the van in many properties in built-up areas would be problematical as many town houses did not have outbuildings or stables to keep the van out of sight. This type of van was more commonly seen in rural areas where many farmers used them as general-purpose vehicles and would blend in more readily, whereas the number of motor vehicles in small towns and villages was still relatively few. Applying the criteria suggested four names from the list to be put in the lowest-priority category.

I now suggested that Sullivan was unlikely to select families with children as suitable for a hiding place and would be much more likely to choose locations where there was only a couple or single occupancy. Ivor readily agreed and we identified three family groups which could also be added to the lowest category but were able to note that there were six locations only inhabited by one or two people, which we added provisionally to the highest category. We decided together that he would be most likely to choose locations in rural areas away from other habitations and untroubled by neighbours and visitors, where there were outbuildings to park the van out of sight, and these were added to the highest category. All the rest were placed in the medium priority. By now, the rest of the team were reporting for duty after a harrowing night at Cwm Farm securing the evidence and returning the bodies to the morgue in town, and I was able to hand over the coordination to Ivor and Rhys whilst I went to visit the police surgeon to discover what he could tell me after his initial examination of the bodies. In just a few days, I had come to respect the professionalism of Dr Roberts and his team and knew that what he told me would be vital in bringing Sullivan to justice and I was a little more optimistic that morning as I walked across the square to the town morgue. Roberts was already hard at work on the second post-mortem examination which was O'Hare, having already completed the autopsy on Bronwen earlier in the day. He was happy to talk if I didn't mind listening whilst he continued to work on the body of O'Hare. I have never been squeamish over the sight of blood and had attended enough post-mortem examinations to know what to expect so I readily agreed. He said he would talk about this cadaver first, which we would refer to as Body 2 until he was positively identified as Rory McCloud O'Hare. "Body 2 is a male of the approximate age of thirty-five years who appears to have been well nourished and in a reasonable state of physical fitness before he sustained a serious bullet wound to the upper chest which affected the function of his left lung considerably. There is evidence of crude surgery to his back, probably to remove the bullet lodged in his body, and trace elements of an antiseptic and painkillers in his bloodstream." He said he was confident that laboratory analysis would show that they were like the substances stolen in the chemist's shop murder in Cardigan several days earlier. "This evidence strongly suggests that he was one of the attackers of Sir Walter and that the wound to his chest was probably caused by the shot from Sir Walter's service revolver but without the bullet I cannot prove it." The cause of death was one shot to the head from a range of fifteen or twenty feet from a high-powered automatic weapon and he had removed a bullet from the brain of the victim which he recognised as having come from a Luger machine pistol. He recognised the round because it bore very strong similarity to the bullets he had recovered from the bodies of Sir Walter and his chauffeur earlier in the week. "I will send this round to the laboratory for forensic examination but guess that they will match, suggesting that they were fired from the same weapon and by inference the same gunman, but we will have to wait for the report to be sure."

Body 3 was lying on the next table, and he had only taken a cursory look when it was brought in the previous night, but he was prepared to say that this was probably Rhodri Owen judging by the farmer's boots and clothing he was wearing. I found all this fascinating and knew that it would prove useful in the investigation, but my patience was wearing thin as I really wanted to hear his conclusions after the post-mortem of Bronwen Phillips. Finally, he came to his conclusions on the examination of Bronwen and he began by warning me that Miss Phillips had been used dreadfully by the perpetrator and there was strong evidence indicating that she had been submitted to severe beating and torture before being brutally raped. He catalogued the injuries he had found on her face and body, pointing out that she had a broken eye socket, a number of cheekbones were shattered and there were bruises evident on her neck where two large hands had squeezed her neck hard, probably during the sex act. Examination of her genitalia showed signs of rough treatment and swelling around her vaginal canal, where he had discovered traces of semen. The location of the injuries suggested that she had been forced to lean forward over the back of the sofa and entered roughly with some force from behind and there was also a large amount of semen in a stain on the cloth of her skirt as if her rapist had cleaned himself on her clothing. Finally, she had been murdered by a single swift slash across her throat, which had severed her jugular, and she had bled to death in a matter of minutes. "The method used by the killer bears all the same hallmarks as the murder of Constable Richards in that the cut is the same direction and of the same depth, only one cut was made, and the blade would have been very sharp and of the same length as the one used to murder the constable." Doctor Roberts suggested that the killer of Richards and Bronwen was probably the same person and the similarities of the wound suggested that the murder weapon was the same. In conclusion, he said he would test both bodies 2 and 3 for traces of semen but he seriously doubted that either of them inflicted the injuries and rape on Constable Phillips and that he was certain that this rapist and killer was still at large.

I felt shaken and a little weak at the knees to hear what Bronwen Phillips had endured at the hands of Sullivan, and I felt the anger rising in me as I resolved to bring Sullivan to justice even if it was the last thing I ever did. My thoughts strayed to Alicia, who I had not seen for nearly a month as we were working in different cities, and I became even angrier as I thought this might happen to her. Roberts could see I was distressed and took me into his office at the side of the morgue and produced a bottle of whisky from his drawer and poured two fingers into a couple of glasses he had placed on the desk. He passed one to me and picked up the other and made a toast to the memory of Constable Phillips and to state our determination to bring her murderer to book. He gave me some sound advice as we drank together that in our jobs, we had to keep our emotions in check because of the jobs we were tasked to do, and he described the horrific sights that came into his morgue on an almost weekly basis and that without the resolve to keep his emotions in check he could not serve this community as well as they deserved. He said that this did not mean he was cold or detached but that he did not show his feelings in public; otherwise, his value as a forensic investigator would be next to useless. I pondered what he had said and remembered the advice George Bennett had given me the day before, which was much in the same vein, and I realised that I must cope with the hurt, shame, horror and guilt of this experience if it was to benefit my development as a policeman.

Ivor and Rhys had completed the analysis of WRP members known to be in that area and sorted them into three categories, and we had ended up with seven locations on the high-priority list for our attention which they had laid out in a table.

1. Albert Pritchard - Farm labourer Mair Pritchard	Coal Pit Cottage, Aber-Giar	Small hamlet, large shed for parking van
2. Thomas Evans, Shepherd	Hillside Farm Cottage, Pencarrag	Isolated house, large barn
3. Mervyn Jenkins - Water Bailiff Josie Jenkins	Reservoir Farm, Lynne Brianne	Isolated house with several large outbuildings
4. Herbert Williams - Road mender Sian Williams	Old Toll House, Cribyn	Isolated house at crossroads on moor
5. Bryn hughes - Forester	Forest Cottage, Tyi Forest	Tied cottage hidden in trees
6. Alan Powell and Raymond Powell - brothers. Small holders	Mossy Bank, Rhydowen	Small holding in remote location, stables
7. Hugh Lawrence, Alice Lawrence, Gareth Lawrence - aged 14	Mill House, Bryn Baird	Small Chicken Farm, remote location, large store sheds, half a mile from nearest neighbours

Ivor had already marked all these locations on the map so we could see easily where they were situated in relation to Cwm Farm, and we estimated the journey time that Sullivan would have to reach each location. Over half of the addresses were over an hour and a half's driving time and we were inclined to discount those and selected the three that were about one hour's driving, with plans to raid them first with a follow-up plan to raid the more distant locations in a second wave if we failed to apprehend our suspect. The names selected were Lawrence at Bryn Baird, Williams at Cribyn and Hughes at Tyi Forest, although we had some discussion about whether we should include Jenkins at Llyn Brianne, which lay only just beyond the one-hour driving limit but decided to put them in the second wave. If I called on the twelve trainees to back up my teams, I would have enough manpower to send seven to each location, which should be sufficient to cope with any resistance that we might encounter and I decided that, given the danger presented by Sullivan with his proven reputation as a murderer, I would issue arms and ammunition to all of my team so he could be taken by force if necessary. I briefed the team leaders that we would arrest all of the occupants found at each house and bring them to Newcastle Emlyn Police Station, where we could interview them at length and see what they knew about Sullivan and the plans of the WRP more generally. I would lead the Lawrence raid, Ivor the Williams and Rhys the Hughes, and we planned to raid each property at 06:00 in the morning. I immediately sent a signal to Major Harcourt-Evans requesting the use of the trainees from Llanthony to reach Newcastle Emlyn by midnight that night for briefing and received an acknowledgement that they would join us that night as requested.

The team from Llanthony arrived under the command of Sgt. Major Martin and Sergeant Gareth Hughes at 00:45 and I began the briefing for the three raids. It would take us approximately an hour to drive to the proximity of each address and I needed each team to be in position within sight of the target property before dawn. At first light, the team leader would go forward and reconnoitre the lay of the land and issue the orders for the raid to begin. It was imperative to cut off escape from all sides of the premises as we needed to apprehend all of the occupants of each property, who were to be arrested and returned to Newcastle Emlyn for questioning with an escort of three of the team whilst the remainder of the team searched the premises thoroughly for evidence of the presence of Sullivan at any time and for additional information about the business of the Workers Revolutionary Party in the area. Transport would leave the station yard at 03:00 to give us plenty of time to reach the respective targets and get into position before dawn. My team was to hit Mill House by the side of the stream at Bryn Baird. It was no longer used as a water mill and the wheel had all but disintegrated with age. The Lawrence family, who had lived there for twenty years, had converted the old grain stores into chicken houses where they farmed eggs which they sold at the local markets to make a living. The local map showed several large sheds on the property, which looked large enough to accommodate the van under cover and out of sight from the road. We moved into a position about five hundred yards from the house and were hidden because a bend in the road obscured the view from the house. I went forward and as dawn broke, I could see that the road passed within yards of the front door, but it was far easier to approach the house from behind the sheds where there were trees and bushes for cover. I decided that two of our number would approach the front of the property in a vehicle which would stop immediately in front of the door and hammer on the front door, shouting that it was the police. At the same moment, we would break down the back door and rush into the house, hopefully to catch the occupants before they were too aware of what was happening. Speed was the key to a successful outcome, and I hoped that we could enter and clear the building with the occupants in handcuffs and on their way to the police station within a couple of minutes.

We had synchronised our watches and at the appointed time I heard the police car screech to a halt at the front of the house and the first heavy knock on the door as we approached the back door, where I kicked the door frame on the hinges side. It took three hefty kicks for the door to give way before we were piling inside the small scullery kitchen and spreading out to search the downstairs rooms and I rushed up the stairs with my pistol in hand, shouting as loudly as I could that it was the police. At the top of the steep stairs there were two doors, one on either side of the staircase, which I presumed were bedrooms and I smashed through the door on the left to find Mr and Mrs Lawrence shocked and dishevelled as they had tried to raise themselves from their bed and within seconds one of the trainees, a burly rugby-playing-type constable, appeared with a boy of about fourteen or so held securely in an armlock. I introduced myself and told them that they were being arrested for questioning about the increasingly violent activities of the WRP in these parts and would be taken to Newcastle Emlyn Police Station as soon as they were dressed. Lawrence asked for some privacy for his wife whilst she dressed but I refused and said she should just pull her dress over her nightclothes for the journey to the police station. A few minutes later, we had the house to ourselves as the Lawrences were sped away under guard to be questioned later in the cells at Newcastle Emlyn. The fact that we had not found Sullivan so far did not mean that he was not there, and we needed to conduct a thorough search of the rest of the house and all the sheds before we could be certain that he was not there. We took our time and searched each room and then the outbuildings, painstakingly making sure that we hadn't missed any clues that he had been there or was still in the vicinity. We were disappointed but found no trace of Sullivan anywhere but were fortunate enough to discover two pistols and a hundred rounds of ammunition, a box of firebombs and a rifle with telescopic sights suitable for use by a sniper hidden in a false cache inside the wall at the rear of the fireplace, which would certainly give us plenty to talk to the Lawrences about back at the station. The weapons were packed up safely and loaded into the luggage rack at the rear of my car and made secure for the journey back to Newcastle.

I hoped that one of the other teams had had more luck than us as I mulled over the events of our raid that morning as I drove back to base, although I had to admit that we had made a significant discovery in finding the weapons cache hidden in the Lawrences' house. Although we had no evidence of Sullivan ever having been there, we were now sure that the Lawrences were more than active members of the WRP and would soon find themselves behind bars for possession of these weapons in wartime. When I pulled into the station yard, I was surprised to see that Rhys' team were already back and I hailed him and asked him how it had gone and he said they had entered the house as planned but found it completely deserted. Hughes was not there and there was certainly no sound of anyone else staying in the house in Hughes' absence. He said that the house was obviously lived in and was neat and tidy but there was little food in the larder and the coals in the fire and range were cold, suggesting that Hughes had not been there for three or four days. One of his team had suggested that foresters tended to move around the forest working in different sectors for several days at a time and that there were specially equipped huts dotted around the forest so that the forester could stay overnight should the need arise. We were not sure that this was the case with Hughes, but Rhys said he would check with the forestry office later in the morning.

It was two hours later when Ivor returned, bringing the Williams family with him plus several crates full of papers relating to the membership and plans of the WRP, and it appeared that Herbert Williams, although he listed his occupation as road mender, was in fact well educated and had earned a good class degree from university and worked as a schoolmaster for over ten years until he was sacked when his political affiliation to revolutionary politics was discovered. He had refused to fight as a conscientious objector and had been sent to prison, where he had shared a cell with Rory O'Hare and they became firm friends. Williams had become the secretary of the

WRP, keeping detailed records secretly hidden in the cellar of the toll house. After only a cursory glance at the papers, Ivor could see that Williams could be a rich mine of information about the activities of the party, which would enable the security service to shut down their operations completely now that their leader was dead. We had not apprehended Sullivan but had made some significant advances against the activities of the WRP and I was sure that this would prove vital to the security of Wales in the future.

I started the questioning of Hugh Lawrence around two-thirty that afternoon and found him angry that he had been arrested and voluble in protesting his innocence. I listened to his shouting and rambling for half an hour and then told him that he was being detained under the Defence of the Realm Act Wartime Measures, which meant he could be held without charge and did not have to have access to a lawyer at that stage. He stopped the noise when I told him this and I swear that his chin dropped and his mouth fell open in dismay when I said that he was under investigation on the charge of conspiracy to commit treason. He went pale and then regained some confidence, calling me mad and stupid as I could not have any evidence to bring such a charge. I sat back and smiled and suggested he sit down and listen, and I would gladly outline the evidence stacked against him. "First, I know from the records of the WRP we have captured that you and your wife are members of an illegal organisation whose sole aim is the overthrow of the government of the British monarch. Secondly, we have discovered hidden in the chimney recess of your house a cache of weapons," and I laid down on the table in front of him photographs of the pistols, ammunition, firebombs and sniper rifle, "which prove that you are an active member of this organisation who conspired with others to hide these weapons so they could be used to further the treasonous ends of the organisation." I waited for this to sink in and when he looked up, I just said calmly that he must realise that these were capital offences which were most likely to lead to him and possibly his wife and son too ending up swinging at the end of the hangman's rope at Cardiff Jail. "However, if you are prepared to help me identify other members of the WRP and particularly help me in my search for a man called Ernest Sullivan, a professional killer and rapist who was a friend of the late leader of your party, Rory McCloud O'Hare, then I can guarantee that that assistance rendered will certainly lead to less severe sentences passed on you and your family." Ivor and Rhys used the same tactic with Williams, but he proved to be a much harder nut to crack and they probably thought that what additional help he could give over and above what we had already discovered in his papers would be negligible. He was thoroughly implicated because throughout all the papers he was shown to be a close associate and confidant of O'Hare, the leader of the WRP, and party to everything that went on.

Before calling it a day, I had a debrief session with Ivor and Rhys and we decided that we would raid the Jenkins place at the same time the next morning and would brief the team before they left for the day to be back on duty by 03:00 for a repeat of yesterday's operation.

TWENTY

Against his better judgement, Sullivan was still at the Jenkinses' cottage twenty-four hours after he had disposed of Jenkins' body in the pigsty, and although he knew he was at greater risk of discovery the longer he stayed in one place, he could not break free from the sexual allure of Josie Jenkins, who was the first woman who had ever captivated him this way. He longed for her body almost constantly at the expense of all rational thoughts in his head. He knew that he would have to make the break soon and was debating in his head whether they should part as friends with the option of him returning sometime soon for more sexual pleasure or playing it safe and killing her before he left. Sullivan had always considered emotions to be a sign of weakness, but he was genuinely confused as to what his next actions should be because he was so captivated by this woman. Josie knew some of the other members of the party locally but was not as deeply immersed in the WRP as her late husband had been, but she suggested a couple of people that he could approach for a more permanent hiding place but also suggested that he could stay with her as she had a secret room at the back of the cellar that no one else knew about, which had been constructed for Jenkins to hide in if the military police came looking for him and also to hide weapons and explosives for the WRP. Jenkins had excavated this room behind a false wall, which was impossible to see unless you knew it was there. She was confident that he would be perfectly safe hiding inside if anyone came to the house and had taken him into the cellar and challenged him to find the entrance to the secret room, and even though he had looked at every wall very carefully, he could not detect the entrance until Josie showed him where it was. She took him into the room, which was equipped with a small bed and chair and shelves for the storage of arms and ammunition, and she said that she would stock it with some provisions and water for any occasion when he might have to spend some time inside. Sullivan was not overkeen on spending too much time in this windowless underground room, which reminded him too much of a police cell, but thought that it might prove useful if the police did come calling.

*

The raid on the Jenkinses' would follow the same format as the previous day except that we were limited to just eight of us from Newcastle Emlyn Police Station as the trainees had returned to their studies at Llanthony House. We were in position on the ridge above the house as dawn was breaking and we had an excellent view of the layout of the cottage with the pathway leading up to a pigsty about fifty yards behind the house. I also noticed that there was something about the size of a small car or van sheeted over to the left side of the house, which could be an item of farm machinery or the missing van. I sent half of my men to skirt around the side of the cottage to be ready to approach the back of the house when I blew a blast on my whistle but stressed that they were not to move before they heard my signal. We lay silently waiting for daylight to slowly brighten up and the time to edge forward to the agreed start. I was watching the house through my telescope, and all seemed quiet and settled until I spotted some movement at the periphery of my vision which materialised into a large black and white border collie, who stretched and then became aware of something behind the house, and I guessed he had picked up the scent of the team hidden behind the house. I cursed that the wind was blowing towards the pig shed; otherwise, their scent would have been masked by the smell of the pigsty, and prayed that the dog would not raise the alarm but settle down again to sleep and it seemed that he was going to do so when something spooked him, and he started to bark very loudly. I knew that any chance of surprise was gone so blew my police whistle as hard as I could to signal for the raid to commence and we broke cover and rushed forward to cover the three hundred yards to the front of the cottage as fast as we could.

*

Josie and Sullivan were in bed asleep but the loud barking from the dog sleeping outside had alerted them to something going on outside the front of the house and Josie shook him awake and pushed him towards the door, grabbing his clothes on the way. They hurried down to the cellar and she opened the secret door so that Sullivan could squeeze in safely and she replaced the door carefully so that no trace of the entrance could be seen and rushed back up the cellar stairs and made it back to the bedroom just as the front door crashed in and a crowd of men in plainclothes piled into the house, waving pistols in their hands. Josie stood in her nightgown and pretended to look terrified as the leader of the men said they were policemen searching for a runaway murderer and revolutionary called Sullivan, who may be using the false name O'Mahoney. More policemen were coming through from the back of the house and they were searching every room in the house and were in the cellar. She just acted timidly and pretended to be frightened as she answered the questions they threw at her, but she admitted that although she was known as Josie Jenkins, the wife of Mervyn Jenkins, they were not actually married, and she was really Josie Richards from Aberporth but had hooked up with Jenkins about eighteen months before and moved in with him in this cottage. For the sake of not causing a scandal in the local area by this impropriety, they styled themselves as man and wife to stop tongues wagging. We couldn't understand why she was here alone and why we had not found any trace of Mervyn Jenkins in the house because we knew that he had certainly not come out of the property at any time since we had been observing from the ridge above. When pressed, she said that Jenkins had gone to visit his mum, who had taken a bad turn and was not expected to live more than a couple of days. We asked for the address of his parents and she wrote it down on a slip of paper. 49 Waterfall Cottages, Bargoed was where he would be found, and she did not know when he would be back. I thanked her for her cooperation and we withdrew to search the outside of the house, where I found Ivor and Rhys looking under the tarpaulin sheet to the left of the house where they had discovered a light van very similar to the one that we sought. Struggling with the tarpaulin to uncover more of the vehicle, they were able to find the registration number and check the rear offside tyre tread and were not surprised to discover that it was the same vehicle that was at the murder scenes and at Cwm Farm. I asked them quietly to sheet it over again and to make no indication that we had discovered what we had been looking for. I went back into the house and asked Mrs Jenkins whom the van in the yard belonged to and she said it belonged to her husband. I asked why he had not used the van to drive to visit his mother in Bargoed and she said that the van had broken down and was sheeted over until he could get the parts to repair it, so he had taken the bus. I asked how long the van had been off the road in need of repair and she replied that she thought it was at least three weeks. These stories seemed just a little too contrived for me to believe them, but I didn't let on to her my true feelings and smiled and thanked her again for clearing that matter up for me. Meanwhile, Rhys had walked up to the pigsty and had a good look round the pen and the sty and had observed what looked like pieces of animal or possibly human bone amongst the muck. Country folk know that the way to dispose of animal matter of any kind is to feed it to the pigs and it was guaranteed to disappear completely within a couple of days. He suggested we let the forensic team have a poke around in the sty to see if there were human remains present in the muck. He said he had taken the precaution of shutting the pig shed door to keep the pigs inside until we could have a closer look.

Before we left, I called Ivor and Rhys together for a review of what we had discovered there that morning and what our strategy should be going forward. We had discovered the van that was present at three murders and was definitely at Cwm Farm and used by Sullivan when he escaped from the farm after killing Bronwen, O'Hare and Owen. "Josie tells us that the van belongs to her husband and confirms that he was unable to use it to go to Bargoed to visit his dying mother because it has broken down and that it has been sheeted up awaiting repair for at least three weeks. We know that this is not true as we can place this van at three murder scenes around Newcastle Emlyn in the past five days. If Josie is lying to us about this van, what else is she lying about?" Rhys' suspicion that there may be human remains in the pigsty was worth following up and may well give an alternative explanation for the absence of Mervyn Jenkins from this property and I noticed when I looked around the bedroom that the bedclothes were ruffled on both sides of the bed but the depression in the mattress of one side was deeper than the other, suggesting someone heavier than Josie had been laying on the other side. I felt the sheets and mattress and both sides were still warm, as if both sides of the bed had been occupied very recently, which could mean Mervyn Jenkins was still there and was now in hiding somewhere inside the house in a secret hideout we hadn't yet found, or what I thought more likely, given the presence of the van on the property and the potential of discovering human remains in the pigsty, was that Jenkins was dead and Sullivan had taken his place in his bed and was now in hiding in this house. I suggested we pretend to be disappointed that we were not able to speak to Mervyn Jenkins but satisfied that Ernest Sullivan was not there and then withdraw as if we were returning to the police station but in fact would only move out of sight and maintain a watch on the house to see what happened next, because I thought Jenkins or Sullivan would miraculously appear sometime that morning.

*

Josie left a gap of ten minutes after they had left to be sure that they were gone before she went down to the cellar and released Sullivan from his hidey hole. He had only been confined for under half an hour and already he was hot and clammy and stressed by the experience. Josie gave him the full details of the police raid, saying that although they said they wanted to speak to Mervyn, their prime objective was to capture him. "They seemed to have no idea that Jenkins was a false name and that he was a deserter named Mervyn Protheroe on the run from the South Wales Fusiliers since mid-1915, but they seemed desperate to catch up with you. I spun them a false story but had to think quickly and I don't think they believed me, but I have bought us enough time to make a getaway from here before they return. I told them that Mervyn had gone to Bargoed to visit his dying mother and they will surely check, but it won't take them very long to discover that the address was fictitious so they will return later today or early tomorrow, by which time we will be gone. They asked about the van and looked at it but sheeted it over again before they left, seeming to have no further interest in it."

Sullivan needed to clean up and get dressed and sent Josie to the kitchen to cook some breakfast as they would need some sustenance to fuel their exertions that day. He packed his few things together and loaded and checked both of his machine pistols, which he felt would be needed sometime later that day, although he was still uncertain what he was going to do with Josie. He was tempted to take her with him because he could continue to enjoy bedding her time and time again, but he knew that taking her reduced his options and slowed him down considerably. He did not believe that the police would have left so quickly without leaving a lookout to check out if what Josie had said was true. He could leave her behind, but the police would arrest and interrogate her and discover that he had killed her husband, or he could dispose of her in his usual fashion, but this time he was not sure what to do and this sense of indecision worried him greatly. Breakfast was on the table when he came from the bedroom, and he sat down to eat the eggs and bacon and fresh bread she had cooked for him. This again disturbed him as he was getting to like having his feet under the table and enjoying living with someone else, and he was sure that this diminished his effectiveness as the cold, calculating killer that he had become over the past decade, and he had never been frightened like this before that his time as an assassin was ending. All this was going over in his mind as he ate, and he seemed to make the final decision like a condemned man eating his final meal. When he had finished, he pulled Josie onto his lap as she stretched over to pick up his plate from the table and kissed her deeply on the mouth and nibbled her neck and earlobes as she moaned with pleasure. His hands were roving under her clothes and searching her body and he was aroused to a fever pitch with desire for her. He stood up and gently pushed Josie forward to lean across the table as he lifted her skirts to reveal her bottom and vagina moist and ready for him to enter, and he needed no further invitation but dropped his trousers and entered her from behind, thrusting his penis hard as far as it would go as she pushed back against him, moaning and gasping with pleasure. He could feel the contractions of her vaginal walls gripping him tighter with each push and feel the moistening of her juices lubricating their union until she arched her back and let out a cry as she climaxed, and he felt the rush of the semen flowing in a gush into her. He was satisfied and stood back and wiped his penis on the tablecloth and pulled his trousers up and tightened his belt. She was still feeling the aftershocks of her orgasms and had not yet retained her composure as he stepped in closer and kissed her gently on the back of her neck and whispered intimately that he was sorry but he had no choice but to do this as he swiped his knife across her throat with one swift movement and stepped back to avoid any blood splatter on his clothing. Sullivan's usual detachment had deserted him because for the first time ever he felt genuine sadness as he watched his victim gurgle her last breaths on the table before him, and out of a kind of respect he waited until she was dead before he collected his bag and went out of the front door to unsheet the van to make his getaway. He knew he needed to be quick as the police would not be far away, but it was imperative that he get to some large village or market town quickly, where he could ditch the van and steal another vehicle.

 Constable Brownlow, who was on watch at that moment, missed the opening of the front door and Sullivan unsheeting the van because he was scanning the other side of the property at that moment but as he slowly moved the glasses around the arc and took in the front of the house and moved on towards the pigsty, he was surprised to see a large man swinging the starting handle of the van and then getting into the van, ready to reverse out into the front yard and drive away. He called for Sergeant Morgan, and Wesley came running to see what had alarmed the watchman. Wesley didn't need the glasses to see that the van was on the move but took them from Brownlow to get a closer look at the driver and passenger. He expected to see two in the van but was surprised to see that the van was being driven by Sullivan, who was already accelerating up the drive towards the road and had caught them by surprise as he would be onto the road and driving away at speed before they had even reached their vehicles.

*

I shouted to Ivor to go down to the house and arrest Mrs Jenkins and send her to the station and secure the property and then come after us as fast as he could. The rest of us mounted up and charged after the van at breakneck speed across the reservoir dam and then down the steep hillside track leading to the tarmac road which led to the small village of Ystradffin. The track was narrow with a sharp drop on one side into the water, which meant that the drivers could not go too fast in case of a mishap and one of our vehicles ending up in the water. I urged them on to go as fast as we could because if we did not gain on him enough, we would not see which way he turned when he came to the T-junction at the bottom of the hill. If he turned right, he would be bound for the village and ultimately back towards Lampeter, but if he turned left, he could disappear into the Cambrian Mountains, where he could hide and not be found for weeks. I studied the map carefully and although I thought the easiest option might be to head for the nearest village, I thought that his chances of finding a suitable replacement vehicle were slim and I had a feeling that he would turn left and take the steep climb up towards the summit of Bryn Cwmn, where I could see there was a tarmac single-track road which led directly down towards the larger town of Tregaron which lay astride the main road between Lampeter and Aberystwyth and offered the best chance of ditching the van and acquiring a replacement vehicle to make a quick getaway along the main road. When we reached the T-junction there was no sight of the van in either direction, so I had to make an instant decision as to which way to go based purely on my gut feeling. I chose the left turning but sent the second car to the right to go as far as the village to see if the van had gone that way whilst we took the mountain road alone. It was a steep climb, but I knew that the police car was a more powerful vehicle than the van and we should begin to overhaul him during this steady climb and sure enough we caught a glimpse of the van much higher up the mountainside as the sunlight glinted off its bodywork. We pulled in and stopped and I focused my glasses on where we had seen the glimpse of the van and I got a clear sighting as it laboured slowly round a bend and was then lost from view. We pulled back onto the road and gave chase again, pushing our car to climb much faster in the hope of closing the distance between us, and I hoped to be able to stop him before he made the turning to the left onto the downhill road to Tregaron, where he would be able to pile on the speed and we would be in danger of losing him.

The road was becoming much steeper as we neared the top and even the powerful engine of the police car was working hard to keep us moving forward at little more than a fast walking pace, but I guessed that we had been making more ground than Sullivan and when we reached the plateau just before the summit, we should be able to see the van. As we came over the last of the rise, we were surprised to hear two high velocity rounds whizz close to the car. I realised that Sullivan had chosen this spot to stand and fight. I knew that he was a quick thinker and had probably thought that he had found a good defensive position where he could pick us off easily since we were exposed and in the open. We stopped the car and the four of us dived out of the doors, rolling into the grass and crawling away to seek out what little defensive cover we could find. Although Sullivan was alone, I knew that he had greater firepower than us and with his Luger machine pistols he could take pot shots at us whilst we were still way outside of the range of our police-issue pistols. We were at a distinct disadvantage, and he held us at bay whilst he fired accurate shots at us at his leisure, and I knew it was only a matter of time before he hit one or more of us and pushed the odds even more in his favour. I signalled Rhys to move towards the right and try to reach the cover of an outcrop of rocks about a hundred feet closer to our target whilst I tried to crawl over the edge of the road and skirt along the edge of the road out of Sullivan's view. I didn't think he had noticed my movements as he seemed to concentrate his firing at Rhys to my right, and then I heard a muffled scream and it looked as if Brownlow had been hit but he did not appear to be dead as he was still moving and making a hell of a noise. I used this distraction to crawl faster until I realised that I had completely outflanked Sullivan's position. I was now behind him approximately twenty yards from his vantage point. He had been so consumed with containing the advance made by Rhys and Brownlow that he had forgotten about me completely. I was now just within the range of the police pistol, but I knew that my shot would have to be bang on target if I was to wound him sufficiently to put an end to his defence. I waited for a lull in the firing as he changed the magazine in his weapon, and I shouted in as strong a voice as I could muster for him to throw down his weapon and put his hands up. This caught him by surprise and he spun round quickly, which toppled him off balance and he was unable to get a shot away before I fired my pistol, hitting him in the hand and causing him to drop his machine pistol and grab his hand in pain. He was in a blind panic and his basic instinct was to run away so without any thought he jumped up and ran towards me, knocking me flying, and headed down the hill. Rhys had reached me by this time and coolly picked up the machine pistol and checked that it was loaded and pulled out the stock and put the pistol up to his shoulder like a rifle and took aim through the excellent sights as he controlled his breathing. He squeezed the trigger once and a single shot rang out and struck Sullivan in the back of his thigh, bringing him immediately to the ground. He struggled to pull himself up several times, so strong was his urge to escape, but the leg wound would not let him place any weight on this leg and he toppled over each time he tried to get up. Rhys and I approached him with our weapons pointing directly at him and whilst Rhys kept the Luger trained on him from a range of six feet, I manacled his hands behind his back and half lifted him to his feet and made him hobble back to the police car for the journey back to Newcastle Emlyn. Rhys accompanied me in the police car and the other constable drove Brownlow in Rhodri Owen's van to get medical treatment in Tregaron. Brownlow did not seem to be badly wounded but needed to be seen by a doctor and to have his wound dressed before he made the journey back home.

I concentrated on my driving whilst Rhys kept Sullivan covered on the journey back to Newcastle, although I could have happily vented my revenge on Sullivan with my truncheon before we made it to the police station, but I kept myself under control and knew that I would not lower myself to his level and would see him pay for all of his crimes through due process. As we pulled into the station yard at Newcastle, the whole watch were around, waiting to congratulate us on our arrest, for Brownlow had telephoned from the Cottage

Hospital in Tregaron with the news. Chief Inspector Bennett was there also to add his congratulations and I was glad to receive their accolades but even happier to see Sullivan booked into the cells and the police doctor summoned to look at his wounds. George Bennett said a few words of praise for the work of our team and reserved some words to highlight the contribution made by Bronwen Phillips before paying tribute to my leadership and persistence in finally bringing into custody the last and most dangerous member of the Wurtenberg spy network. I replied that this was a team effort and without the work of every member of the team and the support of the Newcastle Emlyn police station we could not have achieved this result.

The glow of our success did not last for very long and barely lasted until the following morning when Colonel Stewart arrived with an order to take Sullivan into his custody to be interviewed in London about not only his activities with the WRP but more importantly with the German espionage system and Irish republican movement. Inspector Hughes objected vociferously because Sullivan was suspected of at least seven murders on his patch alone, all within the past week, and I was inclined to support his point of view and made my feelings known to the colonel also. Sullivan had murdered five that we knew of as part of his activities with the Wurtenberg spy ring, two of whom were the wounded British officers, Lieutenants Crawford and King. Colonel Stewart listened politely to both Hughes and me and was sympathetic to our plea for custody of Sullivan but made it clear that it was in the national interest to get access to the information that Sullivan possessed about the wider spy efforts by the German secret service and the Irish rebel movement. He promised us that no deals would be done with Sullivan in return for this information and he guaranteed that justice would be done for all of his victims at the end of the executioner's rope. He guardedly hinted that there were measures that they could apply to put pressure on Sullivan that we as policemen could not use and the constraints of the workings of criminal law would be too slow for us in this case. "You would have to give Sullivan access to a lawyer this morning before you could interview him, and his lawyer would press for you to wait for his wounds to heal sufficiently and would easily get a court order to stop you if you did not agree and if you wanted to proceed. None of these restrictions apply to us and we will remove Sullivan this morning to a secure and secret location where we have specialist interrogators who will get the information. We require it much faster than you would be able to get it," and I knew exactly what he meant as I remembered the two military police sergeants who had interrogated Sir Wilhelm Branden in the basement of Llanthony House and I shuddered but reluctantly agreed. Colonel Stewart dismissed us with the parting words that this was not in any way a slur on our ability, which he respected and acknowledged as being of the highest order, and he was certain that it was our determination and professionalism that had apprehended this most dangerous criminal so quickly and we were to be congratulated. Sullivan was removed later that day by a security team from the security service and I was sure that he was being removed to Llanthony because I thought I caught a glimpse of Sergeants Causwell and Bellamy in charge of the party.

After we had left the room, I could see that Inspector Hughes was still bristling with indignation and I explained to him what the colonel had meant by the hints he had dropped. "They will use torture and violence to get the answers they need much quicker than we would be able to do following our clear set of procedures for prosecuting criminals. They will guarantee that whatever charges Sullivan faces eventually, he will face the gallows, and the murders in the Newcastle Emlyn area will be attributed to him and the cases marked as solved." He understood what I was saying but was still very concerned that Sullivan would escape justice for the murders of two police officers, the local magistrate and his chauffeur and Josie Jenkins. I reassured him that he had much to be satisfied about having arrested some of the very key players in the WRP and discovering a weapons cache and explosives, which proved beyond doubt that the WRP had already stepped beyond the bounds of political agitation and proposed a campaign of violence in that area. "You have in your possession all the secret records of the party, which will enable you to identify and arrest further members in this area and share information with other areas too. I think your station has earned considerable kudos through the whole affair." He asked me if I approved of these methods, and I had to admit that as a policeman I found them abhorrent, but I understood why these extraordinary methods might be necessary in wartime. We shook hands and parted as friends, and I went into our temporary squad office to pack up our papers and complete our reports before returning to Swansea the following morning.

The next couple of days were rather an anti-climax after the frenetic chase across half of Wales and I for one was glad of a couple of days of relative peace and quiet to reconnect with my life. I managed to give Ivor and Rhys a few days' leave so they could relax, and hoped that I would be able to get away for a few days myself at the end of the week. When I got back to my apartment, I found some mail on the mat and I recognised the regular weekly letter from Alicia and one from my mum and an unusual one with French postmarks which looked like the address had been written by my younger brother Derfal, who didn't usually write that often.

Alicia wrote about her continuing work at Cardiff Docks and how the team were different now that there were so many new recruits, but Inspector Howells was doing well in command and relying heavily on her to train the new people so they could be effective operationally as quickly as possible. The legacy of the Wurtenberg affair had proved the necessity for a radical shake-up of security in all the major docks along the South Wales coast, and the ease with which enemy sympathisers and spies had been able to infiltrate into the heart of the dock management system and pass vital shipping movements, tonnage and cargo manifests to the U-boats waiting in the deep waters of our coast had proved a huge wake-up call. The security of Cardiff Docks was now in the hands of Howells' team, but he was now operating with Royal Navy support, who supplied blue jacket support when major searches were necessary. All shipping movement information was now coded, and access was strictly limited to those with a need to know. Alicia hoped my investigation was going well, and she hoped that we could get a weekend away together and said she still had the key to her cousin's cottage in Barmouth if I could get away. She finished with the news that she had applied to take the sergeant's examination but was not hopeful of passing at the first attempt. I thought that a few days at the Barmouth cottage with Alicia was exactly what I needed, and I decided that I would write back that evening and get my letter in the post first thing in the morning.

Mum's letter was the usual family chit-chat and gossip from the chapel, but it was obvious that the affair between my other brother, Gwyn, and Mair Davis was still going strong and although Mum did not approve of their relationship, she was embarrassed to discover that she liked Mair as a person after she had got to know her a bit more when she helped her recover from the beating she had received at the hands of her husband. Mum told me that Mair's husband had been killed at sea when his ship went down so she was now a widow and Gwyn was now intent on marrying her. The chapel gossip was that it was unseemly for a young widow to contemplate marriage so soon after her husband's death and even though Mum liked Mair, she was unwilling to go against the accepted opinion of the chapel ladies anytime soon. It seemed to me that the female holy of holies in our local chapel was even more self-righteous and devout than even old Reverend Lewis and I must admit to thinking of the scripture verse about he who is without sin casting the first stone.

I saved the last letter until last and knew that I would enjoy reading the news from my younger brother Derfal very much. He had written a longish letter telling me about life in his squadron and being promoted to captain, defending an infantry officer accused of desertion and winning the case, transferring to the newly formed Royal Air Force as a flight lieutenant and gaining a second DFC, but he finally got to the reason for the letter, which was that he and Ruby were getting married on May the third and that he would be delighted if I would be his best man. I was so cheered up by this news and knew that there was a second letter to write for the post box in the morning, saying that I would be proud to accept. He had told me that he had secured three weeks' leave so he could be home for a week before the wedding and have time for a honeymoon with Ruby before he went back to his squadron. He expressed an interest in meeting up before the wedding to discuss the arrangements and hoped I would accept his invitation.

The following morning, Chief Inspector Bennett called me into his office and read out a letter from the chief constable commending Constable Bronwen Phillips for bravery in the field and said, "Although someone from headquarters has visited her parents with the news of her death, they do not know that she has been awarded this posthumous commendation and I thought you might like to go down to Penarth and deliver it to them personally, Inspector Morgan." I was astonished because I was only a sergeant, although I had already passed the inspector's examination. George saw the confusion on my face and smiled and said, "Inspector Price, who leads the security team at Newport Docks, is to retire next week and the chief has just asked me for a recommendation for a replacement and I suggested you and he agreed. You will receive written notification shortly and the promotion will be promulgated in the *Gazette* in the usual way with effect from Monday next, alongside the award of the Police Gallantry Medal." He came round his desk and clapped me on the back, shook my hand and then produced his whisky bottle and two glasses to celebrate the good news. He said, "You can tell Ivor Bethal and Rhys Evans that they are both to receive commendations on their record and will become detective constables officially on Monday next. Evans is to be posted to the Swansea team, but you could take Ivor with you to Newport if you wish." I felt light-headed with this news or perhaps it was drinking whisky at eight in the morning, I don't know, but I knew that celebrations would continue throughout the day when I imparted the news to the rest of the team.

It was a couple of days before I received the Commendation for Bravery that had been awarded to Bronwen Phillips by the chief constable of the South Wales Force. It was an impressive scroll that was printed on vellum, and I took it to a picture framer's shop in the High Street to get it mounted in a solid polished wood frame. I was able to collect it the next day and, asking Ivor to accompany me for moral support, I drove to Penarth to meet Bronwen's parents. I was not looking forward to meeting them because I knew that they did not approve of Bronwen's choice of career and may well vent their anger at me as a representative of the police and as her commander in the field who had sent her to her death. I had never been to Penarth before but was impressed at the neat houses with lovely gardens in the obviously prosperous suburban town. I found the Phillipses' house quite easily and could see that Bronwen had come from a comfortable middle-class family background, because her parents lived in a substantial semi-detached house with lawns at the front and side of the house, and I seemed to remember Bronwen telling me her father was a bank manager and he wanted her to have a career in the bank too. The door was opened by a young woman who was obviously the housemaid, and I introduced myself as Detective Inspector Morgan accompanied by Detective Constable Bethal who had come to see Mr and Mrs Phillips. She closed the door and left us stood on the doorstep without uttering a word. Within thirty seconds or so, she was back and opened the door and showed us inside and took our hats and directed us to a sitting room on the right where Bronwen's parents were waiting for us. They were both dressed formally in mourning for their daughter, although I suspected that the morning dress and winged collar worn by Mr Phillips was his usual business attire, and Mrs Phillips was dressed completely in black. Bronwen's father rose and shook my hand and offered us a seat and then sat back down next to his wife on the sofa to listen to what we had to say. I noticed that Bronwen was very like her mother, with the same colouring and facial features. I told them that both Ivor and I were part of the same team that Bronwen was assigned to and that in the short time that she had been working with us we had come to recognise her skills and talents as an investigator and were sure that she would have become one of the leading female detectives in Wales, given time.

"She was one of the bravest young women we had ever met, who was not afraid to enter a man's world and be able to prove that she was as good as and, in many cases, better than her male colleagues. Her astute and analytical mind enabled us to track the most dangerous killer and the last member of a major German spy ring that had been operating in South Wales for over two and a half years. Her contribution helped us to track him to a remote location near Newcastle Emlyn where he was hiding on an isolated hill farm. The whole team assembled a mile or so from the farm, but we could see from the map and with our glasses that it would be difficult for us to make a covert approach without getting a closer look at the layout of the farm to discover the best places to approach the farmhouse with maximum cover. We needed for someone to get much closer to take a better look at the farm for us so we could plan the safest way to raid the farm. Your daughter volunteered to pretend to be a local rider exercising her horse on the hillside above the farm and would ride as close to the farm property and back up to our hiding place with an idea of the best ways to attack the farm. There were other officers who could have made this reconnaissance, but Bronwen persisted and said that her idea would not awaken their suspicions and she could ride past the farm and back again to us without making the occupants suspicious in any way. Reluctantly, I agreed to her plan because it was, simply, the best plan that had been put forward and stood a fair to good chance of being successful. Bronwen was so proud to have been chosen and carried off her part brilliantly. The main problem for us was that we were unable to keep watch on her progress as she got nearer to the farm because of the lay of the land so we are not sure how and why she was captured by the occupants of the farm but as soon as we were aware that her riderless horse had been found, we charged down the hill to affect a rescue but were tragically too late."

I told them with complete frankness that I held myself accountable for what had happened but also admitted to them that as a commander faced with making decisions in the field, I would not hesitate to agree to Bronwen's plan if it were presented to me again. "She was a brave woman and a resolute police officer who desperately wanted to undertake this reconnaissance mission even though she was aware of the risks that it involved. I am proud to have been her commander and to have worked so closely with her on this investigation and can state that her contribution played an important part leading to the arrest of our main suspect, who carried out seven murders, including two police officers in that number, in this past week alone. I am pleased to tell you that this man is Ernest Sullivan, a professional killer, with a long track record of violence within the Irish rebel movement and the German secret service and he is currently under intensive questioning at this moment and will be brought before the courts at the earliest opportunity, where we are confident that the evidence we have against him will send him to the gallows for his crimes." Finally, I said that the name of Bronwen Phillips would always be remembered by the South Wales Police Force with honour and respect and I handed Mr Phillips a copy of the citation that was published in the *London Gazette* that morning promulgating the award of the Chief Constable's Commendation for Bravery in the field. Mrs Phillips just sobbed as the tears ran down her face, but Mr Phillips stoically took the citation and thanked me for my honesty about what had happened to Bronwen. He went on to say that they did not approve of her choice of career but knew that she loved being a police officer very much, and he took a deep breath that was almost a sigh and then continued by saying that his daughter wanted to contribute towards winning this war and, reading this, it seemed that she got her wish.

I handed him the framed commendation and he thanked me and said, "Nothing can bring our daughter back to us, but this will perhaps remind us that her death was not in vain."

I was reunited with Alicia that weekend when we managed to get three days together at her cousin's cottage at Barmouth and enjoyed lazy days in each other's company, renewing our acquaintanceship with each other and making love in the big brass bed in the main bedroom. It was not yet warm enough to enjoy swimming on the beach, but we enjoyed some long walks along the cliff and in the dunes in the blustery onshore winds. I told Alicia about my promotion to inspector and appointment to head the security team at Newport Docks, and I was pleased to be able to take Ivor with me as a detective constable and this could be great for us because Cardiff and Newport were close enough that we could see each other much more regularly than we had been able to do with the Cardiff and Swansea arrangement. I told her the news about my younger brother Derfal's marriage on the third of May to Ruby and asked if she would like to come to the wedding with me. She replied that she only knew me, but she would see what shift she was on and let me know and I thought that perhaps we could invite Derfal and Ruby to meet us for lunch somewhere in the week before the wedding when Derfal came home on leave from France.

And a few weeks later we had the pleasure of lunching with Ruby and Derfal at the Ponturdolais Inn and I was able to discuss the best man duties but also introduce Alicia to the bride and groom. The wedding weekend was excellent, and Alicia met all my family and seemed to be accepted by all, especially the women when she attended the hen party and stayed the night at the Reeses' house. Mum and Dad seemed to like her too and I noticed that Alicia relaxed much more as the weekend went on. I was determined to ask her to marry me, but I thought that I would wait for the excitement of Derfal and Ruby's marriage to die down for a couple of weeks before I popped the question. I was called to give evidence at the trial of Ernest Sullivan in Cardiff which gave me the bonus of being able to see Alicia every evening and that weekend too. It was the Saturday night after we had heard that Sullivan had been found guilty and sentenced to death within two weeks at Cardiff Jail that I decided to take Alicia for dinner to one of the upmarket restaurants in the city. We sat at a candlelit table in a romantic corner position with some privacy from the other diners when after a delicious meal and over brandy and coffee I plucked up the courage to ask her to become my wife. Alicia said that she would have to sum up all the evidence before she gave me an answer and I was initially a little perturbed but then she smiled and said that all the evidence pointed to this being a good thing for us to do and she accepted my proposal. We made a date for the following Saturday to go shopping in Cardiff to purchase an engagement ring and then we could broadcast our happiness to the world. I told her that Derfal had recommended an excellent jeweller in the city where he had bought the engagement ring for Ruby and their wedding rings, which we could try first.

The following day, as I travelled back to Newport to take up my new appointment, I reflected on how fortunate I had been to have escaped from the colliery and to make something of my life. Joining the police had been the making of me and helped me grow and develop as a man. It was just over four years since I had sworn my oath as a constable and here I was, a detective inspector, and even luckier to have found Alicia, who would be my life's partner. We could close the file on the Wurtenberg affair with the conviction of Ernest Sullivan, although I knew that equally challenging cases would soon come forward to trouble us in the future. I suspected that the threat from German spies and sympathisers would decline for, although the war was not yet over, all the signs were positive that the allied victory was secure. The real task for us would be to begin to secure the peace and counter the threats that would come from many different quarters, and many of them probably home-grown and much more difficult to deal with than the agents of enemy powers ever had been.